W9-BJS-142

Hudson Bay

D A

REINDEER L.

NELSON R.

CHURCHILL R.

MANITOBA

Grand Rapids

Cumberland House

L. WINNIPEG

L. MANITOBA

WINNIPEG R.

LAKE OF THE WOODS

ASSINIBOINE R.

Red Oaks Massacre

ASKATCHEWAN

TO MONTREAL

U.S.

*Pemmican*

## BOOKS BY VARDIS FISHER

NOVELS

*Pemmican*
*Toilers of the Hills*
*Dark Bridwell*
*April: A Fable of Love*
*Forgive Us Our Virtues*
*Children of God*
*City of Illusion*
*The Mothers*

THE VRIDAR HUNTER TETRALOGY

*In Tragic Life*
*Passions Spin the Plot*
*We Are Betrayed*
*No Villain Need Be*

THE TESTAMENT OF MAN SERIES

*Darkness and the Deep*
*The Golden Rooms*
*Intimations of Eve*
*Adam and the Serpent*
*The Divine Passion*
*The Valley of Vision*
*The Island of the Innocent*
*Jesus Came Again: a Parable*

NON-FICTION

*The Neurotic Nightingale*
*God or Caesar?*

# PEMMICAN

*A Novel of the Hudson's Bay Company*

BY VARDIS FISHER

1956

*Doubleday & Company, Inc.*

GARDEN CITY, N.Y.

COPYRIGHT © 1956 BY VARDIS FISHER
ALL RIGHTS RESERVED
PRINTED IN THE UNITED STATES

LIBRARY OF CONGRESS CATALOG CARD NUMBER 56-7740

*To* MARGARET *and* RICHARD J. PEAD

*of London*

*A Scot and an Englishman*

*and to all I owe to the cultural*

*heritage of the British Isles*

## FOREWORD

If any reader thinks it unlikely that a white girl could have been on the scene as an Indian I would refer him to John Henry Moberly, an HB factor of a little later time, who says in his *Journal:* "Quite a number of women among the Indians who came to the trading posts in those days had no sign of a drop of Indian blood. Their hair was light, they had blue eyes and good figures and, except for sunburn, were as fair as any white woman. For this there was an explanation: when the Indians raided an immigrant train on the American side they killed all grown people and boys but preserved the female children, who grew up perfect Indians in their ways. Rarely could they be persuaded to leave their Indian friends." In regard to the concluding statement see H. H. Peckham's *Captured by Indians,* which contains fourteen original narratives by captives.

On the virtues and vices of the two companies or on the degree of right on either side I pass no moral judgment. A. C. Laut says, "I can see very little difference in the faults on both sides." All authorities agree on the wanton debauching of the Indians. John Henry was all over the place just before the time of this novel. In his *Journal* he says, "Indians totally neglect their ancient customs; and to what can this degeneracy be ascribed but to their intercourse with us, particularly as they are so unfortunate as to have a continual succession of opposition parties to teach them roguery and destroy both mind and body with . . . rum?" Charles B. Reed says, "Whisky [rum] was poured out in a flood, the naked warriors of forest and plain were totally demoralized, while the struggle for peltries was carried on with a fury and a deadliness that cause it to appear less like a licensed commerce than a wholesale brigandage." Morton (the present secretary of the HB Company calls his history of western

Canada "momumental") says, "In the fierce competition the traders whose posts stood side by side led a cat-and-dog life in which principles of honesty and fair play had no part."

With one exception among the principal characters and with two exceptions among the principal scenes, all the persons and scenes in this novel are the author's own creation and, save in a general historical way, owe nothing to persons or events that actually existed.

VARDIS FISHER

*New York City*
*December 23, 1955*

# I

He was sure for a moment that he smelled the thing but after looking round him he decided that he had imagined it and stretched out on his back in the berry thicket, a late-summer sun full in his face, his hand on either side reaching out to break twigs off and bring the luscious fruit to his lips, each berry a deep blue skinful of juice. No other fruit in the world, and certainly no other berry, was comparable for him in richness and uniqueness of flavor with the huckleberry, high in the Canadian Rockies, away up in the area of deep snows, of the odor of fir and spruce and grapevine. The sparkling music of a finch filled his ears and at last his mind; and turning his head a little, he saw the bird, a brownish-gray-washed-with-orange little fellow; and becoming aware now that he was thirsty, he supposed that water must be near, because this finch built its nest and lived close to pure cool water. But he was in no haste; the berries were almost a drink in themselves, or would have been by the handful. The curse of huckleberries was that they grew singly and were so damned small: it took a man hours to fill his belly and get that exquisite huckleberry feeling all through his senses, until he smelled and tasted full of it. Holding a twig above him and taking the fruit berry by berry with his lips, he wondered if he could hire squaws to gather the fruit for him, so that he could find out if it would blend in pemmican with buffalo hump and moose fat. He sat up and gathered a palmful and poured them into his mouth and crushed them, and the juices gushed against his throat and brimmed over his teeth and burst at his lips.

He had been higher up, for at heart he was a mountain man, not a prairie or plainsman; he had been on top of the world. He had stood on the Athabasca Pass, by a small lake, by a glacier, and had looked on a part of God's earth that was magnificent beyond description; had looked west, where majestic mountainous masses stood in cool remote grandeur farther than a man could see; and north and northeast; and then east across the mists of a vast prairie that unrolled clear to Lake Winnipeg and only God knew to what lands and waters beyond. What a country it was! What an amazing lake that had been at his feet: a part of its water went west and into the great Columbia, that flowed around craggy spurs and through Arrow Lake and south and west to the Pacific, for a thousand or fifteen hundred miles or more; and a part of the water went east into the Athabasca, which flowed north and northeast to hell and gone, until its waters were lost and darkened among the floes of a frozen ocean. And everywhere, all around him, was the finest beaver country on earth, with the accursed pedlars right in the middle of it.

He had been exploring the country at Jim's suggestion, for they both knew that the desperate struggle between the old and honorable Hudson's Bay Company and the interlopers, who called themselves the North Westers but whom HB people contemptuously dismissed as the pedlars, would turn for triumph or defeat on the conquest of terrain or the loss of it. From the heavens to the oceans this was HB land. He was no such explorer and geographer as Alexander Mackenzie, who had gone clear to the mouth of the fabulous Mackenzie River; nor a David Thompson, who went from the Great Lakes to the end of the Columbia, surveying and mapping. Shifting his position and still drenching his throat with juices, he went on thinking.

The trouble with the Hudson's Bay outfit was that it was slower than the Second Coming. Why had its management allowed the pedlars to buy out John Jacob Astor on the Columbia, and so get control of an empire of fur clear to the head of that river's greatest tributary, the Snake? Now, off yonder in the mists, dotted and seamed with nobody knew how many lakes and rivers, was the Eldorado of the fur trade, the broad-timbered Athabasca land. Why had HB let the pedlars get their murderous hands on it? More than half the fortunes the Montreal men had made had come out of there, while HB's sleepy fogbound directors in London sipped their port and vetoed every suggestion for more enterprise and vigor that came from their officials six thousand miles away. The Montreal men could act, at once, decisively, and with terrifying energy, while the HB men had to consult London, across oceans, and weeks or months of time. It had got so bad, Jim said, that a man now had to get permission to fart or blow his nose. Most of the bosses in London had never been out of London. Their idea of a big river was the Thames; of a mountain, Ben Nevis; of a long journey, to Glasgow or Paris. If they had the initiative and vigor of a pedlar postboy they would have seized the immense advantages that came from the explorations of Mackenzie and Thompson and others; but what could you get by writing humble letters to timid and grog-filled old men and signing off, "Beg to remain Dutiful and Obedient Humble Servant to Command, David McDonald"? Though David McDonald, David admitted, plopping berries into his mouth, was not a factor but only the post manager, chief trader, botanist, concocter of pemmican, and bully boy.

HB had followed the pedlars post by post up the Saskatchewan, like men too timid to lead and grateful for another day of life. Pierre Lemoin, with that wicked light in his eyes, that perpetual grin in his sandy furze, said the loss of their dividends had paralyzed the directors' wills. That was it. It made a man sick in his guts when he saw the furs the pedlars brought down the rivers. Jesus, what pelts! And now—David rolled over, then rolled back to bring his gun close —now a queer pale thing named Lord Selkirk had bought control and had no more interest in furs, it was said, than the Dean of Canterbury had in a Cree squaw. The fool was sending settlers to the Red River, their hair standing up. So now you had to fight both the pedlars and this lunatic who imagined that these northern prairies would grow wheat and cabbages. Jim said it would soon be pedlars west and north of you, cabbages and kidney pies all around you, and far away in London the honorable directors dozing over their port.

They reminded David of a greenhorn who had come out. As famished as a wolf in January, he had refused one strange dish after another and at last in a fit of anger had cried that he wouldn't eat bear drippings. But where had he seen bear shit? It was true that pemmican made of pounded buffalo tongues, marrow fat, syrup, and berries sometimes looked like what a bear dropped if he had his gut full in the berry season. This greenhorn—— Suddenly David moved. There was that smell again and there was no other smell in the world like it. In the next moment he had let his duffel slip off his shoulders and over his head. It was strange how a man could feel this sort of thing: he had heard nothing, had seen nothing, but he knew it was there and he knew what it was. The silvertip was meanest when leanest but he was mean any time he saw a poacher in his berry thicket. David softly took his gun, reached around to see if the dagger was at his waist, jerked his blanket around so that he could use it, and very slowly rose to his feet.

Chills went all over him, for there it was, looking at him. God Almighty, he had seen grizzlies but never such a monster as this. The monster, as though to show off all his dreadful size, rose to his hind legs, his small eyes fixed on David, his fury and outrage rising in heat under his deep fur. That was the trouble with a silvertip: the awful beast would attack anything any time, especially poachers in his domains or among his meat caches. David had killed a number of them. He knew them well. He knew that this giant would stand only a few moments and then soundlessly would sink to four feet, and rush forward and rise again. It was fatal to turn your back on this creature. It was fatal to retreat. The silvertip's small dim mind was confused by anything that had the gall to stand and face it; and so, instead of rushing furiously to the kill, it advanced in charges, showing, not fear, but a slight paralysis of its will. It might rise twice or three times. You had to watch it and figure out how it was feeling about things. You knew that when it was six or eight or ten feet from you all you had to do to make it stand again was to toss your hat or jacket or blanket over its face. The stupid monster would then rear up and give you a moment to shoot it right through its brain. Men whose aim was bad or whose nerve faltered left their bones where they stood.

He had rushed twice and he was coming again and there he was, only a few feet from David, this mightiest of all killers; and a moment later he had the blanket over his eyes and with his tiny mind bewildered and his will frozen he got to his hind legs; and in the next moment he had a bullet through his brain and he came down as soundlessly as the flight of an owl and looked like nothing but a huge pelt in a berry thicket. He hardly shuddered but David shuddered and felt a little weak. It took just about all a man had to stand his ground when that monster came charging. Alexander Henry had told of shooting a bear that ran away and hid and of trailing it by its blood and shooting it again; and of how he discovered that his first bullet had gone through the heart. David supposed the man had lied. A deer might run fifty or even a hundred yards after being shot through the heart but it was fantastic to say that a bear had gone a quarter of a mile and was found licking its wound. David rammed powder and ball home, for there might be another; and he stared at the beast and wondered again what a man would do if his gun missed fire. A grizzly could gut a horse or a buffalo from shoulder blade to thigh bone with one stroke of his dreadful talons. One sweep down a man's frame would take half the ribs and all the organs out of him. . . .

Well, there he was, as dead as the bear grease on a squaw's braids. David stooped for berries and filled his mouth. There was a lot of meat and a lot of fat in that monarch but the hell of it with grizzly was that if you put a hunk of it on to boil it stunk you out of the post. It smelled worse than a squaw dying of syphilis. Gathering berries, eating, looking at it, David thought of the grim sports of north country men: they would find coons in hollow trees, or bears, and set fire to the tree and club the beasts to death after the tree fell over. And what they did to female wolves . . .

He looked round him for water but could smell none. He thought for a moment of opening the beast and eating a part of its liver but he only felt into the fur to sense its depth and thickness, then slung his duffel and blanket over his back, rested his gun in the crook of his arm, and turned down the mountain, filling his lungs with relish because he was in huckleberry and fir country. Under a great tree he stopped to gather gum. Exuded fir gum in reddish nodules was too hard to chew alone and soon crumbled but there was a soft sticky kind of the color of prairie water, and when he mixed the two in the right proportions he got a gum that for him was one of the delights of earth. He gathered both kinds and stored them away with his pemmican; and chewing fir gum and marveling at the woods strength of its flavor, he looked out over distant prairies toward Edmonton. He didn't want to go back to the fort yet. This was man country and it was good to get your bones full of it before you went back to the badgers and the buffalo grass. It was good for a man to look at himself in mountain water and give his emotions to the sun.

Choosing a grassy mound, he sat where he could look across forest to prairie, across prairie to the vast dark timber belt of the Athabasca, and yonder through mists to Thunder Bay. It was also good for a man to have a woman, but damned if he wanted a squaw. Nitties, all of them. Dunting cases. Still, it might be smart to take the daughter of a chief, as a man named Harmon had done, saying, "Now I'll get all the furs of the goddamned Crees." It was not only pelts; a man's life was safer in this northern empire if he stood within the approval of a powerful chief. But squaws were such wanton bitches: for beads or vermilion or a drink of rum most of them would lie down for any white man. Unlike white women, they didn't pretend that they were unable to read a man's mind but came right up and looked you in the eye; and if you acted dumb about it they would point between their thighs or right at your cod, as though wondering if you had forgotten you had it. Most white men seemed to like it that way. Maybe it was the Scot in him or maybe the Scot had nothing to do with it; or maybe it was their confounded stink, their smell of rancid fat and lodge smoke and the urine used in tanning and the accumulation of filth ever since their birth. So far as he knew, a squaw never bathed except when she fell into a river or was shoved in by her buck to swim across and catch the horses.

He laid his duffel aside and stripped off his leather shirt to feel upon him the sun like a blessing and the breeze like a woman's fingers. Far away yonder Jim Dugald was worrying his ass off about the pedlars. Perhaps he was saying, "The goddamn French. It was beaver that led Joliet and Marquette and La Salle to the Mississippi and La Vérendrye to the Saskatchewan and the Black Hills. They had trading posts from Montreal up the Lakes and across to the Lake of the Woods and on to Winnipeg and to hell and back. The sons of bitches were as thick as ducks on the Ohio, the Wabash, the Wisconsin, and the Illinois, and they were on the Arkansas, the Osage, the Red, and the Kansas . . . !" To hear Jim talk, the French were a pestilence, but there were more Scots than French among the pedlars—McTavish, McLoughlin, Mackenzie, Mackintosh, McMurray, McGillivray, McMillan, McLeod—there was a whole shitaree of them. Among the officials David couldn't think of a French name.

He drew the duffel to him and opened his skin of pemmican and looked at it. He should have cut that fat silvertip open and eaten his liver. He looked round him for something to kill and eat but saw only the foolish face and wide popping eyes of an owl and heard only the derisive hooting of a bluejay. On the lakes high up in these mountains there were things for a man to see—a thousand swans as white as snow, the high swift V's of wild geese, a skyful of loons, their insane laughter freezing a man's blood, the heavens full of pigeons. The pemmican was dry and looked like boot leather. It tasted like boot leather, for this had been taken in trade from Indians, a bag of pemmican for a quart of rum that was chiefly

Saskatchewan water. Pemmican needed plenty of marrow fat, buffalo tongues and bosses, moose noses and beaver tails, venison, geese, ducks, wild berries, maybe a little sherry or brandy. All the squaws did was pound up old buffalo bull and mix it with any fat they had; and if it swarmed with maggots and with flies and ants, they all got mixed in. David sniffed it.

He dipped his strong teeth into the hard chunk and tore right and left on it like a dog. While chewing he looked down at his leather shirt for signs of lice. Indians, he reflected, knew how to delouse a garment: they tossed it into the hill of the fierce red ants. They had a lot of good tricks. It took a red man to track an animal with nothing but a sense of smell.

A buck would reach down and draw through his closed hand a bough of juniper. He would breathe of his palm as though inhaling incense. He would gently sniff, here, there, and offer the odors to you; and if you were talking in jargon, he would say, "*Tolobus*," meaning that the male wolf had made water there. You could detect dog urine, all right, mixed with juniper incense. He would put a palm low against an aspen trunk and sniff it and mutter, "*Lemora*" —and wild it was, for it was the stench of the wolverine.

A little later, eating and blinking, David thought of his hunger for a woman. He might have had one sent out from back home but for the experience of one of the traders. Fed up to his knackers with squaws, he had asked his people to send him a wife, and when she came he looked her up and down and wrote mournfully to his mother: "Received, one wife in fair shape; hope she will prove good, for God knows she is a rum one to look at." A native wife cost a white man only a little; a bride from back home wanted too many things, including a promise of all the tea she could drink.

David put the pemmican away. A long Saskatchewan feeder burst from the mountain not far from where he was and it was down this stream that his canoe was hidden. He walked briskly through deep forest for most of an afternoon and at dusk came to the first waters. He lay on his belly and drank; the water had the pure unearthy unmineral taste of melted snow. He could spend the night here or he could go down through darkness, and while he was thinking of the matter he heard a beast approaching. Seizing his musket, he turned, rolling, and crouched on his knees, peering out, listening, smelling. It was a mule deer and it was suspicious, for it was looking toward him, ears attentive, gentle eyes wide. He raised his gun and broke its neck. That was better. He would kindle a fire and roast most of it and eat the liver raw and leave the pemmican to the wolves.

The next morning he descended again, alert to the presence of Indians. He was in trapping country now. Somewhere over there was Rocky Mountain House, built in 1802 by John McDonald of Garth, a small man with a crippled arm and the courage of a wolverine. But he was a pedlar. He might have been a relative too. David paused now and then to sniff, for he thought he could smell Indians; the tribes all pretended to be friendly but the white men who had believed them were dead now. This was Blackfoot country. As rum sponges the Blackfeet could be almost as bad as the Crees or the Saulteurs, but they had never welcomed the white man with his fire-water and syphilis. They liked the rum but they hated the trader and, above all, they hated this Lord Selkirk. What right, they asked, had he to take from them their ancient living and hunting grounds to give them to pale repulsive-looking people from across the oceans, who preferred to toil like slaves and grow what only slaves would eat? For an Indian, David had learned, food meant meat: vegetables were for those degraded enough to raise them. . . .

He was going softly on moccasined feet, his senses almost as alert as an Indian's, for he had been in this country since he was eighteen and he was now twenty-six. He advanced softly, but the moment he became suspicious he stood dead-still. It was true that a moose, when started, would run in circles until it got wind of the enemy, it was true that many wild things depended chiefly on their sense of smell; but nearly all of them were like the dull-witted buffalo, dim of vision and hearing: they sensed the presence of an enemy in movement. David had taken one law from a wise old hunter: when in danger, stand still. So he would stand motionless but for the movement of his breathing chest, his nostrils trying to detect and separate the odors.

He had heard a sound and he was standing still, smelling, listening, looking, when he saw a flash, a fleeting moment of color, and knew at once that it was the beast of all beasts that trappers, both red and white, hated with a hate as futile as it was bitter. This murderous thing, with strong sharp teeth and large powerful claws, this thing that was afraid of nothing on earth, seemed to live only to steal bait and to hide or destroy traps. Why it wanted to make off with steel traps nobody knew. No man, Indians said, could hide a cache that the wolverine could not find or build a lodge that it could not enter. David went warily forward, his nose trying to catch an odor that he knew well. He had heard from outraged trappers how this snarling, ugly-faced killer with drooling lips and eyes livid with hate, this thing that alone with the grizzly was unafraid of man and would attack a bear as soon as a rabbit—how with its powerful jaws it wrenched traps out of shape, how it would never back up from any living thing, how it sometimes robbed a camp of every stick of furniture.

He supposed there must be trap lines close by, though he had seen no beaver cuttings and it was too early in the season. He went to the spot where the brown flash had appeared and fell to his knees and sniffed; but everything here was saturated with wild smells—with the odor of skunk and civet, of wolf and bear, fisher and stoat and coyote; with the breath and urine and dung, the matings, the living and dying of countless things down through the ages. You could take a handful of leaf depth and needles and tree mold and smell all these odors in it but never the human odor, as in Scotland and England, as all over Europe; never the human odor in all this land except in human nests, and never, above all, the odor of human dung. People had just about shit themselves out of home and country in Europe and had so fouled their rivers that they were only stench and diarrhea. Over there a man couldn't go off a road or path and fling himself down without leaping up, speechless with disgust and shock; but in this Canadian world a man could fling himself down anywhere. You could stretch out anywhere except where the buffalo had just emptied, but that smell was nothing like the smell of the meat eaters. The voyageurs, the members of the brigades, rowing like galley slaves eighteen hours a day and eating six or eight pounds of pemmican and sweating like men with high fevers were enough at the end of a journey to stink up the whole country from the Grand Portage to Peace River.

He moved off, looking for landmarks by which he had marked the canoe's hiding place, and came to the river just below a series of rapids. Upstream the water was striking stones and rising like plumes of shattered frost, and downstream it was gurgling back under cool sunless banks, where willow and cottonwood and birch, almost washed away in their roots, leaned defeated out over the current. He had hidden his canoe back under a bank, and now, after looking round and listening, he shinned out along a trunk, its lower branches far out smiting the water mighty blows while the straining roots groaned in their depths, and reached under and back to drag the canoe forth. He slipped down to it and shot out into the stream, stroking with noiseless and effortless grace. The river was so overhung that he journeyed alternately through shadow and sunlight.

The next day after canoeing and portaging he was down to the foothills. Now and then he cupped water in a palm and drank. Indians, the fools, thought a white man crazy if he drank water, yet had rum; they had become such drunkards that when earthbound-drunk, eyes glazed, and wills paralyzed, they wouldn't drink water even to wash their guts out but, like La Brute, the half-breed, would beg for more firewater, muttering, "Heap rum big me!" David smiled, remembering a squaw who drank so much rum that she turned stiff and cold and was thought dead for two days.

He was out now where the prairie on either side was like green carpet with knee-deep nap and he was stroking along at about twenty miles an hour when the corner of his eye picked up movement a half mile away on his right. He rested his paddle and looked. At first he thought it was only a buffalo bull, his gut filled, standing alone and sunning himself; but then he saw the paler color, the tawny, and the leaping movements, and like one responding to a reflex, he raised the paddle and shoved for the right bank. He anchored the canoe and climbed out with his gun, and by this time he was feeling a little foolish; for what difference did it make if the old thing just lay down from weariness and died or if the wolves cut his sinews and pulled him down? They would eat him anyway. Would it be better if all old beasts were slain and not left to the pains and loneliness of slow dying? Well, most of them *were* slain: a natural death in this country was not normal, even to man.

At a hundred yards he stopped to look. The old fellow was pretty weak, almost too weak to be angry; he was still turning, head lowered, and the wolves still respected his horns, though they were, David imagined, little more than bone thumbs now. He raised his gun intending to shoot the largest and most energetic wolf but then changed his mind and murmured, "*Paire gaupie!*" If he shot all four of the wolves, another pack would soon be along. Compassion? He had once spoken of this thing to Jim: what a spectacle it was, he had said, with wolves following the caribou herds, with foxes following the wolves, with rats, lemmings, and rodents following the foxes! What in hell was life, Jim had asked, except kill or be killed? The only things not killed and eaten were those whose flesh nothing could stomach. The fisher killed the marten; the mink the muskrat; wolverine, otter, bear, wolf, and lynx killed the beaver; and the beaver, a dumb bastard that killed only trees, had caused an exodus of trappers from the Old World and two companies were now fighting like hell for the poor bugger's hide. . . .

It would soon be over now: the old fellow, whose eyes were never worth a damn, having been dim from birth and soon covered over with forelocks of hair, and which now in old age were nearly blind, had sunk one hind leg into the worst evil of the prairie, the badger hole, and was expressing his helplessness in anguished bellows. The wolves were swift to seize their chance. Two on either side, they were sinking their sharp fangs into tough old bull hide and into flesh, biting in, deeper and deeper, seeking the tendons which, having found, they would gnaw in two; and then the old lord would sink to his haunches and his enemies would gut him open and proceed to the feast.

David moved nearer. In other times he had seen the killing of a weary old bull and he hadn't liked it. He went so near that he could see the color of the wolves' eyes. They were going into the belly now, or two of them were, and two were working into the hams, and it made a man's guts curl to see their eagerness. The shaggy old monster, once a lord of the plains, whose thick skull matted deep with hair had many times driven bone against the bone of his rivals, kept on his spindling forelegs, his head up now because of the agony, his lonely old voice crying to the sky. David raised his gun and took careful aim and fired. The bull sank, not all at once but slowly, as through almost palpable weariness; and four bloody faces turned, with eyes in them as cold as the eyes of the horned owl. They looked at David and snarled, but after a few moments they were feeding again.

Sitting in his canoe, he drifted while eating venison roast and wishing he had salt. The red man wouldn't touch salt, and maybe it was no good for a man; but more than salt he wanted some green succulent plant, for a man got scurvy eating meat four or five times a day. The Crees ate pond lilies and wild potatoes and artichokes and mushrooms; those would do, especially mushrooms, which in cool high country were the champagne of vegetables. Tribes along the Snake collected grasshoppers by the ton, preferably the wingless kind with bloated bellies, and roasted them and rolled them into pemmican.

That sounded as bad as bread which the Okanogans made with tree moss which they buried in a hole with hot stones a day and a night and then molded into cakes. Biscuits of powdered sunflower seeds were better, but what he wanted now was some vegetable swimming in melted butter and a bowl of huckleberry dumplings. A man wondered after eight years, after bear and buffalo and elk and moose and caribou and beaver fat, after fish fat and porcupine belly and otter blubber and deer marrow, if there was such a thing as butter after all. Or a clean woman with her hair just washed and hanging wind-blown and sun-kissed down her back and her complexion clear of grease and vermilion and her cheeks clear of soot and her eyes steady and without suspicion. Or a child who did not look as if he had spent all his time squatting in lodge smoke and bathing in melted tallow. Or a soft bed by an open window that opened on the river Dee and the Grampians and Ben Macdhui. He sighed, for he knew that such things would be his no more. There were good things over in Scotland, things to spend your passion on, but he would forget them, they would fade away into the steady withdrawal of all childhood memories, the hills of home, the river, the smell of the North Sea, the autumn mists on the highlands, the look in his father's face when he said he was going, in his mother's eyes. It was pretty stupid to be drifting along in a canoe and chewing venison and filling up with homesickness. By God, he would get him the cleanest squaw girl he could find and he would skelp her doup, he would put a look in her eyes that she would never get out of them; a princess, of course, who might cost him a jug of rum or a military coat in the time of Henry VIII, with braid and shining buttons and a gold stripe. Many of the white men who came to this country, but not all, not even a majority, married squaws and learned to their horror that a squaw could be as jealous as any white woman, could even go up a tree and hang herself for that reason alone. Big John McLoughlin seemed to have a great love for the Indians; he said that in some ways a squaw was a hell of a lot better wife than a white woman.

If the white man didn't want to marry the red woman, a buck would rent his wife for the night for a swig of rum or a bright ribbon. Now and then a buck had an extra wife, or even two or three, whom he rented out to the white men and kept chiefly for that purpose. If you married a squaw and got tired of her you could just walk off and leave her or trade her: some of the French and half-breeds were forever haggling and bargaining over their sullen spouses, each striving to get boot, if no more than a trifle, for the sake of pride and prestige. But David was not at all sure that he could ever walk away from a wife, even if he felt that she was not a wife really. He would be fond of the children. And he would realize, as so many had, that if you deserted them they would hate you and become so villainous that hell wouldn't have them. Look at the Bois Brulés, whom the pedlars were now inciting to murder!

And so, drifting and eating, he moved down the river, wondering about his future, planning and dreaming.

## II

He had been drifting north but now the river swung east around a great bend and flowed lazily through burnt-over country as flat as a floor. Looking back, he wondered when he had passed Wolf River, or the spot where Piegans murdered a batch of Crees to avenge a murder on the Rivière au Calumet. As he rounded the bend the first thing to catch his eye was a group of Indians on the south bank. Their presence did not alarm him, for he was now in what was supposed to be friendly area and he imagined that this group was on its way to the post to bargain for fall provisions. The next thing to catch his eye was a swimmer at some distance from him. At once he understood the whole picture: the Indians had their horses with them and they were crossing the river; and, as was their custom, they were sending the squaws across first, or the younger ones who were expert swimmers, to catch the horses as the beasts emerged. Looking at the smooth water ahead, he saw a number of swimmers, and on the north bank one who had come out, stark-naked; and then he saw one who brought from him a gasp of amazement.

This one, like the others, was downstream from him but closer to his canoe. The moment he looked at her she dived. He now realized that in the last few minutes she had probably been under water most of the time, hiding from him, for he had not seen her until this moment. And now she was gone. This struck him as being quite unusual: squaws ordinarily did not care if a white man saw them naked and it certainly was not their way to swim under water to hide from his gaze. David seized the paddle and shot the canoe forward. He knew that she would be stroking under water toward the north bank. Then suddenly she shot up and when her head came above water her eyes were like drenched agates under little awnings of black silk. Again he gasped. This, he thought, was no squaw, for in that moment he had seen her eyes clearly and they were not the jet black of an Indian's but the gray of rain-washed sage.

She had come up for only a moment and was gone again, and he saw her deep under like a bronzed image wreathed with river moss. He shot the canoe over to head her off. He bent over the canoe, peering down, and saw that the undulant water distorted her form, as in a series of grotesque mirrors. Six or eight feet under she was going swiftly toward the north bank, and again he shot forward and put himself between the bank and her. Again she came up like a cork and the instant her head was clear her gaze was on him and he saw in her eyes that she hated him. With his paddle he knocked a fountain of water over her and her mouth opened wide to show her teeth and her lids darted up to show the full fury of her eyes, reminding him of the wolverine's face when confronting an enemy.

Jesus! he thought as she dived again. He now headed for the bank and quickly beached his canoe and seized his gun and waited. She came up and saw him and disappeared; and he stood there, thinking about her, admiring her, for she could swim like an otter. He supposed that she would veer upstream or down to try to avoid him and he kept a sharp lookout, and suddenly she made the bank and stood up as if she had never seen him at all. But the moment he started toward her she began to run. She ran so fast that the braids of her hair lay out on the wind behind her, leaving her nape visible to him, and the little valley between her shoulder blades. David stood six feet two, and though he weighed two hundred and twenty pounds there was not a snippet of fat on him; and he also ran like the wind and after a hundred yards overtook her, with the wet smell of her in his nostrils. In that moment, knowing that she was overtaken, she swung to him, her whole face flashing with contempt.

Still astonished, he looked at her. In spite of the way bear grease, and now water, plastered her hair low on her forehead, and of the vermilion washed into fantastic patterns, he thought her very lovely. She was poised in scorn like a wild thing cornered, and while her eyes defied him and her lips curled and her face, yes, and her body, expressed the hate she felt for him, he looked her up and down, observing how fine her breasts were, her belly and flanks, her legs.

He stepped back for a better view. Squaws in general were so short of leg that they looked dumpy, but this girl had legs in proportion to her torso and they were beautifully shaped, from the pubic hair, bejeweled with tiny river drops, to the slender ankles and the arched feet.

"You're white," he said. He knew that it was a custom with Indians to kill all the men and boys among their white captives, and often the women, but almost never the female children. Many tales were told of children who had grown up, not knowing they were white, and of their fierce resistance when, found by relatives, they were asked to return to their people. She was white, he told her again, but there was no response in her face. She still stood poised like a statue—but no, like a wild thing waiting to be slain, and contemptuous of her killer. He could tell that she was white. She was bronzed all over, she was almost as red as an Indian, but her eyes were gray and her hair was not black and her features were not those of the redskin.

"Do you speak English?"

She made a slight turn as though to flee and he grasped her arm to hold her. Almost spitting at him, she looked at his hand and tried to throw it off. Sensing that she could not, she drew a sharp breath and again met his eyes, her own eyes expressing more scorn than he had ever seen, even in a half-breed. Shamed, he released her.

He had only a smattering of various Indian languages. He spoke some Chinook. He had no idea that she was a Cree but he knew the word for woman in Cree and he said, "*Isquayo?*" There was no change in her. "*Aki?*" he said, using the Blackfoot word. He stared at her a moment and said "*Poxaput?*" It was the Blackfoot word for come. At once she stepped back from him.

She pointed toward his post and the word came out hard and small and cold: "*Mistaput!*" It was the Blackfoot word for go.

"Oh no," he said, shaking his head and smiling at her. "*Ketuckhomin?*" That was the Blackfoot word for love. "To post?" he asked, his gesture embracing all the Indians on the river. "Edmonton?" He was beginning to feel a little silly, to feel like one who had caught a golden eagle and didn't know what to do with it. Did she speak Chinook? "*Ka-was?*" he asked, meaning, Are you afraid? Her gaze never left his eyes and never wavered. "Siwash," he said, waving toward the Indians. "You no siwash. No siwash," he said, shaking his head no at her. He couldn't think of an Indian or Chinook word for white.

He felt that he had to keep talking or she would run away from him; he wanted to look at her, to feast starved eyes on her womanly form, possibly to hear a tender word from a white woman's mouth. Where had she been captured, when, by whom? Perhaps by some tribe on the Missouri or Mississippi. Had she been traded or sold from tribe to tribe, as white women sometimes were, until at last she had come into the keeping of the Blackfeet away up here? Was she still a virgin? He looked down over her form and was sure that she had never borne a child.

Turning to the river where the horses were emerging and the squaws were catching them, he said, "*Sichekiekoon*," the Blackfoot word for themselves. "Not you," he said. "You no *Sichekiekoon*. Wigwamming?" he asked, pointing north, meaning, Do they intend to pitch their lodges up there? There was no change in her eyes. "There?—*temolo*?" Then, smiling at her, he asked softly, "*Netokee-mun*?" In the Blackfoot tongue he had asked her if she would be his wife. And still there was no change in her eyes.

There now came toward them an Indian and David recognized him as Horned Thunder, an important chief, whose squaw Tanino had had her nose chewed off to the bone because of adultery. No white man liked this chief, none trusted him. When drunk he was as murderous as a wolverine. He came up, looking at David, his eyes subtly hinting of insolence and menace; and David with studied deliberation moved his gun over to his left side and reached over with his right hand to hold it, so that his hunting knife would be close to that hand. Horned Thunder did not miss the significance of the movement.

He came up and looked at David. One good thing about this chief, David was thinking, was that he spoke some English.

Horned Thunder said, "Squaw *oxi*?" and looked at the girl. "You buy squaw?"

David nodded his head yes.

The menace in the chief's eyes was momentarily effaced by sly mirth. He shook his head no. "Him," he said, and pointed.

So that was it! The girl was spoken for by one of the bucks. "Mucha rum," said David, watching the crafty eyes. Did he understand the word rum? "Mucha high wine," he said, using Alexander

Henry's term for it. "Firewater." He thought the black eyes were laughing at him.

"Him," said the sly rogue, again pointing. The one pointed to now came forward and brought to the girl her leather garments and she slipped into skirt and jacket. The one who had come up was also a chief but David thought he had never seen him before. "Him," Horned Thunder said again, his eyes looking very wicked because of their sultry brooding and their broken veins. In a soft voice hinting of insolence and menace he said, "Squaw him mucha loov."

David looked at the girl. "*Ketuckhomin* him?" he asked. He thought her eyes were looking at him a little more curiously. "She love me," he said to Horned Thunder, pointing first at the girl and then at himself. "She loov me mucha."

There was that sly look in the rascal's eyes as he shook his head no. Then the eyes became hooded and looked twice as insolent and menacing. The chief turned to go and David thought furiously, Go, you teurd, and we'll see how much rum you get next time! But that, he knew, was a childish thought: if the chief didn't get rum from HB he would go to the pedlars, and there he would get more, for the pedlars weren't bothered by Lord Selkirk's scruples.

David now became aware of the younger chief's eyes. There was only menace and hate and threat in them—that look of an Indian who hated all whites.

"Go," Horned Thunder said to David, pointing toward Edmonton.

With deliberate insolence David said, "*Mistaput.*"

"Tomorr," the chief said, but tomorrow for an Indian meant any day in the future.

"Tomorrow," David said, nodding.

David then turned abruptly away without looking at the girl and went back to his canoe. He was resolved to have her come hell or high water—not, he told himself, because he was in love with her (his emotions were not mirrors) but because his manhood had been outraged. That insolent bastard, bloated and swollen with pride! What made a redskin think he had a right to a white woman? A white woman was what they wanted when they could get her, in spite of their contempt, feigned or real, for white skin and fair hair and eyes. Stroking along, he recalled that seven years ago he had been naked by the river, bathing, when a group of half-breeds and Indians came up to look at him. They looked with pity and talked among themselves as though discussing one with some dreadful and loathsome disease. It was true that a white skin when exposed to a hot sun simply cooked and turned the color of copper and became ridiculous pouches full of water. But was it natural for a pale skin to be repulsive, even sickening, and for one golden brown or bronzed or even black to suggest affinity with the good rich earth? It was true perhaps that a white man looked bleached and prematurely born and badly in need of a placenta to cover and hide him. Clothes had bleached him out. This girl, probably at birth as white as any, now looked healthy in a rich and colorful way that was deeper than sun stain on her skin. He recalled too the story of the explorer in Africa who expected on coming again to the company of white folk to be enthralled but who was shocked by the sickly-looking faces and disgusted by their empty and pretentious talk.

David looked back but the Indians were distant by several miles now. He remembered images of the girl which he had been only dimly conscious of—of the churning of her fine buttocks when she was running away from him; of her nipples like sun-darkened thimbleberries; of the intoxicating slenderness of her waist when deep under water she made a sharp turn; of the whiteness and perfection of her teeth and the luscious sensuousness of her lips; of the tapering loveliness of her arms and hands. . . . Why in hell should an Indian want her, knowing that she was white under her tan? His mind turned again to squaws. Some of the men loved to tell about the squaws of the Big Belly tribe whose pudendum hung down four or six or more inches: the longer the labia, it was said, the more desirable the woman. It was also said that they got that way because the men pulled on them with their hands from early childhood up. What customs people had, the world over!

He recalled next something that he himself had seen. Years ago there had come to Pembina one Marie Anne Gaboury, the first white woman the Indians in the area had ever beheld. Even after she had become the bride of Batiste Lajimoniere, a famous HB scout, the Indians were never done with adoring her and caressing her soft skin and hair and gazing into her fair eyes as if into the celestial hunting grounds. David had not seen that but he had heard those talk who had seen it. January sixth of the next year, the year David came out from Scotland to seek his fortune, Marie gave birth to the first white child born west of the Mississippi. That's what men said, anyway. She was called Reine because she was born on a king's birthday.

David did see what followed. When Alexander Henry moved his men north from Pembina to the Saskatchewan, hundreds of Indians all along the way came to look at her. It was true that many of them stared as if looking at a specter, that some faces revealed wonder and disgust; but it was also true that squaws had pressed forward to touch Marie's soft hair or skin, as though touching silk, and that some of the bucks tried to buy her from Batiste. A little later Marie was another thing: she became almost as bronzed as an Indian and she learned to ride like an Indian. Batiste put her on his buffalo pony that was taught to kick and nip and wheel and surge in cutting out choice beasts, and Marie, so scared that she was breathless, had the ride of her life, her hands clutching the mane while her baby jounced up and down in a moss bag hanging from the pommel.

David wondered, as he had wondered so many times, why the bucks wanted white wives. It was not for the erotic part of it certainly; the squaws, wanton even when not ardent, willing even when half sick, did their best to appease their mates, and the white men too; but a white wife lying under a buck dripping with vermilion and tallow fat would hardly be, it seemed to David, a willing partner —though he confessed himself a greenhorn in the ways of women. And it was certainly not for the labor: a squaw would do five times the work of any white woman on earth. No doubt it was a prestige of some sort.

And no matter: he intended to have this girl with the gray eyes and the form of a woods nymph and the spirit of a falcon. He would tame her, by God—not break her but just tame her—and she would be his. He would win her love somehow. He told himself this, stroking along toward the post, eating venison, cooling his heated brow and his wrists with gray river water, slapping at mosquitoes, looking right and left at *mine toba,* the land of prairie water, though he thought a better name was *minnesota,* the land of sky-colored water. He would win her, but he knew in all his bones that winning this girl would take more than manly effort. She would be against him from the start, with all the stable and vigilant strength of the white races, all the fire and craftiness of the red. And she would have accomplices, any one of whom would delight in burying a tomahawk in his skull and not one of whom would fight on the level. It was strange that a people as cunning and crafty and treacherous as Indians should have such a horror of night fighting. They simply didn't like to risk their lives in the dark. Oh, they would sneak around in the night and get at you, as a wolf might, but they wouldn't come in force against you when the moon was up and the sun was down.

Horned Thunder himself was enough adversary for any man, white or red. A man who would seize his woman by the throat merely on suspicion and chew her nose off from the bridge down to the upper lip, leaving her to look like a death's-head—well, that was no man to fool with. He had an ungodly temper, as so many Indians had, including the women. He was ready to kill for small reasons. When he got full of firewater he was ready to kill for no reason at all, but now had the good sense before drinking to tell his squaw to hide his weapons. There seemed to be some fascination for an Indian in feeling around a body and sinking a knife to the hilt in all the soft parts. And there was the other one, the scowling assassin out of hell who was determined to make her his wife. Besides these two were all their blood brothers, who would like nothing better than to sit before a lodge fire with a jug of rum and David's scalp and a sharp knife. With the most painstaking artistry they would trim off every tiny scrap of flesh and even up the edges and comb out the hair; they would soften and tan the inside with their horrible stinking mixture of brains and oils and urine; and then, when it was just right, they would make a tobacco pouch or a fire bag out of it and would sit together and smoke and grunt and stare admiringly at the pouch with its long mane of hair hanging from the scalper's girdle. And David's bones, poor lovelorn fellow, would be bleaching somewhere on the prairie after the teeth of wolves had gnawed them clean.

He grinned. The gruesome picture of his end amused him. He didn't intend to come to such an end but in the *pays d'en haut* you never could tell. He knew in that privacy where only David spoke to David that he would rather face a grizzly every day or get lost in a blizzard surrounded by wolves or shoot the rapids in les Dalles aux Morts in a buffalo skin than dare the treacheries of an Indian brave crossed in love. But he would never back up, not now, not ever. He thought he could buy the Indians with rum.

The next day he pulled up at the post, set on a bluff above the river, with a pedlar post only a musket shot away, and pulled the canoe out and with his gun climbed the hill. He looked all around him but he knew that the Blackfeet were not here yet. They would take their time. They would hunt along the way and let their ponies fatten on grass belly deep and they would keep their terrible eyes open for something to ambush or something to steal. It might be a week before they came.

He saw Pierre first, chewing twist, staining his reddish beard with brown juice, his eyes, as always, full of lights that ranged from the impish to the wicked.

"Well," Pierre said, "you're back. We thought mebbe you come to your end on Peace River." He chuckled at that. He thought it a hell of a good joke.

David grinned. "Jim back yet?"

"Oh yeah, and lookin' like a widder just a few days outta her weeds."

"Worried? A big band of Blackfeet is coming in."

Pierre's face did not change at all. First a trapper, now an assistant to the chief trader, hoping someday to be a factor like Jim, he cultivated the point of view that only those died young who were afraid they would.

"It ain't the Blackfeet we have to watch, Jim says. It's the Bois Brulés."

## III

Jim Dugald had had a servant spit and roast half a fat deer in the huge fireplace of the main hall and Pierre's wife Belle-mere bake some rich biscuits and this evening he sat with David before a blazing fir fire to discuss their problems. Jim had been clear over to Fort Douglas on Red River and had brought back with him a few bottles of fine old brandy and port. He now filled two tin cups. The evenings were already becoming chilly in this northern clime; they sliced off hunks of dripping venison and stretched their legs to the fire.

"Well," David said, speaking through meat and juices, "did you learn any more about this Lord Selkirk?"

A few things, Jim said. He had married a very wealthy woman and she seemed to think he was the sun god about halfway up the sky. With her money Selkirk had bought up control of the HB Company. It was said that he despised trapping and the fur trade and had a grandiose vision of a great feudal barony over here, with himself sitting on its apex. Rupert's Land, the land grant which the directors had given him, was larger than all the British Isles and included the finest buffalo country. That was the big reason the Indians were so furious. It was all prairie land, yes, and damned fools might be able to plow it, even to make a cabbage grow in it, but there was a lot of beaver water in it too.

Jim picked up his knife and cut off another half pound. He licked off drops of juice about ready to fall and turned away politely and broke wind. "Goddamn," he said. "A man lives on nothing but meat he spends half his time farting."

David was looking at Jim. He had learned years ago that the chief factor here was rather self-conscious about his physical functions. That was a little strange, for he was a big bastard with heavy shoulders and with the largest hands David had ever seen, even larger than Donald Mackenzie's and Mackenzie weighed three hundred and twenty pounds and looked like a moose. He could outwalk any man in the whole country, and was so active and restless that he was known from Smoky River to Montreal as Perpetual Motion.

"Rupert's Land!" Jim grunted, for he despised agriculture. It would get bigger and bigger. Rupert's Land would be as big as France and then as big as Europe and there wouldn't be a beaver in it, nothing but the goddamned farmers.

"What kind of people are his settlers?"

He hadn't seen any of them, Jim said. The first batches had been glad to get out of there with their hair standing up and their cabins burning behind them. He had heard that some were Scotch Presbyterians, some were foppish Glasgow clerks; there were a few Irish Catholics, a few red-faced Orkneymen, a few Moravian sisters and brothers.

"You mean the pedlars already have been giving them hell?"

Hell, Jim said, was a pretty mild term for it. Three or four years ago they had been warned; Simon McGillivray had said that the colony would be destroyed. Then when the pedlars turned the job over to such men as Duncan Cameron and Alexander Macdonell couldn't Selkirk read the handwriting on the wall?

"Duncan Cameron," David said, looking at Jim. He had seen that man.

The ringleader, Jim said, dressed himself up in a bright red coat and put on a sword and signed his letters as captain and commanding officer of the Red River Voyageur Corps. Jim looked at David to see what he thought of such gall. And to win their confidence he had talked to their leaders in Gaelic and had had them over to the fort for dinners and dancing. He had persuaded a bunch of them to go up into the north to some godforsaken land where no doubt they were freezing to death. Jim said he thought a lot about these people, leaving behind them forever Scotland and their kin and entering a vast unknown continent. They found it rough on Red River: imagine the poor devils up among the ice floes! Those who wouldn't go north he scared the hell out of with the half-breeds: a man would be out plowing when a bullet would almost take his ear off; or in the dead of night there were wild war cries at the windows and women got hysterical and children had nightmares. Haystacks suddenly blazed up at midnight when there was no lightning anywhere. A cabin would catch fire and its occupants would rush screaming into the darkness. And in the end they had all fled like a moostoos with fire in its tail.

"Just last summer?"

Only a couple of months ago, Jim said, filling his tin cup with port. As he saw it, both companies were getting murderous pretty fast; but what had Selkirk thought he would get when he chose one of the wild Macdonells and told him to enforce orders if he had the physical means? Then what had happened? Why, John Warren led a small army against the pedlars at Pembina and took everything they had. John Spencer went up the Assiniboine to their fort, Souris, and demanded to be let in, and when they told him to go to hell his men chopped down the palisades and his men went in and at gun point took everything the pedlars had there. "That," said Jim, glancing over at David, "is a hell of a way to get along with people."

A smile touched David's features. He arose and looked at the woodpile: he liked to burn different kinds of woods for their different smells and sounds. Douglas fir was the noisiest of them all in a fire; it sounded like exploding firecrackers. It had a fine fragrance but so had spruce and aspen and willow. The French called the aspen trembles or tremblers; he laid a few lengths of it on the fire. What would Prince Rupert, first governor of HB, think of things now?

"I suppose," he said, "that made the pedlars pretty damned mad."

So mad, Jim said, that they rushed right out and found the smartest of all the half-breeds, Cuthbert Grant, who had gone to college in Montreal; and they told him to keep the buffalo hunters in line. They told James Grant to keep the Pillager Indians in line, and they told Cameron to hold the forks at Red River and win the colonists to their side or scare the living daylights out of them; and they told Macdonell to keep the west trail open. Macdonell said he was eager to be at them with all his heart and soul. Then a letter turned up which Cameron had written to Grant: it said the Pillagers were sons of gunpowder and eager for plunder and might be persuaded to pay the settlers a midnight visit. "The letter told them," Jim said, again glancing at David, "that the booty would be pretty good."

David lifted his cup. He had a vision of Pillager eyes when a pedlar told them about white-man booty. "I'll be damned," he said.

Jim cut off another slice of venison. It was now known, he said, that they had tried to get the Crees to wipe out the camp. Then they had tried to get the Chipewyans at Sand Lake to do it: the old chief there said they offered him a bribe as big as the moon. It was known that Cuthbert Grant wrote their governor a letter ordering the settlers to burn their crops and buildings and get out. That letter was signed not only by Grant but by William Shaw, Bonhomme Montour, and Bostonnais Pangman, all half-breeds and as fine a gang of cutthroats as you could find in the north.

"That's pretty dirty work," David said.

"Not much dirtier than ours," Jim said. "What did Colin Robertson advise Selkirk to do? Fight fire with fire. He said you can't sit down in a backhouse if it's full of pissants. He said, 'Go hire Frenchmen, they're tougher.'"

"Not as tough as a half-breed."

"Maybe not. They got the worst from both races."

"Well, it has been bad enough, God knows, fighting pedlars, but now we have Selkirk against us."

Jim glanced around him to see if spies were lurking. It had got so you couldn't trust most of your own men, much less an Indian. "Selkirk's our boss," he said. "We can obey orders or we can get out of it. I've been thinking of getting out."

"You'd come back," David said. "This country is in your blood now. It has crowded out everything else."

"Funny thing," Jim said, "they actually do grow wheat and vegetables over there. They had whole damn granaries full of the stuff."

"It might work out if the farmers would let the beaver alone."

"But they'd kill all the buffalo in time."

They were silent a little while and David was looking back to HB's beginnings. Away back in the seventeenth century some young daredevils, of whom one named Radisson was the boldest of all, had pushed westward from Hudson Bay and found wonderful trapping country—a little later Radisson delivered as many as twenty thousand pelts at a time. A few princes and earls and dukes and plain knights got interested and asked King Charles for a charter and the idiot gave them half a continent. He gave them more than he or any other white man had ever heard of—"The whole trade of all those seas, streights and bays, rivers, lakes, creeks and sounds . . . with all the lands, countries and territories upon the coasts and confines of the seas, streights, bays, lakes, rivers, creeks"—a trade monopoly in a vast area; and for all this the Crown was to be paid "two Elkcs and two Black beavers whensoever and as often as Wee our heires and Successors shall happen to enter into the said Countryes." Its correct legal title was "The Governor and Company of Adventurers of England trading into Hudson's Bay," but the princes and earls and dukes had wanted to be called "Gentlemen Adventurers." Adventurers! Not a one of them had ever crossed the ocean or could have told an elk from a moose.

They had a soft time of it, and so had their successors: incorporated in 1670, by 1682 they had Rupert's House, Moose Factory, Albany Factory on James Bay, and Fort Nelson on the west coast of Hudson Bay. They did all right until the French in the valley of the St. Lawrence began to shoot at them: one Le Moyne d'Iberville, as bold a buccaneer as Sir Francis Drake, gave them dreadful shudders and had them frantically looking into their purses: with just a little more luck he would have cleaned out every post they had. But he came and went and they prospered again and had peace until a half century ago the pedlars came on the scene. Even with them it hadn't been bad for a long time, the country was so big, the fur bearers so many millions; but now the angry Lord Selkirk was reading the seventy thousand words of the charter and discovering that the company had powers of war and peace, that it might send "shippes of war men or amunicion unto theire Plantacions, Fortes, Factoryes or Places of Trade" and that anyone who had the gall to trespass would "incurr our Indignacion" and be hauled off to "this Realme of England" to stand trial.

From time to time Parliament had, of course, challenged the charter, and petitioners had said that the company had made no effort to discover the Northwest Passage, had not pushed their settlements to the limits granted by the charter, had abused the Indians and ill-treated their servants, and encouraged the national aspirations of the French. Thus goaded, the Hudson's Bay Company had sent instructions from the secure comfort of its London offices: "Choose out from amongst our Servants such as are best qualified with Strength of Body and the Country Language, to travel and to penetrate into the country." But it was the pedlars who, braver and far more resourceful, traveled and penetrated, clear to what was to be called Alaska and clear to the mouth of the Columbia. A hundred and four years passed before the Hudson's Bay Company's first post was established on the Saskatchewan, and then only because pedlar vigor drove them to it; and after that they just trailed the pedlars, building post by post as the pedlars built. And now the sole boss of HB was a man more interested in cabbages than in furs!

David said, "Does the HB really own all this country?"

"Hell yes, I suppose it does. The highest legal authorities say that its charter is as good as the bank of England. The pedlars say possession is one hundred per cent of law. Selkirk takes up another hitch in his lordship and says they are goddamned poachers who have incurred his 'Indignacion', throw them out. He thinks it's as simple as chasing a poacher off his estate in Scotland."

David was grinning. He wondered what Selkirk would think if he knew how big this country was. Did he know that men had spent months trying to canoe to the end of rivers that seemed to go clear to China? "Well, we don't like it, the pedlars don't like it, the Indians don't like it, only Lord and Lady Selkirk like it."

"That's all," Jim said. "The directors sitting on their fat asses in London and waiting for their dividends aren't going to like it either. As for the redskins, God help us. They have sense enough to see that if the prairies are plowed up there'll be no more buffalo. Selkirk doesn't know what he's doing. He doesn't know a beaver from a musquash. We might have been able to work out a deal with the pedlars—we could take a part of the country, they a part; but Selkirk's idea is contented cows with milkmaids sitting by their bellies. God, they had a cow and a bull over there they named Adam and Eve."

"The hell they did."

"Multiply and replenish the prairies. Who's going to stop him?"

"Not even the half-breeds?"

Jim shook his head gloomily and filled his cup. "He's on his way now with three or four more shiploads of settlers. There are enough fools in Scotland for a lot more shiploads. The pedlars say skin them alive and feed them to the wolves but they don't realize how many

Scots there are who'll turn their solemn Presbyterian faces into the unknown."

David chuckled.

"His farmers fled in their nightshirts, with their houses burning behind them, and Selkirk puts out from Plymouth with another four hundred. When they are scared north to the glaciers or burned in their sheds, Selkirk will be ready with another batch. Clodhoppers, the Indians call them. A chief asked me who but a fool hops over the clods after a plow when you can get all the buffalo hump you want by riding after it?"

"You didn't get to talk to any of the settlers?"

"All gone. Every building burned, every rick of hay, every field of wheat. Nothing but ashes. And when the next greenhorns from Scotland take a look at that site can you see their eyes pushing out for a better look?"

Yes, David could see their eyes standing out. He could see wives turning to look at husbands, husbands at wives. He filled his cup and cut off another slice of meat. "Well, what do we do?"

"Fight fire with fire, I guess. Treat them as poachers, Selkirk says. Use force when necessary, he says, as if we had policemen here. Use force, he says, under a legal warrant." Jim groaned. He turned to look at David. "The idiot thinks we have legal warrants out here."

David held his port in firelight to show its cherry red. He was trying to remember what it was like to live in a physical world as small as Selkirk's.

Jim rubbed a big hand over his bewhiskered and weathered face. "Legal warrants," he said, and leaning forward, blew his nose into the fire.

"Don't suppose his lordship has any idea of distances out here."

"Oh, Christ. His idea of a long journey is from Glasgow to London."

"Does he have any notion of how far Montreal is from where we sit?"

"If he knew that beaver land lies in almost every direction from us farther than from Glasgow to Rome he'd fall over dead."

"He ought to go with one of the brigades."

Jim's smile was thin and pained. He had a picture of this frail lord journeying for fifteen hundred miles in a canoe, his legs cramped, starting at two in the morning, breakfast at eight, stopping at dark, up again at two, chewing on hard pemmican, fighting mosquitoes as big as owls and lice and ticks as hungry as wolves.

Again they fell silent, each with his thoughts. They were two different worlds, David was thinking, this with its vast spaces, mighty rivers, deep winters, and its whole out-of-doors teeming with wild things, and Selkirk's small prim province fenced by a hedge and smelling of age and weariness, in which a hill was called a mountain, a creek a river, a distance of fifty miles a journey. What would Selkirk think of that trader who, bored with the white immensities and silences of January, hiked on snowshoes a hundred and fifty miles through twenty-below-zero weather merely to spend a night or two with a friend and swap a little gab? Here a man thought nothing of that. That was not a journey, that was only a visit. David reckoned that in the past two months he had covered three thousand miles afoot and by canoe. That was an ordinary part of a man's life here. To get together at Christmas time for drinks and a brawl men thought nothing of journeying hundreds of miles by dog sled.

The stuff about legal warrants revealed the picture in Selkirk's mind. The man seemed to think there were governors here, policemen, courts, judges, jails. Did he realize that there was neither money nor taxes? If his settlers were burned to the ground and driven into the northern winds, did he think he had only to take the matter to court? And to court where? In Montreal?—where the pedlars were a political power, with their sumptuous Beaver Club, in which they entertained every influential person who came there? Did he know that the nearest court of justice to some of the posts was two thousand miles away?

David turned to look at Jim's brooding face.

"I guess," Jim said, stirring, "we'll have to fight just as dirty as the pedlars fight. So from now on around here that's orders. The two companies are making nothing but drunken sons of bitches out of the Indians and the pedlars now are bribing them with rum to steal our food and traps, destroy our snowshoes and sleds, shoot our dogs, bribe our trappers or scare them to death, and set on our men the squaws most rotten with syphilis." He looked over at David. "We've got to do more of that ourselves."

"I reckon."

"It's either give up to them or beat their asses off."

"Fire with fire, Colin said."

"That reminds me but this is a secret: Colin is going to get brigades ready to go right into the Athabasca."

David sat up straight and looked at Jim. "Jesus," he said.

"He's smart," said Jim.

"Smart, yes, but their toughest men are up there."

"Colin will send tough men."

"Does he still talk as much as ever? Doc McLoughlin says he's the most frivolous blabbermouth he's ever known."

"McLoughlin is a pedlar." He filled his cup again. "Colin talks a lot but he has plenty of guts."

"Guts, yes, and plenty, but that's not all a man needs in this country. He has to respect the silences."

Jim looked at his post manager and rubbed a palm over his craggy face. "Is Horned Thunder still loyal to us?"

"How in hell can you tell about a redskin?"

"Didn't notice any change in him?"

"No, not exactly." Should he tell Jim about the girl? Not yet, he thought.

"How did you find things?"

"About as we imagined. They have a lot more posts and forts than we have and they're right in the middle of the best beaver land and sitting on it. Their brigade next spring will take out a lot more furs than ours."

"Some of it will be ours," Jim said. "It sure will if their rum holds out." He chewed a mouthful of roast and muttered, "'If after this notice your buildings are continued, I shall be under the necessity of razing them to the foundations.'"

David grinned. "His lordship speaking?"

"That's what the incredible fool wrote to the pedlars. They nearly laughed themselves to death. Then Cuthbert told the Red River governor, 'Get the hell out of here and leave no trace behind.' He scared him right out of his buckskin. Then Selkirk said that in the name of the tombstones of all the Selkirks he would treat them as ordinary poachers."

"And their brag got bigger?"

"Much bigger—and there's nothing bigger than a pedlar's brag. Cuthbert said, 'Let him come over here and we'll put a buttonhole through him he'll never button up.'" Jim was silent a few moments. Then, "Any more of our trappers gone over to them?"

"None I know of."

"Are the independents getting any thicker?"

"There are a few left."

"The pedlars kick them out with a pound of pemmican and two bullets and let them starve. Guess we'll have to do the same."

"Saw the bones of one of them," David said.

"How did you know?"

"Remember Horn? He had a gold tooth."

"Where'd you see his bones?"

"On the Smoky."

"Well," said Jim, yawning, "when Thunder comes in with his assassins, try to find out if the pedlars have been after him. We're short of vermilion, so you'd better mix a little more flour with it after this. Guess we have plenty of rum, but cut it away down when they get drunk. Make him think we admire him as a great chief."

"How about the dunting cases?" Jim looked at him. Jim had just about forgotten his native language. "The squaws. Half our men have the clap or worse."

"I know it but you can't hold men if they don't have women. If only Selkirk would send us a doctor."

"Maybe he thinks all men out here are pure."

"He'll bring not doctors but preachers. As for the squaws, do you know any that are really filthy?"

"Several."

"Tell Thunder to take care of them or no rum."

Again David's face was touched by mirth. He suspected that Horned Thunder was tickled to death to find squaws infecting white men after the white men had brought the scourge to the Indians. And who could blame him for that? Though Indian faces were impassive, once in a while you saw in them a delight that was infernal and the glow of the fires of hate that it fed on. David said he would do the best he could but there was nothing you could do with a man who had woman on his mind and a trinket in his hand to pay for it.

## IV

David lay awake a part of the night thinking of his problems. If John Spencer and his men marched on Souris and chopped the palisades down and walked in it might be well to look this fort over from top to bottom to see if it was sound. He thought it was. Serving not only as fort and post but as supply depot for a large area, it had been built to withstand attack and siege. The stockade was nearly thirty feet high, with corner bastions from which thrust the muzzles of three-pounders. There was a great pile of flintlocks and Queen Bess muskets. On the inside running all the way around was a gallery, set about four and a half feet down from the top; guards could be posted there and could fire safely from their positions. The interior of this stockade was laid out in squares: one contained the house of the officials; another, the lodgings for the artisans and such servants as did not live outside; a third held the trading shops with a square off it for boat building; and there were forges and a carpenter shop, another square for horses and dogs, and still another for general functions. The stockade logs, squared on two opposite sides, had been set four feet into the earth, and though they rotted away in time David thought they were still sound. He would be sure of it, for in this bitter feud you couldn't tell what would happen: the pedlars might march against this fort or send a howling mob of half-breeds.

In regard to what a pedlar had called Adam's disease he was baffled. As David understood it, the pedlar had not meant that poor old Adam fled the garden with the wrath of God on his terrified head and syphilis in his loins but that if he had not been a damned fool, a weak lusting good-for-nothing, there would have been no man-woman problems. Indian women had come to be more than a problem; they were a curse. In summertime they camped near most of the posts and it was impossible to keep the white men out of their lodges. When the brigades came in, the squaws arrived in boatloads, to do business, as their bucks put it. As venereal diseases had spread, the infant death rate had climbed, and it began to look as if eventually no babies would be born alive. In any case, there would be no Indians left; they would all be mongrels of one degree or another. David found it strange that the married squaws had no scruples at all, for a single girl if she got pregnant plunged her family into disgrace. Customs, he thought, we are all their prisoners!

His worst problem of all might be the girl with the gray eyes. The smart thing was to forget her. David had tried but there was something in the wild and beautiful creature that would not be forgotten. He might be able to buy out the young chief's interest in her with guns and ammunition, or with the kind of finery with which chiefs like to pretty themselves up and put on the dog. But even if he had a free path to her as wide as the Saskatchewan he doubted that she would ever have anything to do with him. Lord, with what contempt she had looked at him, with what loathing! And she had reason. Well, he would win her in one way or another, even if he got scalped for it; he would hold her in his arms and let her flutter and pant like a captured bird and he would kiss all the contempt out of those lips, all the scorn out of those eyes. But right now he had to put sensual visions aside and get ready for Horned Thunder and his thirst.

Late one afternoon the Indians came, but not with the formalities of the Piegans! The Piegans considered themselves superior to all other peoples, white or red, and they had so many elaborate ceremonies that trading with them was tedious. They expected the master of the fort to come out and meet them and to shake hands, and the farther from the fort the greater the honor. The chiefs would come in single file, their place in the line determined by the number of scalps each had taken; and the head chief would take a few whiffs of the trader's pipe and then produce his own, which he would fill and kindle and hand to the trader, who must take a few whiffs. It was a tremendous compliment if the chief allowed the trader to light his pipe. When given rum they were just as punctilious: the chief would dip fingers in and let a few drops fall to the earth and then toss a few drops above—with the Piegans nearly everything was according to form. Well, all Indians loved formalities but the Blackfeet were willing to set most of them aside if their thirst was great enough. They came in and began to pitch their lodges and gather wood; and when smoke was rising from lodge fires, David went toward their camp with the half-breed interpreter named Payette. He wanted to learn how they were feeling.

The first lodge they came to was Tanino's. She was sitting in the entrance, a knife in her lap, a gun across her fat legs, and behind her were stacked the weapons of those chiefs who hoped to get raving-drunk. As so many times before, David looked at her, fascinated; he would never have thought that biting away the flesh part of a nose could make a person look so hideous. The bone of her nose above the lip had no skin on it but was all bone and holes, and the holes were so big and grotesque that David found it difficult to take his gaze away from them.

He turned to Payette. "Tell her . . . no rum . . . three days." He had to speak slowly, not only because Payette spoke only a little English but because he had a thick mind.

Payette talked to her and then said that Horned Thunder was very thirsty.

"He always is," David said. "Listen, they have a squaw . . . with gray eyes . . . who is white. Find out . . . her name . . . name chief wants marry her." He repeated the words, and while Payette and Tanino talked, David looked round him hoping to see her. If he could find her he would talk to her through Payette.

Payette said the chief's name was Brave Feathers.

"What . . . is . . . her . . . name?"

Her name, he said, after talking to Tanino, was Sunday and she was a tame deer.

"Like hell she is," David said. He told Payette to find out if Brave Feathers was betrothed to her, and after a few moments Payette said that he was and David thought that a lie, for the worst liar in the world was a squaw. He asked where he could find her.

Payette talked to Tanino, pointing this way and that, up the river and down, and at last said she was that way; and they went toward a patch of timber on the river. The young squaws, Payette said, had been sent to gather wood and Sunday was among them.

"Why in hell did they name her Sunday? Did you find out?"

"Thank you," Payette said. If he did not understand what was said or if he did not know what reply to give Payette invariably said, "Thank you," or, "Yes, sir."

Speaking slowly, David asked again why she had been named Sunday. Payette said Indians often named children after things that white men thought nice, such as Sunday and Christmas and Easter. He had heard that far south, where many white girls had been captured, a Princess Christmas had married Old Sleeping Bear. They had named one child Sunday, another Monday, a third Easter, a fourth Thanksgiving, and a fifth, a boy, Fourth of July. David turned to look at him. He had never known Payette to jest. Payette was dull-witted and lazy and sly and treacherous, and seemed to live only for copulations and rum.

"Is she a princess?"

Payette did not know but he thought she must be or a chief would not want to marry her.

"A lot of chiefs marry beautiful girls who aren't princesses."

"Thank you," Payette said.

"I've heard," David said, "that Chief Concomly over on the Columbia has a girl named Sunday. But why in hell would they name an Indian girl Sunday?"

"Yes, sir," Payette said. When David slowly repeated the question, Payette said it was to show respect to white folks.

Again David turned on him a curious glance. He told Payette that as soon as they found the girl he was to explain to her that David wanted to marry her. "And tell her I won't stand any damned monkey business. Tell her I'll make her mickle-bookit. You understand mickle-bookit?"

"Yes, sir."

"Like hell you do. Tell her I intend to marry her, and damned soon. And look, Payette, you help me in this and I'll double your rum." He told him this over and over until Payette's face kindled and glowed a moment and went out. David thought it was as if a dead thing had for a moment come to life, and he was wondering about the man, his father, his childhood, his strange apathy, when he saw Sunday reaching up to seize a dead poplar branch. "There she is," he said, and to Sunday he called, "Wait, I'll help you!" And what a hell of a thing that was to say: no squaw respected a buck who helped her with her labor. But Sunday had not understood him and he did not help her with the limb after all, for at sight of him she at once backed away, as from a loathsome object with a dreadful odor. There was again in her face a look almost of horror, and it so annoyed David that he wanted to rush on the girl and seize her and shake the unholy daylights out of her.

He asked Payette to tell her what he had said.

Payette spoke to the girl but she did not look at him. She continued to stare at David as she might have at an enemy about to spring or as David stared at Tanino's nose. As she understood what Payette was saying there was no change in her face, except that her eyes closed a little, as they might have if she had been clenching her hands.

"What she say?"

In a low voice she spoke to Payette. He said to David, "She say she hate white mens, you most."

"Me most. I'm flattered. Why does she hate me?"

After talking to Sunday, Payette said, "She say you kill her people firewater."

"Well, there's some truth in that. Ask if she is princess."

"She say she Princess Sunday."

"Beautiful name, tell her." While Payette was talking to her he saw her shrug.

"She hate what you think, all thing you like, she hate."

"Tell her I love her. *Netokeemun.* Ask her be my wife."

This time David had to wait a full minute. He thought he heard her use the word *ketuckhomin,* which meant love. Then Payette said gravely, "She say you want do to her what white mens do to squaws."

"Well, there's some truth in that too," David said, and smiled at her. Her only response was to open her eyes wider, as though he had called her an offensive name. "Tell her I will buy her from Brave Feathers."

After Payette had communicated these words to her, there was an unmistakable change in her face. It seemed to show alarm, astonishment, disgust and, last of all, fury. Abruptly she moved forward. She marched up and faced David and, drawing a deep breath, looked into his eyes and spit at his face.

"I'll be damned!" he exclaimed, and restrained an impulse to shake her. "You silly damned fool," he said to her.

After spitting at him to show the full measure of her contempt she swung and walked away and resumed the gathering of wood. Some of the young squaws had left their wood gathering and had approached to stare at David.

"He come," Payette said.

"Who?"

"Chief."

David turned toward the lodges and saw Brave Feathers. Payette went over to Sunday and spoke to her but, like a porcupine, she kept turning her rump to him. She would not look at him and she pretended to be unaware of him.

Brave Feathers came up, his lidded gaze on David. He had been making himself handsome. Like all his people, he dressed in leather; he seemed to have on his finest fringed buckskin trousers and shirt and he had stuck eagle feathers in his greased plaited hair.

David told Payette to ask him how much he wanted for the girl. While Payette was talking to him David studied the chief's face, but trying to tell what an Indian was thinking was like trying to tell in pitch-black midnight whether eyes were watching you. Payette shook his head no and said the chief would not sell her.

"I reckon he'll sell if he doesn't get any rum."

"He say she great princess."

"Tell him she is white woman." Payette spoke again, and David saw the Indian's Adam's apple going up and down as he swallowed.

Why was the man so stubborn about it? David had never known a buck who wouldn't sell his squaw, and usually the price was pretty low.

"He say not white. Say daughter Wandering Spirit."

David walked over and looked into Brave Feather's inscrutable eyes. He saw only what he might have seen if he had looked into the depths of a well at midnight. "Tell him . . . I say . . . she is . . . white. She is paleface."

At this moment Sunday abruptly left her wood gathering and approached, her eyes on David, her grimacing face revealing that her emotions were boiling just under the surface. David realized that she had been listening. Her voice vibrant with anger, she spoke to Payette and he turned, visibly agitated, to David.

"She say you lie, not paleface, her father Chief Wandering Spirit."

Admiring her audacity, David smiled at her and her eyes suddenly half closed as though he had touched her. He told Payette to tell Brave Feathers that he was a very great and very brave chief, that there was no braver chief in all the world, and no white man braver. While Payette communicated the message, David looked back and forth from the Indian to Sunday.

"He say thank you."

Now with his gaze on Sunday, David asked Payette to tell him that he would fight him for the girl, in any way that he wanted to fight, the winner to take her. The message was given. There was no change in Sunday's face but for a narrowing of her eyes.

"He say chief never fight over squaw."

"Oh, the hell they don't. They're fighting over squaws all the time."

"He say will fight you one day, not now. He say you be surprised."

"I wouldn't doubt that," David said, looking at the chief. "Does the bastard intend to ambush me? . . . Ask him: ambush me?"

"I would not ask more," Payette said.

"Oh? Why not?"

"I give good advice," Payette said.

What did this mean? What had the chief said to Payette? "All right, you give him good advice. Tell him . . . if he marry . . . Princess Sunday . . . without my consent . . . I'll eat mush out of skull . . . of his grandmother."

David had to repeat the words several times. Payette hesitated. That was the most dreadful, the most unforgivable insult that could be flung at an Indian. And when it was too late, David was sorry that he had flung it. Payette had looked at him, his look asking him to change his mind, to choose a milder form of contempt. He told David that no chief could ever forgive such an insult. Then Payette had spoken to the chief and David had supposed that he had conveyed the insult; and he was astonished when Payette met his eyes a moment and said, "I no tell him that."

"You did not?"

"No, sir."

And it was a good thing, David reflected, that he hadn't. He looked at the chief and considered. "Tell him . . . not marry girl . . . before potlatch." Potlatch was a Chinook term meaning a free feast with gifts and was generally taken by the Indians to mean the Christmas season.

"He say what gift white man."

Give him an inch, David thought, and he would take the whole country. "Tell him fine gifts. Big hat," David said, and held his hand a foot above his hair. "Powder, ball, mucha. Mucha rum. . . . What does he say?"

"He say how many moons to potlatch?"

"Well . . . One–two–three–about three one half. And tell him . . . he can ride . . . my pony . . . buffalo hunt."

That message made the chief shrug.

"He say his pony best. His pony best in world. He say he will wait potlatch . . . if white chief Dugald promise."

"Ask if he promise."

"Chief make promise," Payette said, nodding his head up and down.

"Tell him . . . if he break promise . . . great white father . . . skin him alive."

Again Payette hesitated. He advised against telling Brave Feathers that. He said the chief had promised and all his honor as a chief rested on it.

"All right, fine," David said, and after another look at Sunday, up and down and all over her, he turned away.

That evening, overriding his sense of prudence and his sense of humor, David laid the matter before Jim and Jim turned to look at him as if it were long past time to give his chief assistant a new appraisal.

"Oh, I know that I'm a damned fool. Any man is when he turns baby-soft over a woman. But, Jesus, she's beautiful. She's just like something out of a spruce forest, like something out of lightning in a dark night, like——"

"Yes," Jim said. "If it's just a white woman you need go to Montreal and get one."

"It's a lot more than that."

Jim studied him again and said, "Dave, I guess I've never understood you. Is the loneliness making you a little soft in your head?"

"Goddamnit, no. I like loneliness. Why have I stayed here eight years except to get away from the anthills of people? I don't believe the guff about love at first sight and I don't believe much in man-woman love at all. After you've boiled all the fancy feelings and self-admiration out of it and looked in the pot, what do you have? I suppose——"

"Yes," Jim said, and with that simple word he could silence almost anyone. "You want her because you can't get her."

"Maybe that's some of it. But I intend to get her."

"I wouldn't bet much on that. And look, Dave, what you're doing: right when we have to have these damned Blackfeet on our side you get in a fight with a chief—and, goddamnit, over nothing more important than a woman."

"If you feel that way I'll forget her."

Jim looked over his gnarled hands to see if he had dug out all the thorns. "Maybe I could make a deal with Horned Thunder."

"I don't want it that way. This is no squaw to be had for a trinket."

"She thinks she's a squaw."

"What she thinks doesn't matter. It's what she feels, and a lot of her feels white."

"Well, if all you want is to get her to bed——"

"It isn't that either."

Again Jim looked at him. "By God, you *are* getting baby-soft. Maybe you'd better go over to Selkirk's settlers."

David flushed and the anger came up in him like a fire. "I resent that," he said.

"All right, all right, but keep your ass in your pants. Something's happening to the men of the north. I thought it was Selkirk, but here you are——"

"Rub it in. Jim, didn't you ever feel soft about a woman?"

Jim looked back across the years. "Only once and only a little." He knocked his pipe out and filled it and reached for an ember. "I was about your age or a little younger. I had a squaw. You know, it's a funny thing about Indians. It takes a white man a long time to get to know them. They're children. That's the first thing to keep in mind. They'll smoke a pipe with you and five minutes later will scalp you. They will skin you alive or sit with you at a feast. The beaver will work a hundred times as hard, the squirrel will lay up more for the winter. If it hadn't been for the squaws all the Indians on this continent would have starved to death long ago. You know what the chiefs say, that they don't get out and trap all winter, they don't do all that work and suffer all those hardships for clothes or food or lodgings—or for anything but rum. Except the Piegans. They're too lazy to work even for rum.

"Well, it was twenty years ago and I'm forty-four now. I was just a clerk then and I got me a squaw like a lot of the men do out here; and like about all white men, I thought she was just something to sleep with and do chores for me, like keeping my moccasins soft. Her Indian name was Mourning Bird but I always thought of her and called her Tum-tum—you know, the Chinook for heart. I called her that because the first time I did it to her I thought her heart would jump right out of her chest. I guess she was only about fourteen. She was scared to death. She was like a bird when you hold it in your two hands. Poor little Tum-tum," Jim said, and for a little while was silent, looking into the fire.

"Well, what I was going to tell you is about her and the kid. You know, it's funny the way some men are about their children with squaws. Now and then a man is like John McLoughlin, but he's a doctor. Maybe that makes a difference. He says half-breed children should be just as dear to their father as if they were all white. I guess that's so," Jim said, looking over at David. "But it wasn't so with me and it isn't with a lot of men. Some are worse than I ever was. Some of them don't seem to think the kid is human just because it is part Indian."

He drew deep on his pipe, deep into his lungs. "That's how I was. Goddamn, it makes me ashamed to remember it. I guess I didn't think of Tum-tum as a woman exactly, or at least not quite human. I can recall now so many ways she had trying to make me love her a little. A woman's ways, I guess they were. And I can recall how—"

Jim broke off, and David thought there was a little catch in his voice. Anyway, he was silent, looking through memories into a fire, or perhaps through fire back to memories.

"The kid was born blind," he said, as if he had to say it quick and short and get it over with. "I didn't pay any attention to it, not even when Tum-tum tried to get me to. Least of all then. I guess for me it wasn't a child. It was just a thing that had been born. I didn't care if it was male or female. What I wanted was for Tum-tum to get well fast, so I'd have a woman again. I didn't wait long enough, not as long as a man should, but that's another story."

Again he smoked, looking back. "Well, when at last she got me to look at it I saw that its eyes were kind of white, like they had something over them. We couldn't talk much together. A man don't need to talk to his woman if she means only one thing to him. She knew only a few words of my language—she called me Jeem. I knew only a few words of hers. So she couldn't tell me very well what she wanted me to do but I figured at last that she wanted me to get a doctor or take the kid to a big city. That didn't fit into my plans at all."

He knocked his pipe out and filled it again. "What I mean, Dave, this country does things to a man. '*Je suis un homme du Nord,*' the pedlars brag, but they are right. We all are. *Pays sauvage.* That's it. Weak men don't last long here. Strong men get stronger, I guess, though more and more I wonder about that. We who have been out here for a long time are a long way from the people in Scotland or England. We're a different breed now. I don't know if we're better or worse. God knows we're different. I guess the chief thing that makes us different isn't the distances and the size but that we don't have women. I guess there are things women do for men that should be done for them, or they just don't go on being men."

Jim fell silent, brooding, and David sat thinking of another tragic case. A Frenchman named Trottier had married a Cree. Their daughter Marguerite had become famous all over the northern country for her beauty, and Indian chiefs, eager to own her, had offered the father practically everything they had. Thinking that she ought to marry a white man, the father gave her to a worthless dog named Jutras. With her husband and tiny baby Marguerite had gone with a fur brigade down the Assiniboine to Red River, where the Sioux ambushed and attacked them, and Jutras at once had leaped from the canoe and fled. David had seen Marguerite a few hours after the attack. The Indians had scalped her clear down to her ears and almost as deep as her nape, and her bloody skull was aswarm with flies. One eye had been torn out and hung by a tendon or a piece of flesh halfway down the cheek, and from the socket a liquid was running that seemed to be less blood than water, as though the brain itself were weeping. They had hacked both her hands off. There the poor thing sat, not only alive but conscious, and trying with her one good eye to see her baby. It was at some distance from her, scalped but still breathing. Tough old Dan MacKenzie had wept when he baptized that dying infant, not with water, for there had been none close at hand, but with its blood and his own tears.

David had always felt deeply stirred when remembering it, as he was stirred now, thinking of Tum-tum. He looked over at Jim.

He turned to look at David. "All right, get this girl if you can. I reckon you need her more than you'll ever know. I reckon the way you want her is the way a redskin rips open a belly and digs the liver out and gobbles it raw. Somehow he has a feeling that it's good for him but he doesn't think about it that way, maybe he never thinks about it at all. In some things people seem to be guided by a knowing that is deeper than their thoughts and as old as Adam. Maybe it's that way with you. You been out here a long time, Dave, and I guess you need some liver."

"Maybe," said David, looking at Jim, turning over and over in his mind and emotions the things Jim was saying.

Jim reached for a stick that was out of the fire at one end and red ember at the other. "Well, I don't know how long it went on. I was busy. For days at a time I didn't even see Tum-tum. I had her in a little cabin and one day I went over there for something and as soon as I got to the door I had a feeling. Then I was quiet. I peeked in. There was Tum-tum holding the baby and kissing its eyes, one eye and then the other, over and over; and she was saying to it some words that I never would have known if when I was a kid I hadn't had a playmate who was a Catholic. She was saying, *Pater noster*—I understood that much at once but it took me a little time to figure the rest of it out. *Pater noster, qui es in coelis, sanctificetur nomen tuum.* God. I tiptoed away from there. I was no good for work the rest of the day."

Jim was silent, and David looked at him and waited. At last David said, "I don't know what it means. What was she saying?"

" 'Our Father who art in heaven, hallowed be thy name.' "

"Jesus," David said. "Where did she learn that?"

"I never did know. Maybe from some Frenchman."

"And she was saying it to the child."

"To the child and kissing its eyes, trying to make them well. It took me days to figure the thing out, and I guess I never did figure it all out. It's pretty big," Jim said, glancing at David. "As a redskin might say, it's a hell of a heap of big. I suppose the thing that knocked me out of kilter was that for money and not a goddamned thing but money all of us working for the honorable company were corrupting the Indians just as fast as rum and hell would let us. The white man brought syphilis to them. He brought gunpowder. He brought alcohol. It's a wonder he has never thought to bring narcotics. I'm no doctor. I don't know why the kid was born blind but a doctor has told me that he reckons it was syphilis." Jim drew deep, inhaled, and blew a cloud of smoke up with the excess of his emotions in it. "Tum-tum with her blind baby, blind because of white men, praying to the white man's God. After that she was no longer a thing for me. She was no longer just something in bed. She was a woman."

David had to look away a moment. The way Jim uttered the word woman he filled it with holiness, or something like that, and you just didn't know what to think of this Jim whom you had never seen before.

"The child didn't live long after that," Jim said. "Tum-tum, she didn't either." He knocked his pipe out. "Well, I guess I'll roll in."

David sat until past midnight looking into the fire.

## V

When these Blackfoot Indians came to a post to trade they went first to their campground and pitched their lodges and gathered firewood and water; and then in their most resplendent raiment the chiefs went up to the post. In deference to the red man's sense of dignity and ceremony certain formalities had taken on the sanctity of ritual. No word, for instance, could be spoken before an interpreter had filled a pipe with tobacco and red willow bark. Each chief had his own, which meant a different way of receiving the pipe, and the interpreter had to be a specialist in the etiquette of the thing. The chief accepting the pipe would rise and present it to the north, to the south, to the east, to the west, to the going-to-the-sun. He would then take three whiffs, never more, never fewer, and pass the pipe to the chief on his left.

David, who knew all the etiquette, always stood at a little distance from the interpreter, watchful, quick to correct mistakes if mistakes were made.

After the passing of the pipe the head chief then gave a little talk, which the interpreter translated phrase by phrase, saying that they had done their very best in the past season but would do better in the future; with impassive face but subtle craftiness bringing forth excuses and reasons, most of them invented, to gloss their laziness and failures; and concluding with the air of one who was first among princes and monarchs. David would then make a brief response, gravely thanking the chief and his magnificent people, in the name of the great and honorable company in London; saying that they were well pleased; hoping they would have cause to be even more pleased next time, all of which the chiefs would receive without the movement of a finger or the lowering of an eyelid. They were then ushered into a room and given a drink of a hundred and thirty-three proof rum, which they tossed off as if it were water, and ushered out. The gate was closed, lookouts were posted. The first formalities were over.

Only a limited number of bucks were admitted at one time to the Indian room for trading. They were not allowed to drink there. They had to take their rum with them and leave the room and the fort and go to their own campground to get drunk. The trading might run all night but was never allowed to go beyond nine o'clock the next morning. The big trading time was in the spring, when they came in with their ponies so laden with furs that sometimes only their lower legs could be seen. The Indians were eager to trade at any time of year, if they had anything to offer; besides rum, they wanted tobacco, guns, ammunition, vermilion in small buckskin bags, hatchets, knives, beads, and trinkets. They were not interested in dry goods; they dressed in leather. They did now and then take a fancy to copper kettles or castoff military clothing; and for a stovepipe hat in good condition with feathers attached a chief might give his second-best buffalo horse or the choice of his wives if he had more than one.

For trading they brought with them buffalo and other robes, dried or smoked ribs and tongues—the meat was usually wrapped in a parfleche, a buffalo hide stripped of its hair with wood-ash lye—and wolfskins, bark for canoes, nuggets of ore, and anything else if they thought the greedy white men might like it.

During his first years here David had thought it outrageous the way Indians were robbed. In St. Louis in 1809 an average beaver pelt was worth from two to three dollars. A keg of rum that cost the company ten dollars was traded to Indians for a hundred and twenty beaver pelts. Some men had made fortunes and retired. David had heard of one on the Snake who traded for furs with sugar at one dollar a pound, gunpowder at a dollar and a half, and rum that was chiefly Snake River water at fifteen dollars a gallon. This man had become wealthy in five years.

The company for which David worked, he had to admit, squeezed out of the redskins everything it could get. A five-pound sack of vermilion that was chiefly flour fetched six beaver pelts; a hunting knife or a small hatchet, four. Well, if they didn't squeeze them the pedlars and the independents would. The law of this land was to get all you could while you could and to destroy your competitors if you were able to. Jim said they had stopped smiling at one another; it was blow for blow from here on out. David chuckled on recalling that a century before an HB man had written from London to the posts, "Trade as little brandy as possible to ye Indians, wee being informed it has Destroyed severell of them." Mellow old brandy? This, by God, was raw rum that made an Indian blind-drunk.

As Horned Thunder was admitted on the day appointed for trading, the company's flag was hauled to the mast top and the bastion cannon boomed. This gesture of respect was repeated until all the principal chiefs had been received. Horned Thunder was garbed in his best. Over his shoulders was a buffalo robe, on which crimson spots marked blood from the wounds he had received; and figures shaped like hurdles for the war parties he had led; and an X surmounted by an O, thus, x̊, the scalps hanging from his medicine pole. His chest and right arm were bare. There were many plumes in his war plait and he had an eagle wing as a fan. The other chiefs were in full dress, with fancy beaded and fringed leggings, gay belts, and beribboned and feathered headdresses.

When David met Horned Thunder's eyes he knew that there was trouble ahead but he had no idea what the trouble would be or when it would come. An Indian had little power to dissemble but you still couldn't tell about him. This chief looked into David's eyes for several moments, and in his own eyes David saw nothing that he could have defined, nothing in the face, but just the same, in those black and chilling depths there was a warning for the man who could read it. At that moment the cannon boomed.

The chief spoke and Payette conveyed his greeting. "He say friendship *skoonataps*. That mean strong."

Jesus, what a liar! "Tell great chief Horned Thunder I greet him with friendship heap big *skoonataps*. Tell him we hope always trade with us, not with thieves and robbers of other company."

While Payette communicated the words there wasn't the slightest change in that bronzed countenance or in those fathomless eyes. The great chief, Payette said, wanted David to know that he had always been the company's friend, its loyal guardian and brother.

That was another lie. "Tell him honorable company respects his friendship above that of all other men."

Behind Horned Thunder stood Brave Feathers, watching David. In scenes like this David had always had peculiar sensations, as though he faced wild creatures, ready to leap in and throttle, or to flee. Today he understood a little more fully some of the things Jim had said. You couldn't escape the feeling that these chiefs would be happy to play with you in riding or swimming, or to scalp you and skin you, and that it made little difference to them which they did. That was what so disturbed a white man about an Indian. It was like holding a cougar cub that was playful but would bite your hand off if you didn't watch out.

He told Payette to tell the chiefs that if they had things to trade to bring them to the trading room.

At this time of year they didn't have pelts but the sly rascals hoped to get a bellyful of rum for worthless things that they knew the white men did not want—dry powdered serviceberries, wattape roots for the lacing of canoes, herbs which they presented as infallible cures for every ailment under the sun, from hemlock poisoning to syphilis, wolfskins, fats so rancid they stunk, and maple sugar juice full of insects. They would be hopeful and rather pathetically humble when offering these things, their eyes watching David, their eyes looking round for rum kegs, their tongues pressing on Payette their argument in favor of this or that, and their eyes darkening at last with hostility and menace as wild earth darkened from a passing cloud. Rum, good God, rum, that's what they wanted—enough rum to get blind-raving-drunk. David knew that if they didn't get it here they'd go to the pedlar post and get it. He knew more than that. He knew that he'd have to be as generous as his competitor or a little more generous. He knew that he had to watch them every moment, for as soon as they got rum in their hands they were eager to pour it down right then and there. It was like looking at starving dogs around when he sat at a feast. It was like seeing men five days without water fall to a mudhole to drink. Sometimes he had to get rough and knock the hell out of them and drag them out by their heels. That was bad business, for an Indian had almost as much pride in him as treachery and never forgave an indignity to his person.

They had brought a few robes, which the squaws had made with endless patience and toil. For these fine robes, chiefly buffalo, they took rum and tobacco and a little vermilion but nothing else. After the trading was done they hastened swiftly away, hugging the tobacco twists to them, clutching their rum that was more than half water. They had, of course, held back some things—their choicest things—to trade for rum later; and by the time they were half drunk David could dilute the rum down to thirty, even to twenty, per cent. The pedlars liked to tell of the time when Indians drank nothing but water for forty-eight hours believing that it was firewater.

As David watched them hurry away his face was grave. It was like watching children running off to gaze in wonder at their Christmas toys. The squaws? Some of them got drunk too. They would all have a grand *wabbano* and they would relive in pantomime and song their feats of heroism in battle, they would copulate, they would stab one another: Alexander Henry had told of seeing two bucks seize an infant and pull it in two, though David doubted that that could be done. But they did do terrible things: for instance, a drunken buck chewed the nose off his squaw and spit it out, and bleeding like a stuck hog, she hunted around in the lodge and found the nose and put it back on. It had healed in a way but was a hideous thing to look at. There would be obscenities down there, mutilations, and there might be murders; and if any buck's conscience began to get him down he would calmly cut a piece of flesh from his shoulder and tie it to something invested with astounding potency and then throw it away to propitiate his gods. Some of the squaws, ready to do business, were waiting for the white men. What did they think of the white men? David wondered. They must have thought that he lived chiefly in his knackers, because bedding down a squaw seemed to be his first law of life.

There was Beau Parlez, one of their trappers, a man with so many erotic dreams in his head that he couldn't think clearly about anything. Beau was a half-breed and a Catholic; he had decided that absolution was a miraculous invention and that he could sin like hell up to the last moment of consciousness and still be saved. That was part of it. The other part was that Beau was simply a fool about women in that way. David would have kicked him out long ago but for the fact that Beau was the best trapper in the whole outfit. After he had debauched himself with the women until he could barely crawl he would return to his trap lines and work like a fool for weeks.

The day after the Indians received their rum David went among their lodges to see how they were doing—and to catch a glimpse of Sunday if he could. Tanino was still sitting guard over the weapons, her face enough to abash the drunkest buck ever bent on murder. Before the lodges of the chiefs were tethered their fleetest ponies, so that their masters could mount and make a quick getaway in case of attack. As if most of them could even get to their feet, much less mount a horse! He found Horned Thunder between his lodge and his horse, stretched out flat, senseless, his belly full of rum. David stared at him a few moments and went on. Why, he wondered, did the damned fools drink themselves into unconsciousness? It wasn't for the fun of it: the law of diminishing returns worked here as in all things: a man passed the point beyond which there was no fun, no joy, nothing but stupor and the blind staggers. Jim said Indians thought firewater was some kind of magic. Maybe that was it.

He went to those lodges in which some of the women were doing business and he saw one of his men guiltily slipping away and glancing down to see if his buckskin trousers were closed. Then he saw a squaw hastening toward him. Like all those who had expected to do business, she had got herself up in her gayest ribbons and strips of colored cloth; her hair was braided and plastered with pomatum and bear grease; her cheeks were grotesquely stained with vermilion; her breasts were bare but around her waist she had a wide belt of soft leather. She came up close and looked expectantly at his face, without a trace of shame. How they stank! He imagined there was bear grease in her hair fifteen years old, that there still clung to her some of the smells of childhood. One of these days he would throw Sunday into the river and wash her off.

Still holding his gaze, the squaw pointed to the area of her thighs. He shook his head no. She seemed to doubt him. She pointed again. She put palms under her breasts and lifted them up a little and out, for she had learned that most of the white men were breast lovers.

A breast was only a teat for an Indian, something that a baby drew food out of, and Indians never dallied with breasts or put their lips to them. The squaws never got over their amazement at seeing what white men would do. David wanted to ask her if she knew where Sunday was. Trying to catch his eyes again—he was looking around him now—she became bolder and softly touched his leather trousers in the area of his genitals. Again he shook his head no and turned away from her, aware that her touch had thrilled him, conscious of her lovely breasts. He passed lodges in which he heard heavy breathing and cries of rapture: what a spectacle the human race was in the secret places or under the tent of night! Still, his chief thought at the moment was to be in a secret place with Sunday. . . .

Beyond the lodges of the whores—but dared a white man to think of them as whores?—were older squaws busy at their work. He saw one, shapeless, huddled, bent over, her old half-blind eyes and her old trembling hands busy with a scalp, the eyes looking for tiny pieces of flesh in it, the fingernails scraping them away. A Cree's scalp, David supposed. How many tens or hundreds of thousands of Indians had been scalped in this western world since the first Indian raised a tomahawk?—and how many white people, who now hid their mutilation with a wig? How much would Brave Feathers give for the scalp of David McDonald?

He found another squaw pounding and stretching a parfleche to soften it and he smelled the strange strong odor of the oils and wood ash and brains and urine and heaven knew what that she used, working them all into the hide to make it wondrously soft. He saw a buck sitting off by himself, weeping, wailing; if an Indian felt sad, rum doubled his woes. Then David turned toward the river and went along its bank and presently he came to a group of Indian boys playing in the water. It made him think about his own people when he saw how Indians trained their children. These lads could swim like otter. It was nothing for an Indian boy to dive with the speed of a grebe and come up a few moments later with a live beaver in his arms. It was incredible, David thought, standing to watch the lads play, the way they tamed wild horses. Thousands of wild horses roamed the prairies. Indians would corral a band and choose the fleetest and take them to a river and shove them into deep water; and then they would plunge in and play with the horses' manes and tails, taming them; sliding like seals across their backs as they swam; sitting astride them; caressing their ears and faces and almost drowning them and exhausting them before riding them out. Jim said that when Indians got through with a horse in water it never bucked. There were the Crows, called Crows because they were the master horse thieves of the plains. They were also among the most magnificent horsemen: they would tie a two-year-old boy on a wild horse and turn it loose, and nobody in Scotland, David had written to his people, would believe what happened then. That wild horse went faster than an antelope, with a score of yelling redskins after it, and you would never know if the child's hair stood straight up for you never got a look at it. But the next time you saw the child he was eager to ride again. All the Crow women rode too, rode better than any white man had ever dreamed of riding. The boys out in the river were playing as if water were their natural home: one would dive and fifty yards away David would see his rump come up, but only that, and he tried to see him when he surfaced his mouth for a breath but he never did. Watching them made David feel gawky and awkward, made him feel related to the buffalo and the moose. Sunday, he was remembering, could swim like that.

A squaw was hastening toward him, trailed by Payette. When he came up Payette told David that she had a very sick child and wanted him to make medicine. Thinking this was a trick, David went with them to a lodge to see the boy and found him puking his guts out. One sniff of his foul breath was enough: this kid was sick-drunk. Payette was saying that he had been eating white beaver, which in Indian lore meant a beaver that had fed on poisonous plants.

"He very seeck," Payette said.

"He's goddamned drunk and you know it."

Blandly Payette said it was the mother's belief that rum would cure the child. A white man had to be amused by Indians, for in a way they were so guileless. "Oh yes, rum," David said, looking at the mother, wondering if she was drunk too. He thought it might be well to give the kid a dose of laudanum, though it didn't always work with an Indian: he had known of drunken bucks who had been given as much as a hundred and fifty drops in five or six doses and had yelled louder than ever. Well, the worst thing about the whole business was the way children were becoming drunkards.

"You seen Sunday?" Payette shook his head no. "Brave Feathers?"

Chief Brave Feathers, Payette said, was drunk. He made a gesture to indicate a prone man.

"That drunk? That's good." He told Payette to hustle around and find Sunday and tell her that he had to see her for a moment.

"Thank you," Payette said.

Had he understood? "Tell her . . . must see . . . me. There," he said, indicating a cottonwood grove. "I . . . wait . . . there." He considered the thing a moment. She wouldn't want to come but she might come for a trinket. He went with Payette to the post and filled a small buckskin pouch with vermilion, unmixed with flour. This, he explained to Payette, was to be hers if she came. He filled a tin cup with undiluted rum and handed it to Payette and Payette drank it in choked gulps. David thought a hundred and thirty-three proof rum enough to strangle a moose but it seemed never to faze Indians or half-breeds.

"You bring her."

"Yes, sir."

"Down there," said David, pointing.

"Yes, sir." Payette was looking around hopefully for another drink.

"No more now. Get along."

"Thank you," Payette said, and was off.

## VI

She came with reluctant tread and he could see how her body held back and her will resisted, how she was preparing herself to scorn and detest him even before he spoke. It was hard to believe this girl white, but for her eyes and skin. Still, there was a difference in her, subtle, elusive, as deep as her darkest secret, but he sensed it, he felt it. He felt it in her as she came up, slowly, putting each foot forward as if with a conscious effort, her head high and proud and disdainful, her gray eyes fixed on him where he stood under a tree, watching her. She came to within a dozen feet of him and stopped, and they looked at one another without speaking. The faces of both were grave and set.

David then turned to Payette and told him to explain to the girl that she would not get the vermilion if she did not stay so long—and with his hands he spanned a distance to indicate so much passing of the sun on the sky. Sunday looked up at the sun, now a little past noon. It seemed to David that she was trying to imagine how long that much time would be. She did want the vermilion and she wanted it bad. If a man wanted to woo a maid, David was thinking, let him attack her where her vanity was deepest.

"What does she say?"

"She not say but I think she say yes."

He was now to teach her, David said, her first English word. He was to make her understand the word love. "*Tikeh.*" David watched her scornful face while Payette tried to define for her the English word. He thought he saw her eyes kindle just a little with amusement—and her lips part a little more. "Now say I love her."

Payette gave her the message and turned to David. "She say hate you. Always hate you. Now want color for face then will go."

"The hell she will. Tell her no stay, no color."

Payette told her and she looked up at the sun. Her lips spoke. "She say sun that far."

David now moved toward her, expecting her to flee, but she stood firm, looking at him, and he drew so close that he could have touched her. Again he smelled the odor of her. Jesus, a smell like that almost took all the woman hunger out of a man. He looked down into her eyes and she looked up into his and for half a minute they searched one another's inner thinking and motives. David was looking for the woman. What she was looking for he had no idea; he dared not believe that it was for the man and there was nothing in her eyes to tell him. They were beautiful eyes and, yes, they were gray, a lovely gray like certain things damp with rain, with just a little hazel in them, not green, but almost microscopic jewels of light. They were clear healthy eyes, steady eyes, eyes that looked pretty deep into a man.

Sunday was the one who faltered. They might have looked into one another's depths for minutes or until they were hypnotized if she had not faltered and caught her breath just a little and looked away. The white in her again, David thought. No Indian would have wavered. He now looked down over her form—as though he had need to!—for he had seen it naked turning in the water, running over the earth, standing under the sky. He looked next at her hands because he liked loveliness in a woman's hands and there was none in the hands of squaws. Sunday had lovely hands but they needed a good scrubbing. He moved to take one of them and in an instant she was away from him, and again she was regarding him with that aloof scorn which he now found a little ridiculous. He thought there was some pose in it but he was not sure. Was there any pose in the way a perched falcon looked at the earth?—or a bighorn ram on a pinnacle at the depths below him?

He turned to Payette. "I'm going to strip her naked and bathe her."

Payette's slack jaw fell. He would have been no more astonished if David had said he was going to murder her.

He supposed, David said, that she would get wild and shrill and behave like a mad thing. Was he sure that Brave Feathers was down-drunk?

Payette nodded yes. He bent and with both hands indicated that the chief was flat on his back.

David asked him to run over and be sure—be sure that he was really down and had no weapons on him.

Surly and sulking, Payette turned away. He had seen the chief down, so why should any man doubt it? David, meanwhile, stood close enough to Sunday to seize her if she turned to flee. She did not look at him during Payette's absence. She was looking away at the sky and, so far as David could tell, she was trying to imagine what he intended to do. Beautiful hair, he thought, in spite of its bear grease and pomatum. Beautiful girl. . . .

Payette came back and looked at David and nodded.

"Down-drunk?"

Payette nodded yes.

"Asleep?"

"Yes, sir."

"All right, you listen. When I grab this girl all hell—you understand all hell?—may break loose. You watch that way. Chief. If see chief come with gun, tell me quick. You understand?"

"Yes, sir."

David turned to Sunday and hesitated. He would rather have tackled the biggest man in Christendom or faced a pack of wolves alone in a blizzard than to force this girl to cleanse herself. He hesitated because he was not sure he ought to do it. What right had he? But he wanted to know what she looked like, how white she was. He wanted to get that damned stink off her.

And still he hesitated, while Payette stared at him, while Sunday looked at the sky. She was waiting for the vermilion, he supposed. She was trying to measure the distance the sun had covered. Well, good Lord, was he afraid of her . . . ? Forcing himself to act, he reached out first to clasp a wrist. With a movement that was all hell and venom she flung his hand off. That angered him a little. Swiftly he moved over behind her and took her from behind, with his powerful arms around her. He expected her to begin to scream. She did not scream or cry out at all but she began to fight him, trying to get to his hands with her teeth. He picked her up as if she were a child and with her legs kicking against him and her fingernails digging and tearing and her teeth turning from side to side trying to find his flesh he carried her down to the river.

It made him feel good to hold a woman so close. He pushed down an impulse to draw her head back and kiss her lips. Her waist, he discovered, now that his arms were around it, was small, smaller than he had thought. But how her hair stunk in his face! The whole woman smelled of rancid fat and lodge smoke and old sweat and horse sweat and—yes, there was now another odor and he liked that. She still did not cry out. He also liked that. It showed that she had real spirit.

At the river's edge he set her down. He had chosen his place so that it was sheltered and hidden, a spot almost roofed with lodged driftwood and sun-dried moss—because this river, now low, was twenty feet higher in floodwater and went like hell. He looked back up the path and saw that Payette had taken a position as sentinel. After setting her down he moved around quickly to face her, one hand clasping her arm, and again their eyes met. Her eyes were even darker and more dreadful in their hate than they had been, but he saw no fear in them, nothing but loathing and contempt. Confound it, if he could only talk to her! He didn't know the Blackfoot word for bathe, if they had a word, which he doubted, or for clean. All he knew was yes, no, good, strong, woman, come, go, eyes, mouth, belly, love, eat, food, wife, bed.

"*Netokeemun?*" he asked, and then realized that it was silly to ask her to be his wife. That was not the way to woo her. "*Aki, poxaput!*" he cried, and if he had his words right they meant, "Woman, come!" But when he tried to draw her toward the water she resisted and fought like ten wildcats. She put all she had into the effort, fighting with feet and hands and teeth; and like any captured wild thing, she struggled until exhausted and then was incredibly meek and tame while recruiting strength to fight again. A wolf would do it, or a beaver, or even a wild duck. He merely held her by both wrists and let her kick and bite. When her head moved toward him, eyes popping and flashing and mouth open and ugly like the mouth of a thing determined to kill, he made no move to dodge her teeth but let her sink them as well as she could in his shoulder. She didn't bite very well through his leather jacket, and so, like a mosquito that moves from spot to spot to sink its probe, she tried to bite up and down his arm and then into his neck. On his neck above the collar she sank teeth and drew blood. She pulled her head back and he saw the crimson on her lips and the blood on her teeth. In the instant when she met his eyes he saw that loathing and contempt had for a moment given way to wonder about him. And well they might have, for if she had been fighting an Indian buck this way he would have knocked her head off or buried his knife in her belly clear over the handle.

Gently, as though ministering to a wounded thing, he laid her by the water's edge and sat astride her but not on her and began to unbraid her hair. That was not easy to do. It was so saturated with grease and dust that the hairs were almost cemented together. After he had the strands undone he gathered fine sand by the handful to use as soap and he scoured and scrubbed her hair and she lay and looked up at him with what seemed to him a strange expression. Had the fool thought he was going to do it to her now and here?—or had some memory of her childhood entered consciousness? Or was she so full of womanly astonishment and of wonder about him that she could only stare as if fascinated? He cleansed only the part of her hair that was braided, and when he got the filth off it he saw that the natural color was a kind of golden brown. No Indian in the world had hair like that. He wanted to cleanse her scalp but was afraid the sand would lacerate it. He decided to wash her face.

That was not easy either. The vermilion and the grease were deep in her pores. Using a handkerchief, he worked gently, and though water now and then splashed into her eyes she kept looking at him. Somewhere he had seen an animal looking at him that way. He washed around the base of her nose and below her nostrils, trying to recall what animal it was. Or possibly it had been a bird. Anyway, he knew now that it had been in a trap, whatever it was, and it had looked at him as she was looking, not with fear but with a kind of wonder as if thinking, This is the enemy that will kill me; what is it like? When he had cleansed her lips he wanted to kiss them, for they were luscious and lovely and needed no artificial color. Her eyes were lovelier after he had washed the stuff away from her upper cheeks. "Shut your eyes," he said. He moved a forefinger to the lids and she closed her eyes and he washed the lashes and lids. When she opened them they were beaded like eyes that had come out of a rain. "Beautiful eyes," he said.

He was wondering if he should bathe her all over. He thought it would be too indelicate but knew well enough that the redskin did not have the paleface's sensitivity in such things. Would she mind that any more than his washing of her face and hair? The best way to find out was to strip her down to her waist and find out what she would do.

What she did when in an unguarded moment he left her hands free was to strike him such a blow across his mouth that he felt the blood start. That might have angered him if he had not been thinking of the thing in the trap. A thing in a trap would strike too when it thought it had a chance to break free. Or if it thought it had no chance at all. After she struck the blow he imprisoned both her hands and then removed a thorn at the shoulder and took her leather blouse off. He was getting wet, as wet as she was; and now he got wetter as he used his cupped hand as a dipper to pour water over her. Yes, she had magnificent breasts and he wanted to lower his head and kiss a nipple or feel the breast's wonder against his cheek. He should have told Payette to ask her how old she was. "You're a girl," he said, "and a woman: so much girl in your youthfulness, so womanly matured. And, my dear, what a lovely throat you have." He was very gentle with her breasts, knowing that they were the tenderest part of a woman's body; he softly washed them and her throat and down over her belly, and then rose a little so that he could turn her over. She did not help him, she did not resist. She gave him so completely the sense of a thing in an evil power and despairing but not afraid that he felt shame in what he was doing. Still, he knew as well as he knew his own hungers that this girl would never surrender to ordinary wooing. Not to Indian wooing, not to white, but to wooing that was neither or both. Washing her back, he saw that it was lovely too, with the most delightful curve down over her waist. She had turned her head to one side, with a cheek across an arm: he could not see her eyes and he smiled to think of the expressions in them and his tongue licked out to gather the blood on his lip. He had decided not to wash the rest of her. Maybe she would take the hint. Maybe on the contrary she would so drench herself with filthy stinking greases that she would be unrecognizable the next time he saw her.

When he had her back clean and the hair on the back of her head as well as he could he did not rise at once. He did not want to leave her. He was clasping her with his legs at the top of her thighs and he remained astride a few moments longer to look at her downy nape, the curve of her spine. Then, taking one of her wrists, he got up and drew her to her feet; and, holding her, he put the skin blouse around her shoulders and fastened it with the thorn she had used. Then he looked into her eyes. He was never to know quite what he saw there, but whatever it was, it was to haunt him all his life. There was no love in it, not the slightest hint of sexual ardor. There was loathing, he supposed, though it was different now. It was not active and explosive now but subtle and cunning and indrawn. It was something that would plot and wait. While looking into those eyes, so steady, so full of things seldom seen in human eyes, David felt as deep as certainty that this girl would kill him if she ever got the chance. That made him feel a little sick, weary, dispirited. He gave her a faint smile, released her arm, and turned away.

He went up the path and took the vermilion from Payette. He went back to her and offered it and she took it, but not eagerly, not as if she had full right to it. Again he turned away, and in this moment he didn't give a damn what happened to her or whom she married or how filthy she got. He climbed the hill to the post and went to his room and poured a big drink of brandy. Could he really be sure, he asked himself, that this girl had resolved on his death? Had he sensed it in the deadly quietness of her? Well, no doubt she felt that the washing had been an unforgivable indignity to her person and she had set her heart on his death. He had looked into the eyes of too many killers to have any doubt of that.

He felt so depressed or shamed—he was not sure what his emotion was—that he decided to go for a walk; and he went through the autumn woods down the river and tried to get his mind off himself and the girl by watching the life around him. There was a woodpecker. Jesus, that was a creature with a tool! Its bill was a combination of chisel, pickax, hammer, and augur, and after it had knocked a hole into a hollow tree its long barbed tongue, covered with a substance as sticky as soft fir gum, reached in to the grubs and dragged them forth. The flicker would bore and knock a hole right through the gable of your house if it sensed there was something to eat inside, such as a nest of wasps. Its principal food was ants and David wondered why, for he had tasted several kinds and they were all bitter. Well, there was the dragonfly, its legs too short for walking: it would eat thirty fat houseflies in an hour; it—it—— But this was no good. He didn't give a damn about the dragonfly or the flicker.

He returned to the post and at the stockade door a group of Indians in different stages of drunkenness and all clamoring to get in came eagerly to meet him, to show their friendliness by shaking his hand. He shook hands with them in turn, and by the time he was done his own right hand was smeared deep with grease and vermilion. This made him think again of the girl. He gave a signal for an aide inside to unbolt the door, and when it was opened a little David moved quickly but was not quick enough. A murderous half-breed named Latude pushed in ahead of him and entered. David then entered and shouted to those inside, "Shut the gate!"

It was swung to and the bolts were shot.

To Latude he said, "What in hell do you mean pushing ahead of me that way?"

"High wine," said Latude, his eyes inflamed and wicked and barely in focus. "Heap big thirst me."

"When I open gate," David said, "you better get out. I want no trouble with you."

"Trub-bull?" said Latude, and David could see the man's furies coming up. "Hell and a squaw's tits! You think you get girl Sunday? You no get."

David turned to his assistants and said, "Get ready to open it." To Latude he said, "Will you go or do I have to throw you out?" Then he saw it but he had known it was coming and he was ready. Latude's right hand moved to draw a dagger but in the same instant David stepped in and clubbed him with a fist on the jaw. Latude went down, and in the next moment the bolts were shot and two men seized Latude, each by a wrist and ankle, and heaved him outside as though he were a bag of pemmican. David went out, calling to Payette to follow. He had learned the lesson that all white men had to learn about Indians if they were to get along with them, if they were to live: you never argued with them, and if you valued your life you never showed fear or weakness. He stepped out to face the bucks, among whom were several chiefs; he folded his arms and looked at them, looked from face to face, meeting those eyes that would meet his; and he told Payette to ask them if any of them wanted the same medicine.

Payette put the question and David watched the faces. Most of them looked a little abashed, for they were in desperate need of rum and willing to indulge a white man's bravado to get it. Latude was crawling away on hands and knees but nobody looked at him. A chief then spoke, and Payette said:

"Chief Long Serpent say very friend, like trade little."

"Tell him no more trading till tomorrow."

"Chief say potlatch, want know."

"Tell him yes, if they trap many pelts, don't trade with pedlars."

"Chief say trap many."

"Tell him that is fine."

Payette now talked to the chief and turned to tell David that he had no tobacco, only rose leaves, willow, kinnikinick bark.

"Ask what he has to trade."

"He say squaw."

David shook his head no. He told Payette to get it into Long Serpent's head that he cared nothing about squaws.

"Say has young squaw you like."

A thought came to David. "Tell him I trade rum . . . tobacco . . . Princess Sunday."

Chief Long Serpent's face turned tragic. He came as close to talking with his hands as an Indian could, while his lips spoke to Payette.

"He say Sunday, she Brave Feather."

David asked Payette to make a trade for Sunday, if he could, and he went to his room. He was thinking that he ought to write a letter home. The clan Donald was the oldest and the most famous of all Scottish clans but that was no reason to write. In his breath he was murmuring, *"Lui-ya longtemps que je t'aime, jamais je ne t'oublierai,"* and then he thought, The hell I won't! It came to him that what he really wanted to do was to write a letter to his people and tell them about Sunday, though he did not for a moment believe that Sunday would ever be his to love and never forget. He had too many enemies against him who would stop at nothing.

He was thinking about them when he heard a sound. One Ear, the squaw wife of Latude, her appearance wild and bloody, had rushed into his room, supplicating him with eyes, tongue, and hands. Astonished, he got to his feet and looked down at her, for she had thrown herself to her knees and was begging him in her gibberish of English and Indian to take her as his wife. He supposed that Latude, the miserable coward, had crawled away to find his wife and knock the living daylights out of her. She had blood over her face and skull, she was bruised and torn.

"Get up," he said.

She was clutching at him. She wanted to kiss his hands. She was babbling to him about the horrors of her life with Latude, and Lord God, he had no doubt of that. Almost any Indian buck could be unbelievably brutal with his wife but a half-breed was worse. A half-breed reminded him of the Saulteurs: their squaws lived in such terror that they would climb a tree with a rope around their neck and tie the rope to a high branch and jump. They would sometimes hang themselves rather than live any longer with the brutes who beat them almost to death for no reason at all.

Well, he guessed he would have to call a couple of men and have them take her back. That was a cruel thing to do but there was nothing else to be done. Latude might kill her now. A few years ago he had cut one of her ears off and many times he had beaten her until she was bloody and senseless. Poor thing! She wanted to be his wife, with tears washing with the blood down her face she was begging him to take her; and while he was wondering what to do with her she tried to win him in a squaw's pathetic way. She leaped up and stripped her clothes off and then appealed to him with the ageless coquetry of the female who had only one thing to trade for her life. She was naked before him, a squaw perhaps thirty years old, shapeless, ill-smelling, scarred from head to feet. It was more than a man could stand, to see this bloody pathetic thing, so close to tears, so full of terror and grief, yet trying to use on him a woman's wiles. He went to the door and shouted, and when a man came he said, "Bring Pierre." When Pierre came he said, "What in hell are we to do with her? If I send her back to him he'll kill her." Or he might do worse than that, David was thinking: sometimes when a buck suspected his wife of adultery he would throw her down and with glowing red fagots he would burn over her face and even her eyes until she was horribly disfigured and maybe blind.

"Latude's wife?" Pierre asked, looking at her.

"Latude, the son of a bitch. I had to throw him out, so he goes over and beats his woman. And now she wants me to marry her."

Pierre said, "You should get rid of her fast. He'll be thinking things."

"That's right, he will. Well, get a couple of men to take her." While Pierre was gone she put aside the coquetry and again beseeched him, her tragic eyes blind with tears. It was a hell of a thing to do, this sending her back, but maybe a little rum would help. When the men came he told them to put her garments on and she did not resist for she knew that she had lost. He said to Pierre, "Send Payette along with some rum for him and tell him that if he beats his wife again he'll get no more rum." It was easy to say that and it was no good: when Latude got drunk he would beat her again and someday he would kill her. That was why a man hated trading with Indians, all the rum and drunkenness, the brutalities and murders and all the torture and heartbreak. It made a man wish sometimes that he had never been born.

## VII

David hated trading because of the grand *wabbano,* the *boisson* or drinking bout which had become an inseparable part of it. In the fighting it was usually the defenseless wives and daughters who were beaten and sometimes killed. It was true that after a drunken buck had murdered his daughter or wife or mother he would, after sobering up, be plunged into such inconsolable grief that he would beg a white man to kill him; or if his own people thought he deserved death he would make no move to escape it. He would throw himself at your feet and turn up to you such a picture of shame and woe as you never saw in a white face.

When the post opened the next morning for trading there was Brave Feathers decked out in a military coat adorned with gilt braid and buttons of the Henry VIII period, an elaborately embroidered and very long vest, red military trousers with gold stripes down their sides, and a high beaver hat with an immense plume and a fox tail in front. David let him inside and told Payette to ask him what he wanted. He was closely watching Brave Feathers, particularly his eyes, because an Indian revealed his designs in his eyes, never in his mouth, if he revealed them at all.

"Say trade rum. How much for coat?"

"Ask him how much Princess Sunday."

Then Payette was shaking his head no. The chief would not trade her, he said. He would trade the coat.

David knew there would be no advantage in pressing the matter now. He would wait until the chief had traded everything he had to trade. "One quart," he said, and he intended that it would be chiefly Saskatchewan water.

But the chief said no. He looked terribly offended. He said there was no other coat like this one in all the north country. He said it had cost Horned Thunder—and Payette held up, as Brave Feathers had done, his ten fingers and thumbs twice—twenty made-beaver. David did not doubt it. They really turned the screws into a chief when he took a fancy to something. "Two quarts, no more. I won't argue it."

Brave Feathers and Payette talked back and forth and David could tell that the chief was outraged but very thirsty. He wondered how he had got these garments from Horned Thunder. Had he given him Sunday for them?

"Chief say you rob him. He will accept."

Brave Feathers took off the coat. David brought a two-quart measure of rum that had been cut to about twenty-five proof and the chief hugged it against his belly and went away. When that was drunk he came to trade the vest for another two quarts, and then the trousers for two quarts, and staggered out stark-naked but for his moccasins and hat, looking red and hairless and grotesque, with the huge beaver hat wavering on his greased hair. David followed him out to see if he would fall. He almost fell again and again; he would pause to get his bearings and clear his wits; and again he would go weaving and staggering, clutching the rum to his naked gut as if it were all the treasure of heaven and earth. At the bottom of the hill a group of thirsty bucks awaited him. They ran up to him, afraid that he might fall and spill the precious fluid, and they took him by his arms and one and another tried to take the rum away from him. But Brave Feathers clung to it as to his life. David looked all around, hoping that Sunday would see the ridiculous ass, staggering around naked with that absurd hat on and imagining that he was fully dressed.

The chief never came back to trade the hat. Payette said that he never would, for it was his dearest possession now, even dearer than his Cree scalps. Payette said he had passed out again and was lying stark-naked under a swarm of insect pests and snoring at the sky like a bull buffalo. Would David be interested in a contest of barter over wives?

"Down at the camp?"

Payette nodded.

"Who?"

One, Payette said, was Latude, who had decided that it was smart to get what he could out of his wife rather than to kill her. The other was a brave whose name was Fierce Wolf. David was not particularly interested in watching an Indian and a half-breed swap wives but he was interested in Latude. He expected trouble from him. "All right," he said.

They went to the lodges and Payette then took a path to a cottonwood grove. The two men were there with their wives and a group of onlookers. Latude at the moment was speaking, and Payette translated for David: Latude said that his woman was younger and fatter—and why, David again wondered, did the Indians like fat women? Then Fierce Wolf spoke. He said his woman was a harder worker and liked to copulate as often as any man. The two husbands seemed to be very angry but David knew that their show of heat and scorn was intended only to convince the other that he was a fool.

The two women, sitting, were paying no attention to their men. They both looked fat and shapeless and apathetic. On perceiving that David was present, Fierce Wolf came over and told Payette to ask David to judge the women; and then Fierce Wolf rushed howling at the women as if to kill them, and they turned over to their hands and like fat cows thrust their rumps up and got to their feet. Fierce Wolf told them to take off their clothes. When the women were naked the Indian gestured to David, meaning that he was to walk around them and note their good and bad points; and he kept pointing to the side of the woman's head from which the ear was missing, as though convinced that David through obstinacy or blindness would miss the imperfection. David obligingly walked around the women, neither of whom even looked at him, much less tried to draw her paunch in a little or in any way put on a better appearance. They were both dumpy and short of leg and bellied out from childbearing.

Fierce Wolf was talking to Payette. Payette told David that he was to look into the mouths. Fierce Wolf then shouted and the women opened their mouths for David to look in but David had no notion at all of what it was that Fierce Wolf wanted him to see. Payette now told him that Fierce Wolf wanted him to take the women away and try both.

"Say no, thanks."

Payette said that Fierce Wolf was offering his wife for a keg of rum.

"Tell him no."

Payette said that Latude's wife had only one ear. Had he perceived that?

"Yes," David said.

Latude now seemed to be outraged; he was shouting wildly and pointing at Fierce Wolf's woman as though she had leprous spots all over her. Then Fierce Wolf began to shout and leap up and down and point out imperfections in Latude's woman—the side of the skull with no ear first, then a maimed toe, which David had not noticed, and a scar down one flank, and at last a piece chipped off a tooth. David knew that the men cared little about such things: what both wanted was a work horse and a night whore.

Well, which man ought to have boot?

David saw an opportunity here to breach the ill will of Latude. He looked at the two women, gravely, up and down, shaking his head no at this, yes at that, over and over; and at last he said that Latude had the better wife and should get boot.

Latude was triumphant. Fierce Wolf slobbered with chagrin and rage.

David went on to say that Fierce Wolf had a fine wife too; and he proposed that he should use Latude's wife two moons and if he then wanted to trade back, Latude was to return the boot. The boot was to be a quart of rum.

Again Latude was frenzied in expressions of joy. Fierce Wolf suspected that he was getting the worst of it but David calmed him by having Payette explain that he could trade back after two moons and get the return of the rum. David wondered if the Indian's wild and childlike mind could see the advantage to him in that: he could use the other woman and then, if he did not want her, he could be even. As for Latude, he could get drunk and have a fresh embrace. The two men were trying their best to figure the thing out, each fiercely suspicious of the other; but at last they accepted and Wolf seized his woman and took her away. He was eager to find out if he had been only a pitiful dog.

David went up and got the rum and sent Payette with it to Latude. An hour later Payette came to him eagerly. It was his habit to look round him for things that might divert David and relieve his boredom, for then David would give him an extra ration of rum. He now confided that two drunken bucks were betting on their wives, each shouting to the heavens that his wife could piss the farthest.

"What?" asked David, doubting his ears.

That was it, said Payette, his face glowing with excitement. They were down there behind a lodge——

"I didn't know they could," David said, amused at himself. There was a lot, he told himself again, that he didn't know about women.

"Come?"

"No," David said. But he went outside and looked away toward the lodges, wondering about the thing. It was funny what a white man didn't know about Indians, and particularly about their love life. He had heard Beau Parlez tell of his experiences with both white and red, saying that the red in the love embrace was much better than the white. There was no shame in them, Beau said; if they liked you they did it like hell and damnation. And you could tell in a lot of ways if they liked it. The nostrils would flare and quiver and sometimes turn a deeper red; the ear lobes would become redder as they filled with blood; and there were actually some squaws, he said, who could be brought to a collapse by sucking the lobes of their ears. That had all been news to David. It was news when Beau said that a man could tell if a woman wanted him by the way she looked at him after an absence: her face would change color, and oftentimes the throat and ears, and you could see the nostrils begin to quiver. When you had a loving squaw really yearning for you, said Beau, her genital area would become a huckleberry purple. David found it all a little fantastic but he admitted that he didn't know much about such things; and his reflections now colored his attitude toward Sunday. He doubted that her nostrils would ever flare for him.

"You mean," he had said to Beau Parlez, "that red women are more ardent than white?"

"Orden?" asked Beau, and the lecherous illiterate rascal was not feigning.

"Like men more that way?"

"Ohhh!" Beau exclaimed, opening his eyes ecstatically. Had Mister McDonald never tried them?

David had admitted that he had not and he had felt pretty silly about it. What kind of white man was it who spent years in the north country without lying with a woman? To tell the truth, he was afraid of squaws—afraid of their disease, their jealousy, their murderous passions. He had learned with amazement that among Indians the women were crueler than the men. He would never forget the picture of a squaw on the warpath because her buck had tried to ditch her. Lord God! That woman had had a scalping knife in either hand and had been so eager to kill that she had crouched forward like a beast instead of standing erect, and her jaw had been thrust out, pulling the lower lip away from her teeth, and her eyes had had half the fires of hell in them. Whether she ever got the knives into the guts of her lord David never learned but he told himself then and there that a squaw on the warpath was not for him. Any man he would face, red or white, or any beast in prairie or jungle, but a woman with all her fires kindled was too much for David McDonald. Thinking of it now, he found it strange that he should be enraptured with such a fireball as Sunday.

One of his men who had been preparing beasts and equipment for a buffalo hunt came to him. He said David's favorite horse was limping.

"Why?"

"His hoofs is all worn away."

David went over to look at the beast. He picked up a hoof, resting the beast's foreleg across his thigh, and examined the hoof and found it so worn away that it was raw and bleeding. There was nothing you could do with a foot like that.

"Just one?" he said.

"Right hind one too."

David took the hind foot up and examined it. It was worse. It was really down to the quick and the frog was nearly all gone. David put an arm around the horse's neck and his cheek to the big flat jawbone and with a hand stroked down the nose to the sensitive nostrils. This had been his favorite of all animals since he came here. He had ridden it hell for leather over badger holes and prairie dog villages and never once had it stumbled, much less fallen. He had ridden its sure-footed balance high into mountain goat country. And once when his life was at stake and he had to make a quick getaway he had all in one movement flung the saddle and caught the cinch and made one turn with the latigo and then astride had ridden at full speed for miles, cinch and latigo flying like the beast's tail, his heels dug in to keep the saddle seated. Now the poor thing had to die.

"You shoot it," he said, and turned away.

Inside the post to forget about it he turned to his work, provisioning a trapper who in lying with the squaws had tried to cram six or seven long months of woman into a few days and was ready to go. David measured out the powder and ball, tobacco, a little sugar and said, "Pemmican, how much?"

"One bag," the man said.

David went for a bag, thinking that one bag would not last long. Nothing had astonished him more on coming here than the amount of food the men ate. In a week, Jim said, a dozen trappers had eaten seven bear, two moose, several bags of pemmican, and God alone knew how many beaver. Four men could eat a caribou at a sitting, and the story was told of a feast at which ten men ate at one meal a ninety-pound bag of pemmican. These things surprised David no longer. He could eat with any of them. Men of the north country reminded him of that tribe of Indians called Big Bellies, not because they had protuberant guts but because one of their tribal signs was a gesture over their stomach which meant that they were always hungry.

A bag of pemmican would feed this trapper into the north woods country, home of the Crees. He would then eat almost nothing but beaver. Oh, he might get a woodland caribou now and then or a red deer or a few grouse but week after week and month after month it would be beaver; and sitting alone in loneliness by his own little campfire, he would smack over beaver tail and swear to God that it was the finest delicacy in the world.

"Anything else?" asked David, throwing down the bag.

"How much that?"

David added up the sums. A trapper was allowed a hundred and fifty dollars in credit and woe to him if he took his pelts to the enemy. "You have twenty dollars yet."

"Rum," the man said. "The Crees ain't as friendly as they were."

Going for rum, David reflected that the Crees had formerly been quite friendly to the whites, though a few years ago, on coming into possession of guns, they had resolved to chase all other Indians out of the Churchill and Beaver rivers area. Even the poor Dogribs. That had led to all kinds of trouble. And more and more they liked their rum too. Thomas Nashe, a playwright in the time of Shakespeare, had divided drunkards into ape-drunk, pig-drunk and sheep-drunk. The Crees now, like the other tribes roundabout, wanted to be ape-drunk if they could.

"There you are," said David. "Remember that you're an HB man."

The man nodded. He knew what David meant. He knew that if he went over to the pedlars his bones would be lost and forgotten somewhere between Red Deer River and Little Slave Lake.

David had done a little trapping during his first years here. He knew the hazards, the deep snows, the smell of beaver and beaver-house and steaming beaver ponds; the naked thickets and the shadows and the alluring shelters under overhanging snow ceilings; the conical stumps made by beaver teeth on aspen and willow and alder and poplar; the smell of the castors; the feeling of the thick soft fur and the cries of forest birds and of wolf and of the thousands of ducks and loons and snipes; and the sight, when in early spring you kicked the snow away, of flowers deep under the snow pushing their way up to light and melting the snow around them with their own living warmth; and the cold, oh God, the cold, and the loneliness like an envelope on a man's soul. Forty or fifty or sixty below zero sometimes and a man out there in a frozen wilderness trying to keep warm with buffalo robes and a little fire. How his bones had ached, how he had flailed himself as he grew numb, how he had piled up the larch and spruce and fir needles and burrowed into the pile, with robes around him! Some of the trappers built themselves a little cabin but others did not bother. Cabin or not, they were, it seemed to David, the most rugged tribe of men on earth and he never looked at one without admiration and wonder.

Now and then one broke and went down, even after years of rigors and solitudes. A half-breed named Louis had gone into the moon, which was Jim's way of saying that he had gone berserk.

"Everything ready to take him out?" Jim asked a little later.

Everything would be, David said. The redskins said it would be a late fall; the fur wasn't thickening yet and the buffalo were not at their fattest. "Now what about Louis?"

He was in irons, Jim said. When one of the buggers went into the moon it cost the old HB the packs of two trappers.

"I guess one man could take him out."

"What man? Would you try it? A lunatic in a canoe with one man? And how in hell would you portage?"

"Well, that's right. A man might handle him in irons in a canoe but it would take two for the portage."

"He's a goddamned nuisance," Jim said.

"Violent all the time?"

"Just about. Slobbers and screams and thinks he's being scalped. I reckon the Indians must have run a finger around his head."

"To show him where it would come off."

"Yeah."

"It's a hell of a long way out," David said.

They were silent. David was thinking of Old Man Barlow. Old Man had trapped for years and years and got himself one squaw and then another, until he had six; and they helped him trap and he became prosperous and he began to drink too much rum. He began to beat his women and one by one they stole away and fled, and when he was left desolate he went into the moon. Since then he had become a legend. From time to time a trapper would see him drifting down a river on a raft, for he had no canoe any more but tied two or three logs together. He had no tobacco any more, no rum, no woman, no companion but the wild things of forest and river. That, David supposed, might happen to any man here if he didn't keep his two feet right on the ground. You'd become a Louis or an Old Man Barlow. . . .

"Want me to choose the two men?"

"But don't take any trappers."

"No."

"They should be dependable, I guess. Still," Jim said, knocking his pipe out, "if it wasn't for the dumb bastards sitting on their asses in London we'd just send three out that we want to get rid of. But the honorable directors would write long folios to find out what happened to them. And they usually find out."

"The pedlars," David said.

"How you getting along with your woman trouble? No snoodless lass, eh?"

"Not getting along."

"Can't trade Brave Feathers out of her?"

David shook his head no.

"Well, maybe there's one thing, Dave, you don't know about Indians yet. I don't know so well how it is with the Slaves and the Dogribs and the Wood and Assiniboins and some of the others but the Blackfeet always have a chief who is boss. That chief might be

Horned Thunder or it might be old Mink Tails. If you made a trade with him Feathers would have to pretend it was spruce beer and swallow it."

"But the girl hates me, I reckon. And now Latude, the son of a bitch, is against me."

"What does he have to do with it?"

"I had to throw him out of the trading room."

"He's a mean one," Jim said. "He's the dog that just barked. You know, the thing I like least any more is the way we have to handle the redskins. It used to be that if they didn't behave we could knock a few of them down or give them a physic and let them do the backdoor trot a night or two. Why did you have to toss him out?"

"Same old thing. Drunk."

"Watch him, he's a mean one."

"Behind a man's back."

"Well, choose a couple of men and get that bastard off down the river. They'll have to force food and water into him and keep him in chains all the way; but if he gets so he just won't open his mouth tell them to dump him where the river is widest and let him go."

## VIII

It took a lot of buffalo to make enough pemmican for men who could eat two fat geese at a sitting or four or five mallard ducks or the hindquarter of a deer or a caribou. Indians did most of the hunting for both companies but David liked to go in a big hunt when he could get away. He knew of two immense herds in the northern area. One of them wintered in the brushlands of the Coteau du Missouri, westward from Pembina River, drifting northward in springtime to the lush open prairies where it crossed the valley of the Qu'Appelle and foraged as far as the Assiniboine when it turned south to Red River and its winter home. That was the larger herd. That herd was so damned huge and dense and tame that Selkirk's settlers had complained that, like a flood, it overwhelmed their fields and stood black and immovable farther than human eye could see. The other herd moved up from its summer lands to make the areas upon the two Saskatchewan rivers its winter home. It was now moving up and the hunters would try to intercept it when it was at the farthest point north in its great annual circle. Snow would be falling then. It would be a cold wet journey, particularly unpleasant for the poor squaws, who were only beasts of burden when not whores in the lodges. Somewhere on that hunt he would meet Sunday again.

Formerly the Indian hunters had killed the meat and made the pemmican and brought it to the post but you couldn't count on that so much now. Now the pedlars not only sent their men far and wide to find and deal with the Indians but to live with them all winter long, to learn their language, to become as like Indians as they could. And everywhere, even within musket shot of where David stood, were their bully boys. With iron fist and gun brag Sam Black and his thugs had scared the unholy daylights out of Peter Fidler, then in charge of an HB post: they had carried off his firewood, stolen his fishing nets, trampled his garden into the earth, and at last dared him to show his face outside the palisades. That had been too much for Peter. That might be too much for a lot of them.

"But not for you," Jim had said to him a couple of years ago. "You're chief trader now. You're more than that. The pitiful dogs aren't going to bluff anyone at this post."

"You mean John Bowman's bully?" David asked innocently.

"Or any other."

Well, he probably ought to go over and see Bowman. He never knew whether it was better to have a heart-to-heart talk with a man or to put a spy on him. He hadn't seen John Bowman's face for weeks but the man was over there at Augustus, as full of zeal and schemes and conspiracies as ever. He was a nice warmhearted likable guy if he liked you but if he didn't like you he was all wolverine and wolf teeth and as bold as any man from Astoria to Thunder Bay. When he dealt with Indians he would back the chiefs right up against their buckskin even when they were surrounded by warriors with drawn tomahawks. "Too bad he isn't on our side," Jim had said one day.

It was funny, David thought, the way the damned fool companies did with one another. If one built a fort the other moved right in and built a fort, sometimes almost alongside, never more than a mile or so distant. Of course that was a good thing in case of Indian attack but they followed one another fort by fort up and down the rivers not because of Indian fear but to be in a position to bribe or intimidate or shoot the other's trappers and hunters. And everywhere orders had gone out from both companies to match the men—to measure bullies against bullies, craftiness against craftiness. David was not dead-sure in which category they had placed him. He did not think of himself as a bully, he did not feel crafty, and he knew of bolder men. This John Bowman, for instance, seemed to him to be as bold as a famished wolf with his muzzle lifted into a blizzard.

Trying to decide whether to go over and learn how Bowman was feeling, he went to a keg which the barber used as his stool. He had thought to get a haircut and shave but, hell, he didn't want that. Sunday would think him ridiculous. He ought to braid his hair and soak it with hump fat, and it might be a good thing to thin his beard out, for the redskins were not well-bearded men. He decided instead to write a letter to his people back in Scotland—Jim had said an express canoe was coming—and he went to his own small room, now gloomy with early-autumn chill. But what was there to write home that had not been many times written?—that because of the murderous feud between the two companies and the raiding and pillaging and the fat-bottomed British habit of postponing as long as possible anything unpleasant—hadn't Elizabeth almost brought the nation to disaster that way?—the fat bottoms hadn't been paid a shilling of dividends in five long years. How did the bastards like that? "If you get down to London will you please go in and ask them how they like it and if it is possible for an Englishman to make up his mind about anything? The pedlar bosses are only as far away as Montreal and in a crisis they make up their minds fast and shoot an express canoe over. We have to wait on a slow ship to Plymouth and on old fiddle-doups in London and on a slow ship back—and imagine how fast the pedlars are moving in all that time!" Should he tell them that he had taken to dreaming of delting with a lassie?—that instead of tending to his affairs he had gone away splunting?

"I'm courting a lass," he wrote, shivering as he scratched over the paper, "a wild thing, neither white nor red, but as dirty as a buffalo in a mud wallow and with a stink like that of buffalo bush drenched with wolf urine. I guess she must have been captured by some Indian tribe when very small. Jim says down in the States a lot of stories have been written by those captured as children, usually girls, who survived and at last were freed. She seems not to know a word of her own language, though sometimes I suspect her of pretending. An undichtet wean she is but as beautiful as anything out of doors. She is strange and dark and buried and as unpredictable as an Indian."

He was idle a few minutes, nibbling at the tip of the quill. Then,

"She's about five feet and five or six inches tall—a trifle short for me but, like so many Scots, I'm too far up in the air; and she has grace—Lord, she can swim like whatever it is that swims best, otter or seal, and run like the wind and ride a horse, I have no doubt, in a way that will make me feel awkward for life. In regard to that I shall see, for we are soon to go on the big hunt. Jim wants me to go along this year because he's afraid the Blackfeet might double-cross us and leave us pemmican-destitute, and what would our outlying posts do if our depot was empty? We'd all starve to death, as we may anyhow when we push up into the Athabasca, into the great woods belt. The woods Indians seem always to be half starved. Prairie Indians have the buffalo and that is all they need—its hide for clothing, its sinews for bowstrings, its belly for their cooking pots, its flesh for food along with spruce beer—and that reminds me that I must get some spruce beer made up, for I see signs of scurvy in some of the men."

He paused again in thought and went on, "Jim said something the other day that troubles me. Some of the Mandans, he says—they're to hell and gone south of here—have fair hair and complexion. Is it possible that my princess is a Mandan? I don't want to marry an Indian and I tell myself I have no prejudice against them, but that is not true. I can't determine if I wish to remain here all my life. Scotland is too small now, the British Isles too small; a mountain man of the north could never again live on the moors. It would be folly to take an Indian wife among people who think it important what tools they eat with. This country grows in you and fills you out and becomes hard in your muscles and emotions, and your mind becomes a map. If I were back there I'd have to stand up some morning and look off west to Thunder Bay and remember how it was when the northern winds came in, and water and earth and sky each howled and fought for its share of living. As these two companies are fighting, more and more, with a showdown inevitable.

"Jim thinks our company may be destroyed for lack of boldness. A hundred and forty-five years ago it was established and, so far as I can learn, has operated in peace nearly all that time, while corrupting Indians to make them more useful and destroying animals by the tens of thousands for their skins. But now its rights and its very existence are challenged, and a man like Jim, who has been with it all his adult life, feels as Lord Selkirk feels, that all other trappers are poachers. I can't feel that way but I must be loyal as long as I am with it. I suppose what I'm trying to say is that the struggle is going to become violent and men on both sides will die. I want to get this letter off——"

Oh hell! he thought, getting to his feet. He stared for a few moments at the pages he had written and then tore them up. He had wanted to write about the girl but he couldn't think about her without getting steamed up like a bog in the first frost. He had wanted to write about this desperate struggle that was shaping up—but why? Was he afraid? It didn't make much sense to tell himself that he was afraid of anything, yet he was feeling angry, almost furious, and after a little reflection he decided that he was angry because he had been thinking earlier about John Bowman. The thing to do was to go over right now and see how the bastard was feeling. The partners in Montreal might shape the strategy but it was men in the field who would execute it, and none more than Bowman.

Not big and powerfully muscled, not a bully boy, but a rather droll and slightly whimsical man who liked to read and speculate and quip, and who like all the top men in both companies was pretty well educated, John Bowman, unlike David, was on fire with ambition. He was so ambitious that he cared nothing about his own personal comforts when these got in the way of doing and climbing, and so ruthless that he would stop at nothing. He preferred guile and cunning and gentleness in dealing with men, red or white, but when these failed and he was thwarted he backfired like a faulty musket and was all flame and gunpowder.

"Why, hello," he said in his soft way, his eyes narrowed, whimsical, alert, searching. "David, my friend, how are you?"

A hell of a lot you care! David was thinking. But his voice was gracious. "As every day. And you?"

"As weary as a kultus klootchman after the third night."

That was Indian jargon for whore. "Maybe you need a regale," David said. He hated this fencing and feinting and feeling out an opponent but that's the way you had to be with John, who to all the tricks and deceptions of the whites had added those of the Indians. He knew that John was not weary at all: the man would get you off guard with absurd statements or chitchat until he found out what was on your mind.

"Had one," John said, meaning regale, which was a cup of brandy or rum. "Huzza-huzza *pour le pays sauvage*." He narrowed his eyes a little more and added, "*Je suis bien aise de vous voir.*"

David looked at him, thinking, He knows damned well I speak very little French. He said, *"Oui, monsieur."*

In Bowman's face there was the suggestion of a smile. *"Le pays!* It's worse than pissants in a backhouse, isn't it?"

"Mean you're tired of it?" asked David, watching John's eyes.

"David, I'm all ganted up with loneliness."

All his talk so far, David reflected, was woman talk in a man who usually made big brag. There was something here that didn't show on the surface. "It's the winter coming," he said.

"It'll be a deep one, the redskins say, and so cold a man's piss will freeze before it hits the ground. I plan to find a place where I can shiver comfortably and then shiver all winter."

"I've done it," David said. "Fifty below and no fat in the belly."

John looked at him with quick alert interest. He was about to say something but changed his mind and let it pass. What he said was, "Got all your pemmican bagged up?"

"We're short and you know it."

"I don't know how in hell I would know it."

David met his eyes and said, "John Bowman knows everything that goes on around here and John Bowman has plenty of pemmican."

*"Mais peut-être c'est pas vrai."* He was surveying David, his eyes mocking. "Would you like a bag or two?"

"I'm muckle obleeged to ye," David said.

"Thank God for pemmican," John said. "You suppose they eat the stuff in heaven?"

"It's not so bad if you know how to make it. Come over sometime and I'll give you a sample."

"I'm muckle obleeged," said John. "Any news from the outside world? Are there still clean beds in which a man feels the tanino?"

"Wars and rumors of wars," David said.

John's face sobered. "You know what is going to happen? Our two companies will kill one another off and the United States will grab everything clear to the ocean. Look at the lower Columbia, a lot of beaver there."

"I hear that you people are moving that way."

"You mean that you people want everything."

"Oh no—"

"You mean the United States and HB are to divide it."

"No—"

"That's what your honorable directors in London mean. That's what Selkirk means. Look," said John, gesturing at the distances, "whose men explored it? Did your old HB send Samuel Hearne and Alexander Mackenzie and David Thompson and all the others out there?"

"Hearne?" said David. "He was before your time." It was like John to include Hearne. He was so ambitious, he was at heart such an empire builder, that he got his own accomplishments mixed up with those of other men. But it was true, Lord yes, it was true, that the vast areas out yonder were explored and mapped by pedlars.

As if reading his thoughts John said, "We map and explore it, you take it. Is that it? And Selkirk doesn't even thank us. Yonder," he said, again waving an arm, "is the Athabasca. We explored it, not you."

"But our charter——"

"Oh, to hell with your charter. A bunch of princes and earls smelling riches went to a king who divided his time between wenching and drinking and said, 'Give it to us,' and he gave it, all the lands beyond the ocean. What in hell did he know about it?—or care. And if you have a right to everything over here why don't you call the United States poachers and tell them to get out?"

"But all the best trapping is now up there."

"When was your company founded?"

"In 1670."

"How far is it from here to Hudson Bay?"

David hesitated. The sly rascal had something in mind.

"Fifteen hundred miles? How broad is it? A thousand miles? All right, for a hundred and forty-five years your company trapped that broad expanse. Generations have come and gone in all that time. Men grew wealthy and passed fortunes on to heirs who are now in the fourth or fifth generation. If another company organizes and goes out beyond you and builds posts and explores and maps, then you cry to Christ and heaven that that's all yours too. Just because Charles II thought he had a right to give some of his favorites all the continents he had never heard about but imagined might exist."

"You make out quite a case for yourself," David said.

"No trouble at all," said John. "A thousand times fifteen hundred is a million five hundred thousand square miles. Isn't that enough for you? Are we to have no right to what we have explored and mapped? If we got to the Athabasca first, is that to make no difference? I'll tell you something," John said, again speaking quietly, a little mockingly, "if you come snooping up into the Athabasca, as I have heard you intend to, you're going to get a lot of surprises."

"Such as what?" David asked.

"If I told you," said John with a faint smile, "they wouldn't be surprises, would they?"

Jim Dugald, meanwhile, was laboriously and painstakingly communicating his views (by the next express out) to what he thought of, privately, as the fat asses in London. They hadn't received any dividends for five years. Their purses were gaping. They were worried, for they had at last got it into their dull British heads that the men from Montreal were standing right in the middle of the best beaver land on earth and intended to stay there. The directors were sending their anxieties in words insufferably polite and pompous; they were wondering in their confused and fumbling way what must be done again to fatten their purses. After scratching out the stiffly polite salutation Jim went on:

"The North West Company is plotting some major move that shall be intended for the utter extermination of all other interests in the entire Athabasca forest belt. There can be no doubt of that. But no vigilance on the part of your humble servant has divulged any details of their sinister plan. Lord Selkirk and his honourable Committee know what desperation will invest their purpose, to the end that their profits may be greater and ours less; for you must by this time have a full picture of affairs on the Red River last summer."

He sat in thought a few minutes and puffed his pipe. This was not the kind of letter he wanted to write. He wanted to say, "You fantastic blockheads, your men here, including me, begged you for years and years to explore and map and push out with new posts. The whole world acclaimed Mackenzie's discoveries and the North Westers leapt to seize their opportunities. David Thompson was once your man but you couldn't make up your mind to anything and the North Westers grabbed him and he explored and mapped the areas where they now are. It's nobody's fault but yours, and nobody with a grain of sense can deny that these men are entitled to what they had the vision to seize and you the timidity to lose." But humble servants did not write that way to their masters. He smoked and deliberated and looked at a list of words in his big smudged dirty notebook. He had jotted down a number of big words that he liked to use on the directors and he now chose one:

"With what prescience we have we will anticipate and prepare.

Hard blows will be struck, more deadly blows than any that have yet fallen. I think it essential to lay in an unusually large store of pemmican, and I urge you to send with the spring brigades at least one and a half times the amount of rum you sent over this year. We, your servants, are aware of Lord Selkirk's wish to deal with Indians without rum but until we have another and adequate way we shall have to persist in the old grooves. If the honourable company is ever again to pay dividends . . ."

He broke off and knocked his pipe out. "You dull snoring bastards!" he muttered. As a chief factor he participated in profits, when there were profits, but his want of profits for five years was not what disturbed him. It was the lack of vision and resoluteness that had allowed the Montreal men to possess a beaver land as big as half of Europe. He pushed his disgust down and enumerated various bookkeeping details, taken from the clerk's record, and poured a cup of brandy and drank it off. He wished they would send West Indian rum instead of the inferior product back in New England. The New England rum cost less, of course, and the pinchfists in London had always been primarily interested in keeping expenses down and profits up.

Having completed a rather long letter, he closed:

I am, Dear Sirs,
Your Dutifull & Obedient
Humble Servt to Command

Jas. Dugald

He then leaned back, feeling that he was growing old in his bones and mind, and called a servant and sent him to find David. When David came he stared at him a few moments through tobacco smoke and then said:

"Learn anything?"

"He says they will hold the Athabasca. He says if we go up there there will be surprises for us."

"We knew all that," Jim rumbled. "What surprises?"

"He said to reveal them would be to spoil them."

"Murder he means. Ambush. Starvation. Well, I've told Horned Thunder we're going to want a lot more pemmican and the reason I want you to go along is to see that we get it. If we don't have a big supply of meat we'll be sunk. He say anything else?"

"Oh, the old fiddle-doup. If the directors had just given David Thompson the supplies and told him to go ahead—"

"Yes, yes. That's an old story now. The company could have had all the beaver land clear to the ocean if the directors could have seen farther than the nearest alehouse. But that's all dead Indian now. We've let them grow fat and strong and now we have to fight."

## IX

When he came out David looked down to see if everything was all right. He felt around for his pistol and knife. When in the saddle he liked to wear a girdle of soft buckskin, about eight or nine inches wide and long enough to go around him three times. When it was wrapped around him, firm against his gut, he felt more trim and ready, as he supposed a woman felt in a certain kind of corset that gave support to her torso and breasts. He had had the tailor make a sheath in it for his hunting knife and another for his pistol. Now, pistol and knife in place, he went over to his horse, where his men were waiting.

Putting foot to stirrup, he swung up easily, looked north for a moment at the Athabasca country, and then moved around in the saddle, adjusting his hams, measuring the stirrups for length, examining the duffel to see if it was securely tied. Looking at the sky in the southwest, he said to Pierre, "A big storm coming."

He was not familiar with this horse and he now tried it out. Putting it to the gallop, he would turn a little to the right and with his left knee put gentle pressure to the shoulder; and turn to the left and press with his right knee; and the horse turned, with no guidance from the rein. He was delighted. That was the kind of horse to have, one that felt and responded to the movement in the rider: you could give both hands to your gun and it was a mighty good thing to have both hands free in the midst of buffalo or with redskins after you. This horse was fat and without saddle sores. The backs of some Indian ponies were stinking masses of flesh wounds, and when the Indians mounted, the poor suffering beasts would flinch away sidewise almost to the ground.

"Ready?" he asked, facing south. A breeze was blowing through autumn and he could smell the first yellow on cottonwood and aspen and the first scarlet of maple and wild rose and the smoky sweetness of aster and goldenrod and diamond willow. He could feel the autumn, he could taste it. Summer was fine, when the hot afternoons steeped the air with the odors of saxifrage and heather and bear grass, but autumn was a man's season, for then he stepped out of summer loafings as from a chrysalis and felt the tang in his nostrils and the impatience in his blood.

He was looking south. The Indians had gone ahead and were out of sight or were lost in the protective russet-brown coloring of the prairie. It was best, for they liked to be alone. Before riding out of sight he glanced back to see if the pennon was flying and there it was, red and black and white with HBC in white on red down in the lower front corner. Down under it Jim was worrying his head off about Athabasca land. "We've got to have a hell of a lot of pemmican," he had said. It would be rough on the buffalo this fall.

Pierre was riding on his right, Payette on his left. Behind came servants with camp and hunting equipment, horses and dogs, but he didn't have enough white men to make a stand if Horned Thunder got an itch for scalps. David had a feeling that his life would be in danger from the moment the post fell out of sight and he was not sure if he had a single man with him in whom he could put complete trust. Pierre was the nearest to it but he had to admit that he didn't know a hell of a lot about Pierre. The man was chewing twist and browning his sandy stubble with it. He now and then looked at David out of tiny pupils in pale green eyes and David thought he saw amused cunning; and as often as David wanted to listen to it Pierre would tell him in his soft voice that he never raised or lowered that only those died young who were afraid to die. David thought it a piece of silliness but that was Pierre's philosophy.

"Horned Thunder in good humor?"

"Kinda," Pierre said, and spit straight ahead between his horse's ears. "But Brave Feathers, him?"

"Don't ask me. Latude with them?"

"Couldn't say for Jesus."

"They all Blackfeet?"

Pierre shook his head, meaning that he didn't know.

And what man would? Who but an expert could walk among Blackfeet, Bloods, Crees, Piegans, Gros Ventres, Sarcees, Dogribs, Shuswaps, Stonies, Sioux, Slaves, Chipewyans and say this man is this and that man is that? David had been studying their red skins for years but could see no more difference among them than among the Chinese. The Piegans were possibly the fiercest, or the Sioux; and maybe the gentlest were the Dogribs or Crees. The Indians seemed able to spot one another a mile away but how they did it was a riddle to white men. It wasn't the way they rode: they all pounded their ponies and kicked in with their heels. The pedlars had bluffed and bulldozed the Chipewyans and the Crees but they had never had the face to try that with the Blackfeet. Well, David was now in Blackfoot land and tomorrow he would be in the land of the Bloods; and westward on the foothills of the Rockies the savage Piegans would be shading their eyes and watching him.

The breeze was from the southwest. "I can smell them," David said.

Pierre lifted his nose like a dog. In that low voice, so deadly in its quietness, he said, "Heap big stink."

That, David reflected, was true, for the buffalo was a filthy beast. It had reason to be. In springtime it shook and shuddered and itched and rubbed itself against stones and trees, trying to shed the mattings of dead hair, alive with vermin and caked with old sweat and mud and scabs; and when patches fell off, leaving naked and bleeding areas, clouds of its enemies moved in, chief of which was the one men here called the bulldog, a large vicious and bloodthirsty fly that, like a tick, was never done with feeding until it was all gut and stupor. And there were ticks by the millions: they dug in so deep that in dislodging one you pulled its body off its head, leaving the head buried; and the itching was horrible. There were fleas and wood lice and monstrous black horseflies and deer flies and mosquitoes—in fact the pests in certain seasons were so dreadful that men dared not sleep at all but sat choking all night in a smudge. Horses sometimes were so desperate with pain that they would hurl themselves into water or roll in mud. The buffalo, poor old bastard, had dim eyes at best, and when matted forelocks hung over them or hordes of insects fed and drank at their rims, it might better have had none at all. David had often looked with astonishment at the ravages the buffalo had made in woods with its rubbings and the great piles of hair at the foot of trees and the bark brightly polished as high as it reached. And if it wasn't a skyful of pests eating him alive it was the early-summer sun blistering hell out of his naked skin where the winter mats had fallen, or flocks of magpies or crows riding his raw back and eating until, goaded with pain, the grotesque monster went bellowing into the wind or tumbled like a hog into the first mudhole and burrowed and snorted until he was sheathed over with prairie clay. Or it was the prairie fires, set by lightning or by Indians; David had seen the wretched creatures with the hair burnt off them and their eyes burnt out, staggering round and round, knocking themselves senseless against trees, falling into rivers, and drowning by the hundreds or thousands or toppling over to die. Men here told of having seen so many drowned buffalo that a flowing river was continuously full of them for more than two days and two nights, and the stench along the shores was something a man had to smell to believe; and he had to see the squaws opening the bellies to take the fat out of the stinking things to believe that.

David had used to watch the bulls fight, but no more. When he first came from Scotland, his emotions green and tender and credulity like altar candles in his eyes, he thought the monsters would kill one another. In the rutting season when struggling for the cows their bellows shook the heavens and their feet tore the earth into clouds, blowing snot and rage from their nostrils, their flanks heaving, their dim eyes inflamed and bulging with erotic ardor, and their thick skulls crashing bone on bone with such power that the impact could be heard a mile away. God, how they fought and bellowed! David had expected to see crushed skulls and gutted bellies everywhere, but never once had he seen a bull hurt by another bull. Like the pedlars, they packed an awful lot of brag.

And what ridiculous things they were to look at! Most of a buffalo, almost four fifths of its bulk and weight, was from the penis sheath forward, rising into the enormous and largely useless hump of the shoulders and the massive depth of the neck and the skull, all covered over with enough hair to fill a half dozen mattresses; while from the middle on back the monster looked naked, as if it had been shorn, because the hair was so short compared to the shaggy manes and masses and beards of the front half. Even more ridiculous was the smallness of the rear quarters, compared to the front: the grotesquely tiny thighs, with the great pouch of testicles hanging between them and flinging wildly back and forth and all around when the beast fought or ran; and the short useless tail; and the absurdly small feet, so small under the huge bulk that they cut narrow trenches across the prairie, a foot or a foot and a half in depth, and no wider than that. And to top everything there were the silly little horns, looking like two tusks growing out of the skull.

On seeing the skulls opened David had been surprised to learn that the beasts actually had brains. They had brains but most of the time they never used them. Back from the precipice the Indians would set a V-shaped ambush of pickets, and then by waving robes and uttering a cry that the dull-witted creature thought friendly they would stampede a whole herd into the V and over a precipice; though if the cow who led refused to jump but turned back, as now and then she did, the Indians behind the herd had no chance to escape being trampled to death. And what a sight it was to see the squaws rush in with hatchets and knives like avengers ejected out of hell, to strike and stab and thrust until the whole pound under the precipice was wet with blood and guts and the squaws were red and wet too, while stuffing their mouths with raw liver; and the whole earth steamed and stank of the gut and kidney and heart and womb and testicle smells of living creatures, living a few moments ago, roaring and bellowing, but now hacked and laid open and still, eyes glazed, black tongues hanging down over lower-jaw teeth and only the muscles in thigh or neck still twitching. But that was not where he had seen them at their most stupid: after all, even a man could be ambushed.

He had seen Indians with fire or with plain whoop and holler stampede them into a river, where they drowned by hundreds as the moving masses behind shoved forward in snorting and terrified violence and beasts made a bridge for beasts or pontoons, and you saw a big bull standing precariously and amazingly upon the bulls and cows under him, as if walking across and resting a moment from his labors, and in another moment down he went under, never to come up until dead, but you could see the air from his lungs coming up, and the Indians there behind the dark and heaving and rolling mass, driving them on, beast upon beast, a bridge drowning, and beasts falling through the bridge, until the whole damn river was black and choked with them and the air from dying lungs was making a multitude of tiny fountains in the rolling tides and the Indians were giving no mercy, no quarter until the last hapless, unlucky, dimwitted and filled-with-terror thing lost his footing and went down . . . And then you saw the acreage of them, dead, drifting with the current, beaching; and Indians out among them, pushing, shoving and yelling like mad; and then the beach heavy with them, the heavens steaming with heat from their insides, and red people choking down raw livers, eating like dogs. . . .

David preferred the flesh of the red deer or of young moose or of mountain sheep; though in the early fall, when the rear short-haired part was smooth with fat and the great pelage of the front half had shed all its mattings and scabs and accumulated filth from mudholes and wallows, the flesh was pretty good, particularly from the older calves and the young barren cows. Indians were fond of the *dépouille,* or back fat, which they melted to make pemmican but would eat raw, though of all fats they ate raw their favorite was that around the kidneys. They thought it was good for sore mouths. And, hell, maybe it was, David had told himself; you could call it superstition if you wanted to, but the Indians had a lot of fine remedies besides spruce beer for scurvy and cankerroot for canker and balsam sap for flesh wounds.

Indian dust had been in sight all the way, and now as they rounded a hilltop the Indians came in view. Beyond them a body of water shone like a mirror and David thought of the unbelievable loveliness of Maligne Lake, high up against mountain grandeur. This in view now was the lake where all the bittern were; there were thousands of them, and more ducks and geese than an army could eat in a lifetime. It was funny about wild things. Before geese learned that man was an enemy they would come honking and whistling almost to his feet, and David had seen men club their heads off. The young and foolish ones, anyway.

He turned to look at Pierre. "How many lakes you think there are in this country?"

Pierre gestured toward the northeast. "Tens of thousands."

"But around here."

"Hundreds," Pierre said.

"And rivers, Jesus. Thousands of lakes and rivers in this country. Up in the top of the mountains there, that's where the beautiful lakes are." Pierre looked westward at peaks misty with distance and autumn. "Like huge sapphire jewels in granite settings," David said.

Pierre looked a little funny at that. "Clear up on top?"

"Some right on top. Maybe twelve, maybe thirteen thousand feet up."

"Rivers there?" asked Pierre, staring at distance.

"Headwaters. Glaciers. The Columbia, Saskatchewan, and Athabasca all rise from the same snows."

"Beaver?"

"Not that far up." David felt moisture on the end of his nose and wiped it away with a buckskin glove. He returned his hand and sniffed. He loved the smell of this soft leather and thought he would love to hold Sunday in his arms if she were dressed in buckskin from head to feet. The chief odor was of the smoking but there were other and subtler odors that a man couldn't distinguish. He put the glove to his nostrils and breathed: it was a fine clean strong odor, the smell of Indians and lodge fires and an untamed earth. You dressed in leather from head to feet and slept under buffalo robes and after a while you forgot about these strong smells until you were naked and at some distance from your clothes and then you missed something, as if all the strength had departed from life. Or it was like watching naked Indians, red and full of sun and weather, and then peering inside your shirt at your own pale skin.

"Storm coming," Pierre said, and filled his mouth with twist.

David looked up at the sun. There was a nimbus around it. "Snow," he said, and filled his pipe.

The Indians wouldn't like it so well if it snowed. Though superb horsemen they still preferred to hunt afoot with bow and arrow, for then they could walk among the beasts and they wouldn't stampede; but if the earth was white they would stand out as enemies and they would have to crawl on their bellies. It wasn't much fun crawling a mile or two on your belly in snow.

Thinking of snow reminded him of another thing he had seen. The snow even on the prairies had been six feet deep, yes, deeper than that, and the cold had been so pure from the North Pole that men had got lockjaw. That was the first he had known that a person could get a locked jaw from freezing. And that was a winter in which God alone knew how many buffalo had perished because of their great weight and foolish sharp little feet. The snow's crust would support a horse but not a buffalo, and the poor things had fallen into the soft depths and been as securely imprisoned as if they had dropped into a well. The Indians had found a lot of them and stripped them to their bones, but hundreds or thousands had never been found until the snows went away. Then there they were, scattered over the prairie, and if you hadn't known the reason you could never for the life of you have imagined why they died. If a man fell through and found the crust maybe two feet above him he could tramp snow on snow and build a mound to stand on and crawl out but a buffalo just stood there and died.

"That's Sunday," Pierre said.

"Where?" asked David, rising in his saddle and staring.

"The bay pony with the white in its tail. That's Brave Feathers."

"I'd better remember that horse."

"She is on his left."

Well, David thought, he couldn't tell from this distance. He studied her pony. It was like most of the ponies in size and color, and the only thing he could study was its gait and there wasn't much of that. She was a quarter of a mile ahead of him. He thought for a moment to take Payette and dash to her side and ride with her but he had promised Jim to be prudent. "If you're not," Jim had said, "an accident will be pretty easy. Get your liver if you can but let's have the pemmican first." Well, Jim was right. Even without treachery men were always wounded in a big hunt and sometimes killed. He would wait.

"Seems to be talking to her," David said. "Telling her, I suppose, what a fine tobacco pouch or fire bag my scalp will make."

Pierre looked at David's hair falling from under his beaver cap to his shoulders. "And she says how fine she will tan it." Pierre grinned, and when the man grinned his eyes were twice as bright and his whiskers twice as red.

"Wonder why they like to carry their tobacco in a white man's skin."

"Reminds them how brave they was every time they smoke."

David looked at Payette. Payette pretended that he was not listening.

"If twenty times a day he smokes, twenty times he thinks, I killed and scalped this dirty dog."

"Some like fire bag of white man's scalp."

The fire bag was a leather pouch in which was carried flint, steel, and punk. "Maybe," said David, "he hopes to get both a fire bag and tobacco pouch out of me." He glanced again at Payette, but the wily half-breed was looking away.

Pierre was gazing again at David's hair. David stripped a glove off and with thumb and finger pinched his forehead.

"Pretty thin," he said, "for pouches."

"But tough," Pierre said. "He will brush your hair and grease it and stink it up with beaver."

Pierre meant with the castoreum, an orange-brown substance with a very strong and penetrating odor, secreted by the beaver and used by trappers as a scent. David managed a grin but he didn't feel like grinning. He knew that when Pierre jested he was in dead-earnest and he knew that Payette was tickled silly. In his own way Pierre was telling him that Brave Feathers had resolved on David's scalp for a tobacco pouch.

That evening when they all camped at dusk, the whites at some distance from the reds, Pierre made his belief plain when he said to David, "You better sleep back in there, I will pitch my bed here."

David looked at Pierre a moment and then turned to see what he meant by "back in there." It was a recess against the riverbank, overhung with stones and thicket.

"He'd never bother me in camp," he said. "He would make it look like an accident."

David opened his duffel and cut off a hunk of pemmican and sat by running water to eat. He wondered if Brave Feathers could be prevailed on to accept him as a brother. If a Blackfoot adopted a white man as father, brother, or son he got himself up in his most resplendent raiment, his leather shirt heavily fringed with ermine or with eagle feathers and with human hair; his leggings and trousers fringed and beaded and his headdress huge with feathers and adornments; and he then stripped all these things off and gave them to the adopted one and put on the adopted one's garments and sat with him to smoke a pipe of peace. David had once seen the ceremony and had been impressed by it—impressed, above all, by the feeling he got that this new brother, the red one, was moved to the bottom of his emotions and under no provocation would ever betray you. In some ways it was good to be their brother, in some ways it was bad. It removed from a man the threat of scalping and death, but it put upon him the burden of stealing rum and tobacco for his brother, who then demanded of him all things in the red man's code.

No, that was no good. He would simply have to see this thing through. An accident could work either way: perhaps he could keep a sharp eye on this chief and contrive a little misfortune for him. There was no telling when an Indian was ready to strike, there was no way to read the red man's mind. David doubted that Brave Feathers would try to kill him in this hunt. It seemed more likely that the crafty rascal would wish to ambush and capture him so that he could put him to torture and degrade and humiliate him, and if possible frighten him, for nothing so delighted an Indian as to force a white man to show yellow. Of all the triumphs he could achieve over you by far the sweetest was to blanch your face with fear.

That's what Jim said, and Jim knew Indians as well as John McLoughlin or Colin Robertson or John Clarke. Jim had said, "If by chance you ever become their captive show contempt. Spit on them, curse them, insult them. Courage they admire more than anything else on earth and only courage can make them show any mercy. If a man shows any fear he can expect the worst."

He put a hand out, palm up. Snow so cold that it was powdery light was falling. South of him in the woods was the Indian camp and he could see smoke from the lodge fires. Behind him was his own fire, around which his men had gathered, and he went over to it and at once all the men looked at him. One of them, bap-faced and fat and pretty dull in his mind, asked David if he would tell them some stories. David did not fancy himself as a storyteller but now and then he told stories, because these men had little to read at the post or no minds to read, and suffered from boredom. David sat in firelight and filled his pipe.

"Well," he said, looking up at the sky, which now was no sky at all but a low ceiling of storm, "I don't think I know any more stories."

"Tell the same ones," said Bapface.

"This storm," said David, reaching for an ember, "reminds me of the time when a white man and a red man were walking along in the dead of winter. The white man had three times as many clothes on but was shaking like a constipated dog. 'Look how warm I'm dressed,' he said to the Indian, 'yet I'm freezing to death. You have no robe on but seem all right.' The Indian asked him, 'Is your cock cold?' 'No, no,' the white man said. The red man grinned at him and said, 'Injun all cock.' "

A few of the men snorted. "By God," one said, "I never thought of that."

"Me neither," another said.

A third said, "Why don't a man's cock ever get cold?"

"Haven't any idea," David said.

"Everything else does," the man said, looking round him at faces in the firelight. "Ears, nose, hands, feet, God, they'll freeze right off. Even your jaws freeze. You'd think a man's cod would be the first thing to turn blue."

"By God, you would," Bapface said.

They were all silent a little while and then Bapface asked for another story. David puffed his pipe and tried to think of stories the voyageurs told.

"Well, this is about a white man who was making love to a squaw when her buck came in. That buck had a scalping knife half as long as the Saskatchewan and it was so sharp that you could drop a handful of hair across it and cut every hair in two. He had so much war paint on that he looked three times as big as he was and he had two wet scalps hanging from his dagger pouch. Well, that white man was right busy making medicine when the red man let off a war whoop and that white man went right up through the lodge roof faster than Elijah went to heaven. The first foot to touch earth came down on a hill about a mile from that tepee, and the second foot just barely touched a hill two miles beyond that. That man was doing all right getting away from there when a rabbit jumped up and streaked out like lightning, and the man stumbled over it and almost fell. 'You goddamn rabbit,' he said, 'get out of the way and let somebody run who knows how!'"

One of the men had been chewing pemmican and he now exploded, blowing pemmican over the fire. "God!" he said, uttering the word like a prayer.

Another man, convulsed, had fallen backward and made the sounds of one strangling. David had told this story over and over but the men always nearly died when they heard it, laughing loudest when the hyperbole was most fantastic. They were children hugely magnified. Some of them were now wiping tears away and others with choking gasps were retelling the highlights of the story—" 'Right up . . . through the roof . . . a mile away . . . two miles more the next foot . . .' Oh God!" Pierre said quietly, "Some white men go almost that fast if a buck goes after 'em with a scalping knife."

"Lord God!" another said, as if suddenly recalling a close shave.

"It's best," Pierre said, "to pay for it and have it honest-like."

"By God, yes," another said. "Specially as how it's so cheap."

They were talking about their experiences with squaws when David stood up and Bapface cried, "Tell us another one!"

"Guess I don't know any more," David said.

"The hell you don't. You could tell stories all night. Tell us the one about the Irishman."

David looked at the men. "Any Irish here?" When there was no reply he sat and stuffed his pipe again. "Well," he said, lighting his pipe, "this Irish, he was as busy as hell shingling a house when another Irish come along and stood and watched him awhile. The second Irish saw that the first Irish was throwing about half the nails away and he went over and tapped him a little whack on his skull and said, 'What in hell are you wasting all them nails for?' 'Why, you doggone idiot,' the other Irish said, 'you must not have any more brains than a Englishman. I throw half the nails away because they have their heads on the wrong end.' 'Why, you pitiful dog,' the other Irish said. 'Them nails is for the other side of the house.' "

The men never exploded over this story. They merely looked at Pierre and nodded their heads in agreement when he said quietly, "That's just like a Nirishman."

Grinning, David got to his feet and looked up at the storm and around him, smelling, listening and wondering if the Indians were yet asleep. "I wouldn't be surprised," he said, "if even that part of us freezes tonight."

## X

He had more memories of sleeping cold than of anything else in this country. He knew everything that a freezing man could do to try to imagine that he was warm and this night he did all of them. He went back into the shelter where Pierre had asked him to sleep and there, standing, enfolded himself with his robe, the hair side in, and lay down. Almost at once he felt the chills of night. He had learned that it did no good at all to turn or to draw your knees up or to hug yourself or to contract your muscles and shudder or to blow breath into the interior or to chafe your flesh; but he did all these things, wishing all the while that Sunday were with him, her rump in his lap and his lips at the nape of her neck. He became aware that it was snowing harder, and to protect them he put his weapons under an edge of his robe and dozed off and awoke and found his weapons exposed to the storm. Disgusted, he stood up and left the shelter. It was funny, he thought, how physical unpleasantness could make a man contemptuous of danger: little he cared if Brave Feathers or Latude was waiting out in the night to get a shot at him. The men had scattered their fire over a considerable area to heat the earth, and after raking all the embers away had lain down close together. Their snoring said that they all slept. He saw some embers still glowing and scraped them together and soon had a fire, and he sat in firelight under a deep silent storm, tenting himself with the robe, thinking, his guns within reach. The flakes now were as big as luna moths, and whiter, except where he saw them glowing with firelight as if a sky of butterflies were descending. For David there were few pleasures deeper than that of opening mind and emotions to the soft and graceful loveliness of falling snow. Turning, he saw that the sleepers were now white mounds. They would be buried deep long before morning and in a white pure way would look like a small graveyard.

He filled his pipe and smoked. Was Sunday asleep, and if asleep was she dreaming, and if dreaming, of what? Indian dreams or white dreams? Of love or of killing? Tomorrow they would be in buffalo land and the hunt would begin. David did not like this kind of hunt. He liked the kind that was organized, with captains, each with ten or twenty hunters; the whole camp under military discipline, with a flag and signals, with swift and drastic punishment for the thief. So it used to be, but now you had to baby the Indians and let them hunt in their ancient and favorite ways or they would run over to the enemy. They would kill hundreds of beasts and the squaws would make up tons of pemmican to trade, and you could be damned sure that they would keep all the choicest meat and you could be sure that in the pemmican for white men they would pound in not only maggots but flies and beetles and any living thing that got in their way. He wondered if the voyageurs would eat pemmican if they saw how it was made. There would be plenty of old bulls and cows in it and some of it would be so tough that it would swell in your mouth as you chewed and fill your mouth, and after a while you would drag it out and look at it with disgust.

Later he thought he must have slept, for he was lying on his side and the fire was out and covered with white. A man could get warm if he had enough snow on him. He reached out and down to measure the depth and thought there was about four inches; and it was still falling, the whole world above him was one of infinite variety in light and shade and movement. Not a single dog had barked all night, there had been no sound, nothing but this depthless softness filling the earth, this pure wonder of frozen vapor. He closed his eyes and slept again.

A little before daylight he stood up and went over to look at the men. The snow depth now was seven or eight inches. The men were white mounds. Not a man had yet broken the snow above him, nowhere did the bedding show. David gathered dry grass and sticks and opened his fire bag and made a fire and sliced off pemmican and ate. In a day or two he intended to eat an entire raw liver, for he had been feeling groggy lately, a straight meat diet was getting him down. It would get even an Indian down. Most Indians had sense enough to eat roots and wild fruits and the viscera of their beasts and to lick the juice from spruce cambium and in other ways keep up their health. David had seen them eat purslane, dandelion, water cress, sumac, sheep sorrel, leek, and still other things that most white men spurned. "You think I'm a moose?" they would ask, and stuff their guts with nothing but meat.

David went over and put a moccasined foot against what he took to be a hinder and pushed. "Up!" he said. He was startled by what happened. There was an eruption and snow flew everywhere and Pierre came bolt upright, his gun in his hand and his finger on the trigger. "It's daylight," David said.

They were packed again and mounted and riding south through a storm. The Indians had left at daylight and were now a mile or two ahead of them, but David could tell where they were, for above them was a slightly luminous area, caused by the warmth of them and their beasts. It might snow a foot or two but it really didn't matter, for in this kind of prairie grass a horse could winter all right in deep snow and the dog with his travois load would find the going easier. The bad thing was covering up all the badger holes and prairie dog villages.

It was afternoon when he first saw them. A person who did not know what to expect might have thought he was looking at an immense darkness of timber or at a vast shadow upon the snow. How many were there? he wondered. Thousands. They were in the southwest and the wind was coming from the southwest and they hadn't smelled the enemy yet and with their dim eyes they hadn't seen him.

Horned Thunder with an escort of his boldest braves came riding back and David was startled and alarmed when he saw Latude among them. His presence could have only one meaning. The chief talked to Payette and Payette then told David that the Indians wanted to do their killing first and they wanted to enter the herd on dog sleds or crawl.

David had expected the chief to make this request. It was usual. But he doubted that they would be able to kill enough that way. The chief had asked how many bags the white man wanted. Jim had said they would want about a thousand ninety-pound bags and it would average out about a buffalo to the bag.

Chief Horned Thunder had been told that they would want a thousand bags but possibly he thought he had misunderstood. That was a lot of pemmican in one order but Jim in his shrewd way had said, "This fight will be won with pemmican or lost without it." It would be smart to have a huge supply on hand. While Payette talked to the chief David was studying Latude out of the corner of his eye: the scowling half-breed was staring straight at David with a wish to kill him written all over his face. Yes, his presence here could mean only one thing, that John Bowman had sent his spies along. That was the thing David detested about this struggle between two mighty companies, almost none of it was out in the open where a man could see his enemy and face him: no, it was night skulking, it was sneaking around to shoot dogs, to steal traps and scare the hell out of trappers, and to turn the Indians against you and bribe them not to trade you pemmican or to put enough poisonous plant juice in it to physic your guts out. David met Latude's black eyes and they didn't waver, they were looking at him straight and hard, as a stupid man would look who saw what he took to be an enemy or who had a secret assignment to kill. I'd better keep my eye on that son of a bitch, David thought, and turned to look at Horned Thunder.

The chief was talking and his braves were talking and they had all become excited. Huge numbers always excited an Indian. The Piegans had such fondness for big things that when trading with them David would put their rum in a vessel, such as a keg, that was ten or twenty times bigger than it needed to be, and the Indians then seemed to feel that the keg was clear full.

The chief, Payette said, thought that was a lot of buffalo. "Palefaces *o-lo,*" David said, using a word for hungry; and when this was explained to Horned Thunder he and his braves looked David up and down, as if for signs of hunger. It was time for flattery now, and David asked Payette to tell the chief that he and his braves were the mightiest buffalo hunters on earth and would have no trouble at all killing enough for a thousand bags. As the meaning of this penetrated their minds they exclaimed, "Huh!" or gave off satisfied grunts, as a pig in a wallow might, but their faces did not become any friendlier and Latude still stared straight at David.

"Chief say much buffalo much rum."

With an effort David restrained a smile. He said to tell the chief that there would be much rum, for he suspected that the pedlars had already made an offer. "Tell great chief kill moos-moos . . . to-morrow . . . all moos-moos his skinners can skin . . . his squaws can handle."

Payette communicated that. He then said that the chief wanted the white men to go back out of sight.

"Tell him yes," said David, nodding. "We keep upwind."

The chief swung and off he and his braves dashed, hoofs kicking up the snow, Latude riding last and turning after fifty yards to look back.

It was four or five miles to the herd. David and his men followed the Indian snow path another mile or two until they came to a huge wooded area by a river and they there concealed themselves, though David intended to find a lookout point and watch the hunt. The storm had abated but the whole sky was ominous with darkness and a wind was rising. He wondered if Sunday was going into the hunt.

It was a little after noon when David's men concealed their beasts and equipment in a thicket. David then rode upwind to a hilltop to watch. The Indians, many of them lying flat on dog sleds, some of them hopping and crawling along, none of them mounted, went downwind to the unsuspecting herd. They would move right into it and the dim-witted monsters would think only that coyotes or wolves had invaded their feeding grounds. David supposed that the Indians had taken no guns with them, that they would use only bow and arrow, tomahawk and knife, and that they would make tremendous slaughter before the beasts became aware that an enemy was among them. With their strong bows they would drive arrows clear through the heart chamber if they didn't hit bone; and if they hit bone then the bucks with incredible agility would dance around the snorting and infuriated beast and pull their arrows out. The red man's skill, yes, and his daring, in this kind of thing was simply fantastic.

The Indians were among the buffalo now. David could see that they had scattered widely to be in positions so that if an alarmed beast were to throw its head up and snort they could drop it swiftly. They would not allow a stampede if they could help it . . . Yes, they were killing now. Beasts here, there, all over the wide area were going down. He could see a buck leap to seize an imbedded arrow; could see another poise, bow taut; and in the wind came the sound of triumphant human cries, the bellowing of things in agony, the bawling of calves whose mothers had fallen, of cows who had lost their calves. It was a wild and furious scene but there was no sign of stampede anywhere in the vast herd. The Indians would kill the number they had in mind and then let the remainder of the herd drift away from the fallen beasts, and the squaws then would go out, their knives sharp and shining, their throats giving their chilling cry of exultation. God, what a thing it was to watch the squaws!—and he would presently, for as soon as they went out David and his men would go to get fresh meat. David would go because the squaws with their knives fascinated him and because he wanted to see if in this situation Sunday was white or red. . . .

He could make out a buck who seemed to be having trouble getting his arrow out: he had driven it into a huge bull, possibly into a bull that weighed almost a ton; and the beast was in a foaming and murderous fury, his hoofs throwing up snowballs and earth while the Indian raced around him and around, trying to retrieve his arrow. Now and then, David remembered, a bull drove one of his funny little horns into a buck; or with blood bursting from his nostrils he would charge suddenly and knock his enemy down. But it was a wounded cow with a calf who made a man almost take to wings or shin to the top of a tree.

There they were, the squaws on their way out.

David swung his horse and dashed over to his men, who were sitting on their beasts and waiting. Then they were off, taking with them pack horses on which to bring meat to camp and heads and viscera to the dogs. The buffalo herd had moved away into the great white loneliness, and upon the prairie where it had been were some hundreds that had fallen and the Indians were running among them with hatchet and knife.

By the time David reached the field of slaughter the squaws were there and they were busy. He stared at them with wonder, with astonishment—looked at the light in their black eyes and the passion in their faces as they rushed to a writhing and wounded beast to plunge the knife in and draw it out, red and streaming, and plunge it in again, deep into the throat or against the heart. He was looking round him, watching, when suddenly his eyes popped wide open, for there was Sunday, a red dagger in her hand! He galloped over. She had a cow. Its haunches were down but its fore part still rested solidly on its front legs and it was swinging its head in agony and fury from side to side, blood pouring from nostrils; and Sunday, unaware of him, was trying to get in past the weaving head and plunge for the kill. It was plain to him that she had sunk the knife once or several times. He thought she was trying to open its throat or strike for its heart, he could not tell which, as with amazing agility she darted in, sprang back, darted in again, the knife always poised and ready. He was looking hard at her face. He was trying to determine all the things he saw in her face, things that he had never expected to see in the face of a white woman—not passion so intense and focused that it was hypnotic, not the stripped athletic singleness of will, but the cruelty—was that it?—the absolute lack of pity and compassion, the absolute indifference to a mother's dying agonies. That was Indian, that was even female Indian, but was it white woman? Yes, he saw now that this woman could kill—could kill without mercy, without batting an eyelash, as a squaw could kill. Would she always be that way? Would her natural tenderness, her motherhood, always be overlaid and buried by this ferocity, this evil passion that now disfigured her face and was like trigger steel in her whole being? There, she got in! She went in swift, so swift he could hardly believe it, and buried the knife into the throat, and in the same movement and instant cut down, cut down and then the blood came out in a torrent, drenching a part of her. She seemed not to be aware of that either. In the next instant she was back and away, her hand wet and bloody that held the wet knife, her eyes watching the cow's eyes, watching them for the flickering of the will, the glazing over, the death. Death came, but not quickly. Slowly the beast sank, its forelegs giving way, its eyes glazing as the lifeblood poured out of the severed jugular. It sank, the head fell forward; and the girl, still so intent on what she was doing that she was unaware of this man barely a hundred feet distant, with deft strokes opened the belly, turning the hide back, showing up the storm-gray fat and then the red flesh, with stroke after stroke, even though the beast was still twitching and jerking, even though, with its belly wide open, it seemed to come to life and struggle to get to its feet. She paid no attention to all that. She knew that if she stayed away from the hind legs she would not be struck. He knew that this girl had opened the jugular and turned back the hide of many a beast. Her skill with a knife few but Indians had. She was rolling the deep hide back and working inside, through the diaphragm and in, into the guts-smelling steaming depths, toward the liver. Without cutting a gut she worked over and behind the mass of intestines, thrusting her arm in deep, feeling, drawing the arm out wet and glistening with gut moisture, reaching in again until she felt the liver; and without seeing it but feeling it only she went in with both hands and the knife and cut off a deep red slice of it and lifted it to her mouth. She bit in deep, like an animal, and began to chew and gulp it down, and only then, glancing round her, did she become aware of David. In that moment her mouth was open, her hand raised toward it with liver, and she did not close her mouth or swallow but stood stock-still, a girl frozen in a gawky posture.

The man who thought he loved this woman and the woman who was sure that she hated this man stared at one another.

They stared for perhaps half a minute; and then David said, with a wry smile, "Princess Sunday love moos-moos liver."

She now swallowed and closed her mouth and straightened, for she had been bent forward to keep the blood from her garments, though she was already bloody from head to feet. She stood, the hunk of liver in one hand, the knife in the other, and looked at David's smiling face, with no change in her own. He slipped down from the horse and let the reins fall. He walked over to her, slowly, as he might have approached any wild thing when expecting it to flee. He opened his mouth and pointed, indicating that he wanted her to feed him a piece of liver. *"Ohyoyet,"* he said, using her word for to eat. She cocked one brow a little at that and on her face was an expression that had delighted him—of impudence, as nearly as he could come at it, mixed with a little of the female's natural and spontaneous coquetry. Like a child, she then looked at the knife, the liver, and at his mouth, and he would have sworn that in her face or eyes he caught the faint light of a smile. Then, abruptly, she proffered both knife and liver to him.

He shook his head no. He made a movement of slicing it and he opened his mouth wider and moved a little closer to her.

She seemed perplexed. When feeding herself she had raised the liver to her mouth and sunk her teeth into it and then sliced with the knife. That had left a wedge of liver four or five inches long hanging from her teeth and she had chewed and sucked it in little by a little in the way of a beast, without assisting with her hands at all. Was she wondering if the piece would fall to the earth when she sliced it off? Was she thinking how easy it would be to cut his throat?

He reached over and took the liver by a corner and nodded his head yes. Again she cocked that brow. She looked so adorable, with blood smeared over her face and even on her eyelashes, with blood over her leather garments, with such sly amused knowledge of him in her eyes and with that brow rising in an impudent gesture of mockery that he wanted to crush her to him—yes, to do more than that, for something in her was stirring all his manliness. She sliced liver off and he plopped it into his mouth, a piece as large as one of his hands, and he chewed and gulped and choked, with liver juices bursting out at the corners of his mouth, his eyes winking at her contentedly.

"Good," he said, after swallowing the last of it. Again he seized a corner and she sliced it off and he ate, wondering meanwhile what to say. Just for the hell of it he tried the Dakota word for buffalo: *"Taceezi?"*

She turned at once to the dead and steaming cow and laid the remainder of the liver in the open belly. Then with a skill that again astonished him she pried open the huge unmanageable jaws and got back to the root of the tongue and severed it. He had tried more than once to take a tongue out without mangling it and knew what a difficult thing it was. With a deft turn of the knife this girl took it out and presented it to him. He supposed then that she had thought he had asked for the tongue.

"Thanks," he said, accepting the black tongue and trying vainly to think of an Indian word for thanks. He decided that he might as well again tell her that he loved her, for his mother had said that no woman ever wearied of that declaration. *"Nika tikeh, Princess Sunday."*

Her face changed instantly. It became cold and suspicious and again she was hating him.

He laid the tongue in the open belly and bent over to wash his hands in snow. Payette was sitting on his horse a hundred yards away, looking at him and waiting, but a lover's wisdom told David not to summon Payette, told him that he was doing better without a third party. Where was Brave Feathers? Latude? He straightened, his hands full of snow, and looked all around him but could see no sign of his enemies.

Sunday now resumed the skinning, and David thought that if he were tactful enough he might assist her, and win a little friendliness. She was going down the inside of a leg, incising from the flank to the ankle, and he grasped the foot to pull it away and hold it firm, to make it easier to open the hide. At once she paused in her work and looked at him. He remembered then with a shudder the contempt in which squaws held men who did a woman's work and he let go of the foot. He thought that he ought to return to camp but his deepest desire was to linger here, in this female warmth, in this presence of woman, in this smallness on a vast prairie where they were together and alone. He stepped back and was silent while with the same extraordinary skill she took the pelt off. All around him squaws were busy skinning and gutting but most if not all of the bucks had gone to camp, the man's work done, the woman's beginning. When Sunday's hands became too chilled for comfort, because of the beast moisture freezing on them, she plunged them deep among the guts to warm them and then wiped them in the long hair. David began to feel foolish, standing there, a big man watching a girl labor; and presently he took the tongue and walked over and gave it to Payette. Getting away from her a few minutes would allow him to corral his emotions and decide what to do.

He decided that he had better mount his horse and get back to camp. If he waited around here like a dull bashful schoolboy the Indians would come with dog sleds to load the carcass and wonder what he was doing there. On the way to his horse he watched her to see if she would look at him. She did not. He watched her while mounting and then as he turned the horse away, but never once did she give the slightest sign that she was aware of him. Still, it seemed to him that she did not hate him, not really, or she would not have allowed him to eat, she would not have given him the tongue. A squaw's giving a white man a buffalo tongue was about equal to a white man's giving a squaw a pouch of vermilion. Or was it? He would ask Payette.

Payette looked as if he had been asked the meaning of life and death. He said that possibly it had meant something, possibly nothing; when a buck gave such a delicacy it expressed a hope for rum. But a squaw, and a white squaw at that? He shook his head, meaning that the riddle was too deep for him. Had she said anything?

"Not a word."

How had she looked at him?

Well, David said, not exactly as if she were dying of love for him. In fact, he didn't know if she had looked at him at all.

"No look white man, mebbe love, mebbe no love. Sulluks?"

"No, she didn't seem angry. Just doesn't like me. Tomolla and tomolla and tomolla I may find out. *Mamook* tomolla?"

Yes, Payette said. The Indians would move south tomorrow downwind from the herd and chase it back up for another kill. Then they would not have to drag the flesh so far, or the pemmican.

David looked up at the sky. It was snowing again. "They'd better hurry," he said.

## XI

The Indians needed no urging; their nerves and bones were far more sensitive than the white man's to the approach of storm. The next morning David sent Payette to their camp to ask what their plans were and they said a big storm was coming, a storm that would fill the sky and bury the earth and leave a harvest for the wolves. The bucks had already left to get south of the herd and turn it back, on their fleetest ponies, leaving the older males and the women and children in camp. Had Latude gone with them? Payette said he had but David didn't like the look in Payette's eyes.

The two camps, a half mile apart, were against a river in the sheltering depth of a forest. A great storm was coming. It had turned colder and David imagined that it would not be an ordinary storm but one of those insane hell-roaring blizzards that rose suddenly out of nowhere and went howling over the world. Of all things that men feared in this northland the blizzard was the worst.

He decided to spit and carefully roast the tongue and send it to Sunday with his compliments. He hunted around to find the right size of green willow, because willow, unlike some other woods, did not infect meat with an unpleasant odor or flavor; and then he rigged up tripods and suspended the tongue and carefully turned it over and over, basting it with hump fat, listening to the juices softly sizzle, breathing the delicious smell, and now and then thrusting into it with the sharpened point of a willow to learn if it was done. When he thought it roasted to a king's taste he laid tree moss, heated at the fire, in a piece of soft leather and the tongue on the moss and wrapped it fold on fold to hold the warmth. He then told Payette to take it to her. He didn't know if she would like it that way; some

Indians did, but most of them preferred it raw or smoked or pounded up with marrow fat.

When Payette returned he did not look at David. David asked him what the trouble was. Hadn't she liked it?

She had taken it, Payette said, as if it were something with a frightful odor and had given it to a dog. No, she had said nothing, nothing at all.

"I'll be doggoned," David said, staring at Payette's dark face and small sullen evasive eyes. Had she acted as if it smelled bad?

"Yes, sir."

"I'll shake all the lightning out of her one of these days." Was he sure that Latude had gone south?

He had gone, Payette said. He said the old bucks were worried and scared: they thought the herd had gone so far south that it would be in Piegan country.

"And no more than two hundred bags yet!" He went to find Pierre. It was a policy with white men never to interfere in the wars of red men but neither company wanted the Blackfeet and the Piegans to be scalping one another when they should be making pemmican.

Pierre said he was not sure but he thought the herd had entered Blood country. He figured Blood country was about twenty miles from where they were, but it might be forty.

David said, "I guess I'd better ride out to see if there's any sign. It's going to be hell if we get only a couple hundred bags."

"You go far," Pierre said, "the blizzard will catch you."

David looked up. It was snowing and the wind was rising. "I'll be careful," he said.

He chose what he thought was the fastest horse in their outfit, a long-legged four-year-old bay, and he saddled it himself, for he wanted to be sure that the cinch was right. If he had to ride for his life he wanted no more trouble with a flying latigo. He tied his duffel behind the saddle and over it a buffalo robe and looked up again at the sky. There was nothing much to see but you could feel it. It wasn't that you heard it in the wind, it was that you felt it or sensed it and you knew it was coming and you knew it would be a howler but you didn't know how soon it would come. Where, he wondered, would it catch the great herd of beasts? A buffalo had no time for a blizzard either, and when he felt it upon him he turned his dim gaze to the nearest woods, if any were in sight.

With his pistol and knife but without his rifle David mounted and rode south past the Indian camp, his eyes looking for Sunday, and then into the deepening gloom. He told himself that he would ride until he came to a hill, but he knew that even on a hilltop he wouldn't be able to see anything. He couldn't see a hundred yards away now. He was on a fool's errand and he knew that he ought to turn back but he didn't turn back. Now and then he would dismount and kick the snow away and put his ear to the earth and listen, but there was not even a hint of that deep-in-the-earth rumbling that foretold the approach of a mighty herd. There was nothing to hear but the wind. The wind was picking the snow up and mixing it with the snow that was falling and the air was full of it. He would have no tracks to guide him back, for his tracks were obliterated almost at once, and no landmarks, nothing in sky or earth, and he had never been any good at finding his way without marks; but still he rode on until he thought he had covered three or four miles. There was no sense at all in going on. Hell, everything was lost in a storm such as this one coming, the herd, the hunters, the camps, everything but the wolves. But Jim said they'd have to have a lot of pemmican and what else could he do?

He rode another mile or so but had lost all sense of direction, and he had stopped and was listening when he heard a sound. He knew instantly that it was the sound of a galloping horse and a chill ran through him, for he thought it was Latude out here to kill him. What a perfect setting for ambush and murder! He could be shot here, the storm would bury him, and nobody would ever know what happened to David McDonald of the Donald clan. . . . There was no sound now, the rider had stopped, and the silence was twice as chilling as the galloping had been. Was the bastard sitting somewhere looking at him? David stared all around him and could see only moving snow. He felt of his pistol and his knife to see if they were firmly anchored in their sheaths and if they were ready, and he decided that the quickest way to find out what this invisible person intended was to put his horse into a dead run. Which way was north, where was the camp? He looked up to see if any part of the storm was faintly luminous because of sunlight on it but none was. He turned his horse to face what he thought was north and it leaped from the movement of the reins and David bent low to protect his face from the storm driving in. It would be one hell of a note if his beast hit a badger hole. He could see himself thrown and plunging end over end, losing both pistol and dagger and feeling Latude's hands in his hair. . . .

He went at top speed for what he took to be four or five hundred yards and suddenly reined in, and there the sound was, as clear as a bell under the heaving and breathing of his horse. It was the racing feet of another horse, and as abruptly as before the sound ceased. The rider was now on his left, which he thought was southwest, for it seemed to be downwind. If it was Latude why didn't he come in, why didn't he fire? He rode off again, almost at full speed, and again stopped and heard the other horse running, and then swung to what he thought was east and rode again. Now when he stopped he heard the other horseman on his right, which he thought was southeast. Then there was silence but for the labored breathing of his horse.

He stared all around him but could see only snow. He tried to imagine what in hell purpose this other rider had in mind. He had begun to feel that there was something very strange about this and he wondered if he was hallucinating. A man did sometimes in wild weather. Had he only imagined that he heard the running feet of a horse? Or if another person was actually there, why did he stay off at a distance, out of sight? While sitting and listening and staring and thinking he got the idea that this other person seemed to be herding him toward camp. He couldn't be sure of that. He didn't know where the camp was. Or was the person herding him away from the camp? He looked up, though it did no good at all to look up; he sat still and tried with all his senses to determine which direction was north, but a white man's senses weren't as good a compass as a red man's. After many years in this country some white men developed a feeling for such things and some did not. You couldn't define it, Jim said, but you knew when you had it, and David knew that he didn't have it. If he fired a shot in the direction of the other rider what would happen then?

If the wind had not veered he was sure he knew which way was south, and he now rode south, going for possibly half a mile before realizing with amazement that the other horseman seemed to be racing to head him off. Doubting his senses, he stopped. Yes, there the sound was, south of him if that was south; this mysterious person had outrun him. But why? In the name of heaven, was this a phantom rider, had he lost his mind, had he gone loco with snow blindness, had Payette slipped some poison into his food? With anger rising in him he turned to what he thought was north and galloped off, pausing again and again to listen. He heard the horseman, and if he veered to right or to left the unseen rider moved over to outflank him. He was beginning to feel fear and fear was an emotion strange to him. He was beginning to feel that he had lost his mind when, suddenly, he found himself at the edge of his own camp and his astonishment was boundless.

He sat a few minutes looking back but there was nothing to see, nothing to hear. The storm was deepening and closing in. The other rider, if there had been one, was gone now and there was only the silence, and the mystery.

He found Payette and asked him if anyone had been out riding while he was gone.

"No, sir."

David asked him to go to the Indian camp and see if anyone there had been out. While Payette was gone David unsaddled his lathered beast and then went to his men, sitting by a fire.

"How far you go?" Pierre asked, looking up.

"Not far."

"Find anything?"

"No." David thought it best to keep his mouth shut about the mysterious rider. His men would laugh him out of camp. Strange tales were told in this north country and neither white man nor red could say what was true and what was not.

There was the one about Astor's ship, the *Tonquin.* The damned fool Thorn, who had known less about Indians than Indians knew about Cape Wrath, had ignored the advice of everyone with him and sailed up the coast to trade. He had then let so many Indians on deck that every white man had three red men around him, each armed with long knives. That must have been one hell of a slaughter! Only four men escaped death. One of the four, mortally wounded, had been left on the ship, and after luring a hundred warriors to the deck, had blown the ship to hell and gone, Indians, himself, all. The other three, it was said, had been found hiding in a cave and had been tortured most horribly before they were scalped and killed. That was one story. The other story said that one of the three had escaped and had become a wild man on the upper waters of the Smoky. There were men who swore they had seen him, his hair long and white and his beard down to his belly, but Jim said it was some trapper who had gone loco.

When he saw Payette returning David went over to him, his eyes on the man's surly impassive face. Payette shook his head no.

Had he asked around? Had he searched the camp?

He had asked the old chief, Payette said, and Tanino, and Sunday.

"Sunday? And what did she say?"

"She say no."

"Did you look at their horses?"

"No, sir."

He sent Payette to see if one of the horses was lathered, and Payette returned shaking his head no.

"You see Sunday's horse?"

He had seen all the horses, Payette said. They were in a corral.

A little later David slipped away and went over to the Indian camp. On his way over he walked through a dense growth of cottonwood, spruce, willow, aspen, birch, and through falling snow that was riding down on a wind. He liked to walk through woods when it was snowing for the many changes in light and shade and the variations in coldness and warmth. You walked across an open place where the snow had come down and now lay undisturbed and there was more light there and more cold, and then you pushed your way into a thicket or under overhanging laden branches and the world darkened and it was warmer, almost so cozy in its warmth that you wanted to linger. And there was the wildlife: today it was a sleepy owl, and he went up close and it looked at him with its huge crazy eyes; and when he moved to right or left its head turned to keep its dim gaze fixed on him; and when he moved still closer suddenly the great wings unfolded and it was off, and again he marveled how a thing so dim of vision in daytime could go so swiftly through a forest, touching nothing.

The Indians had many fires burning, for the squaws were busy smoking or drying the meat. Girls and boys were dragging wood to the fires. Eyes of both male and female fixed on David as he approached; they were neither hostile nor friendly, just suspicious, alert, watchful. They all knew that at the Edmonton post he was the chief trader, he was the one who said yes or no, he was the incredible being who had custody of all the tobacco and rum, who said a crossed fox was not a silver fox and you could argue all day but the price was two made-beaver and you couldn't change it. If you stroked a pelt and argued that it was an extremely fine one, and if you said it was worth three but he said it was worth only one and a half, that's the way it would be; and most of the time you knew he was right and that you were trying to outfox him, but that didn't make you feel any friendlier toward him, not at all. You came at last to resent his power, his control of so many things you hungered for, his will, his mighty fists, his way of looking at you, and you wanted to kill him but you did not let him know that. . . .

They thought they didn't, David reflected, feeling their eyes on him, the way their eyes were sizing him up and taking his measure, as though he were a bear entering their camp. He thought he had learned to read the red man's eyes. In the trading room, it seemed to him, he saw in his eyes just about every emotion an Indian could feel.

For a few minutes he walked around in the camp, his eyes seeing more than they seemed to see. The squaws were at their drying racks. The racks were covered with ribbons of flesh and under them were fires, not to smoke the meat but to dry it, the fires being so laid that the wind drove the smoke out and away. Only the heat went up. A few younger women were digging marrow out of the bones. Marrow was by far the best fat for pemmican, but the marrow pemmican the Indians would keep, trading to the white man the hump fat or the faintly yellow walls of tallow that hung down over the kidneys or the grease from beaver and bear.

From the corner of his eye he was looking for Sunday. She was a big squaw now and she ought to be working, even though a princess, but there was no sign of her. Hearing a snort, he knew where the horses were and he ambled over that way, followed by a couple of Indian lads, curious and suspicious, and an old buck who helped himself with a stick. The old man, he supposed, thought he intended to steal a horse. The Indian stole anything he could make off with and looked with contempt on people who did not. They had never heard, Jim said, that civilization was built upon the sanctity of private property.

The horses were in a pound, sheltered against wind and storm, and boys had been bringing buffalo grass to them and aspen branches with the leaves still clinging. David went to the corral and looked in. About thirty ponies were there but not one that had been ridden and lathered this day. One had just dropped his dung and it was a golden mound steaming in the cold. I must be losing my mind, he thought, or my hearing, for he would have wagered his life that a horseman had been out there riding herd on him. Neither

Latude nor Brave Feathers would have done that. It was inconceivable that it was Sunday, for she hated him and would rather see him dead than alive. It could not have been one of his own men, for none of them had such skill in storm darkness, none but Pierre cared much whether he lived or died. Lord, was it the phantom from the *Tonquin*?—or some Old Man Barlow out of the past?—or nobody at all! He looked around for other corrals but could see no sign of any, and he walked beyond this corral thinking he might find a horse hidden but he found none. What would Jim think if he were to tell him? Jim would turn in his slow deliberate way and fix steady eyes on him and possibly say at last, "Maybe I should have sent you along with the other lunatic." He wouldn't tell Jim. He wouldn't tell anyone. He would solve this mystery, somehow, someday.

Returning, he walked around the corral but there was no horse that had been sweating. He looked at the boys' faces and the boys looked at him but there was nothing in their eyes to see. There was nothing in the old man's eyes. All three had closely watched him when he looked at the beasts, as though they might tell by studying his face which one he intended to steal. He went back to the Indian camp, looking round him for someone who could speak a little English, wondering where Tanino was. In some lodge, he supposed, sitting in her timeless brooding way, her eyes sad above the horror of her nose. He turned to one of the Indian lads who had been trailing him and dug from a pocket a few beads.

"Sunday?" he said.

The boy took the beads eagerly, and for a moment looked up at David's eyes.

"Sunday? *Kah*? . . . *Yahka kah*? . . . *Yaw-wah*?" David asked, pointing this way, that way. The boy looked this way, that way, then up at David's eyes, then at his beads. The other lad had pushed in to look at the beads too. "Papa pe Mama?" said David, using the words for parents.

The boy understood that. He looked up. He moved off, beckoning David to come. He led him to a drying rack and David knew that this squaw was his mother; and the boy pointed south and he knew that the father was in the hunt.

"Princess Sunday," David said to the squaw. She didn't even bother to look at him. When a squaw was doing business with white men, that was one thing, and when she was drying meat that was another, and she never mixed the two kinds of business. It took David a little while to realize that she thought his approach to her was amorous.

He turned away and the lad with the beads followed him. Then, looking over at the lodges, he saw Sunday—saw her for an instant only—saw her standing between two lodges looking at him. Then she vanished. He hastened over and thought he knew which tepee she had gone into and he looked at the trees standing over it to mark the spot. "Sunday!" he called, but he did not expect a response. He knew that if he looked into the tepee there would be no sign of her, and he knew that he had no right to look in. He turned to the boy, pointed, and said, "Princess Sunday there?"

The boy went over and looked in. He turned to David, shaking his head no.

David gave him a few more beads and went back to his camp, feeling weary, feeling a wish to sleep with Sunday in his arms, even if her odors were wild. He felt foolish too, he felt absolutely silly, and he shook his head to clear his wits and looked up at the sky, saying to himself, It's coming soon and it'll be a ring-tailed snorter, a mighty grist of a storm, a godforsaken letting loose of all the wrath in heaven!

Well, he had work to do. Knowing that pemmican would be more precious than gold, Jim had sent him down here to be sure that there would be enough and he was spending half his time thinking of a wench. He had been thinking of her as a woman with child, the child his own, and now he must put her out of his mind and get to work. The damnedest storm a man was ever to see was bearing in from the southwest and there would be hell to pay.

## XII

It had been coming all the while, in the way of the kind of storm it was, up out of the Columbia basin, up out of the west, taking its time to gather its furies and hurl its strength, wrestling and tumbling over the mountains, over the Piegans, over the Bloods, and upon the vast prairies, heading hell-bent across the Saskatchewan and the Athabasca and the Churchill, to spend itself across the empty and desolate wastes of the Arctic. But it did not announce its dreadful presence until about midnight. David was sound asleep then, dreaming of Sunday, dreaming of sweet intimacies, or dreaming of a wild race through nameless land with a phantom rider. He was warm, he was snug, he was deep in sleep, sleeping to the music of night winds and the crying of coyotes and the baying of wolves and the answering cries of his own dogs; sleeping under falling snow that had become driven lunacy through a blind frozen night; sleeping and dreaming. He had heard the faint sound in his dreams but it had not awakened him. It had been changing his dreams, filling them with the racing hoofbeats of horses, muffled by snow depth; and at last in a dream he thought he had been thrown and had landed on a shoulder, but it was only Pierre's rough hand. It was Pierre's hand shaking him and his voice saying, "David, wake up! Listen . . . !" until David came out of sleep and said, "What is it?" and Pierre, his voice not even now but vibrant with anxiety, said, "Listen!"

"What in hell is it?"

"Will you listen?"

With an effort David came wide awake. He pulled a robe away and put an ear to the earth, and, yes, he heard it at once, heard it and felt the chills come up through him as if he had thrown covers off and lay naked in winter air, felt the chills over his flesh and in his scalp.

"What is it?" he whispered, but he knew what it was. He listened again. "How far off is it?"

"God knows."

"Coming this way?"

"I reckon so."

"How long you heard it?"

"Long enough."

David hurled the robes back and leaped to his feet. There was no need to dress, for a man in this country slept dressed, slept in his leather suit, with his moccasins or boots on, and often with his beaver cap on. Even in the moment of rising he said to Pierre, his mind flashing like lightning over the situation, "Hop your horse, quick, go a mile north, a mile south, listen, get the direction!"

Pierre hastened away and David ran to his men, standing huddled, awed, waiting for him. "Ed," he said, speaking fast, "choose twenty, grab the axes, there, where the trees are thick and tall, there: drop them that way and that way. Understand?" He meant to fell them so that they would form a huge V, with the apex to the southwest.

"Angus!" he said to another man, and Angus at once said, "Yes, sir!" sharp and quick. "Take Bill, get all the horses saddled, bridled, ready, and off to north or south, as Pierre tells you. Alan," he went on, "you and Hugh go out with the dogs—out there beyond the woods," he said with a quick gesture, "but don't risk your lives. Pierre will get in touch with you later. You will get on the right flank or the left—understand?—and try to make it veer, make it turn north or south, whichever is best—but you and the dogs keep safe." Alan and Hugh hastened over to the dog pound. David turned to Payette and Bapface, the only men left. "Get all our camp stuff inside the V."

How far away was it, how fast was it coming? A hell of a lot a man knew about that but maybe Pierre would be able to gauge it. Which way had he gone? Only two or three minutes had passed since David had risen from his bed; he now dropped to his knees and swept the snow away and put an ear to the ground. He could hear it plain but he did not think it was any louder than it had been. That kind of sound would ride a long way in a wind. Behind him was a crash as the first great cottonwood, towering a hundred feet into the sky, came down; and a few moments later another fell; and David was thinking that if at right angles, a hundred by a hundred would be ten thousand and half of that would be five thousand square feet, or less, for the angle would be acute. Two hundred feet on each side of the V would give plenty of room for all the horses, dogs, and people. What were the Indians doing?

He ran to Payette and seized his arm, crying, "Come!" and they hastened to the corral.

"Angus, my horse!"

"Ready, sir!"

"Payette's!"

"Just a moment, sir."

David liked the semi-military discipline under which the company operated; it made for quick sharp responses and decisions, and in time of emergency such things determined whether a man lived or died. The beasts were led out and the two men mounted. Another tree was falling. David told Payette to ride at full speed to the Indians to see what they were doing and to come back fast. Payette rushed away and David went north. Pierre was just returning.

"Yes?"

"I think this way more than the other." Pierre meant more to the north.

David slipped off and kicked at the snow and put an ear down. Getting up quickly, he said, "More north, that would be good. Is there any doubt it is buffalo and not storm?"

"Both," Pierre said.

"Yes, both," said David, feeling the lash of the wind. "Go find Alan and Hugh with the dogs and tell them. Stay out here. Take soundings back and forth all the time."

"Yes, sir."

"Off with you!"

Pierre was off, his beast's hoofs flinging snow but not snowballs, for this snow was dry and in a wind blew like something out of hell. The wind was high now, and loud. It was a roaring and terrible thing up above the trees, and somewhere yonder in the night was the wild and mighty herd, fear-crazed, and what were Horned Thunder and his bucks doing? But no need to worry about them: they were children of all the weather's treacheries and had found a woods or river embankment or were riding upon the herd hell for leather. They were sometimes reckless enough for that. When their passions were stirred they had no sense of danger and would follow a herd right over the rim of the earth.

He rode toward the Indian camp, his eyes searching the dark for Payette, and when he heard him coming he shouted and Payette rode over.

"What doing?"

Nothing much, Payette said. Many of them were still asleep.

"The goddamn fools! Are they cutting trees?"

"No, sir."

Well, that was because the leaders were gone. The old chiefs were sunk in weariness deeper than sleep and the squaws merely obeyed orders.

"Have they heard it?"

"Yes, sir. They say go that way." Payette meant to the north.

Yes, they said, and went on snoring! They knew better than that, for a gulch or any major obstacle could swing the herd. Still, David thought, slipping to the earth to listen, the red man knew more about such things than the white. It was louder. He asked Payette to listen. He wanted him to listen because he was half Indian and his sense of hearing was keener. "How far?"

Payette shook his head, meaning that he had no idea. David glanced up at the sky. The night was deeper now, the storm was growing stronger. How far away was it? Five miles?—ten?—fifteen? How fast was it traveling? If it was ten miles away and traveling twenty miles an hour it would be here in half an hour, but its speed would slacken as it wearied. They might have forty minutes yet, they might have an hour.

He ordered Payette back to the Indians, to persuade them to come to the shelter with all their dogs and ponies. "Hurry! Go!"

Payette swung back to the Indian camp and David rode west, intending to leave the woods and look for Pierre; but the moment he left shelter and faced the wide prairie night and the wind and the storm he was almost hurled from his horse, and his beast was so stung by the driven snow and the force of the wind that it tried to turn back. Well, good God, he had forgotten: with a wind like that on the rumps of the beasts they would move faster. There was nothing here that a man could see, but he lingered because Pierre was somewhere out there and he became anxious for him. He would not have sent him out or the men with the dogs if he had known it was so dreadful, and now he felt that he should go find them, but how could a man find anything in that? He shouted, and his words were flung back and carried into the woods.

He swung east, galloping as fast as he dared, for if a man went too fast he would get his brains knocked out by overhanging limbs. Without moon or stars, with only the light of snow, he could not see much, especially when the snow was darkened by a driving wind and its own driven self. He swung right and rode to the Indian camp and found Payette there, trying to get them to move to the white man's camp. He had got them all out of bed and they were standing around, chilled, frightened, but suspicious and stubborn.

Had he explained that they were felling trees to make a shelter? Payette talked to an old feeble chief and then said to David, "He say go north."

"But what if the fool is wrong? And ask him where Sunday is."

Another old chief came up and Payette talked to the two of them, and they peered at him or at David or up at the storm and the trees and the night, and then seemed to listen. Payette turned to David and said that Sunday was standing there, a robe over her head.

David looked at the hooded figure. He wanted to ask her to go back with him but he had no time for woman foolishness and no time to squander here with stubborn Indians. He told Payette to keep after them, to try to get them to come, people, dogs, ponies, all; and he rushed back to his camp, thinking that the old Indian, helpless and afraid because all the young bucks were away, figured that this might be an ambush, figured that with the warriors gone the white men would steal the ponies and squaws and buffalo meat. He couldn't argue with him about it and he had no time to argue.

He found Pierre back in camp. "Jesus," he said, leaping from his horse, "I thought I'd lost you!"

He almost had, Pierre said, again speaking in his soft way. He said he had gone north and south and had taken soundings and he judged that where they stood would be about dead center.

Again David dropped and put an ear to listen, and he felt the chills come up his legs and then up his body, and his ears, his cheeks, his scalp were alive with the strange sensations of alarm. "Coming!" he whispered. "A little louder now—a terrible sound under the storm." He could now feel the whole earth shuddering. He could feel it come into the soles of his feet and shudder up his legs and through his whole being; and faintly, without listening at the ground, he could hear the vast muted thundering hum of it, and there was no other sound in the world like it. For it had its own deep beating rhythms and its steadiness, as if not a hoof missed time, not a beast faltered, as the immense herd, desperate with terror, rolled forward, straight, unswerving, maybe smelling the Indian smell behind it in the wind or hearing the Indian yells, maybe smelling the wooded belt ahead or the water it stood by, or maybe just propelled by dumb instinct to go on and on until safety was reached and the terror was no more. The shudders came up him when in his mind he got a picture of that broad dark avalanche of deadly hoofs and horns thundering toward him and knew that nothing could stop it, nothing could turn it now.

He dashed over to the men felling trees. On either side, he thought, they had enough to split open any stampede but he told the men to keep felling, to make it stronger, told another man to get all the horses in, told Angus to take two or three men and rush to the Indian camp and hurry them along, and mounted again and rode away. He felt no alarm for the men out with the dogs: they would keep listening and moving and they would get out of the way, and if they got lost the dogs would lead them back. He did feel alarm for the Indians and for Sunday, and he rode hard toward them, with Angus and the men on his heels, and he met the Indians halfway over. But not the old chief. Not Sunday.

"Get them moving fast!" he said to Angus, and was off.

With the distant thunder of the herd humming in his ears now he forced his horse to top speed, riding low with his face to its neck until he reached the Indian camp; and he shouted her name as he rushed from lodge to lodge of the few who remained and suddenly she appeared, looking hostile and bitter in the dim light, and he hastened toward her, leading his horse; and he wondered what the damned fool thought she was doing here, except to be gutted and obliterated by a thousand feet. Then at the tepee he understood. The feeble old chief whom she looked on as her paternal grandfather was there, inside, resolved not to leave, and she had remained to persuade him to go or to die with him. For a moment David had the insane notion that he might take them both. For a moment he listened to the sound. Then, aware that it was to be a race between him and death, he seized her and swept her up and set her like a child on his left forearm, his right hand grasping a wrist, and an instant later he was astride with her and off, with the thunder so loud and imminent now that even the trees were trembling and the wild blizzard wind was howling inside the louder sound that had enveloped it.

He felt an impulse to swing back to try to rescue the chief but knew it was madness and pushed it down; felt Sunday struggle to be free; in a moment of rage broke her down against his belly, against the pommel, and roughly felt for and found her lips and pressed his own lips in hard and deep, kissed her while riding at full speed until she turned as inert as a corpse; and then held her back under his chest as he bent forward and down to dodge the limbs. He knew it would be the end of him if the horse struck a hole or a buried tree and fell. He just prayed a little in a case like this and trusted to God or to the horse; and, his senses numbed now, his whole being chilled, his imagination fired with one evocation after another and the woman he loved like a dead thing against him, he rode on, trusting to a horse, as in other situations he might trust his life to a dog, counting the seconds, hearing the thunder up and over him and knowing that the first of them had reached the woods, the small dim eyes seeing nothing, the small sharp feet killing everything they touched, all things fleeing before this stampede as before a fire; and then he knew it was there, just ahead of him, the V, the only thing that stood between him and death; and he gave his horse its head and trusted it and fumbled down to find the face of his woman and kissed her again, and then he was within it barely in time, for now the whole woods and the earth around him and the sky were full of blizzard and thunder and the pounding of fear-crazed beasts and his senses were so overwhelmed that he could not think about it at all but only submit to the wind and power of it in a mute helpless way as a man submitted when he had done all he could to save himself and felt himself go under death. . . .

He knew he was inside with her and safe if the V held. *If it held!* Sitting on his trembling lathered horse, still holding her against him, this girl so quiet that she seemed to be dead, he listened and waited, as they were all listening and waiting, their lives in the balance. He was remembering how hard it was to turn the dumb plunging things: Indians could drive a whole herd over a precipice and they would go down and the sky would be full of them as they fell and their legs would still be pumping as if they were only leaping a narrow crevice and would soon be running again, the earth hard and eternal under them. He had heard the first terrific impact against the apex of the V, the sound of splintering timbers and breaking bones; and he had waited, breathless, to see if it would hold. Then he knew it was holding, knew that if it was not holding he would have been under now; knew that beasts had been piled up dead against that apex and that the herd had parted and was going by now on either side, with the sides of the V spreading it; and heard at some distance what he took to be the splash of the first of them hurled into the waters. His breath came hard then, gratitude in swimming ecstasy was all through him and, holding her, he slipped down and stood her on her feet and drew her close to him.

There was no pressure returned and he knew that love nested only in the returned pressure. Amidst the thundering death around him he thought about her, and something in him that he had tried to save, the small core of him that would be the last to die, felt that it had not mattered much; that whether he had gone under the hoofs or had stood above them had not mattered much; and in that moment he recognized, in the way of the old, that the difference between living and dying was no more than the first light in a baby's eyes. He pressed her hands again just to be sure of it and, getting no return, took his hands away and looked round him, convinced that death could have no more terrors for him, knowing that having been cheek to cheek with it, he had won a supremacy for all his years that would remain over its final triumphant moment. But he suspected, next, that he was pitying himself, that the terror of the last hour had left him weak; that perhaps it had left her weak and will-broken too; and so he bent low to her where she stood against him and with a finger under her chin raised her lips and kissed her again, and kissed her eyelids and her hair. He gazed at her face in the dim light and he thought she was looking at his eyes, and he thought her face was very white and still.

The thunder was dying now, not the wind, not the blizzard, but the heavier frenzies and terrors. All the sounds of a convulsed earth still swept overhead, but no longer the sounds of living things like himself running down the winds to outdistance dying. In that great recognition was a night of peace, with chores to be done. The stampede had spent itself, the thousands of beasts terrified by Indians racing south to head them off and then by the storm had found shelter and were now all around him in the deep woods, packed shoulder to gut. He wondered if the herd had gone far enough north to miss the old chief or if he was minced meat now. He looked up into the storm and wished that daylight was nearer. The Indians, and his men, except those out with the dogs, were all jammed together in the V's apex, with the horses next to them, restless now that the beasts were still. He called to his men to quiet them. Sunday then moved away from him, and he did not try to hold her but watched her go over to the red people, remembering the velvet softness of her lips on his lips. He felt sick inside and worn out, but a little proud too for having managed the thing in a way that Jim would approve.

When morning came, when the bucks came in, God upon Sinai, what a slaughter there would be! The killing would be so easy, for the buffalo were helpless things after they had stampeded and found safety. You could just walk among them and take your choice. He thought that possibly the storm was wearing itself out, for the world overhead seemed a little lighter now, and quieter, and he could hear either white men or red men snoring. Some of them had just sunk where they stood and were asleep, sitting up. When he heard a sound at the apex he supposed that the men had pushed their way in with the dogs, and he went up that way, shouting, "Alan, that you?"

"Yes, sir."
"You and Hugh all right?"
"Yes, sir."
When daylight came David climbed up over the fallen timbers on one side of the V and looked around him; it was just a darkness of buffalo everywhere, just buffalo and trees and no snow at all. And what pictures of contentment the beasts seemed to be! They felt, he supposed, that they had won through against terrors and were now safe, with no enemies near, for some of them were chewing the cud and some were asleep. After he had looked all around, with amazement deep and quiet in him, he turned to the huddled group of Indian females but it was impossible to tell which one was Sunday. He climbed down and told his men to bring in some fat calves for breakfast; after such terror and strain people needed hot food and blazing fires and rum in their bellies. He had other men move the horses and dogs farther out and bring in a bull for dog feed; and still others he sent for wood and water. He wondered if he ought to have them set up some sort of privy—not that Indians had much delicacy in these matters, or Sunday either, so far as he knew.

Within an hour two huge fires were staining the gray morning, one for the whites, one for the reds, and dead calves were being roasted. Then hands were cutting off slices and feeding starved mouths. David cut off a pound of half-cooked meat and strolled over to the Indian fire and stood there, looking casually at the women. When he saw Sunday peeking out at him from her hood he went over and said cheerfully, "Good morning," knowing that she did not understand him but feeling a need to talk. "Someday you'll be a mama and our baby will sleep on swandown and it won't be blind." That, he thought, was a hell of a thing to say, but a man said foolish things when he stared hard at a woman and tried to realize that only a few hours ago he had kissed her. "Will the red men be more loyal to us now that I have saved the lives of their old, their children, their women?" She seemed to pay no attention to him at all. She was standing close enough to the fire to be warmed and she was watching the meat sizzle and fry. "*Netokeemun,*" he said, and a brief glance swept him, and in her eyes he saw something besides hate. He wanted to hold her and kiss her, the hunger in him was so great, the passion in him feeding on memories. When he offered her a morsel from his roast she pretended that she did not see it.

He called Payette over and told him to make it plain to her, very plain, in simple words that she could not possibly misunderstand, that he, David McDonald, would always be a friend to the red people; that she ought in gratitude, now that he had saved so many of their lives, to prevail on her people to be loyal to him and his company; and that someday she would be his wife and they would have babies and he would always love her and they would be happy together. Twice while Payette was telling her these things she looked at David but he could read nothing in her eyes and face.

"Does she understand?"

"She say yes."

Then abruptly she turned and walked away, and David knew that she would listen to no more now. In the wild ride that saved her life, in the moments when he kissed her, in these moments at daylight he knew that he had won her or lost her but he had no idea which it was to be. He stared after her as she went among the Indian women and then turned to his men.

About noon Horned Thunder and his braves came in and a little later all the red men were in the midst of the bloodiest steaming and stinking slaughter that David was ever to see. He thought it pathetic the way the dumb beasts made no effort to escape; having fled one enemy and found sanctuary, they seemed unable to understand that another and more deadly enemy was upon them. The Indians simply went among the great herd, spread out through the woods, and chose the largest calves and the fattest cows. Then the skinners were busy, and the squaws were busy stripping meat off bones and getting it on the drying racks. The days and nights that followed were almost sleepless for the women, Sunday among them; and David walked back and forth in the gore, smelling the tons of raw flesh, the guts, the dung, the bones and hair in fires; watching the squaws handle the meat with filthy hands, seeing them blow their noses without turning their heads, smiling to observe how many things went into pemmican merely because they got in a woman's way. But what the men did not know about would do them no harm.

For the post he would make the pemmican; and one day he told his men to pack the horses with all the flesh they could carry, and leading the beasts in single file, with the dogs racing ahead, they turned north. It felt as if it would be a hard winter.

## XIII

As he plodded along David was thinking of his next duties and chores. He would now have to get winter food for the dogs, going with a number of picked men, taking horse-drawn sleds of birch boards a foot or so wide and fourteen feet long, fitted with shafts. Such a sled could haul the meat of a big buffalo or of enough fish to feed a dog all winter, and one man could manage four or five sleds. It seemed to David a clumsy way to do the thing but in both companies that was the way it was done. Nor did he approve the way fish were caught.

Many of the streams were literally choked with whitefish and pike and it was true that a man could drive a lance down and usually spit two or three. But there were faster ways. Some of the streams had trout weighing up to twenty pounds, and they were so hungry that a man could cast a line with three hooks and often catch three trout. In some of the lakes and in the more sluggish rivers there were sturgeon, varying in weight from ten to a hundred pounds or more, and he wondered if it would not save time and expense to seine sturgeon and trout for dog food, or for man food, so far as that went. A trout taken from a high cold stream was a tasty dish if you knew how to cook it, and sturgeon steaks were so rich that they turned a man's stomach. Seining would be easy in a stream where dozens of trout up to four and five pounds leaped out of the water to a baited hook. Over on the Columbia, men said, salmon were so damned thick that you just waded in and killed them with clubs; or a bear went in, and after tossing a dozen or so to the bank, climbed out to make its meal. Whitefish were the poorest in flavor and David wondered why their good and faithful dogs had to eat them when richer food was abundant. But he was only chief trader, not the boss. They would go out and spear and clean and split them by the thousands and suspend them in air to dry and then store them like cordwood. When that chore was done he would have the men dress bull moose skins down to parchment-like fineness and make canoes. Even now he could smell the leather as they rubbed it with hot tallow, he could see the grease glistening on hairy hands as they punched holes and sewed with sinew. He would bend over and sniff a man and say, "Which one of your bigs do you have on now?" but he would know. He would know that the idiot had scented himself with the castor glands from beaver in the belief that it would make him more virile and manly. Men talked about the vanity of women but men did the damnedest things. One of them, for instance, had confessed when dead-drunk that he thought of his cod as His Majesty; and, Lord, what a red face he had had!

When David arrived at the post he learned that a small crisis had developed. It would not have been a crisis a few years earlier, but times had changed. Earlier an Indian horse thief was given a quick trial and a dozen marksmen were warmed with rum and led to the execution spot and told to fire, and the thief was riddled. It was not that way any more.

Jim asked David to his room and there David found Colin Robertson, said by some to be the smartest man in the HB Company. Dr. John McLoughlin, himself as solemn as a tomb, had said that Colin was the most frivolous man on God's green earth, but under the banter and the use of preposterously big words David had felt that Colin was more serious than most men and about ten times as shrewd. His presence here, so many hundreds of miles from his base, indicated that he had come to plot strategy or bear bad news.

"We have problems," Jim said, and nodded to a table on which were port and brandy. "You think the Blackfeet will deliver the pemmican?"

"I've no idea," David said, pouring brandy into a cup.

"They steal anything?"

"Not that I knew about."

Jim turned to Colin. "You tell him."

"Jim means that these goddamned outmaneuvering and circumventing fiends of imposture——"

"We'll understand you better," Jim said, "if you cut out that fancy Edinburgh talk." He turned to David. "He means they tried to steal a horse. They've listened long to the winds of pedlar brag and they don't cow like they did. So we don't know what to do."

Colin turned his round twinkling face on David and said, "I hear you have developed *totoosh* trouble."

David grinned. *Totoosh* was jargon for breasts. "Fine *totoosh,*" he said. "A man just has to look at them to make medicine."

Colin filled a cup. "Jim says she's white."

"As white as any Scot and just as mean."

"Is it bigs, littles, or possibles?"
"Just possibles."
"And Brave Feathers is yearning upon her?"
"I reckon."
"Goddamn," Colin said, turning to Jim, "we might trade these two thieves for her, except if you don't punish the red man when he does wrong you'll have the whole tribe in your tepee. Yet, if we punish them——" He shrugged and drank. To David he said, "This fight between the two companies is getting to be as ugly as a face-scratching whore. Lord Selkirk, what do we do now? They are poachers and thieves, says his lordship; punish them. My Lord, the Blackfeet have a gargantuan hankering for white scalps and it wouldn't take them long to clean our trappers out from the Qu'Appelle to Peace River. His lordship, who weighs a hundred and ten pounds and is bleached from never having seen the sun, shakes his head and quotes Shakespeare: Thrice is he arm'd that hath his quarrel just." Colin drank, wiped his bearded mouth, and said, "David, soon now, maybe next summer, certainly by next fall, my lord intends to kick the pedlars clear out of the Athabasca. We can do it, he says, because we are thrice armed—with rum, powder, and pemmican. It's going to be a hell of a fight, all hidden, out of sight, without a blow struck. Our men will disappear, our men will starve maybe—for I don't think that even Fighting John Clarke can do it. The country is just too big.
"Well," he went on, filling his cup again and knocking out and filling his pipe, "we know damned well we'll all be tomahawked and scalped if the pedlars turn all the Indians against us. They've got the Blackfeet hating us and the Crees afraid of us. This battle is going to be fought upon the innocence of the red man and the avarice and treachery of the white. And when we invade the Athabasca we're going to be in trouble ass deep to a moose, while his lordship searches the poets over in Montreal for appropriate quotations." He was smoking and looking back and forth from Jim to David. "It occurs to me," he said, "that it would be a big boost for us if David married this girl and got adopted into the tribe. That would be worth a small army."
"Might be," Jim said.
To change the subject David said, "So we have thieves and don't dare shoot them and don't dare turn them free."
"It'll be bad," Colin said, "no matter what we do. For the pedlars it's an ace in their tepee."

"Why don't we put it up to Horned Thunder?"
Jim grunted and looked at David. "So that he would know he had us running?"
David flushed. "Then give them a trial and shoot them."
"We've talked the damn thing over and over," Jim said, reaching for his pipe and tobacco pouch. "Maybe three or four times we thought that was best. Maybe three or four times the other was best. A hell of a lot of pemmican might depend on what we do. How do you size Brave Feathers up now, and Latude?"
"Latude was down there spying for them. They're both on my trail." David emptied his cup and looked at Jim. "If you two think it's best I forget the girl, say so."
Jim and Colin looked at one another. Jim said, "We don't think it would make much difference now. The thing has gone too far. Colin says the pedlars are just busting out of their britches over at Fort William and betting all comers that they lick us. The side that has the pemmican will win, but you can't have pemmican without Indians."
"That's right," Colin said. "We don't want you to give up the girl. I've just been wondering if she could help us some way."
David said, "I don't have her yet."
"That can be arranged."
Jim spoke up quickly. "He don't want her that way."
Colin was looking at David. "You mean you're in love with this squaw?"
"She's no squaw," David said.
"Well now," said Colin, who took pride in his learning, "it's a Massachusetts Indian word that means a woman." Observing that David was angry, he quickly changed the subject, saying, "Lord Selkirk wouldn't know an Indian if he saw one. He has read Rousseau and believes in the noble savage. Would to God he was on a horse and headed across a prairie full of badger holes with a buck after him waving a tomahawk."
Jim was looking at David through tobacco smoke. "You figure they intend to let John Bowman have a lot of that pemmican?"
"I wouldn't be surprised."
"They kill enough for them and us?"
"Plenty."
"Colin says they're piling a lot of it up at Brandon and Cumberland. Next year, he says, will be pemmican year."

"If we don't get enough pemmican we could lay in some fish."

"Not yet," Colin said, "it dries out too fast. We probably won't be going into the Athabasca before next fall, and when we get there, as I figure it, John Bowman will have the red men so damned scared they won't trade with us."

"You mean we'll need a lot of pemmican to take in there."

"We won't have it, not the way Selkirk sends his settlers in. For how do they come? Stripped down to their knackers. Can you see the picture?—the goddamned greenhorns standing there and gawking around them and wondering if anybody is getting their dinner ready! My lord has no idea how men eat in this country. A spot of tea and a wafer for breakfast. Huzza! A spot of tea and a scone for lunch. Huzza! What a mighty grist of eating!"

Jim leaned back to let off a burst of laughter. "By God, Colin, you're making me hungry."

"One thing I want to do if I can, get that pale dreaming lubber out here and walk his weak legs off and starve his lordly gut empty and let the Indians do a war dance around him. We'll never get anything into his head writing him letters. He thinks this is a piece of Scotland that the wicked British stole and shipped over here."

The three men chuckled. They were all Scots.

David said, "If we're not going to kick them out of the Athabasca before next fall what do we do meanwhile?"

"Get all the pelts we can, all the pemmican. Keep the Blackfeet friendly with rum. See that they don't scare our trappers to death and steal our traps."

Jim said, "Colin has a new job for you this winter. He wants you to sort of travel around and see what they're up to."

"Would you make a good spy?" Colin asked.

David shrugged. He didn't like the proposal at all.

"That way," Colin said, "you could kinda keep your eye on your girl too. By spring you might have her."

"We know what they're up to," David said. "What could I do just snooping around?"

Colin narrowed his eyes a little. "That depends on what kind of man you are."

Jim spoke up quickly. "Don't get funny ideas. Dave is not afraid of anything."

"Fine, then there are a lot of things he might think of to do. Now let's decide what to do with the thieves."

"Have they admitted it?" David asked.

"An Indian never admits anything, not even if you catch him with your scalp on his medicine pole and your teeth in his fire bag."

David was looking at Colin. Jim had said that this rather fat and quite jolly man had no superiors and few equals in handling the half-breeds. A man who could handle them should be able to handle Indians. David was also thinking that Colin Robertson used to be a pedlar, but why he had left that company no man seemed to know.

Colin was saying, "They've always handled Indians better than honorable old HB. They encourage their men to talk Indian, sleep Indian, think Indian. That," he said, turning to David, "is what I'd like you to learn to do this winter—and it should come easy if you've got your heart on a girl. In fact, if you moved right in with the Blackfeet and kept them on our side you'd be worth all the directors in London."

"Sort of kill two birds with one stone," Jim said.

David said dryly, "I was beginning to get the idea. Have you said anything to John Bowman about all this?"

"Not yet," Colin said.

Jim said, "Colin thinks John is the one who is to figure out the death of all of us."

"Why don't I just give the thieves to John?" Colin said. "He might appreciate a gift like that."

The next day when the two Indians were brought out of the dark room where they had lain in irons David was there to have a good look at them, though to him all Indians looked alike. They all had the same red skin, braided black hair soaked with grease, black eyes, high cheekbones and Roman nose, almost beardless face, impassive mouth. You smelled in them the smoke of lodge fires and you felt in them all the treacheries of nature. He recognized neither of the bucks. The irons were taken off them and they were allowed to walk into the trading room, but they were sullen and hostile and they looked round them like things that had been flushed out of their holes. They believed, David supposed, that they would be shot and they were trying not to show fear—for it was a piece of nonsense to say, as some men did, that Indian braves never felt fear. Still, it was true that they would have gone to their death without flinching, without revealing a trace of emotion in those faces that were so much more intimate than a white man's with wind and sky and water.

His eyes squinting, Colin was studying them, his shrewd mind trying to read their emotions and thoughts. He turned to an interpreter and said, "Ask if they confess."

The interpreter talked to them but they made no response at all. David was thinking, If I am ever the captive of Indians I must remember to act this way.

"I still like the Sioux best," Colin said. "There isn't so much sullenness in their pride." He told the interpreter to go on talking to them, to try to get a reply from them. "Ask if they speak with a crooked tongue. Ask them if the pedlars want them to be their *coureurs de bois.* Ask them any damn thing but get them to talk." An Indian, Colin said to David, would make no response to anything that he felt was calculated to degrade or humiliate him or to soften him. In his world and among his values if you got something in your power, whether moos-moos, grizzly bear, or man, you did with it what you wished to do. Was not that the way with all things in nature? Such things in the white man's world as compassion and pity and mercy he had never heard of, or if he had heard, it was only to be astonished and contemptuous. You could get further with the half-breed because he was half white.

Stolid, impassive, sullen, the two bucks stood and waited.

"Better come with me," Colin said.

With Colin leading, the two bucks in the middle, and with David bringing up the rear, a hand on his pistol butt, they went across the white chilled earth to Augustus, the pedlar post and fort. Looking at the leather trousers of the two Indians, David saw that they were stiff and out of shape from sweat and he knew that they had recently been riding far and hard; but whether they had gone south with Horned Thunder and returned or had been left concealed here, he had no idea.

At the big gate Colin sent up a hullabaloo and a guard looked out through a peephole to size him up. "John Bowman!" Colin roared. "Tell the son of a bitch he has guests!" While they waited, Colin tried to peer between palisades into the compound. "You suppose the old toom-the-stoup is lying with a squaw?"

"He's no toom-the-stoup," David said. "He rarely drinks."

"I think I hear him coming, like a man who is all spent." Then Colin was shouting, "John Bowman, you merry-begotten, open up! Your best friends in all the world are here!"

The gate was opened a foot and Bowman's face, always prudent but always a little sly, looked out. "Skin me alive and feed me to the dogs! If it isn't my dear old friend Colin Robertson!"

"And more your friend as I get older," Colin said, extending a hand.

"Damn my hide and taller, what have you got here?"

"A couple of your pals," Colin said. "They got a little mixed up in their minds in regard to horses. Must be the brand of rum you give them."

David had advanced and was studying the two men. It had been said that no other northmen could blow up such a wind of brag or sweeten insults with such wild honey as Colin and John. David had never before seen them together.

"The great North West Company gives high wine to its red brothers? Where do you pick up such shameful lies? As for these two, Colin, my dear friend, they're not ours."

"That's not what they say, John. They say——"

"Nothing at all, nothing at all. I can tell by their faces they haven't said a word. I've no idea, Mr. Robertson, why you honor me with this visit but I see that you have David McDonald, your bully boy, with you. Will you have a drink?"

"The same Christian gentleman," Colin said, "with his emotions in a pupa. But no potlatch today."

"By the way, this season do we potlatch at our post or at yours?"

"Ours," Colin said. "Now, as for these men, I've heard you need trappers. These two——"

"I simply can't allow you to be so generous."

"Why not?" Colin said. "You have half our trappers now, a few of them still alive. Next year——"

"Ah, next year!" John said. He smiled. He smiled and he seemed benign, almost beaming, but in his eyes David saw something that chilled even a bold man. John had been standing in the gate. He now stepped out and behind him came a huge scowling creature whom David recognized as his chief bully boy.

"Colin, I just don't understand why you bring these two braves to me. We've no more need of trappers than we have of pemmican."

Colin lost his temper for a moment and that was bad. Dropping the feinting and the pretense of friendliness, he said, "John, my friend, we're getting pretty goddamned tired of having you set the Indians on us to steal our traps, our horses, our pelts, to intimidate——"

"Intimidate?" said John, picking the word up fast. He was still bland and self-controlled. "I didn't know an HB man could be scared. As for the charges you bring against us, you're my dear friend, I'm sure I have no better friend on earth, but there are things that not even friends should say to one another. I think you should apologize. I have heard that your motto is, 'When among wolves, howl,' and I have heard you do some pretty fancy howling. But we men from Montreal have been taking care of wolves a long time."

Colin was again in possession of himself but he did not speak.

John was looking him straight in the eye. His own eyes full of craftiness and menace, he looked at him steadily for several moments before he said, "It would be too bad if we who have been dear friends so long should become enemies. But let us understand one another. It is said that you advised this Lord Selkirk to fight fire with fire. It is said that you intend to march into the Athabasca and throw us out. We want only our fair share of trapping, we would live in peace; but if you are going to use fire that doesn't scare us a goddamned bit. If you're going to come into the Athabasca we'll be ready for you—and *you* will be among those who come, won't you, Colin?"

The insolence, the intimation of cowardice, was so plain that Colin's face reddened. He said, "If you meant what I think you intended to mean we could settle that now."

"So we might, my dear friend. I might kill you or you me but would that settle anything? If that is the way you want it I'll not say no but I'd prefer to match more than fists or pistols against you. This is big country, it gives a man a lot of room, it opens him up wide and puts sunlight and distance on his guts. Is my meaning clear? Your funny little lord from Scotland says he's going to have the Athabasca. We say he isn't. We've heard you're going to be his spearhead. So would you like to settle the matter in a bigger arena?"

"Suits me," Colin said.

"Suits me. Meanwhile, let's be friends, and as an act of friendship take these Indians with you. I know nothing about them. Sure you don't want a drink?"

"Thanks, no," Colin said. He was trembling a little.

"Good day," John said. He nodded slightly, his bully bodyguard, scowling at David, slipped behind him and into the post, John followed him, the gate was shut.

Colin turned to David. "Well, that's that. It's going to be rougher than I thought."
"Looks that way," David said.
"He's going to put his bully boy on you."
"Had the same thought," David said.
With the Indians between them they went back over white earth to the post.

## XIV

David was in the general workshop making pemmican and thinking. It had been a deliberate insolence to take the two thieves over to John and John knew it, and John would make somebody pay for it. He wondered why Colin had done it.

As for pemmican, a man got so tired of the Indian kind before the long winter was over that he felt like eating the mooseskin canoes. It was funny that the red man was content with the same old buffalo meat, fat, and saskatoon berries, for in other ways he showed that he did have a taste for food. Jim said that down south certain tribes had a food which was called corn or maize and this they prepared in more than forty different ways: parched it in hot ashes, baked it, simmered it in broth, ate it on the cob, or mixed it with various berries, fats, vegetables, and the seeds of wild plants. . . .

*Would he like to move the thing to a bigger arena? John Bowman wasn't bluffing and he wouldn't forget the insolence.*

Well, there was the camas, which Jim said was a damned fine dish if done right. The Indians dug it up by the ton in June and July and then made a pit two or three feet deep and a few feet in diameter, lined with dry wood on which small stones were heated. Earth and grass were thrown over the stones. Bushels of the peeled camas roots were then piled on the grass and covered with grass, water was thrown on, the whole of it was covered with earth and upon the mound of earth a fire was kept all night. This treatment with heat turned the roots black and gave them, Jim said, a deliciously sweet flavor. They were then pounded between stones and the meal was baked in huge loaves or steamed and made into cakes that were smoked or dried in the sun. Jim thought it better than bread. But pemmican!

*He is going to put his bully boy on you,* Colin had said. It was said that John's bully was the biggest human brute west of Cumberland House and could lick his weight in tigers. David guessed his weight at about three hundred pounds. . . .

Pemmican was a Cree word that meant mixture, but the Indians didn't have enough mixture even when the squaws pounded flies and maggots in. David had sent his hunters out for elk, deer, and buffalo, and after they had stripped the flesh off he had had them boil the big bones to free the marrow; and now on the bench before him he had a number of vessels made of skin, wood, or metal, in which he had various ingredients with which he was experimenting. He had experimented many times but hadn't yet concocted a food that really pleased him.

He had used practically everything in the area, for seasoning and enriching—even boiled or roasted pine seeds, the cambium of fir and spruce; hawthorn berries, which the Indians dried, pulverized, moistened, and molded into cakes; plum, chokecherry, various currants, grapes, even mint and other leaves of fragrant wild plants. He had mixed buffalo or elk or moose flesh with other kinds of meat—with pigeon, partridge, turkey, grouse; with beaver, raccoon and porcupine; with frog legs, rattlesnake meat, crab; and with every kind of fish in the area.

*And you will be among those who come, won't you?* He had been looking at Colin but after a moment he turned to meet David's eyes and include him in the question. *Oh, I'll be there,* David thought, *but I doubt that Colin will.* . . .

Lord Selkirk figured that his Red River colonists would grow huge quantities of grain and vegetables to feed the fur empire, and so make it unnecessary to slaughter wild beasts by the thousands, or for men to live chiefly on meat. Soon after coming here David had got so sick of meat at every meal and nothing but meat that he had experimented with making bread. He had had men gather the seed of sunflower, of buffalo and brome grass, of bedstraw, of wild carrot, parsley, parsnip, and caraway; and he had pounded the seeds into meal and had baked bread, and some of it he thought better than any he had eaten in Scotland, but it would have taken an army of men to gather the seeds. He had experimented with the roots of pond lilies, with wild potato, artichoke, and mushroom but always had come back to the same old pemmican that after a few weeks or months was as tough and tasteless as bull buffalo hide.

*He didn't want any trouble with bully boy but he knew that trouble was coming. He knew that if he was sent out to spy on pedlar positions it would be trouble and nothing else. . . .*

But today, thank God, he need not worry, he could make pemmican. He reminded himself of an irresponsible old woman in a duke's kitchen—mixing ingredients, tasting, blinking his eyes over flavors, again mixing. For his principal meat he had hindquarter of elk, dried out and pounded into a kind of flour; for his principal fat he had marrow; and among the many things around him, to enrich and season, he had the juice of various berries, including chokecherry and huckleberry; he had leek, wild garlic, mushroom, a heavy soup stock from beaver tail, raisins dried and ground into powder, brandy and port, macerated mint leaves, powdered partridge and grouse breasts, various wild seeds molded into tiny cakes, sugar, salt. He also had *tripe-de-roche* or rock moss, which some Indians boiled and ate with relish but which David thought tasted exactly like rock moss.

He had no thought of making pemmican in sufficient quantity to feed a host of men but only for himself and Jim and Pierre and his family back home. Back home? There was no back home any longer, this was home now, he would live here and here he would die. All the more reason then to concoct food a man could relish rather than merely gag down in line of duty. He had seen men gag when eating pemmican a year or two years old. He had seen them slowly chewing, jaws opening wide, open mouth revealing a grayish mass, eyes wide and popping as a man's eyes might be if he were looking to his hidden emotions and expecting to explode. The only time he saw men eat pemmican as if they enjoyed it was on a portage when, carrying ninety or a hundred and eighty pounds up mountains, they seized a hunk of the stuff and tore at it with their teeth as they climbed. Doing that kind of work a man would eat anything, even his moccasins.

"Got something good?" Jim asked, coming up behind.

"Try this," David said without turning.

With a knife Jim fed a juicy blob to his mouth and chewed, his eyes winking. "God hanker me," he said, "it's damned good. What you got in it besides elk and marrow?"

"Lots of things. Beaver-tail stock, garlic, some berry juice."

"Better not let the men taste this stuff," Jim said, and sampled another.

"Too fancy for them," David said. "This is for his lordship."

"Like hell it is," Jim said.

"Colin tell you what Bowman said?"

"Yeh."

"What are we going to do when we get in the Athabasca?—shoot it out with them or just sit in the snow and starve to death?"

"Build forts, Colin says. Trap beaver."

"And what will the pedlars be doing?" After Jim had gone away David turned to the east, as if by some effort of will or sight he could look in on the pedlar partners in their sumptuous club, two thousand miles away in Montreal, and hear what they were saying. Just what were the bastards up to, anyway . . . ?

At that moment, in Fort William on Lake Superior, Alex Macdonell and Duncan Cameron were talking. They had raised unholy hell with all of Selkirk's first settlers and they were proud of it, and they intended to exterminate them as fast as they were sent in. Alex, a cousin of Selkirk's governor, Miles Macdonell, had said, when assigned his task, "Here is at them with all my heart and energy." His heart had held no pity and his energy was inexhaustible. Duncan was telling him that in the future nobody in the HB Company, from Selkirk down to the laziest trapper, was to be received into any of the North West forts unless it was clear that the person was almost dead of starvation.

"And in regard to that," Duncan said in his dry way, "a man will use his own judgment."

Alex's florid cheeks and bearded jaws softened into a smile. He said, "Any man's judgment is likely to be bad in such cases. I'd never trust mine."

The two rogues grinned at one another. "For your cousin you'd bring out the fatted calf?"

"Oh yes," said Alex, brushing with a palm over his weather-toughened face. "Feeding cousins is a law of life with me."

"If we just keep the rum in Cuthbert and Peter they'll feed your cousin."

Alex chuckled. "Them half-breeds are never so happy as when they have a few white men to kill. About as many," Alex said, making a whisker sound across his chin, "as Selkirk sends out each time, and about as often."

"It's funny," said Duncan gravely, "how them two things fit together."

Alex laughed a soft wicked laugh and reached for the liquor. Fort William had celebrated like hell on fire after the destruction of Selkirk's most recent colony and some of the men there had never sobered up. It was believed at first that they would hear no more of farming in the Red River Valley, and the half-breeds had been poured full of rum as pay for their victory. But only the other day Fort William had received the dire word that his lordship was getting up a migration twice as big.

"You know," Duncan said, also turning to the liquor, "one of the first things is to get rid of Colin."

"Right," Alex said.

"No man in this country makes such big brag. Does he mean it?"

"My beloved cousin says he does."

"Well, he'd look good to me full of Saskatchewan water. I've hated him ever since he turned traitor to our company."

"That's right," said Alex, drinking. "Used to be a North West partner, didn't he? What turned his color?"

"I never did know. Bigger job, I reckon."

For a few moments Alex seemed to be brooding. Then he said, raising his cup to his lips, "I got a suspicion that next year the Red River is going to be a little redder."

In the same week a group of North West partners were lounging in their Beaver Club in Montreal and spitting into the winds from Thunder Bay, as one of them put it. Among them were Dr. John McLoughlin, a physician by profession, a fur trader by choice, a man as big as a hill and as stern as a granite crag in zero weather, who when he could not elbow opposition aside walked over it; Ben Frobisher, as reckless and headstrong a man as ever came to the north country, so reckless indeed that he would come to his end frozen as stiff as a poker over the dead ashes of his own campfire; and Simon McGillivray and his brother William, the brains of the pedlars and as canny a politician as ever came out of Scotland.

William was saying, in a kind of aggrieved, muttering, inconsolable way, "Their gall! In our company we're all Canadians. We're the men who are developing this land. Yet these foreign poachers, these thieves with a charter, think they own this whole goddamned country because a wenching scoundrel called Charles II gave them a piece of paper. Not a decade ago, gentlemen, not a generation ago, mind you, but a hundred and fifty years ago, when Charlie thought this new land was an island of about the size he slept with Nell

Gwyn on. He and all his drooling sycophants thought it was chiefly water. Water and beaver. For Radisson never got halfway to the Athabasca. If it is found to be ten times as big as Europe they still think they own all of it. Suppose Charles had given them a charter to the moon, you think Selkirk would be trying to get settlers up there?"

Some of the men were growling. The canny William knew how to get their wrath up.

Frobisher rumbled, "He claims a lot as his. How much?"

"Over a hundred thousand square miles."

Frobisher looked at William down his beaked nose. "All on the Red and Assiniboine?"

William's heavy-lidded, too-close-together, and sharply cunning eyes were looking at Frobisher. "Not if there isn't enough of it."

"The son of a bitch," Frobisher said. "Does he realize we took the worst part? It's two thousand miles between us and our best trapping. They started right out from Hudson Bay and cleaned it up as they went. We have to go up over the worst portage in the world and then to hell and gone, and now they want that."

"They won't get it," someone said.

William turned to the speaker and asked softly, "How we going to lick a charter?"

"You think the courts will uphold a charter that gave away a continent?"

"They might," William said. He had not felt so cocksure since hearing that the pigheaded Selkirk was going to send over a bigger colony and soldiers with it. As if trying to clarify something for himself he resumed his muttering. "Says he has unimpeachable validity. Says his claims are universally considered to be clear and indisputable. Universal, my schoolteachers said, is a hell of a big word. He must mean that the Russians accept his claim, the United States, even the Chinese, even the people on other planets, if there are such people. It's universal, gentlemen. Charlie's colossal theft. Selkirk says he will stake his fortune and his life, and though his life may be shorter than ours his fortune is a lot bigger."

"The one he married," said a contemptuous voice.

"Well," growled Frobisher, "we're here to decide what we'll do."

"We'll fight him," said McLoughlin in a voice that belonged out-of-doors.

"Of course. How? Have we a plan?"

"Half-breeds," said Simon, "don't need plans."

William looked further into the future. "We can't use them forever," he said. "Selkirk has the money to hire a small army—and soldiers from the Indian wars are everywhere for a drink of rum."

McLoughlin said, "What we did last summer won't stop him?"

William put a hand to his forehead as if such questions made his head ache. "He's a Scot too," he said.

"Stop him?" said Simon. "My God, John, he's getting up a force three times as big as the last one. He's going to march in with it."

"The trouble," said William, "is that these poachers from London intend to fight fire with fire. That's what Colin told Selkirk."

"We have to get rid of that man," Frobisher growled.

"He's only a hand," said William. "We have to cut off the head and the head is Selkirk."

"If he goes out to Red River——" said Frobisher, looking at William.

William shook his head no. "Not that. We mustn't go too far."

"But how about it when John Clarke marches into the Athabasca next year? Are we going to feed him?"

William's smile was sly. "John Bowman will have his orders. Something could happen to any man up in that wild country, but a lord from Scotland? No. We could never wrestle that one down. We have to make everything we do seem as if we had nothing to do with it. We'll hope the old fighting spirit is aroused to great anger—somewhere under the level of the top leadership," he added softly. "If the Indians won't trade with Clarke or his men or have nothing to trade will that be any fault of ours?"

The men looked at one another. Under Frobisher's stern brows his eyes lit up with twinkles.

"Holding the Athabasca," William went on, "is the easy part. It belongs to us, if there are any rights left in this world. The hard part is Red River. We can destroy another and even bigger colony but we can't go on destroying them forever. And if Selkirk isn't stopped he'll push out farther and farther. He isn't content with a domain bigger than Europe, God no, but must have the Athabasca; and if we gave him that and went over the mountains, soon he'd want that too; and if we moved down the Columbia he would follow us. He'll never be satisfied until he drives us into the ocean."

Silent, musing, he looked around at his partners. Then he said,

"I've a feeling that the two companies will soon have a choice of only two things, destroy one another or merge."

"Then we'll destroy one another," Frobisher said.

"And be bankrupt?" asked William, looking at his angry face.

"I'd rather be bankrupt than take orders from that arrogant bastard."

"They haven't licked us yet," Simon said.

"We haven't licked them either."

Simon said, "If we could only persuade all their trappers to desert them."

"That," William said, "is our big project this winter and the next. . . ."

David looked east but he was unaware of their plans and he went on making pemmican, his thoughts with a wild girl down in buffalo country. After all, he did not belong to the policy-making committee. He was not a partner, not even a factor, but only the chief trader at this post. He sometimes thought that those who determined policy looked on him chiefly as a bully boy, whose principal duty and chore was to knock the living daylights out of the big brute at Augustus if he got out of line. He had known why Colin took him along.

It was not that he was ambitious to become a big man in the company: vanity in him burned with a low flame. It was not that he wanted to lord it over other men; he had seen enough of that since coming here: he had learned that most human males seemed to delight in nothing more than positions of power over their fellows. He was remaining here because he had fallen in love with the country, with its rigors, its disciplines, its great distances that invited a man to look, to listen, to breathe deep. If he had a home of his own outside the post, with his girl in it, with a garden, maybe with a bit of Scotland somewhere . . .

Hell, he guessed he was feeling a little sentimental. A little anxious maybe, knowing that bitter days lay ahead; and possibly a little afraid, for he had dreamed repeatedly of the phantom rider and always in the dream he was racing with death. He went from under the roof and looked up at a wonder world, at a great snowstorm, windless, silent, beautiful, and decided to take a walk. He liked to walk in this kind of storm. It gave a man privacy, it gave him depth and reach within himself. He liked to be warm, to feel cozy under his clothes: he put on heavy stockings and waterproofed boots, his heaviest leather, a beaver cap that snuggled low around his ears, and a kind of cape that was warm, stormproof, yet light. He did not take weapons. His mood today scorned them.

A few minutes later he was following the stream, taking his way through cottonwood and birch and aspen and looking at the mirror slate and the shattering lights of the moving water, at the millions of flakes touching it like moths alighting and instantly disappearing. It seemed to him that in this kind of storm, so immense and deep and still, the earth was at its fullest flowering. The earth then received a carpet that was softer than any carpet anywhere and so pure and fresh that he could think of nothing to compare it with, except the very first flowers at alpine heights, such as the caltha. He loved to walk in it when it was a foot or even two feet deep; to feel his booted feet moving softly through it; to look back on his path in dim-world snow light, at his own and at the paths of wild things which now wrote in the wonder of storm the plain evidence of their being. He could walk for hours, every part of him snug and warm, the flakes so huge and dense that he could see only a little distance, the sky above him a marvel of design and movement, the earth as quiet as a sleeping mother; he could walk, aimlessly, all his senses a little drowsy with contentment; and he could trace the path of grouse or partridge here, of weasel there, of coyote, of a dozen or a hundred different things. As the years passed he had come to know the kind of tracks they made, their smell, their way in wintertime of looking for food; and in a snowstorm like this in a world like this he looked deep into some things that city folk, he supposed, were not even aware of. Maybe that was why he had left his weapons behind.

What a time of magic, this soft replenishing of the earth's waters! What a time of gentleness, a gentleness that took him back to the first memories of his mother. And what infinite softness and shadings and patterns of light! David could not have said which of all these sensuous things he liked best—whether to sink to his knees and examine the torn snow, to tell what a rabbit was doing here; or to stand, head bared, face up, mouth open and eyes open, looking, breathing, feeling the flakes touch him so softly and melt, the caress the gentlest of all caresses in life; or to fling himself down on his back, legs wide, arms outstretched, eyes closed, his mind and senses filled with this vision of a world without wind or barrenness or emptiness and without sound—so completely and utterly without sound—yet so completely full of movement. There was no other situation in life to compare with it. Or to lie on his back, outflung, his eyes open; then he saw such variety in light patterns that wonder grew and filled him, and this kind of wonder, so rare in the adult, made him a child again.

A conifer forest in a storm like this was for him a deeply religious experience. There was no such forest near the post. Here he had to be content with such magic as snow could make of cottonwood and aspen and birch, mixed with spruce and pine. He liked to walk up to a willow or an aspen and put his arms around the trunk and shake it and feel its burden of snow tumbling over him; and then to walk back and look at the tree's stark beauty against a world of white. The darker the tree the better. An old dead aspen made a lovely picture if it stood so that he could see it against both earth and storm. What he needed was his girl with him, his woman, to walk at his side, her warm hand sheltered within his palm and her fingers returning his pressure, her tongue mute. If only Sunday were with him now and feeling not like an avenger but like a woman when first touched by love!

He chose a position where he could most fully use all his senses, though there was nothing for a man's ears to do in this world. The river, now in low water, now twenty feet down on its banks, was soundless unless he went to the bank to hear the lipping and gurgling or the faint muted tone of the deep reluctant waters under the swifter waters on the surface. He sat in the open, so that the descending softness could find him and cover him; so that he could see the slate sheets of river water like dull mirrors, the darkening depths and recesses of river thickets, the open prairie being smoothed and mounded over in gently rolling symmetries. If on a day like this a man didn't have a woman who loved him he wanted a book. Up at Chipewyan, it was said, the pedlars had a fine library; in these things the company was more generous than HB. The directors over in London seemed to feel that books and journals would make the men lazy and shrink the profits. What a hell of a library it was at the Edmonton post! David had read all of it two or three times and had asked for books against his wages but none had come.

A half dozen times he had read *The Tempest*—of a certain island in a certain sea, of an old man named Prospero, and his daughter Miranda, so very lovely, like all Shakespeare's heroines. "Knowing I lov'd my books, he furnish'd me from mine own library with volumes that I prize above my dukedom." He was recalling now her words, "with my heart in 't; and now farewell . . ." He felt like that today. He foresaw, more clearly he was sure than Jim, if not more clearly than Colin, the dark months ahead, the strife that would "run upon the sharp wind of the north" and "set a mark so bloody on the business"; and he was not sure that he would not meet his end in it. It was not too hard to die if you had known your woman, but it was hard if you had not known her and were still young. When Jim sent him out into the frozen winter he would be on the very spearpoint of danger and, unlike Prospero, no woman's nor any person's indulgences would set him free. It did no good compassed about with storm to try to decide what to do, nor in the chilled loneliness of his bed, nor when making pemmican or sitting before a blazing fire. Shakespeare knew what it was that carried a man to the tide's pitch, he knew that once you were thrown in you were a fool to buck the current if you hadn't the strength for it. All his plays told you that. They all carried the same lesson, that passions ran at far greater depths than reason, ran in mindless darkness like that of slow senseless waters in moonless midnight. Jim didn't know that. He did not know that far from persuading the Blackfeet to come with peace offerings to HB, David McDonald would be lucky if he got out with his life. In Jim's world there were no Mirandas. In his world man-woman love was not allowed to get in the way of profits or a good night's sleep.

He lay back and closed his eyes and did not stir for an hour or more. The white gentleness covered him, all but his face; it melted on his face and ran into his ears and mouth and with tiny cold fingers down his throat.

## XV

David kept the post on the alert day and night and he was not surprised one morning when a scout came to tell him that Indians were hiding in the woods down south and drying their buffalo robes. The way they acted they were up to no good.

The same day a band of young bucks rode up to the post to announce the presence of the Blackfeet with goods to trade. David gave to each, as was the custom with both companies, about six inches of tobacco twist. They begged for rum, and when he refused it they swaggered up to him, showing off their arrogance, their contempt. In their menacing gestures he saw trouble lurking.

"It's the pedlars," Jim said after David had reported to him. "Send the chiefs a quart of rum each."

David sent the rum, cut by half, and at once word came back that the chiefs were angry. He had sent rum for only six and there were seven.

"Who in hell is the other one?"

"Mink Tails."

It had been two or three years since Mink Tails came to the post. He had grown so fat and gross and lazy that he reminded David of Chief Gros Blanc, now dead, who had been seventy-six inches around his middle but who in spite of his monstrous fat had been able to ride his white mule almost to the day of his death. David sent a quart of rum to Mink Tails and went to find Jim.

Jim said, "You know what it means?"

"Trouble."

"If Mink Tails has come along it means he's trying to hold the young bloods back. He used to be the only one who could do it. Maybe he still is."

"I'll go out and see how they're feeling."

"I wouldn't. You'll find out soon enough. Post more guards."

David had a half dozen men put on extra clothing and examine their guns and take positions on the gallery, with instructions to fire into the air if, when the Indians approached, they shot off their guns and made war cries. That is exactly what they did. The braves, led by the more reckless chiefs, came in a rush, shattering the white world with their war whoops and firing their guns; but when the post's guns answered them their behavior abruptly changed. At the gate one of them who could speak a little English pretended to be very abashed and friendly. He said Horned Thunder had complaints to make.

"About what?" asked David impatiently. He didn't like the way the red men were looking at him.

Payette said, "He say much complaint."

That was an old ruse, but an Indian was a child and even when his complaint was the most audacious invention, as it usually was, you had to listen to him. David said that Horned Thunder would be admitted to the trading room to make his complaints if Mink Tails came with him.

The Indians listened with their faces while Payette was speaking. They seemed almost to smile. They turned and ran away.

The two chiefs were admitted and at once began to talk to Payette; and David, who was now trying to learn the Blackfoot language, recognized several words.

Horned Thunder, Payette said, was furious because he had lost his fleetest horse. His grief was great. It happened last September when the bull moose were in the rutting season and a big bull mistook the chief's horse for a cow and mounted him. That much, David reflected, could be true: a bull moose in ardor would mount anything that at all resembled his mate. But he doubted that the horse had been injured.

He said to tell the great chief that he had many horses to choose from. He said to tell him that he shared his great grief. Had he any more complaints?

He had many, Payette said. The grizzly bears had eaten most of the buffalo. There wouldn't be much pemmican.

David looked at Horned Thunder and with difficulty restrained a smile. It was true that grizzlies in some places were almost as thick as red deer and did devour buffalo carcasses before the Indians could skin them and get the flesh away. But this was something the pedlars had told him to say.

David asked if they had brought any fresh buffalo.

Yes, Payette said, after talking to the chief. They had a huge quantity of fresh meat to trade—buffalo, deer, moose, caribou.

He said to tell the great and brave chief that his hunters would kill many more buffalo, make much more pemmican. Had he any more complaints?

Yes, indeed. The Crees had been debauching their women.

Jesus, what a lie! The Crees were scared to death of the Blackfeet; if any women had been debauched it was Cree women. This wily chief was building toward something, lie by lie, and David knew what it was but he had to pretend that he didn't know. He looked at the fat impassive face of Mink Tails but read nothing there. Mink Tails was a gentle soul, as Indians went; a diplomat in his way, almost a statesman. He was waiting to see what kind of case Horned Thunder could make out for himself.

Horned Thunder was again talking to Payette. Then Payette was saying that the Blackfeet had been so degraded and shamed by the Crees that they were going on the warpath against them. Well, John

Bowman had been busy. The hell of it with this struggle between the two companies was that you couldn't get anything out into the open.

David said to tell the great and brave chief that his wars and quarrels with the Crees were no business of white men. Had he more complaints?

Many more, Payette said. There had been fresh trouble and bloodshed and much flashing of knives between the Little Girl tribe and the Saskatchewan Assiniboines, and the hunting grounds of the Blackfeet were imperiled.

Lord, what lies, what lies! David said again to tell him that quarrels of red men with red men were none of the white man's business. That seemed to set Horned Thunder back. He was silent a few moments but the crafty fellow had a mind full of lies and the hell of it was that being a trader, you had to listen until all the lies were told, until the rascal had depleted himself, or he would feel that his person had been insulted.

"Has he any more complaints?"

Payette said the chief, to save buffalo and make pemmican for David, had killed many grizzlies and must now appease their spirits and could do this only by drinking. That was too much for David. The smile came out.

"Any more?"

Yes, Payette said. The great chief had seen in a dream that his people would take ten times as many pelts this season and he would lead them to fine trapping waters; but meanwhile his son, Tall Eagle, was very ill and needed rum to ease his pain and his woes.

David looked at the chief. His son had been at the gate only an hour ago. "Any more complaints?"

Horned Thunder moved close to Payette and whispered, and Payette said that Latude had gone. He had deserted, had vanished, and Horned Thunder wondered if David knew where he was. David felt a chill. He looked into the chief's crafty half-lidded eyes and thought, You sly bastard, you're out to get me, aren't you?

David said to tell the chief that he had a complaint—to ask Mink Tails to listen carefully also. Payette was to tell them about the two horse thieves. He was to tell them how their lives had been spared because the Sichekiekoon and the HB Company had been good and loyal friends; how these thieves had been put up to it by the pedlars, who themselves were thieves and scoundrels.

David had coached Payette in what to say on this matter and Payette now talked easily, as though he had memorized what he would say. David studied in turn the faces of the two red men but they told him nothing. The Indian's capacity to conceal his emotions and thoughts was for David one of the marvels of life: not in the slightest way, not in eyes, mouth, face, or movements did they usually reveal anything at all.

Did Mink Tails think this was the way to treat his paleface friends?

"He say bring thief, he will punish."

David called to assistants and told them to bring the thieves out. Still surly, sullen, impenitent, outraged, murderous, they were brought forth and the two chiefs looked at them. David knew that if they were punished it would be not for having tried but for having failed.

He now gave to each chief a quart of rum, cut to about fifty proof, and indicated that the conference was at an end. The gate was opened a little and swiftly a rogue whom David had not seen for a year or more, one Buffalo Dung, notorious horse thief and killer, who boasted of the fifteen scalps he had and who now was stark-naked but for moccasins and headdress, pushed his way in and swaggered up to face David and sneer as only a half-breed could sneer.

In the next moment David was astounded to see the villain swiftly draw a bow from behind him and present an arrow at David's heart. No one moved. David had no doubt that this was the end of him, for Buffalo Dung was drunk and even when sober killed with no provocation at all. It gave a man a queer feeling to expect an arrow through his heart any moment and to be helpless, though unfettered. He had goose flesh. At the top left side of his heart he felt a twinge of pain, a kind of twisted corkscrew stab; and he heard a gurgle in his bowels. Never in his life had he been so vividly aware of fear.

He was convinced afterward that it was Mink Tails who saved his life. Mink Tails said something, a few words, quietly, but there was no change in Buffalo Dung, at least no change that a man could see. He stood there with the bowstring far back, the arrow pointed straight at David's heart. Mink Tails spoke again. David did not know what he said but Payette knew. David had been looking into the half-breed's eyes but he now turned to Payette. Then, just as swiftly as he had drawn the bow, Buffalo Dung relaxed it and swung to look at Mink Tails, and in the next instant Pierre had moved forward to snatch the bow from his hand. Mink Tails ordered him out and he went almost abjectly; and then the chief, speaking through Payette, asked David to give Buffalo Dung a dose of poison.

David was conscious of moisture on his brow. He had not quite recovered. "Poison?" he asked, looking at Payette.

Mink Tails, Payette said, was sick and tired of Buffalo Dung. The man was a thief and killer and no-good who gave trouble all the time; white man had many kinds of poison and could put enough in a cup of rum to make Dung be good.

David shook his head no. He said to tell the chief that white man had no poison and never killed people that way.

"He say you no kill Dung, Dung kill you."

"Tell him I'll have to take my chance on that." He saw Mink Tails looking round him. When an Indian looked round him that way he wanted something, and David supposed it was rum, and he gave the old man another quart and again indicated that the visit was terminated.

David then went to Jim's room and poured a tin cup full of uncut rum and gulped it down. He moved a hand across the moisture on his brow. He had faced grizzlies and wolves and enraged bull buffaloes and all kinds of men but never before had he been so unnerved. He told Jim about it. There had been a funny thing, he said. Dung was naked but for moccasins and headdress and somehow he had shoved his private parts up into his body and apparently had kept them up by tying the folds of hide with a string. "It's pretty damn queer to have a naked man about to kill you who has no sign of cod and knackers."

Jim grinned. "Never heard of that trick before?"

"I guess there's a lot I've never heard of."

Indians did it sometimes, Jim said, but he had never known why. They did a lot of funny things.

"I wouldn't have thought a man could do it," David said.

"Try it sometime. As for this Buffalo Shit, watch him."

That was his name in the Indian tongue. Indians had no such euphemisms as white men had and Jim scorned euphemisms. Any man did who lived in this country awhile.

"They say Latude has deserted. What would that mean?"

"Just a trick to throw us off. That's the half-breed you knocked down, isn't it?"

"Yes."

"Well, when you go out this winter you'll need eyes in the back of your head. You'll have to be damned careful or they'll get you."

"I reckon." The two men looked into the fire. Things had taken such a turn that David doubted he would be alive in six months. Well, he was determined to sink his being deep into Sunday's before he died. Thinking of her reminded him of what the chief had said about the Crees. "They say Crees have raped their women and they are going to war against them."

"I guess they already have. They have a Cree woman—hair parted and bunched up in knots behind her ears and tattoo lines on her chin. It's all pedlar work."

So it was, David supposed. The pedlars had made notorious drunkards of the Crees—they were almost as bad as the Saulteurs. "But why should they set the Blackfeet on them?"

"To scare them. Then when we go into the Athabasca the Crees won't dare trade with us."

David nodded. Jim saw through these things.

Jim said, "What have they got?"

"Fresh meat . . . swanskins . . . dried berries . . . wolf hides . . . women. Horned Thunder has made it plain as moose lip that we're to do a lot of business with their women this time."

Jim stretched a leg and heard the knee pop. "Just don't feel like the mawsie wench myself. You?"

"No squaws for me."

"You'd better watch the sons of bitches this time, they're splashing over for trouble. Mink Tails might handle a drunken half-breed but he won't handle the bloods."

David knew they were splashing over for trouble. Instead of going to bed at his usual hour he stayed up to receive reports from his scouts. The Indians, they said, had many fires among their lodges; and when David went to the gallery it was quite a sight that he looked down on, the lodge village, the fires, the reflections from firelight on snow and river waters, the immensities of the white frozen world. At midnight some of them were still drinking rum and making pantomime of old battles around the fires, using their pipes or sticks as guns, some of them so drunk that they staggered and fell. At two o'clock it was reported to David that Indians in small groups were lurking here and there around the post, and he could imagine John Bowman's glee when his scouts reported this to him. Rum and pedlar encouragement had made the red men bold. Drunk and reckless, with their hair crawling forward to the fight, they might try to fire the palisades or to climb them or to chop them down. Indians were like boys who made a big show of their courage; when full of rum they were full of brag but under the brag it was chiefly bluff. A lot of the rum, he supposed, was coming from Bowman.

The next morning Pierre came to him with bad news. One of the guns which had hung in its sheath in the trading room was gone and in the sheath was a stick of wood. David was amazed. The theft was bad enough. The stick of wood was the last word in Indian gall and insolence.

David went to the trading room. It was true, but how under heaven had the gun been stolen right under his nose and who had stolen it? One of the young bucks, he supposed, who had come in first. He reported the matter to Jim and said he would go find it.

"Alone?" asked Jim, looking at him queerly.

"Alone is best, isn't it?"

"First thing I know I'll need another chief trader."

David went unarmed and alone. He was thinking of Donald Mackenzie, the giant who weighed three hundred and twenty pounds and could outwalk any man, red or white. Everyone in the north country had heard how, when a rifle was stolen, Donald went boldly to the lodge of the chief and marched in unannounced and came out with the gun. Perpetual Motion knew his Indians. David did not know them so well but he was aware that if they were allowed to steal a gun and get away with it not all of hell would then contain their arrogance.

He went among the lodges, looking round him, wondering how to go about the thing. This for him was a new experience. The word for gun among Indians was musket, from the French *mousquet,* and the common jargon for steal was *kapsualla.* He went among the fires and the lodges shouting, "*Kapsualla* musket!" making his voice sound very angry, making his eyes kindle like fires on all those who looked at him; and presently Mink Tails appeared. Pretending not to see him, David went on shouting and making menacing gestures, and his voice seemed to choke and puke upon the most horrible wrath. In the jargon he was now saying, "No musket, no rum!"

Mink Tails understood that and waddled over to explain it to Horned Thunder. While David shouted and looked round for a glimpse of Sunday the two chiefs talked excitedly together, and then Horned Thunder hastened away and vanished into a lodge. In only a few moments he flushed a sheepish young buck out, who came toward David with the gun, shame in him, but under the shame humiliation and anger and visions of vengeance. David looked at him, hoping to remember that face, and then took the gun and climbed the hill.

He had hardly reached the post when a scout dashed up on a horse to tell him that another band of Indians was moving in. That was bad.

"Who?"

They might be Bloods or Piegans but he thought they were Crees. From a distance they had looked like a herd of red deer.

David hoped they were not Piegans. Some of the Piegan chiefs had many wives, whom they were willing to debauch for rum, and all Piegans were among the world's worst horse thieves. Not even the Crows could give a white man more trouble. But the worst thing about the Piegans was their haughty contempt for barter and trade. Why, they asked, should water be paid for?—meaning rum. Too lazy to trap, too arrogant to trade, nevertheless they would brook no refusal: when they demanded rum they expected to get it. They also demanded a great deal of ceremony, and innumerable gestures to their bravery and prowess and eminence, these loafers, with their filthy cooking and shameless use of women, who thought themselves a chosen people, far above all other Indians, or white men either.

David sent scouts out and posted more guards in the gallery. It would be a hell of a note if there was an Indian war right in the post's own yard.

But it was not the Piegans or Bloods, it was the Crees. David took the information to Jim.

Jim grunted. "The damn fools," he said. "Many?"

"More braves than the Blackfeet."

"More pedlar work," Jim said. "Send for Horned Thunder and Mink Tails. We'll see if we can talk some sense into their rummed-up skulls."

The two chiefs came, with Payette, to the chamber where Jim and David were waiting. Speaking slowly, pausing often, so that Payette could communicate his meaning, Jim said that a band of Crees was moving in to trade, and since all trading was completed with the Blackfeet they should move on. Wars between Indians were none of the white man's business but the white man did not want them shooting and scalping near his posts. If the Blackfeet were going on the warpath against the Crees, white man cared nothing about that, so long as they did it in Indian lands.

Horned Thunder then talked and Payette translated. The chief said the Crees had no right to come here, this was Blackfoot trading country——

"Tell him to hell with that. Tell him the pedlars told him to say that."

The chief and Payette again talked. The chief said his people had many things yet to trade, yet white man would not trade, nor lie much with their squaws for rum; and this was so because white man had known Crees were coming, those pitiful dogs and cowards——

"John Bowman!" Jim exploded, and looked at David. David thought, Does he expect me to be as two-faced and double-dealing as that sneaker?

Jim asked what they had to trade, and Payette said they had many kinds of berries——

"No more berries, no swanskin, no old wolf hides, no wattap roots, no balsam gum. Tell him beaver, otter, mink, marten, lynx, bear."

The Cree pelts, the chief said, were no good.

David smiled. Jim stared, speechless.

The chief said if they did not trade with him he would trade with Bowman.

Jim shrugged. They simply wore a man out. The directors in London were lamenting their empty purses and writing to their factors, "You have not persuaded nor sufficiently attempted to persuade the Indians of the advantages in trading with the Company. We believe it will be good for the Compys. interest . . ."

"Tell him we'll trade more. Will they go then?"

"He say when potlatch."

"Oh, a moon. Tell him all go away trap. Tell him pelts good now, buy much rum."

Payette talked to the chief. They would go soon, he said, they would trap many.

But they did not go soon. They moved along the river to a thickly wooded bottom that offered windbreak and abundant wood for fires. They pitched their lodges and gave every sign of intending to spend the winter there. At least till Christmas, Jim said; they seemed to have a hell of a rum thirst this year, though of course John Bowman had put them up to it. He could hear John telling them that the HB had thousands of kegs of rum and were dying to trade it for dried berries and skins from which the hair was peeling.

"Watch them," Jim said.

David kept such a sharp eye on them that he went daily to their village to see what they were doing. Or was it with the hope of seeing Sunday? He had been trying to forget her and for days at a time he would be so absorbed by his duties that he would not think of her, when suddenly there she was in his thoughts like a rainbow, or in the night like something walking through his sleep. He would then smell her, he would see the loveliness of her swimming or running naked, the touch of her as he sat astride her and washed her; the unbelievable softness of her lips, the sound of her voice, the sheen of her greased hair. The smell, the touch, the sound, the beauty would not be put away. Then he ached for her as a big strong man aches, when young and charged with health, a man who has not known a woman for months, for years; and he vowed again to possess her before he had to die.

One windless forenoon a lovely snow was falling and he went for a walk toward the camp. He followed paths close to the river because so much snow had fallen in the past month, almost three feet of it out on the prairie and around the post. There were paths along the river made by Indians who had come to beg rum or to offer to lie with the white men. An old squaw with drooping pus-filled eyelids, as filthy a drunkard as any, had come, begging rum; and she reminded David of a story told in this country, of a squaw who in twenty-four hours drank up more than a hundred beaver skins and a whole pile of buffalo robes. That was a gross exaggeration or the old woman hadn't got more than a thimbleful for each pelt.

David had three small buckskin pouches hung from his leather girdle, each filled with dried berries, and he ate berries as he walked. Most of the men would not eat dried berries, they thought them squaw food, they said that as likely as not the squaws pissed on them to show how much they loved the white man; but David felt need of more than meat and he ate them with relish, particularly the serviceberries. These when dried still had body, unlike raspberries, which became all seeds, and a nice flavor of earthy things. Dried elderberry or squawberry or wild currant he did not care for—they were little more than seeds and skin; but he liked gooseberry and huckleberry and these he mixed with serviceberry, blending the flavors in his mouth. Gooseberry was only skin and seeds, too, but it had a nice tartness that spiced up the dull serviceberry.

He liked to walk in snug warmth, his feet well encased, his hands deep in mittens except when feeding his mouth, his face framed with the soft fur edging of beaver cap—to walk and wonder how long he would live and if he would have his woman before he died. He was about a mile from the village when suddenly he saw her, and he would have sworn by the confusion in her face that she had been out looking for him. But no doubt that was only a man's vanity. Still, for weeks, for a long time, he was to remember something in her eyes at this moment, something female, something as natural and eternal as the rutting seasons.

At a distance of fifteen feet he looked at her and she looked at him. This astonished him: almost never before had she met his eyes. She did not look friendly but neither did she look hostile; he wondered desperately about her, trying to read the meanings in her face, telling himself that in a moment the contempt would return and she would leave him. He removed a mitten and fed berries into his mouth. Her gaze was steady. He would have sworn by God and heaven that this girl wanted him in the way of the female for the male, that he could have taken her; but he told himself that this could not be so, that it was something else.

He had been learning the Blackfoot tongue from Payette and in a fumbling groping way he now talked to her. He said, his gesture embracing the whole world, that her eyes were the most beautiful he had ever seen, her lips the sweetest; and he pursed his own lips and made a kind of kissing sound and smiled. It occurred to him that possibly this was silly, because Indians, so far as he had observed, never kissed one another's lips. In the fury of the embrace they did scratch and bite and draw blood; and Jim had told him that once his gentle Tum-tum, carried away, carried deep into animal passions, had risen under him, her mouth open and wet and her teeth seeking, her face distorted, her eyes on fire.

Eating berries, watching her, David told the girl that he loved her, but there was no change in her face. He tried to tell her that soon now he had to go alone into the frozen winter and he might be killed, but she was to wait for him. Her expression did not change, but it seemed to him that she was wondering about him, thinking about him, yes, *feeling* about him, as a female and a woman might. Then, eating only a berry at a time, for his words at best sounded wholly unintelligible to him, he said that at potlatch there was usually a belle of the ball and Sunday was to be the belle this year. He wanted her to be at her loveliest. There was no way of knowing how much she understood of what he was saying, and now and then he stepped over into English, as when he said, "Dress up all in buckskin, for you're the finest-looking woman in the whole north country. Princess Sunday of the Sichekiekoon!"

He stopped abruptly, for pride was such an obstacle in love. He had made up his mind that she would not move first this time. He had decided that if he was to win this proud contemptuous girl, so many of whose ways and values were Indian, he would have to show more impudence, more indifference. Then something told him that she was about to go, and at once he swung and walked away from her, without looking back. Let her figure that out! Maybe he should have used simple English words, baby words, the kind parents spoke to a small child: next time he would mama and papa and baby her to death and perhaps then in darkness would shine the lights of memory.

As the Christmas season drew near he prepared a message for her and went over and over it with Payette to be sure that he understood it. Payette was to tell her that she would be the belle of the season (surely she was vain enough to be flattered by that); that she was to make herself as beautiful as she could—but what if she smeared herself all over with bear grease!—and that he would send to her the company's finest sled and dog team. Payette was to tell her that this was a great honor. He thought he would send Payette with the sled, but after looking into the rascal's eyes he changed his mind about that. He said to tell her that she would come with Mink Tails.

He then filled his pouches with berries and went for a walk, not toward the village but away from it. It was a gloomy world under a heavy dead sky. David walked for an hour, for two hours, and found himself in a grove of very large aspen. He chose a tree whose bark was a smooth silver green and upon it as high as he could reach he cut these words:

PRINCESS SUNDAY
DAVID McDONALD
18 Dec.
1815

# XVI

Men in long winters with time on their hands liked to do different things. A very few liked to read and to write journals or long letters home; a few liked to make furniture or gunstocks and knife handles and pipes; and those who worked with dogs and sleds liked to have, if possible, the gayest dog train in the whole land. Such men spent countless hours adorning the harness with silver and copper and beadwork, embroidering saddle cloths, engraving legends on silver bells, working feathers and quills and all sorts of things into buckskin mantles, with the result that those who came a hundred or several hundred miles to the holiday revelry came in style. Long before they appeared in sight those expecting them could hear the music of bells in the frozen air; and then the sled would come in sight, drawn by four or six husky dogs, all glittering and splendid in holiday attire, with their master sitting so deep in the sled in buffalo robes that he was only a shapeless thing with a face. Some of the hardier men, the bolder men, would journey for days to participate in the holy season; the sled laden with dog food; men and dogs burrowing deep into the snow at night; the man shooting a deer or caribou or elk if one showed up, or turning the dogs loose, if the wolves became too menacing, to tear a few of them to pieces; covering forty, fifty, sometimes sixty miles a day, depending on whether the snow was frozen hard enough to support dogs and sled; sometimes pausing for a day or two under a blizzard and burrowing and waiting for it to pass over; sometimes making a fire to roast a deer or a beaver or to thaw out the dog food if the cold had gone through the robes; arriving at last eager to get drunk and raise hell and bed a squaw down and swap yarns and brag in fellowship by great blazing fires.

To have seen the men come in and greet one another and those in the post nobody would have dreamed that the two companies were in a war of extermination. Whether pedlar or HB they came up or down the river over the frozen snows or south from the Athabasca, their bells merry with Christmas music, the dogs gay with bright ribbons and ornaments, the men snuggled deep in their pile of robes, tiny icicles in their brows and beards.

After a sled had come up the river Jim poured a brandy for himself and another for David. "A new governor at Red River," he said. "Semple, they say his name is, but I reckon it is Simple, for the damned fool wants to bring in a lot of priests and ministers. Priests——"

"Priests!" said David, staring at Jim. "In this country?"

"In this country, where a man learns to pray as God intended."

"Priests to pray or to plow?"

"To tell us and the red men what sinners we are. Until Governor Simple has stood on top of the Rockies or gone fifteen hundred miles up one of these big rivers what in hell will he ever know about praying?"

David was looking at Jim. Jim always talked this way during the Christmas season. "And Selkirk?"

"He has come over. I guess he's in Montreal."

"A wintering partner," said David maliciously.

"In Montreal's finest hotel with his shinbones up to the fire. Next summer his lordship's education will begin."

And mine this winter, David thought. He then heard a hubbub in the big room and dashed out. This was the revelry room, with guns and deerhorns and elkhorns and pelt rugs almost covering the walls, with a huge fireplace at one end where cooks brewed warm drinks and roasted whole carcasses. Pierre was at the main door. David rushed over to him and Pierre said that it was Brave Feathers, hog-drunk. "He wants to see you."

David went into the trading room where Brave Feathers, with HB men all around him, was sitting in a stupor, hands on a bench to support himself, his glazed black eyes looking round him. He was about the drunkest Indian David had ever seen and he suspected that the rum in the chief's belly had come from John Bowman. He called Payette in and told him to find out what the chief wanted.

Payette talked and Brave Feathers tried to talk but his tongue was thick, he drooled, he bunched his nose up and stared round him as if for rum. He was weaving back and forth, bending over and then back, supported by both hands that were palms down on the bench top. When he slobbered he thrust his tongue out and explored his chin as though to recover the spittle, and his eyes, settling at last on David, were out of focus.

"He say potlatch."

"Potlatch, hell. Tell him begins tomorrow. And goddamn it, doesn't he know he's drunk?"

Payette talked again to the chief and then told David that he was ready to trade Sunday. How much was offered for her? Before David could reply the chief was again speaking, or muttering, far down in his throat, and Payette was standing close to him to make out what he said.

"He say ten kegs rum."

"Oh, is that all? Tell him he has to go back to his lodge. My men will help him."

Payette spoke close to the chief's ear and the chief angrily wagged his head no. He decided to stand up and face the thing, but when he took his hands off the bench he pitched forward onto his red face, and David's men helped him to his feet and held him.

"Who let him in?" David asked, looking round at his men. He knew it was a fruitless question. Most of his men were already half drunk. That was the hell of it with the holiday season: the bars were let down, the gates opened, and the Indians might have ringed their medicine poles with scalps, except that they got drunker than the whites. David told two of his men to take the chief back to his lodge.

One of them said, "He'll stagger right back up here."

"You heard the order. Tell Mink Tails to tie him down."

It was like this for a week until the final debauch New Year's Eve and the following day. Red man or white, there wasn't much difference. Men who risked their lives through sub-zero blizzards to find holiday cheer wanted cheer: they ate like gluttons and drank like drunkards, and some of them went almost daily to do business with the squaws, staggering along the frozen path, falling, floundering in the snow, cursing. And every day there was trouble.

Christmas morning David was told that he was wanted at the front gate. He went reluctantly, thinking that it was Brave Feathers again; but no, it was a squaw and she had murder in her brain and murder shone in the black windows of her eyes. Payette said that her buck had left her—or anyway she thought he had left her—and she wanted to go inside and find him and cut his heart out.

"Does the fool think he's in the fort?"

"Yes, sir."

"Is he?"

"No, sir."

David looked hard at Payette, wondering if the man lied. Then he looked at the squaw. He thought her rather pathetic, in spite of the murderous lights in her eyes, for she seemed sick and tired and she had been beaten horribly. She was filthy and she stunk like hell. Her eyes were bloodshot, as if she had sat all night in lodge fire smoke, and they were blacked, both of them, and her broad fat face was cut and bruised all over it. David could see no weapon but he knew that she had a dagger hidden.

He told Payette to bring Pierre. When Pierre came, grinning in his sandy furze, David said he thought Payette had lied about the buck, that probably he was in the fort. "See if you can find him."

While they waited David tried to pass the time with talk. Why had the buck left her? Payette asked her the question and then said that her man was in love with Princess Sunday. David's brows shot up. With Sunday? What was his name? When Payette seemed reluctant to put the question David swung to him, his suspicions ripe and his anger mounting. He seized the half-breed by his shoulders and looked into his sly treacherous eyes. "Just what are you up to, anyway?"

"Me?" Payette whined, writhing under thumbs that dug in against his bones.

David shook him. "Who is this woman?"

Whimpering, Payette said her name was Blue Flower.

"Who is she?"

David now seized the man under his armpits and lifted him and plunged him against the palisades and held him there, his feet off the earth but sunk in snow. He brought him out a little and then hurled him back hard, so that his head struck. But then, shamed by his loss of temper, he set him down and in a voice shaken by anger said, "Get out of my sight." Payette vanished and David turned to the squaw. So far as he knew, she had not moved or changed expression.

Pierre now returned. He said he was unable to find anyone hiding inside. The two men went into the post and closed the gate, leaving the woman standing there, her face looking bruised, bloody, and frozen.

An hour later Pierre came to tell him that the woman was dead by the gate.

David stared at him. "Dead . . . ? How?"

"I haven't seen her yet."

David called to Jim and the three of them went to the gate and unbolted it and stepped outside. The squaw was lying about where she had stood and her throat was cut from ear to ear and blood was all over her, and blood redder than David had thought blood could be dyed the snow all around her. As if moved by a common signal the three men looked away toward the pedlar fort.

Jim said, "Did she kill herself or was she killed?"

Pierre bent over her and found a bloodstained knife under her where she had fallen. He handed it to David. Then he felt over the woman, turning her as his hands explored, and said at last, "There's no knife on her."

David said to Jim, "Can a squaw get jealous enough to kill herself?"

"Oh God, yes," Jim said. "If they've been drinking."

"You suppose she did?"

Jim stooped to look at her throat. "If we could tell which side the knife started from. But I guess it would be from the left no matter who did it. I reckon I'm no good as a detective," he said, staring. "If her man did it would he leave the knife under her? And what in hell would be his motive?"

"Fear that she'd kill him."

"Might be. But if he slipped up behind her he had a knife. Didn't she have one?"

"Must have. She came to kill her man."

"Or only to find him? Anyway, she's dead. Notify Mink Tails," he said to Pierre. To David, "They might use this as an excuse, so see that your guards are awake."

David said he would have a look and he went up to the gallery, climbing a ladder whose rungs were as cold as ice. He found the two guards looking down over the palisades at the slain woman. Had they seen it happen? They said no.

One of them said, "Who is she?"

"A squaw," David said. Feeling shame, he corrected himself, "A woman. The wife of one of the Indian men." That was better: she was a wife, her husband was a man. "They might get their blood up, so be on the watch here and don't stand around together."

The men moved off.

"I'll send you up a hot drink."

"Thank you, sir."

He had no business sending hot drinks up but it *was* Christmas Day. He had heard or read that some people set up a tree they called a *Christmas* tree; and, taking an ax, he left the fort and went to the river bottom and cut a small fir. He felt confused and deeply vexed with himself. The murder or suicide of the squaw—*of the woman*—had upset him and he walked around in a kind of emotional paralysis, looking at other trees, telling himself over and over that this was Christmas Day. He took the tree to the post and had a carpenter set it on a base, and when it was ready he wondered what he could enliven it with. He went to the trading room and stared round him, thinking of buckskin fringe, beaded leather, colorful feathers, red buffalo berries still on the twigs, kingfisher crowns, mink tails—but all such things seemed mere trumpery and rubbish. He decided to let the tree stand in its own simple unadorned beauty and he was looking at it when a group of men came up.

They looked at the tree and one of them said to David, "You feeling all right?"

"What in hell is it?" another said.

"A Christmas tree."

The men walked round it as they might have walked round a white buffalo, looking the tree up and down with exaggerated interest, their eyes bugging. Jim came up.

"A Christmas tree," one of the men said to him. "The north country is fairing off."

"It gets me all ganted up with hanker," another said.

"Go on, get out of here!" Jim cried, feigning anger. "You cynical bastards, I say go on!" Grinning sheepishly, the men moved away. They went over to the fireplace, where the cooks were serving rum grogs. Jim looked at the tree and at David. "You'd better write a letter home."

"Why?"

"It might make you feel better. And on my table there's something for you." Jim watched him go till he was out of sight, then called a man and said, "Take this tree to Mr. McDonald's room."

"Yes, sir."

Goddamn it, you couldn't have a Christmas tree in a place like this. The men wouldn't know what to make of it. You might as well ask them to go to church or to confess their sins or put in the pin or stop whoring.

On the table was a bottle of champagne—David had not known that there was any left—and under the bottle was a piece of paper on which was written in Jim's strong slow handwriting:

David:

Just a few notes on things I might forget to tell you.

Mink Tails says the dead squaw is one of Brave Feather's wives. He thinks she was murdered. Keep your eye open for that red bastard. He's after you.

I had hoped that you wouldn't have to go out this winter but all the reports tell the same story. Our trappers are being bluffed out. God knows if we'll have any pelts to ship next spring. . . .

There were a few other notes but David did not read them now. With his heart sinking he understood that Jim had taken this apparently casual way to warn him that when he left the post to go alone into the frozen winter his life would be in danger. He would go with four dogs maybe, a sled half filled with dried fish, a bag of pemmican, a gun, and a knife—and cold might not be his deadliest enemy, even cold that might reach forty below or even fifty. In that kind of weather men got lockjaw, axheads shattered like glass, and trees burst open. That was an enemy to daunt almost any man, but Jim had meant to tell him that he might have a deadlier enemy than that.

Latude, he supposed, and, flanking him, such villains as Buffalo Dung. Either of them would give his favorite pony and all his women for David's scalp. They would know of his departure and their eagle eyes would follow him day after day; he would never see them but they would be watching him. He might want to write a letter home, Jim had said!

David plopped the cork from the bottle and drank.

## XVII

The revelry began just after Christmas Day. Every white man in the post was there because he had far more than average hardiness and courage. His hungers were bigger, so big that filling his stomach with food and rum and his loins with woman did not fill the man. These men ate as if they had been starved all their lives—great feasts day after day, of venison, roasted ducks and geese and swans, smoked and salted buffalo tongues and bosses, moose noses, a half dozen kinds of fish, beaver tails, together with various delicacies brought from the Old World and stored away for this season. They drank as if a hundred and thirty proof rum were only water. If they wearied of rum they had sherry and port, wines fermented from local berries, and brandy as special treats.

They would gather, fifty or sixty of them, before the great fire and roast whole sides of buffalo and elk and slice off succulent hunks and feed their mouths with their hands and swap stories and roar with laughter and obscenities. Made bold and malicious with rum, an HB man, acting out each part, would show how the pedlar partners in their sumptuous Montreal club dressed for dinner—his big weathered fingers dancing round him to suggest ruffles and gold lace, his whole body straining and looking anguished to suggest the tight knee britches, daintily pretending to fasten the gold clasps on the garters or straighten a huge silver buckle on a shoe, with mincing manner putting finger tips up to see if the big powdered wig was in place—until he had all the HB men hooting with scornful laughter and the pedlars looking gravely at one another, or at the HB men with feigned amazement.

Then a North Wester, his voice stricken, would exclaim, "What! No dividends?" imitating and exaggerating the prim British accent; and he would act the part of a director in London, threadbare, physically emaciated, running feverishly through his mail to learn if the payments had been resumed; jumping up and down in ineffectual squeaking fury and cursing the pedlars with gentle well-bred oaths. Then the pedlars began to roar with glee; or, as if to a signal, they would cast off their boisterous mirth and turn grave sympathetic faces on the HB men; and one of them, looking maudlin with brotherly love, would inquire, "No profits in your company? How sad!" Then the pedlar men would all reach into their pockets as if for crowns and sovereigns and pretend to take up a collection for the directors in London.

It might be murder the week before or the week after but the holiday week was always like that.

When David came up to listen, John Bowman looked at him with feigned sadness and seemed to be wiping a tear from his eyes. "David," he said, and for a moment seemed overcome, "David, we've learned that your company hasn't received a copper tuppuns since 1798——"

"Seventeen ninety-eight!" a voice broke in, and the huge lubber belched and collapsed over his knees.

"The tragic part," John went on, moving the skin up and down between his eyes, "is that it'll get worse before it gets better."

As though all their emotions were controlled in common the pedlars exploded, and among others, John Bowman had to stand up and fight for air. Confound them, David thought, they had no more daring, no more stamina, no more hair on their muscle, but all in all they were of coarser fiber, closer to the earth and to their physical functions. You just couldn't get a wind up against their brag. You just couldn't match them in malicious give-and-take.

David drew a handkerchief and offered it to John. "Wipe your tears away."

John looked solemnly around him, again flirting the skin up and down between his eyes. "David, my dearest friend—and he is my dearest friend," he said, staring round at the owlish faces. "David, you make me think of the bravest Hudson's Bay man I ever knew. He was a Scot, of course"—he gave a sly wink to a French Canadian—"and like our friend here, he belonged to the Donald clan, greatest of all the clans in the finest country on earth. His name was Don Donald." For a few moments John looked at the faces, and the pedlars looked at one another, their faces almost bursting with glee.

"Now this Don Donald was a mighty hunter. He went out to get himself a buffalo, but all he had was his six gun and his horse was afraid and it was barren country, without a tree from sunup to sundown. Well, after a while he saw a nice fat bull standing all alone and he got off his horse downwind, and soft as an Indian with goosedown in his moccasins he slipped up. He got within thirty feet. He aimed his pistol."

A pedlar erupted in a violent snort. "Goddamn!" he gasped. "It kills me!" He blew slobber into his hands.

John Bowman went on, his eyes turning from face to face. "He aimed his pistol, just like I said. He fired, and nowhere around him was there a better shot than Don Donald of the Donald clan. He saw the hair part just behind the shoulder, just about where the heart should be. The big bull swung around and tossed his forelocks up and took a good look. Don fired again. He put that bullet right on top of the first, and a third bullet on top of the two; and that big bull began to snort blood and his eyes turned red. Don emptied his gun, and the bull figgered he'd had enough of this kind of play and, snorting blood as high as the moon and digging his chisels into the earth, he took in after Don lickety-split and Don took out for the horizon. Men, I swear by our mothers, that was a foot race. The bull was so close to Hudson's Bay's mightiest hunter that he painted the back of him red and almost blew him down, and after a couple of miles Don could tell by the wind that the bull was gaining. He calculated he had another good ten miles in him at about the same speed."

The big lubber threw his arms out, sobbing, looking strangled, his moans begging for mercy. He staggered to his feet, his eyes bulging. It was killing him, he said.

"At about the same speed!" another pedlar gasped.

"Approximately," John said blandly. "But the bull was picking up a little, for as he unloaded a part of his blood he had less ballast and got lighter——"

"Oh my God!" another pedlar cried, and got up and staggered off.

"Besides the dung he was blowing out."

"Ohhh, you're killing me!"

John turned to David. "They always feel bad this way when one of your men gets in trouble. Still, this story doesn't have an unhappy ending. Now Don, he was telling himself that if he who runs away lives to fight another day, he who shins up a tree does a lot better and up a tree he went."

"You liar!" a pedlar cried, feigning great anger. "You said there wasn't no tree from sunup to sundown. These here lies sours my stomach and my drink starts fermenting all over again."

David was grinning. He suspected that a few of the pedlars had rehearsed this story before coming over.

John was scowling at the one who had interrupted. "Have you never seen a mirage lake or a mirage tree?"

The big fellow faced John, hands on his hips, eyes glowering, lips turning out with disgust. His voice thick with scorn and rum and buffalo hump, he growled, "I suppose you'll tell us next it was a mirage buffalo!"

John turned an innocent face on David. David's own face had turned a little red. No, you couldn't match these bastards in cunning and malice. John had fixed his bland innocence on other HB men, looking at them around the circle; and at last with a slight shrug he said, "A mirage buffalo? How preposterous!"

David turned away, thinking the double-entendre not bad. He was also thinking that the HB Company ought to keep all its eyes on John Bowman.

For a week the men drank and feasted and slept and entered hell at varying depths, depending on the man. La Brute was there with his squaw wife, and in one mood he would make a courtly bow to a woman and kiss her hand (on the palm, never on top) and inquire after her health in his highfalutin jargon, and in another mood he would beat his wife so brutally that David would have him tossed out into the snow. That did no good. The wife then set up a frenzied wailing, and white men looked at her and marveled at the devotion of some squaws to the husbands who flogged them. A squaw would bow her neck, forehead on the earth, and the man could kick all the hell and lightning out of her, yet if he did not knock her senseless she would be up presently, his slave again, his mistress and tool, her eyes mutely regarding him with what white men took to be love.

If not love, they said, what was it?

La Brute's woman was a fat shapeless dirty thing but she seemed to love her man. Was it because most of the time he was such a gentleman, with courtly ways and tender kisses? Was it because he seemed so educated and mannered?

It was a riddle, the white men said, looking at her bruised and bleeding face. The Indian was a riddle, that was all. Maybe Donald Mackenzie and John McLoughlin and Colin Robertson and a few others understood them, but for most white people they were a language that it was a waste of time trying to read.

And so, some said, were the half-breeds. La Brute fancied himself not only as a lady-killer but as the champion drinker in the north country, though half the men there could drink him under the birch canoes. He was chiefly swagger and brag. On being readmitted, frozen almost stiff, his hands turning purple, he would walk in his outlandish courtly way over to the fire and thaw himself out and then challenge any man, red or white, to a drinking bout. He would look round him, John Bowman said, with the air of Lord Selkirk. His face was scarred, one side of his lower lip hung repulsively open, and the hazel-brown band encircling the iris of his eyes gave a man the feel of frost on his spine. He would shout a few moments at Payette and Payette would say:

"Can drink down any man."

"Any man!" roared La Brute fiercely.

Day after day the two companies tried to satirize one another. They had all heard not only of the feasts but of the hell-roaring drinking bouts that the North Westers held at their club; and of how when a number of them got drunk they would sit on the floor, one behind another like men in a canoe, and pretend that they were rowing. When the HB men pantomimed this before the big fire the pedlars made up another brigade and challenged them to a race; and a dozen men in each of two rows bent forward and straightened and pulled with their arms and groaned and flung taunts, as in the actual brigades they so often did, on the Saskatchewan or Clearwater or Churchill, on Lake Winnipeg or the Lake of the Woods. At the head of the pedlar line was Bowman's bully boy, his face dark and scowling, his eyes fixed on the HB men with the kind of contempt that a stupid man reveals.

Some of the men pretending to row had been oarsmen and all of them had been with brigades. It was inevitable that a pedlar should soon burst into the "Canadian Boat Song," which a grateful Tom Moore had written for the North West Company on his visit in 1804: "'Faintly as tolls the evening chime—'" He paused, waited. "All right, men!" And all twelve of them, some tuneful, some tuneless, now roared through the verses:

> *"Faintly as tolls the evening chime,*
> *Our voices keep tune and our oars keep time.*
> *Soon as the woods on the shore look dim,*
> *We'll sing at St. Anne's our parting hymn!*
> *Row, brothers, row, the stream runs fast,*
> *The rapids are near and the daylight's past. . . ."*

The HB men could only listen, for they had no boat song of their own. It was a hell of a note that a company which had been in existence since 1670 had no boat song, while the pedlars, a gang of upstarts and poachers, had a song written by a famous poet:

> *"Blow, breezes, blow, the stream runs fast.*
> *The rapids are near and the daylight's past. . . ."*

Jim had come up to stand with David and listen. "This is better," he said. "They were getting too damned friendly."

"Look at them. You'd never think they were dying to cut one another's throats."

"A man's a funny thing," Jim said. He was staring at the bully boy. In a lower voice he said to David, "I've heard the bully is going to pick a fight with you tonight."

David turned to look at him.

Jim said, "Don't hurt him too much. Leave him a couple of teeth and his collarbone."

Those who had been voyageurs knew some French songs, and a few men in both brigades were now singing:

*"J'ai cueilli la belle rose!*
*J'ai cueilli la belle rose!*
*Qui pendait au rosier blanc:*
*La belle rose*
*qui pendait au rosier blanc*
*la belle rose du rosier blanc. . . ."*

Those who did not know the French songs became impatient and one, regularly bending forward and sweeping back with his arms, burst forth above all the voices:

"'My darling, smile on me!' Hey, you bastards, shut up that rose stuff and sing with me!" Then a dozen voices were roaring:

*"My darling, smile on me!*
*No, no, good sir, I do not dare!*
*My dear papa would know, would know!*
*But who would tell your papa?*
*The birds on the forest tree. . . ."*

Jim turned to look at David. "Your girl here yet?"

"No," said David, shaking his head.

"Why in hell isn't she?"

"No idea."

"Well, damn it, we have to have a belle rose. I thought she was to be it."

David shrugged. "I'm forgetting her."

Jim rumbled. He said once a man imagined himself in bed with a woman he never forgot her until after they had been in bed.

David looked at him. "So that's the way it is."

"With most men. You'd better get her over here New Year's Eve. I want a look at her."

That was the rub: how was he to get the wench over here? Was he to allow Brave Feathers to bring her, or if he did not would the chief come fired with murder? Should he go with a dog sled and ask her to come with him? He liked the thought of riding four or five miles with her to the music of bells but he knew that she would not come with him. He was not sure that she would come at all, though women, both white and red, thought it a great honor to be la belle rose at this season.

Perhaps he should put the matter up to Mink Tails. He was an intelligent chief, statesman more than warrior, indulgent, humorous, wise. So with the help of Payette, David explained his problem, and Mink Tails, almost twinkling at him, said he would take care of it. "Tell him she is to be beautiful, very beautiful."

Payette communicated the words and Mink Tails said, "*Kapsualla kopa kloochman?*"

David understood the Chinook jargon: the chief had asked if he wanted to elope with the girl. That astonished him, because Indians in general did not approve elopements and severely punished them.

"No," said David, shaking his head. He thought Mink Tails looked disappointed.

It was arranged that Sunday would come in a dog sled with Mink Tails, to arrive about eight o'clock in the evening; and David was amused to discover himself as eager and impatient as a young man with his first love. Over and over while doing his chores and trying to maintain order within the stockade he wondered about her: would her hair be drenched with bear fat, would her face be hideously smeared with vermilion, would she stink to high heaven, would she be in a vicious mood, would she dance with him, would she try to humiliate him by playing up to Brave Feathers?

Should he do something special for Mink Tails? He decided to make up a Christmas parcel for the old chief, of his finest pemmican, a quart of uncut rum, a few pounds of powder and ball, a staghafted dagger, a silver buckle, a few specially fine golden eagle feathers that he had intended to send to a sister. In his room he made it up as carefully as though it were a treasure to be sent to Scotland, wrapping each item separately in the softest buckskin and all of them together in a fringed leather cape. He had an uneasy feeling that he was being pretty free with HB property—and a feeling that he was being pretty damned silly. Was he trying to bank insurance against the hazards that awaited him this winter? He supposed he was.

He was annoyed to find himself trembling a little as the hour of her arrival drew near. By God, but he was stupid! In the past hour he had climbed the ladder three or four times, ostensibly to see if the guards were at their posts or to smell out the weather but really to scan the path leading to the village. Twenty minutes before eight o'clock he was at the post gate, the parcel in his arms, blood singing in his ears. He knew that promptness was not a red virtue: the sled might not come for an hour or two. Then it occurred to him that he should have made up a parcel for Sunday and, like the most lovelorn man on earth, he dashed to the trading room and in frantic haste looked at shelves, into bins, at bales of supplies and at last said to hell with it. He could do it later if he wanted to do it.

He returned to the post gate and stood there shivering, waiting, peering out. When he heard the sound of bells his emotions would have been no closer to the surface if he had stepped over the threshold on the river Dee and found his father and mother in their old familiar places. Trying to seem unconcerned and casual, he opened the gate and went out.

## XVIII

He thought at first that Sunday had not come but that was because she sat behind the monstrously fat chief. When David walked up to the sled he saw her, with only a part of her face showing, she was so deeply bundled; and he bowed to her and asked wryly, "How is my wife tonight?" Mink Tails could not have understood the words but his fat gentle face spread into a grin.

"Papo," David said, looking at her. "Mamo. Babo." He pronounced it bay-bow, drawing the vowels out. "Baby babo," he said, and rocked his arms back and forth, smiling. Mink Tails tried to turn to look at her but was unable to. He said something to her in his own tongue and swiftly she looked up to meet David's eyes in the moonlight.

David presented the parcel to Mink Tails and the old chief beamed up at him, his eyes agleam with anticipation. As a child might have done, he shook the parcel, trying to tell what was inside; and he must have heard a gurgle of rum, for his face became a picture of delight.

"*Kaso?*" he asked.

David nodded yes and said, "*Kaso—muckamuck—polally.*" Mink Tails was solemnly nodding. "*Otchoos.*" The chief grunted and opened his eyes a little wider. Food was all right, yes, but he wanted rum, mucha rum. So again David said, "*Kaso.*"

Reassured, the chief grinned and cradled and rocked the parcel as if it were a baby. David had not known that an Indian could be so playful. He then helped the old chief rise from his robes and leave the sled, and when he was out of it he turned to Sunday and rocked the parcel and made cooing Indian sounds. Her face softened. There came to her eyes a deeper warmth than David had ever seen there.

He stepped over and put a hand out, indicating that he would assist her, but she moved away from him and left the sled by the opposite side. At the gate he called one of his men and told him to feed and shelter the dogs and then stepped back so that Sunday and the chief could enter first. Mink Tails preceded her. That white men let their women go first Indians took to be a sign of foolishness in the head.

David took them to the central hall, bright with firelight and loud with sounds of revelry. There in firelight he turned to look at Sunday, beginning at her hair and moving down to her feet; and he thought how stupid he had been to imagine that she would try to look like anything but a squaw. Her braided hair shone as if it had been pulled out of a barrel of bear fat, her cheeks were grotesquely brilliant with vermilion, and under her eyes and across her forehead she had daubed some blackness, possibly soot from lodge fire embers. But in her leather jacket and skirt and moccasins she was a trim figure. She stood, looking round her as he sized her up, and though she knew that he was sizing her up she gave no sign of it. A few moments later a servant called him away.

Bowman's bully boy had become unmanageable. He was pig-drunk. For an hour he had been roaring a challenge to all the HB men, the loser's life to be the winner's award; and when no one would drink with him he said he could lick any HB man in the post.

"He says he'll lick you before the night is over." It was Pierre speaking. "Mebbe you better knock him out."

"I never hit a man who's drunk if I don't have to."

Pierre's eyes were looking hard at David. "There are pedlars and Indians waiting to see what you'll do."

David's anger came up. "A woman, too, why don't you say?" It was the custom with both companies to strap unruly men to their sleds and send them off to their post. If he did that, would they think he was afraid of this braggart? Was vanity to be allowed to rewrite rules and overthrow customs? "Have him strapped to his sled and send him home."

Pierre was still looking at David.

David lost his temper. "Goddamn it, man, did you hear me?"

"Yes, sir," Pierre said. "But this is no ordinary time."

It got a man's guts up in the north country to be thought a coward. "What do you mean?"

"The fight that's coming up and all that. You going out alone this winter and all that."

David looked at Pierre a long moment. "All right, where is he?"

Pierre led the way and David followed him to the far side of the hall, where men were drinking and roaring, and on seeing David approaching, Bully Boy stood up and shook his head as a buffalo bull might that was getting ready to charge.

David looked round him at the men and then at John Bowman. "John," he said, and his voice was resonant with anger, "you know as well as I do what our companies do with men who get out of line. But it seems some of you have the idea I'm afraid of your—uh—bully boy. I'd thought it was quite well known that I'm afraid of no man." He paused a moment. He was looking into Bowman's eyes. "I don't like to fight a man in his liquor. Do I knock this fool out or do you put him in his sled and send him home?"

John Bowman's eyes were hard and steady for another few moments. Then he flashed a quick smile and said, turning to one of his men, "Strap him to it and send him out."

Pedlar men at once seized Bully Boy and bore him down. David turned away. The Indians and half-breeds, he supposed, would not learn at once how the matter had been settled but they would find out and it would be all right. In this country every man was on call twenty-four hours a day to prove his courage and it got pretty damned tiresome. Courage was a hell of a thing when it became an obsession. That was what made the red man such an awful bore: as soon as an Indian boy could think he began the ordeal of proving to his people and to himself that he was one of the bravest of the brave and this became an obsession that dominated his life and ceased only with his death.

David was so upset and so deeply angry that he went away by himself a little while to recover his poise. He thought it pretty silly that every post should have a bully and that he had been chosen as the bully here. He had never felt like that kind of man and he suspected that that kind of man was a coward at heart. Looking into a mirror to see if his face was all right, he again noted the hint of a dimple in his strong chin, his wide straight mouth, his handsome nose, his steady hazel eyes that seemed to have been washed with blue, his fine forehead. It had been said that David McDonald was the handsomest man in the north country but he had never thought about it save now and then when he looked in a mirror, and then he was curious rather than vain. He had on his finest buckskin suit, fringed and beaded and with the delightful smell of woods smoke in it, and he was a figure of a man, tall and deep and broad, his belly flat, his legs straight, six feet two in his moccasins. He was wondering if Sunday would dance with him. He supposed she didn't know how to dance any of the white man's dances, that she would think the skirling of bagpipes pretty infernally silly. Well, one of the men had a fiddle and its music might suit her better.

With his emotions at their normal temperature he returned to the main hall and stood with his back to firelight, his eyes searching the revelers. Nobody seemed to be very gay tonight. Most of the men had been drinking for days and had exhausted themselves, and some of them sat back to the wall and dozed and some lay stretched out snoring. The Indians were in a group, the squaws almost out of sight behind the bucks; it was always that way with these people: the white man had to be faithful to Indian customs, and if he invited them to eat with him the squaws had to be seated so that it was plain that their men occupied a social level far above them. It was hard to know how to woo a creature who had been taught that her sex was inferior and who looked with contempt on anyone who questioned it. Customs, he reflected, ran deep. It seemed possible to teach a child to believe practically anything and the more contrary it ran to reason the more tenaciously he would cling to it.

"Soon be 1816," Jim said, coming over to him. "How you feel?"

"A year older."

"Where's your girl?"

"With the squaws, I reckon."

"Can't see you're getting very far delting with the lassie."

"I'm not much good at splunting," David said.

"You bashful?"

"I just don't know much about such things."

"Me neither," Jim said. "But I learned this much: the thing a woman likes best in a man is boldness."

"The hell," David said, turning to look at him. "I thought you had to be kinda gentle with them."

"Boldness can be gentle. Be bold, be tender, then no woman can resist you. That's what they tell."

"I'll be damned," David said. "You seem to know a lot about these things."

"In Scotland they say it. The lassie in Scotland, she likes her man bold."

"And big," David said.

The fiddler was tuning up. "You might introduce me," Jim said.

"Sure," David said.

They crossed the big hall to the group of squaws and at once the eyes of the red men were on them. David glanced at Tanino's nose and then looked at Sunday, who was sitting behind her.

"How do I do it?" David asked, looking at Jim. "Mr. Dugald, may I present the Princess Sunday, granddaughter of Mink Tails of the Sichekiekoon?"

Jim looked round him and called to Payette. When Payette came up Jim said to him, "Tell her to get out here."

Payette spoke to her, and the moment she understood what he was saying she looked up at Jim and her face darkened. But she stood up, for she thought of herself as a squaw, and she came out past Tanino and stood before Jim, and he looked her up and down, his gaze lingering at her breasts.

"Goddamn," he said, "she really has a pair of whirkins!" He looked at Payette. "Tell her to turn. Slow." Obediently Sunday turned, her lids sinking halfway to hide the contempt in her eyes. "She's white," Jim said, "all white and as pretty as a picture. Well, see if she'll dance with you." He told Payette to tell her that David wanted to dance with her.

When Payette spoke to her she began to back away. She looked round her, at the squaws, over at the Indian men, at Jim, at David, like one who felt herself trapped and was looking for friends. David thought it was that but was soon to realize that it was not that at all. Jim was looking deeper. He sensed something, for he turned to the fiddler and called out a tune and said, "Let her go!"

David did not understand that by *her* Jim meant Sunday.

Jim turned to Payette and said sharply, "She dance . . . order . . . me order."

Jim then touched David's arm to indicate that he was to move back, and the men moved back, leaving Sunday standing alone. There was no sound but the fir explosions in the fire, the zany frenzy of the fiddle, and the snoring. When Sunday still made no move Jim called to the fiddler, "Change your tune!" and he changed to one and another and still she did not move. Jim stepped over and looked into her eyes in what David thought was a queer way, and raised a hand to silence the violinist. He then had Payette speak to the nine or ten squaws huddled together and almost at once they began a low mournful blood-chilling dirge—for though Indians might have thought of it as singing it was a dirge for David, a wild sad lamentation without words, a music as ancient, as timeless, as nationless and raceless as the first cries of the first women.

Sunday moved now. She did not move quickly, as a white woman might have, throwing herself abruptly into a dance, but with soft feline movements, as though relaxing her will and her passions. Her first gestures seemed to say that she was a furtive slinking soundless treacherous thing—that she was a woman of the night, of the forests . . . Or was that what she was saying? David looked uneasily at Jim. Jim seemed to be hypnotized.

There was something so barbarous in the chanting and in the dance that they took hold of David, and he thought that rather strange, for he was a white man, he had been out of the jungles a long time. Yet he thought he saw the jungle rising in Jim's face; it was something ugly and primal and terrifying, and it was in the faces of the chanting squaws. David looked away. He looked at the Indians, and away; at Sunday, and away. His emotions mixed and confused and darkening, he tried to look at her with detachment; to note her incomparable grace of movement; the passion she put into certain gestures that were, he supposed, symbolic—but again and again his gaze returned to her face, for deep emotion had distorted it, had made it look murderous, and he wondered dully what her dance meant. In one brief scene she seemed to be tomahawking. She seemed to be slipping up, as silent as a weasel and as deadly, and then she was killing, she was striking with all the savage force of her being; and then she spun and seemed to look down at a slain thing, contemptuous, her lips ugly with scorn. Were the red men destroying the white, or what did it mean? It meant something that had brought passions to the surface in the red men—and the chanting, he now realized, had deepened, had quickened in tempo, darkened in fury, until he had felt choked and was breathing hard—a white man looking at a white woman dance. Then the chanting was falling away into a wailing withdrawing and hushing, so sad, so mournful that it was like a mother's dirge above the death of all her children, for she had slain, this woman; she had strewn the prairie or the village, and not a gaze had left her to wander, to question and speculate, not a gaze but David's; all the others seemed fascinated, spellbound, as this white woman who had become red dramatized for them with her vivid and impassioned and chilling symbols something almost too primitive for a white man to think of without shuddering. David could feel the darkness of the jungle falling over him and sense the deeper meaning of blazing fires and marrow dug out of bones, and he could imagine that death stood at the windows looking in. He didn't like the way he felt, not if he thought of himself as a civilized man, and he didn't trust himself either. He'd not have been surprised if the room had burst into jungle cries and killing.

Jim went forward and seized her arm and shook her and David saw then that she seemed to be in a kind of trance. She came up to her full height, stiff-like, as though her passions had run cold. Jim had Payette speak to her, then Mink Tails and Tanino. Tanino spoke to her group. The quality of their singing or chanting changed and Sunday changed with it, as if she were only a thing of moods, instantly responsive to the mood you asked for.

Her first move astonished David. She came up to him, in a kind of slipping dimpling movement, in her soft catlike way, the way that put frost in his blood; and when for a moment she stood poised and looked up into his eyes his heart leaped and all his blood seemed to pour and he was about to obey an impulse and seize her when he became aware that one of her hands had lifted the fire bag from his girdle. In the next instant, with the pouch in her hand, she swung, tall then to her full height, head up and back, and tossed the bag about thirty feet out onto the floor. There was a rumbling from the throats of the white men around John Bowman.

What was the meaning of the chanting now? It was more mournful, sadder, lonelier, and her dancing was that way now, her dancing around the fire bag, her eyes looking down at it; and what in heaven's name was the meaning of this? David asked himself the question and felt his face turning red. This grieving mother for her child—this female that sees—but no; God, no! He turned swiftly to look at Jim but Jim had eyes only for Sunday, they all had eyes only for Sunday, dancing around David McDonald's fire bag, with only heaven knew what menace or intimations or haughty scorn: was the mother in it somewhere, was there grief in it, could he feel sadness in her movements and hear it in the voices of the women?—or was it contempt? Lord, was it contempt! It made David feel unspeakably foolish to have a girl dancing around his fire bag that way as if around his corpse—no, not that but as if around——

She stooped swiftly and picked it up and emptied its contents, and flints, balls, and powder spilled over the floor and she flung the pouch away, and then—he almost doubted his senses—she threw herself down in a position of grief, of grief over the contents; and if her hair had not been braided it would have spread over them in a protective covering, as she was protective in the position she had taken. His face redder, David glanced round him and saw John Bowman staring at him, his eyes cold and curious. Then Jim was going out to her and he took her arm and helped her rise and, as if all this had been rehearsed between them, led her back to the women and stood with her a few moments, his bold Northern eyes looking into her eyes, over her face; and in a way that was fatherly but not fatherly at all he pinched her chin and turned back to David.

They needed a drink, he said. But first he had Payette thank Sunday and tell Mink Tails that hot drinks would come over soon and there would great roasts and feasting a little later. Then with David he went to his small private chamber that served as bedroom and office. It had a small fireplace and a servant to tend it; the room was cozy, though the temperature outside was twenty below zero. From its hiding place Jim drew forth a bottle of fine old brandy and set it on the table. "Help yourself."

David poured a tin cup full.

Jim poured a smaller drink and sat and looked at David. "A lot of woman there," he said at last. "You in love with her?"

"I reckon so," David said, still feeling foolish.

"Want to marry her?"

"I reckon."

"I'm a little daft about her myself," Jim said. "I could go a-winching right now."

"What's holding you?"

"She's your girl. Did you understand the dances?"

"I don't know. Did you?"

"Some," Jim said. "I've seen the Blackfeet dance a hundred times but I never know how much I understand. My people lived too long in Scotland." He studied David a few moments. "You know, Dave, I think I'd better send somebody else out to the posts."

"Like hell you will." He was looking at Jim. "So that's what you think the dance meant."

"Hell no, not that."

"You think it meant——"

"All I know, Dave, is that they were death dances. It doesn't mean they had anything to do with you."

"We both know they had something to do with me."

"All right. I'd guess the girl's in love with you."

"And so does a death dance for me."

"Well, love's a queer thing, don't ever think it isn't. Why do the muskrats chew one another all to hell when they mate? Why does the spider eat her lover? Why did Tum-tum come up at me with her teeth bared and her face snarling?"

For a few minutes the two men were silent, Jim looking at David, David looking at the fire.

At last Jim said, "All right, you go if you want to but be damned sure that you come back."

## XIX

As the old year died everyone fired a gun who could afford powder and ball. It had been a custom to fire three-pound metal carronades but two years ago the man assigned to fire the gun and a part of the bastion he was in had been blown to pieces. This year after the firing of guns there was gift giving, a New Year's custom with Scots; more drinking, feasting, handshaking, boasting; but many of the celebrants were too weary to see the night through and rolled into buffalo robes and slept. David sent Jim to bed but himself stayed awake to oversee matters, and to keep himself from getting too drowsy he drank hot rum and stayed on his feet. Among the sleeping squaws was Sunday, lying on one side, her cheek on a palm, her buckskin revealing the slenderness of her waist and the rising curve of her hip. Once when David stood looking down at her he became aware that a squaw had one eye half open and that the eye was looking at him.

At daylight the Indians were sent to their lodges, the men from the Augustus post went home, and the others got ready to depart.

Those who had come from distant posts had carioles, sleds of birch boards twelve feet long, the sides covered with parchment skins painted with bright colors. There were four husky dogs to each sled. The departing official wrapped himself so deep in buffalo robes that he could barely move, and sitting bundled up in the sled, he looked cozy enough. If he was an important official and the trail was difficult he might have a man on snowshoes to go ahead and another on snowshoes behind to drive the dogs and see that the sled did not upset. It was their custom to depart about three o'clock in the morning, as the brigades did, but these were not ordinary times and some of the men were gone before noon of New Year's Day.

The truce was over, the war between the companies was resumed.

During the long night awake David thought about his own imminent departure and of the vast country into which he would go alone—up the Saskatchewan first and into the ganglion of tributaries, the Scab and Ram and Clearwater and Wolf and Biche rivers; and maybe northwest to the Sturgeon, Anne's Lake, Paddle River, the Muskeg, even the Smoky, even the Athabasca. He told himself he ought to get his feckless mind in kilter and be sure that he was taking everything he would need. He would have to go by cariole, of course; the rivers were frozen over now save in their rapid waters and the snow crust was frozen deep enough to hold a bull. Just the same he would take a spade, he would write down a list of the things: dog feed for two months and plenty of it, because some days he might want to journey eighty miles or more; six or seven hundred pounds of dried fish, and for himself two ninety-pound bags of pemmican, for a man ate like hell in deep-zero weather. He would need twenty pounds anyway of powder and ball, a few gallons of rum, a pile of trinkets, two long sharp knives but no razor, for he would let his beard grow; enough robes to keep him warm, and extras to make windbreaks for the dogs—it looked as if it would be a hell of a load for four dogs.

After breakfast he talked with Jim. Some of the men coming in had given Jim a picture of certain areas and Jim said he should go first to Acton House and the upper reaches because things looked bad there. Then he could swing up toward the headwaters of the Athabasca and on, depending on how he smelled the thing out, river by river. The honorable company had to get its share of the furs in any way that it could.

David said he could be at Acton House in a couple of days.

"Maybe."

"Why do you say maybe?"

"You'll be going through Blackfoot country and Blood country. Better keep under the hills as much as you can . . . along streams and timber."

David shrugged. A lot of difference it would make if the Indians were out to get him! A man couldn't hide from them; he might as well get on the highest hill and run up a banner with his name on it as to slink along in the shadows of timbered streams. David figured that his only protection would lie in being always on the alert and having his gun ready.

Was he forgetting anything? He asked himself the question over and over. He would stand and look at his feet and think up his body: footwear, it was usually the feet that froze first but he had furlined boots and socks with the fur turned inside; trousers, he had heavy underwear and an inner pair of leather britches, fur inside; shirt and coat and greatcoat, beaver cap, two pairs of mittens furlined; several flints in his fire bag; a pair of snowshoes; a pistol besides his musket and leather straps to repair dog harness, with needles and thread; materials to repair his cariole. What else? All one day he packed, checked and rechecked, and all the next day, turning the things over and over in his mind, curious to know why he felt such concern, eager for a last glimpse of Sunday. It was true that a journey alone into the dead of winter was a gamble with death but he had gone in other times without feeling such anxieties. Yes, but never for so long, so deep, and never with bitter enemies waiting for him. What else did he need? He would need soot to protect him from snow blindness and he gathered a pouchful at the fireplace. An ax, of course; an extra powder horn; some balsam juice in case he got wounded; some writing materials to make notes. And what else? He could think of nothing more.

He went to bed at dark and slept soundly and was up at two in the morning. There was a full moon. He went to Jim's room to see if there were any last-minute instructions or advice. Jim said he would be out in a minute. He said he didn't suppose David wanted any bells or things on the harness and he had had them soaked extra good in grease so there would be no leather squeaks. It was such remarks that made David wonder about Jim, for Jim knew as well as any man in this country would know that the harness might as well squeak as loud as Red River carts and it might as well have bells on it. Ordinarily if a man thought he would be trailed he wanted a silent harness and dogs with cat feet but it made no difference now.

The dogs were set and ready to go when Jim came in. He bent over the sled and felt down among the luggage and shoved a parcel down, saying, "A bottle of old brandy, but never drink when you're cold."

David thought, He isn't meeting my eyes the way he usually does.

"Sure you have everything?" Jim asked.

"I reckon."

Jim put out his hand and he met his eyes then and he said, "Be damn sure you come back." Then he turned quickly away, David crawled into the sled, the gate was opened, the dogs strained at the leashes and he was off—out of the post and into the immensity of a moonlit frozen night, the snow like a prairie of white stone with millions of tiny frost points scattered over it. This was one of the best dog teams in the north country; he had only to speak softly to the leaders to guide them, and he spoke and they swung and he was off into the southwest, where he thought he could see distant mountains looking like slightly heavier sky. There would be no streams to speak of for some time, no water but small creeks buried deep under snow until he came to Pigeon Lake and Battle Lake, and they might be frozen over; and then there would be—well, Buck Lake or Gull Lake, depending on which way he veered. He had no idea where he would spend the coming night: a man and his dogs didn't need water, they could eat snow; but they needed shelter. He didn't know how far it was to the posts far up the North Saskatchewan: if a man spent most of his time traveling by canoe, following all the meanderings of a river, he had little idea of distance as the crow flew. He looked up at the stars to fix his direction and judged that he was going almost exactly into the southwest. He looked back but knew that there would be nothing to see. He reached down to be sure of the exact position of his gun. As long as he was out in the open this way the Indians would never molest him. They would wait until he entered timber.

It was cold, colder than he had realized. A man got soft in wintertime living in a post and sucking his pipe by big fires and sleeping four or five deep under buffalo robes in a room sixty degrees warmer than out-of-doors. He felt delightfully snug: his feet were warm, his hands were warm in big mittens full of fur, he was warm all over except the exposed part of his face. Off on his left a half mile distant three wolves were standing, bellied down, their eyes on the dogs. They looked gaunt. He turned again with difficulty to have a view of the country behind him; it was a gently rolling wonderland of white. Even in moonlight the world was so dazzling that his eyes ached and a part of the time he kept them closed and was then conscious only of the swaying of the cariole, the rasping sound of it on snow, the smell of fresh grease in the dog harness, the smell of dogs and the soft sound of their feet.

Daylight came so gray that the world looked wasted. An hour after sunup he gave each dog a dried fish and was off again, until mid-afternoon looking round him or closing his eyes and dreaming. He guessed it was Pigeon Lake three or four miles on his left and he guessed Buck Lake was some fifteen miles straight west of it. Earlier in the journey he had seen the marks of sleds that had come in and gone but there was no sign of them now. He supposed their line was farther north. This was open prairie country and sometimes its winds were so bitter that even the wolves froze to death. The pedlars in parts of the Athabasca were lucky dogs, for they had hot springs. There were a lot of hot springs yonder against the mountains; he had heard it said that a man could travel for seven days and camp by a hot spring each night. But there were no hot springs in this prairie land, only frozen rivers and lakes, frozen earth and trees and winds.

A little before dusk he saw wooded growth on a creek that flowed north to Buck Lake and decided to spend the night there. The country ahead looked open and timberless. A wind was rising and both man and dogs needed shelter, and though the creek was frozen over or snowed over he pushed back into a thicket and unhitched and unharnessed the dogs and caressed down their strong faces and over their eyes. These north country dogs were a marvel: they were stronger than a wolf by far and more cheerful than a bluejay in April. All they asked was their daily ration, a little affection, a place to sleep, and day after day they served a man more faithfully than anything else under the sun. These were Jim's dogs and he had named them for islands off Scotland: Eigg, Canna, Rum, and Coll. Coll was the leader, and the biggest and smartest dog at the post. Jim said he was a lot smarter than most men. "Coll, old boy," David said, patting over his face, "would you like a little fight with a wolf tonight?" Coll looked up, his eyes questioning.

David put the cariole back against overhanging birch and willow and spaded a clearing alongside it, so that the dogs could sleep there and be between him and Indians or wolves if they came. Wolves would come, of course. They always did. Then with the ax he cut through to gurgling water so that the dogs could drink. He was not thirsty but he forced himself to drink a tin cup full; Jim said the trouble with cold weather was that a man didn't drink enough water and got his bowels all buttoned up. He then ate a hunk of pemmican, pausing now and then to listen, and arranged the robes in the cariole and stretched out, his weapons close to his right hand. A journey in the dead of winter was tough, but not so tough as in the heat of summer, when insect pests made life hell on earth for man and beast. The mosquitoes in this country were so big that they stung like wasps, and men had written home so many times to say they were nothing but knots and bumps that wags in Scotland called it the knot-and-bump land. David had seen men in the muskeg country with their eyes swollen shut. . . .

He guessed he must have dozed off, for he became conscious of low deep growls and he said, "Coll, old fellow, what is it?" But he knew what it was. They were howling and they would howl all night. With an effort he got his face up so that he could see. All four dogs had arched backs, their hair rising, anger rumbling deep in their throats; and out there only seventy-five yards distant was a pack of wolves that looked as thin as shadows. The nice thing about dogs like these was that they never attacked without orders; they might growl like the devil and work up a prodigious rage but they wouldn't leap to a wolf even if it came within a few feet. Unless it was a female looking for a mate. David had never ceased wondering why the female wolf preferred to mate with a dog or why some men were so fiendishly brutal. When copulation-bound both dog and bitch were helpless and it was then that certain men, and by no means always half-breeds, would rush in and club the bitch to death.

"Coll, be still."

What fights wolves and dogs had in the rutting season! They disputed possession of mates with a savage fury and a rending of flesh and fur that made a duel between two bulls look gentle. The wolves out there were softly trotting, stopping to look, trotting, back and forth in the way of creatures famished but afraid. They could smell the food. He could shoot one of them and the others would tear it to pieces and devour it and then trot again, their jaws loose and drooling.

"Go to sleep," David said.

The dogs didn't intend to go to sleep. Without looking he knew how they were—lying on their bellies, their lower jaws resting on their forefeet and their eyes fixed steadily on those slinking shadows out there against the sky. They tried to obey him but they couldn't help growling a little and he smiled to hear them. If he were to say, "Go get them!" they would rush forth and shake the living daylights out of the wolves, but that was not a good thing to do. That sort of thing brought the wolf up in a dog and made it forget its training.

"Go to sleep now," he said, and snuggled back into the depths of his bedding. Jim had been traveling by dog sled one winter when about twenty wolves began to circle him, around and around, and they had made him so furious that he had turned the dogs loose. He then had hell's own time getting the dogs back into harness. That was about as close, Jim said, as he had ever come to death. David had heard it said that wolves sometimes entered tents to seize persons and he knew that most people, including Indians, lived in fear of them, but he had never had any serious trouble with them. He knew that they would move in closer. He knew that he might have to shoot before morning but he didn't want to shoot because he was deep in Indian country.

"Go to sleep," he said.

The howling became such a wild mournful thing that he was unable to sleep. He looked up at the stars and waited for daylight. When morning came he fed the dogs and examined their necks and heads for swelling, set them in the harness and was on his way, with a pack of wolves trailing him. He knew this country fairly well: Wolf River fell into Rivière la Biche and then he would ascend the Wolf Hills and he would be in pine forest and the mountains would seem quite close; then there would be Rivière à l'Eau Claire and the post would be near. . . .

It was dark when he reached it and hammered on the gate. It seemed an hour to him before Jake—David always thought of him as Silent Jake—peered out.

"Let me in!" David shouted.

The gate was unbarred, and opened wide enough to admit the sled. After caring for the dogs David went with Jake to a small room with a fire in it and said, "How are things here?" Jake shook his filthy bearded head. "No pelts?" He shook his head again. In his slow muttering way he said that the pedlars had left their Rocky Mountain House and gone out to the Indians.

"To live Indian, talk Indian, sleep Indian, think Indian," David said.

Jake nodded.

"Let's see what you have," David said, and they went to the trading room. Not much had come in—a few beaver, two otter, a half dozen fox and lynx. "This all?"

"All," Jake said.

"Jesus!" David said. "The directors in London will have a fit if it's like this everywhere."

Jake said that Indian trappers who had always trapped for the HB Company were trapping for the pedlars now. It was that way all over here.

David stared at Jake's bearded mouth, at his pale unemotional eyes. Jim had said that this man wasn't worth his pay but he would go anywhere, he would live alone all winter in the most godforsaken and dangerous outposts, he never got drunk or whored, and there weren't many men like that. You couldn't have everything in a man, Jim said. Jake was about fifty now and this north country had gone into him so deep that you couldn't see the human being any more, but only his kinship with the silent earth and its wild things. He had almost forgotten how to talk and David always felt a little queer just being around him.

Well, John Bowman's men were busy here, and the son of a bitch had probably sent Latude to the Piegans and Bloods as well as to the Blackfeet. When Bowman looked David straight in the eye and proposed a toast of friendship his plans, already formulated, called for an end of David McDonald. Was Latude in this area? Jake said he had been.

"Did you see him?"

"I smelt him."

David stared at the man, wondering if he meant that literally. You could never tell about Jake.

"Which way have the pedlars gone?"

"All over."

"Nobody in their post?"

Jake shook his head no.

"Any independents around here this winter?"

He shook his head no.

The pedlars, David supposed, had by this time taken care of all the independents and their bones would show up here and there, man by man. They had destroyed all their competitors now but HB and HB's number was up.

Looking at the gray in Jake's heavy unwashed beard, David said, "Weren't there any independents at all?"

"Was one."

It was better not to inquire into such things; Jake said there had been one, implying that there was one no more. The independents, the poor foolhardy bastards, had had a rough time of it and their bones were scattered from the headwaters of the big rivers clear to the Lake of the Woods and Thunder Bay.

"Well, guess I'll roll in," David said, and went to his cariole. It seemed to him that things looked bad, very bad.

## XX

He remained at the post a couple of weeks exploring the area roundabout, as far west as Scab River and Cripple Creek, as far south as Burnt Timber Creek and Red Deer River. He thought it a rather melancholy scene, a scene everywhere of old beaver ponds, beaver dams, and beaver houses, empty now, and trees cut down by beaver long ago. There wasn't enough trapping in this area for one post, much less two. The Piegans and Bloods were trapping far up the streams now and the Blackfeet had moved farther north. It was as plain as the gray in Jake's beard that in this area the pedlars had things their own way.

Several times he saw a man at a distance and hastened toward him, but always the man disappeared, and the glimpse of him was too brief to tell if he was white or red. David was convinced that it was one of Bowman's spies. He suspected that it was Latude. When he mentioned the matter to Jake he got only a shrug.

The cold had abated and snow was falling when, seated again in his sled, he looked at the loneliness in Jake's face. He had lived with him for days and together they hadn't spoken a hundred words. As silence went deep into such a man, year after year, words became as alien to him as shattering glass to the depths of a cathedral. David tucked the robes in and looked north, for it was into the north now, into Blackfoot land and danger.

"Which way is dog-easiest?" David asked.

Up Scab River, then across and north, Jake said.

"Well, keep your fire bag dry."

"Yeh," Jake said.

You got so out of patience with such a man, David reflected, riding north, that you wanted to kick his stupid ass, but you knew that would do no good. You wondered how he kept from losing his powers of speech altogether. Jim said that a long time ago Jake had had a squaw but for some reason she left him and there went with her the man's need of speech. There was a dark and terrible sadness in the man that made David ache to think of. Once, while smoking, he had caught Jake looking at him, and then had the feeling that Jake wanted to talk about something; but he never again caught his gaze on him or felt that the man had anything to say. When he got older he would be found dead someday, they would bury him, that was all.

He passed the black coal beds a little way down the river and then the cascades. In the afternoon he jumped a woods buffalo but never got sight of it, and he camped not more than twenty miles from the post. He felt safe there. By midmorning of the second day he jumped a red deer. He brought the dogs to a halt and picked up his gun. The deer ran from him but stopped about seventy yards away, and he took careful aim and fired, and was sure that he saw the hair part high on the shoulder. But the deer ran again. David got out of the sled and called the dogs after him, and he walked until he came to timber along a creek and there he secured Coll with a leash. Then he went after the deer. If he had shot it through the lungs it would never get up if it lay down, for it would choke to death. He thought it would lie down soon. It had taken its way through goose grass and juniper and scrub pine and willow, following the creek, and he trailed it, pausing now and then to study the signs: on a branch that had touched it in passing he saw a spot of blood and judged by the height of it that he had shot close to the heart. Or he studied the footprints when he could find them to see if the front ones showed signs of unsteadiness, or a pool of blood left at a spot where it had rested. If most of its bleeding was internal it could not go far but it did go far, it did go on and on, until he became alarmed. He would look back, wondering how far he had left the dogs behind—a mile, two miles, three—and the confounded deer still kept out of sight ahead of him. If there were Indians lurking around, or Latude, they might try to steal the sled but they would have to kill the dogs if they did. He told himself over and over that he ought to turn back but he went on and on, saying that surely the deer would be just around the next bend—for never had he seen a lung-shot deer go this far. But it was not around the next bend. The damned thing kept going, on and on, and he judged that he was now four miles from the dogs, or farther, and over forty miles from the post, and he was in Blackfoot country. He didn't like it at all. If Indians were in this area they had heard the shot, they were hastening in. Everything that he had learned in nine years in this country told him that he was being a fool, that he was placing himself in deadly peril, all for a little fresh meat. Four miles and a half now, he judged it was, and he hadn't even caught a glimpse of the beast. But he knew by signs that it was only two hundred yards ahead of him, never more than that, sometimes less; he knew that it was weary and sick; he knew that it would have to lie down, and he trotted fast, hoping to see it.

He had again come to a tiny pool of blood, and after setting his gun against a tree, had knelt to examine the footprints when he heard a sound and stiffened, his whole body rigid. In that instant even before he saw them he knew—he knew with such certainty that chills went through him like currents of ice, and in the next moment when he looked up and saw them they were just what he expected to see—a half dozen red men, one in the act of lifting his gun as the others closed around him. A lot of things go through a man's mind in a moment like that, a lot of recognitions stand big and plain. He recognized that these were Blackfeet and that they were on the warpath, for their foreheads and eyes were blackened, the rest of their faces was blood-red. He recognized that they were returning and probably had captives and that he was now their prisoner.

They had fenced him in but they hadn't touched him. He got to his feet. He looked at their faces and recognized none of them; but, hell, he couldn't recognize a redskin with his war paint on. One of them could be Brave Feathers and he would never know it. One of them could be Latude. . . . Now a hand touched him: it felt around his waist and found and lifted his dagger, and then his fire bag. Then with gestures and cries they indicated that he was to march with them, and two of them went ahead and he followed them, and the others followed behind. When he saw that they were not taking the direction to his dogs he tried to explain to them in their own tongue that his dogs and cariole were down the creek; and when they jabbered to one another, yet did not change their direction, he realized that they knew where the dogs were. Now and then he listened for shots; they would never take those dogs alive: Coll himself would tear two Indians to pieces before they could untie his leash.

Well, it was just his luck to cross their path when their blood was up. Did they know who he was? If they knew who he was and his capture was deliberate, it looked bad: it meant that the pedlars had won them over, it meant that they would torture and then kill him. Never show fear, Jim had said. . . . If they didn't know who he was they might turn him free after he had explained matters to their council of chiefs. There was no way to tell, not now. You just couldn't predict what Indians would do; they might get drunk and hack him to pieces just for the fun of it. Would Mink Tails be there? Would Coll be able to break free?

They were taking him northeast, and after a half hour or more he could see far in the distance the frozen irregular line of timber upon the Saskatchewan and he supposed that they had a winter camp there. After another mile they were joined by a band of warriors with snowshoes and dog sleds, and David looked everywhere but could see no sign of his own sled and Jim's dogs. He was sure Jim's dogs would never be taken alive. He knew that Jim would be broken-hearted if he never saw his dogs again. These other warriors were also so hideously painted and daubed that he couldn't recognize one, even if he had known him all his life. They were all on the warpath. They now went northeast toward the river with David among them, and he counted seven sleds and he thought there were twenty or twenty-one warriors. He began to feel a little more hopeful, for it seemed to him that they were treating him with unusual respect, as if uncertain of the quality of their prisoner. If that were so, Latude and Brave Feathers and Horned Thunder were not here, nor any Blackfoot who knew him as chief trader at the HB fort.

Those ahead of him were about thirty feet ahead, those behind an equal distance behind. So it was that he walked alone, feeling foolish. He wished he knew the Indian mind and heart as well as Jim or Colin or John Bowman knew it. He hadn't a ghost of a notion of what they intended to do with him. He now knew quite a few words of their tongue and wondered if he should try to talk to them; and, wondering, looked behind him at the faces and was silent. How could a man talk to such monstrous things, their foreheads and eyes as black and mysterious as Africa, the rest of their faces looking as if they had been skinned! They didn't look like men, not even like

Indians, and he sensed in them a pride in accomplishment that demanded silence. He remembered that his beard was now two inches long; possibly those who had known him could not recognize him now. He put a hand up to feel over his face: yes, it was a heavy beard all right and it covered his face high on his cheeks.

After plodding along another mile or two, listening all the while for shots that might mean the death of the dogs, he decided to speak up. In a voice they could all hear he said, "Me David McDonald! Me chief trader HB Company!" Not a face ahead of him turned. He looked behind and not a face there looked at him. The lack of any response at all was sinister, there could be no question about that: he suspected that they knew who he was and that they knew exactly what they were going to do with him. If he could only be sure of that he would make a break for it and die now. He figured that he could outrun any man here but he could not outrun their bullets. Would they shoot him or let him go? It was insane even to think of it, for if he got away and his dogs were gone he would freeze to death before he could reach a post. Still, he could burrow in snow. . . .

He would feel them out a little, if he could. "*Ohyoyet!*" he shouted, using their word for eat, and then their word for food, "*Otchoos!*" No face turned to look at him, no feet paused. Some of the warriors were riding in the sleds up ahead. There were five behind him, each with a gun in his hand; and ahead of him were six walking, two abreast, then three, then one in the lead. Those ahead of him were of about the same height and breadth and they all walked with the lazy Indian stride, as though their legs had been born weary.

Again and again his gaze swept the white prairie to the south and west for sign of his dogs. He was convinced that they had not found the dogs or had decided not to bother them. If that was so, then Coll would chew the leash in two and the dogs would set out for home. When, drawing to his fullest height, his eyes swept the distances the Indians behind him did not turn to see what he was seeing but out of the tail of his eye he saw their hands tighten on their guns. He tried to make sense out of that. They must have figured that he was thinking of making a dash for it and they must have had orders to shoot him if he did.

He could see smoke from the lodges now and he thought he could smell it but perhaps he was only smelling the smoke in the leather around him. Twenty-one braves were heading into camp with a single prisoner! He had never seen the red men enter camp with a captive but he had heard Jim and others talk about it and it was a picture to blanch just about any man's mind. Courage, Jim said, they admired above all things. Or was it fortitude? He must prepare himself. It was the squaws, the infernal murderous bitches, who came howling and shrieking to meet the captives, to spit on them and hack at them to get their blood gushing. After you learned what squaws would do you modified some of your ideas about women. Women were no longer all gentleness and compassion and pity, nor even chiefly: they were more nearly the female of the mink, the weasel, the wolverine.

While he was thinking about them and swallowing hard and trying to steel himself for what was ahead of him he heard the first shrill cries. He supposed that someone had gone on ahead with the news and that the squaws were already screaming for him; and if that was it, then by God he could expect the worst. Again his gaze swept the dazzling prairie behind him, again he wondered if he should make a dash for it while he was unbound, and again red hands tightened on their weapons and red men stepped up close to surround him.

The cries had become shrill with eagerness and a group of younger women now came running from the village, and they closed around David and began to tear and slash at him, their convulsed faces eager for the blood gush. One of the men was shouting at them and then rushing at them, tomahawk in hand, and they fell back, abashed, as wolves might, but still drooling in their way, frenzied in their joy at seeing him helpless, their savage blood up, their wild black eyes fixed on his face like the eyes of famished wolf or lynx. The experience had chilled David. For him it was so much more horrible to find women slavering in their hope of hacking him open than to find men eager to scalp him. He searched their faces to see if any was familiar but no face was, though he might have seen some of them or all of them before. He could remember a Tanino and a few like that but he couldn't remember all the red faces he had seen. Besides, they were so distorted and hideous with passions, so ugly with a wish to strike him and open him up and get his blood gushing—and then the warriors were hustling him away and into the camp and the squaws were shrieking and squealing behind, their cries wilder and more chilling than the voice of any wild beast, than even the wolf; and other squaws were coming and other braves, and they were all around him now and he could smell them as if there were a million of them as they forced him over with his back to an aspen and bound his wrists behind it. What a pitiable thing hope was; he should have made a break for it and died a decent death! Now he was bound with leather laces that had been softened in warm water and not all of hell could ever untie them nor the power of a bull moose rend them. His wrists were across one another, the right one against his back, his right fingers over toward his left side, his left fingers on his right. Squaws singly or in twos were dashing up close to peer at him with black eyes full of hate and murder, to spit up at his face; and they would have been slashing at him with knives if the men had not driven them back.

David looked at the hatred in those out-of-shape female faces and thought of all the syphilis and gonorrhea, all the rum, all the crass adulteries of the white men, all the babies born blind like Tum-tum's, or deaf or dead, all the "wives" broken down under a man's passion and dishonored and deserted, and he shut his eyes against what he saw, against the vast obscenity of the north country, feeling that if they were to tear him to pieces it was no more than he or any other white man deserved. He thought he understood more fully now Sunday's contempt, which was only her contempt for all white men. In all the other times he had seen squaws they had been cowed, they had been doing business for a trinket; he had never seen their souls as he saw them now: those who had come running out to open his veins now stood back like female beasts, crouching awkwardly, looking as if held by leashes, their black eyes on him, their red faces full of loathing, their hands twitching with eagerness to get at his throat. What a picture it was! But then he told himself that he was being sentimental: a vast obscenity, yes it was, but they would have been just as eager to see blood gushing from captives who were red—from Slave, Piegan, or Cree.

It was uncomfortable standing with your back to a tree and your hands behind it, and he began to realize that it could become torture —to realize that his hands might freeze, and his feet. He could churn his feet up and down as long as his strength lasted but he could do nothing about his hands. He could wiggle his fingers, he could clench them, he could roll his wrists a little from side to side, but that was all. If deep cold set in he would freeze as stiff as a tree. He looked up at the sun and thought the time was about two o'clock and he wished they would make up their minds about him and get it over with. He would rather endure torture than stand here like a fool tied to a tree. Tied to a tree like any simple greenhorn, knowing that John Bowman had known when he offered the toast that he would be.

Did they intend to leave him here all night? If so, he would freeze to death, and that was an easy way to die; or would the squaws come skulking out of their lodges to slice him down with their hatchets? Many years ago Jim had seen Flatheads torture Blackfeet and he said their savagery was simply incredible—but not incredible, David thought, not if you remembered the Romans, the Syrians, the Turks, the Chinese. Just the human male—and, as he understood now, the human female—or just male and female, neither human. He would be patient a little longer, for they might be holding a council to determine his fate. A little longer, and then he would make a hell of an outcry, he would curse them with every destroying curse under the seven heavens and demand to know if they had killed his dogs, to know what they meant by this insolent degradation of an official of a great company. Most of the bucks had disappeared soon after he was tied and he thought they had gone away to powwow until he heard sudden shrill wild barbarous cries among the lodges up north. He could not see what was happening there.

He stared north and waited, hoping that white men had come to free him . . . But it was not white men. It was a war-raiding party of braves coming in with captives; they brought them down past the lodges and to the area which David faced. Two bucks, bleeding, staggering, exhausted or half dead, David recognized as Crees from the lines of tattooing on the chin. Cries that would chill the blood of a wolf went shrieking skyward as the squaws pushed in to tear and hack. In the way of hope, of desperate hope, David had been thinking that the pedlars had set the Blackfeet on him to cow and intimidate him or to bring him over to their side. He had wondered if they had tied him to a tree to force him to witness their barbarities. He felt quite certain that so it was as he watched the preparations before him.

The two half-dead bucks had been gouged, slashed, trampled, beaten, and were now dragged forward until they were no more than forty or fifty feet from where David stood. The gantlet was now formed. Two rows of warriors stood about fifteen feet apart, and between them were two rows of squaws, the squaws who had been most eager to kill. The two captives were stripped to their waist and forced to grasp a slender pole with the scalp of one of their tribesmen at its top. A little way off a buck began to pound a drum. The two rows of warriors began to dance, alternately moving sideways, chanting, shouting, shrieking; and the squaws began to dance too, with what David took to be copulatory movements. They were also shrieking with such infernal ferocity and bedlam that he thought his eardrums would split. Other warriors came up to the captives and smote them with tomahawk blades, driving them into the spirit of the dance, forcing the pitiable bloody half-dead things to laugh and shout, and then to run back and forth between the two rows of women so that the women could riddle them with knives and brain them with clubs.

This savage dance of triumph over captives steadily gained in passion and violence until the whole woods area was ringing and the dogs were howling as if tortured. Both the captive bucks were weak when the torture started, and one of them from the beginning tottered and fell and got up under blows and slashes to try again like a poor feeble creature hamstrung to run between the clubs and the daggers. David thought his powers of endurance more than human, for after running seven or eight times down the gantlet he was naked to his moccasins and blood red all over and blood was gushing from a hundred wounds, yet he fell and got up to stagger along again, and still again. If there were mercy in savage hearts there should have been mercy here, for greater fortitude than this no man could have, white or red, nor greater call on pity. But there was no mercy here. David watched, hoped, prayed almost, for some sign of compassion, some move out of gentleness from buck or squaw; but there was none—only the primitive lodge smoke wildness of passions from which all human traits had blacked out; and two drums, booming out of the woods and over the frozen prairies; and squaws screaming in their savage lust to hack off a piece of living flesh and hurl it toward a fire blazing at the north end of the gantlet. Though hurt from a hundred or a thousand wounds it was from loss of blood that he was dying, this young Cree; and when he staggered still again along the gantlet, to the end toward David, he fell and was unable to rise. A buck, shrieking furiously, lifted his tomahawk to threaten him; kicked at him, smote him with the head of the ax; and then, overcome by his murderous lusts, buried the blade into the Cree's skull. The Cree heaved himself up then, with a new and dreadful and last burst of strength; heaved himself clear up to his feet, his feet spread, his knees shaking, the tomahawk in his brain, blood cascading down over him, his hands outstretched, groping; and for a moment stood thus, when, like a bull buffalo hamstrung by wolves, he sank, and almost before his rump had touched earth the brave who had tomahawked him leaped in with dagger to take the scalp.

Was the fate of the other the same? David did not know, for he had closed his eyes. He was not a man who quailed at sight of brutalities: this was brutal country, only brutal men survived here, but he was sickened to see with his own eyes in what a shameful way brave men had to die, as he had been sickened when men clubbed the brains out of a bitch wolf for no more than her mother-mating instinct and her helplessness when stuck. He was enraged now, he trembled against the tree and strained at the thongs; if he could have burst free he would with his bare hands have attacked the four lines of torturers and at least for a few moments bucks and squaws would have been going end over end. When at last aware that the awful clamor had subsided he opened his eyes to look and saw that the four lines had broken up. Over to his right, thrown out into the snow, naked, red, scalped, lay the two dead warriors. Not once, so far as David knew, had a moan escaped them, no cry of pain, no plea for mercy. Savages, yes; in a way he had to admire them, in a way detest them. Would he have the fortitude if this was to be his lot? Well, he would not take it that way. No white man would, no white man worth his gumption. He would seize a knife or tomahawk and wade in and there would be dead people all around him when he died. . . .

The chilling cries told him that they were coming forward with another captive. There was tremendous outcry down among the lodges while she was out of sight and then she came in sight, driven by kicks and blows from behind—a girl, a Cree girl, her eyes hugely open and terrified, her lips so tremulous that David thought she was about to cry. She had been so cuffed and knocked around that her garments were half off her, and her breasts, which seemed as firm and lovely as Sunday's, were exposed and smeared with blood. There were bloodstains over her chest and throat and arms and streaks like thorn wounds across her face. She was forced to the gantlet area and then stood there, trembling, surrounded, with black warrior eyes looking her up and down. One buck, bolder than the others because this was his captive, his slave, his property, stepped close to her and peered, as though to study her eyes or some other feature; lifted one of her hands and in a queer way looked at it; pulled her leather skirt aside or up to stare at her flanks; seemed to sniff; and then quickly stepped back when cries indicated that someone was coming.

It was the bold warrior's wife. It was a law among these people that if a buck captured a girl or woman she was his property, but his wife, or his chief wife if he had more than one, had to accept her if the captive was to be taken as another wife; and if the wife did not accept her, the captive was then the man's to hack to pieces on the spot or to sell or to give away. David knew all this, and recognized what a moment of drama had come. Lord God Almighty, what a misfortune in a captive woman to be lovely! This squaw wife, this stugger waddling up, this flotch looked middle-aged and dirty and mean and miserable, coyote or wolf bait, a fit mate for a wolverine. She pushed her way roughly among men and women to the inner circle, where snow and earth were red with the blood of dead men, and looked at the girl; and in that moment the poor frightened thing appealed to her, eyes wide and eloquent, tongue supplicating. She was telling her, David supposed, that if she would spare her she would be her slave for life, her drudge, the thing at her feet. That is what her eyes and tongue were saying. Because he stood on earth above these people David could see her: she was beautiful, he thought, one of the most beautiful Indian girls he had ever seen, a girl snatched away from her parents, her people, possibly her husband, with only her bitter and ancient enemies around her, some eager for her degradation, others for her death. And even if spared, what could her lot be? The whore of a brute who would always hate her as a Cree, the slave of his flotch, who would starve her, beat her, and make life a hell on earth for her. It would be better if she died. It looked as if death was her lot, judging by the way the fat filthy crone was eying her up and down, her head thrust forward as though at the end of her mean and murderous will, like something ugly on a bent stem. . . .

David did not see her give the sign. He saw her break away from the group and he knew by the violence in the Cree girl's trembling that the sign had been no. The buck whose property she was now shoved in, and David, afraid that he intended at once to hack her to pieces, shouted over at him, "Wait, I'll buy this woman!" The shout was enough to stop the buck even if he did not understand the words.

Blackfoot words were what David was trying to think of—the words for woman, wife, rum, gunpowder, tobacco; and piling them one on top of another, he offered all those things and more. The girl was looking at him now and the bucks and squaws were looking at him.

Then the one who owned the girl came toward David, his movements menacing, his eyes hardly visible in the warpath black around them. He came up close and looked at David's eyes, and again David was explaining as well as he could that he would buy the girl. "*Netokeemun,*" he said, meaning that she would be his wife. "*Sahhookkattook,*" he said, meaning that she would share his bed. He said he would give rum for her, tobacco, a gun, vermilion, powder, and ball; and then waited to see if the Indian's expression would change. "*Aki,*" he said, nodding toward her. Not sure that the buck had understood him, David now spoke in jargon, not with eagerness—that would have aroused contempt—but with a kind of sneering shrugging interest in her.

The Indian stared up at him, his face expressionless. He then turned away and went to a lodge. While he was gone the girl stood, as before, trembling a little, her gaze on David. He wondered if there was any hope in her breast, or only fear, and what she thought would be his fate, bound there to a tree. The warrior came back with an old feeble Indian who came up and peered at David, squinting, and spoke.

"Wan woe-man?"

David was so astonished that he did not at once understand what the old Indian had said. Then, nodding his head with vigor, "Yes, I wan woman, will buy woman. Give rum for woman, tobac."

The old man's face was a parfleche of seams. He squinted, as if looking at a bright sun. "Room?" he said. "*Kah?*"

"Yonder," David said, nodding in the direction of the post. "*Kaso*—room—mucha." The old Indian, he reflected, knew that. Perhaps he was being too eager. He looked over at the girl, shrugged, turned his head aside to spit, and said, "Potlatch room."

The old man turned to the warrior and they talked together. Then the old man fixed David with his tired yellowed half-blind eyes and said, "Hooo moocha?"

David's heart leaped: if they did not intend to turn him free, why bargain with him? How much? If he could have brought his hands forward he might have shown him. He knew no Blackfoot word of measure, nor Chinook word either. "*Huehu,*" he said. "*Mokah.*" He said he would swap for her, he would buy her. And his heart was racing.

The old man asked again, "Hooo moocha?"

It now occurred to David that if he talked at length in English the old man might understand a few of the words and get the drift of his meaning. He said, "Will give rum . . . *kaso* . . . rum . . . moocha . . . enough *kaso* heap-big droonk . . . two big droonk . . . *kwinnim* big droonk . . . for moocha brave . . . room one night one day . . . bellyful room . . . parfleche full room-*kaso* . . . two quart, three quart . . . and tobac . . . powder . . . musket . . . *temolo* . . . suga, now make wah-wah . . . Make wah-wah?"

There was no change in the old face. "*Kah?*" he asked again, meaning where.

"Yaw-wah," David said, meaning yonder, and nodded toward the fort. "*Kaso* yaw-wah."

The old fellow turned to the buck and talked to him and the buck shook his head no. Then the old man peered again at David and asked, "Room?"

"Room," David said, nodding. "Aha." Maybe the buck wanted rum and nothing but rum. "*Tiye,*" David said.

The old man grunted. "*Tiye?*" he said, opening his eyes wide.

"*Tiye,*" David said, nodding down at himself, indicating himself, telling the old man that he, David, was a chief, a master.

The Indians were talking when the squaw who had rejected the girl came from the lodges. She came running and it was plain that she was furious. She rushed up to her husband, shouting at him and shaking both hands at him. Abashed, he moved back, and the old man with him; and the wife, still shouting, ran back to the lodge. She returned at once, and with her was an Indian lad, perhaps five or six years old. Something flashed in the boy's hand, and looking at it more sharply, David thought it was a knife. He was wondering what this turn of events meant when the squaw came up to him, talking to the boy. The boy looked up at David's face. His own face was not mean or eager but only curious, wide open and curious and interested, as it might have been if he had been looking at a beast in a trap. Then he went behind the tree and David felt the boy's hands grasping his left thumb.

# XXI

A moment later a cry of amazement escaped him. He had had no idea at all of the squaw's intentions and never in his life had he been more astounded than when he felt the blade of the knife cutting into his thumb. He was about to roar out with prodigious anger when he saw that a lot of the Indian men were watching him. The squaw, the ugly, mean, and brutish flotch, was facing him, looking up, with the studied, impassive, almost ageless contempt and scorn that he had so often seen in Indian faces. The Cree girl still stood surrounded and looked at him. The old Indian and the younger one stood together, looking at him. David saw all this while the first pain shot through him, while astonishment faded and rage came up. His first impulse was to preserve himself, to fling himself around the tree and kick the lad with all the power of a booted foot. Just what in God's name did they intend here, anyway? Up till now he had been convinced that the whole thing was only an effort, prompted by the pedlars, to scare him back to the post. But this steady hacking at his thumb was something more. He turned so that he could look back across his shoulder at the boy; he looked down and saw him there, busy, intent, cutting through hide, through flesh at the first joint. Then David felt something sharp and a flash of pain in his belly, and swinging back he found the squaw thrusting at him with a dagger.

So that was it! It all came to him now in a flash, all the horror of it, all the savage brutality of it: because he had interfered in this matter between a husband and wife, the wife had resolved to punish him. This recognition now ran through his tortured brain as the pain went deeper and deeper. The dreadful bitch stood there, the dagger at his belly. Remembering Jim's words, he was about to spit in her face, but did not, for in the next moment calmer judgment told him that if he did she would push the blade in clear to the hilt. This was no buck, no warrior, for whom courage was the greatest thing in life, but a damned nasty bitch of a female whose vanity had just been outraged and who in her perverted mother's heart was twice as savage as any man on earth. So many things were flashing through his mind now as the earnest lad applied himself to his task—so many impulses came up, only to be shoved down and away—as when he thought to make a fight of it, to kick the bitch in her filthy gut as hard as he could and then swing around and kick the boy, telling himself that they would never dare to torture or kill an official of the powerful company; but in the next instant he knew better than that, knew that they could do what they pleased with him; knew that they could feed him to the wolves and burn his bones, that they could sink him in a parfleche of stones into the river; that they had many ways to get rid of him. . . .

A slight groan escaped him. Merciful God, the little fiend was now hacking at the joint. Convinced that the intention was to cut his thumb off, David stood taller to ease the pain a little, to let the bolts and flashes of it scatter and spread up his arm, through his shoulder and chest, down into his bowels, which felt full of gas pains and diarrhea; to let rage, blind murderous fury, more fully possess him, as anesthesia; to let thoughts of vengeance fill him with their lightning; to figure out if he could in the next few moments what to do. But what could he do except to bear it? The sons of bitches stood back there watching him, watching as only Indians could, to see if he would whimper, if he would writhe and wince, if his face would show agony, if his fortitude would falter. And the dirty little bastard was patiently, patiently hacking away! What if he intended to take off more than a thumb? What if he intended to take off both thumbs and all his fingers, and possibly the hands off at the wrists? —for there was no savagery too primitive for a red man or a red woman. He knew, with the sharp bitter pain of it now all through him, that whether they stopped with one thumb would depend, and perhaps depend entirely, on the kind of response he made to it. Show your contempt, Jim had said. He decided that when the squaw looked up at him he would meet her eyes, he would look into them, he would express all the contempt and disdain that he felt. All right, Indians bore such ordeals: among the Big Bellies every youth on reaching manhood had to go naked into the winter, to a far hill, and neither eat nor sleep there as long as he could stand it, but leap and howl day and night and make dreadful sounds, and cut one of his fingers off. Yes, they stood it, a white man could. If only the little whelp were more skilled with a knife, if only he had a sharp blade, if only he did not hack and hack and keep feeling into the wound to see how much remained to cut through! All right, you little savage and butcher out of hell, go after it—and gawk, you sons of the devil, and be damned sure you never set me free . . . !

He wanted to close his eyes—for some reason closed eyes were a barrier against pain—but he forced himself to look around, to meet the eyes of warriors or of those coming from the lodges to view him. He must prepare himself: cutting through flesh, hacking around bone joint put on a man's heart and soul just about all they could endure, but cutting the tendon, he knew, would be worst of all—would be a slow, fumbling, hacking, beastly thing that would darken his senses, that would demand all he had to keep from fainting. . . .

He could feel the blood running from his thumb and he supposed the aspen was red now from his wrists to the snow. He thought by the feel of it that it was all done but the tendon. Steeling himself, he looked into the eyes of the animal who stood before him, never moving, her gaze never leaving his face, her hand that pressed the dagger point against his belly as steady as a surgeon's hand. So this was a woman! This was a wife, a mother, this thing! This, and those over there, they were said to be human beings, these—God, the pain was now coming from his legs up, into his loins as from a hard blow on his testicles, into his belly as if she had the dagger in and was turning it around; and then he was full of nausea and the pain was around his heart and he was choked, his throat was so full of it that he felt strangled, it was in his eyes . . . her face now seemed to be dancing before him, and then there was a kind of release . . . then the Indian lad was there before him, bloody all over his hands and his front, holding the piece of thumb for the woman to see. She looked at it and up at David, but he was too numbed to try to tell what she was thinking. Dully he was wondering if the other thumb would be cut off. . . .

But she took the piece of thumb and turned away and the boy went with her and he saw them vanish among the lodges. Then the buck who owned the Cree girl came over and looked at him and David held back an impulse to spit in his face. You son of a bitch! he thought. If I ever get free and meet you again! Show your contempt, Jim had said, but hope beat in a man like wings, hope made him feel that if he was gentle his enemy would be gentle! Did the rabbit feel that when running blindly round and round from the stoat? Turning, the Indian spoke to the other bucks and they hastened away and returned with hatchets; and they went behind David and began to chop the tree down. Did they intend to topple it while he was bound? He decided that they did. About eight inches through, it was twenty-five feet tall and it was green; when it fell it would carry him down with it and it might break his wrists or his arms. He looked round at the two men hacking away and he put his legs out from the bole lest a blade glance off and strike him. He would have to watch it. When he saw which way the tree was falling he would go down with it. . . .

He managed it somehow but he was never to know how. He found himself lying alongside the tree, still bound to it, and he worked his arms down the trunk until released and got to his feet, his wrists bound behind him. He realized that they had cut the tree down so that they would not have to untie the knots, or sever the thongs and waste a part of them. He was grimly amused by such ingenuity. The armed warriors gathered around him and indicated a direction and he was marched away to a lodge. At a large tepee they encircled him, dagger blades pointed, and forced him inside. He was conscious first of warmth and then of smoke, for a fire was burning. They prodded him in and over to the fire and surrounded him, jabbering all the while, and David became aware, with a sudden flash of insight, that these Indians didn't know what to do with him. No doubt they knew what they wanted to do but they were afraid to do it. They were afraid of white man's vengeance. Or perhaps what the pedlars had told them to do had got all mixed up with their own savage impulses.

That they were confused became certain a little later. One of them went away and returned with pemmican, and the buck who owned the Cree girl offered pemmican to David's mouth. He refused it. He shut his lips tight and shook his head no and in the gloom he saw the bewilderment in their faces. Or perhaps he did not see it but only heard it in their voices. Like children, they furiously argued the matter: he understood only a word now and then but it was plain to him that some wanted to punish him further and some counseled prudence. The prudent ones seemed to prevail: two of them left and returned with a buffalo robe and they draped it over his shoulders and indicated that he was to lie by the fire. He lay down, with the robe around him. He understood that he was to sleep here, at least until they could make up their minds what to do with him.

They all left the lodge but one, who sat on his rump across from David and stared at him through the flames. David was trying to tell if his thumb was still bleeding. He did not want to lose much blood, not with an empty gut and a sleepless frame; yet dared he imagine that he might escape? He knew it was out of the question. They would torture him and then kill him or they would turn him free. Some of them, he suspected, were clamoring for his scalp: an Indian brave with his blood boiling up coveted a scalp above all things, and a white man's above a red man's. What a triumph to raise David McDonald's scalp like a banner and carry it through the village!

Now a fresh hazard occurred to him. In the dead of night one of those determined on his death might sneak up to him with tomahawk to bury the blade silently, and what could he do, even if awake, with his hands behind him? He could cry out if he had time. Yes, if he had time! A skulking Indian in the dark of night was as soundless as a kitten. He would have to stay awake and keep his eyes open, wide open, all night.

There was light from the large hole above, through which the smoke escaped. There was firelight. Lying with his hands behind him was so uncomfortable that he sat up, and through smoke and flame he and the red man looked at one another. This brave had been among those on the warpath and it was impossible to tell what kind of face he had behind all the soot and vermilion and grease. But his eyes were plain, eyes alert and watchful yet strangely brooding, now and then catching firelight that illumined their depths, as lanterns looked into jungles. The light from flames danced over him and seemed to reveal changes in his eyes and face, but David knew there were no changes. Not once had he seen him blink. . . . The pain in his thumb was sharper now; it flashed up his arm and was a terrible ache in his shoulder. He knew that it had stopped bleeding. He had a picture of it with the rounded ball joint exposed and the tendon and flesh frayed out; if only he could thrust it into balsam gum. God, how he hated the pedlars! If he ever saw John Bowman again he would hit him once so hard that he would break his neck. He would hit the son of a bitch so hard that his head would hang down his back. Colin was right: you had to fight fire with fire, you only got your thumbs chewed off if you tried to be a good fellow. He had never fully believed Colin and Jim and others, but he saw now that they had been right, that this was war to the death, with the Indians, the poor savage children, caught between. The pedlars, shrewder and more ruthless than the Selkirks, had had the right idea from the beginning, knowing that the way to win was to turn the red men against the enemy. If they wouldn't bring their pelts to you, if they ambushed you, stole your horses from their winter grazing lands, scared the daylights out of your lone trappers and hacked off your thumbs, you wouldn't last long, would you? About as long, Colin had said, as a fart in a blizzard.

What would they do with him? What would they do with the Cree girl? If Jim knew what had happened Jim would say, "Women will be the death of you." What a sentimental romantic lubber he was! He should have kept his mouth shut and let the buck kill the girl as a gesture of rage and frustration against his tyrant wife. John Bowman would have done it. Most of the men of the north country would have done it. But he wouldn't do it, not if it cost him both his hands. A man was no longer a man, or even a decent animal, if he could see a girl trembling all over and looking round for the coming knives and keep his mouth shut. And such a pretty thing, though David told himself that even if she had been an old squaw he would have spoken. He wiggled his thumb to see how it felt. Both his shoulders were aching now. His hands had been behind him for hours and they might remain there until he was paralyzed. The tepee was darkening as night came in. He tried to figure out what was ahead of him, but trying to guess an Indian's mind was a waste of time; they would turn him free or they would torture him and that was all. If they turned him free they might strip him naked. That would be a sentence of death. Or they might send him forth as independent trappers were sent forth, with a pound or two of pemmican, a thin robe, and enough powder and ball for two shots. In that case he could make it to the fort. Or they might send him without weapons or food or robe, and in that case he could make it if a blizzard did not come over him, roaring down from the cold mountains. Turning him free would certainly draw vengeance upon them; for this reason he thought they would decide to kill him and destroy his bones.

He looked at the face through firelight but no answer was there. No answer was there for the reason that none could be there. The answer was in the hearts of the chiefs here, and perhaps even now they were sitting in council. Was Brave Feathers among them? He could have no doubt of that. The Blackfeet knew when he went forth in a sled and they had kept their eye on him. Or had they been north on the warpath? It was so utterly useless to think about it, yet a man had to think when facing torture and death, for he then stood on the deepest and darkest and most primitive things in him and he was like a man of long ago, he had to brood and plot and connive, even if bound hand and foot, even if the dagger was at his throat; for then life was as ruthless as death, and as desperate as beauty struggling to keep a petal hold in a world not made for flowers, or a Cree girl hoping for motherhood in a world not made for mothers; for then all that human striving had fought for and preserved, all the little of it, the tiny precious essence of it, was there before you in your gaze and your hearing, in all your senses, in the sound of your heartbeat, in the shining brilliant needlepoint of your thought; and there was in you, all through you, the wish for one last free unfettered blow. But it was useless to think about it, as useless as giving the fumes of cooking food to one dying of hunger.

Night had come. Above the hole at the apex the ascending flames and smoke made witchery of twilight. Sparks went up the smoke wind and into the sky like flakes of candle flame, and the smoke thinned and was a pale blue and was gone. It was a nice fire. The wood in it was dead dry aspen and cypress and these were steady burning woods that did not spit embers at you or startle you with explosions. Three Indians came in and stood together and talked and went out. He supposed they were discussing his fate, and again he wished they would make up their minds and get it over with. The one sitting across from him was quite a picture in firelight now that deep dusk had come: his vermilion-red face from his eyes down was touched with shades from pale pink to scarlet and his eyes were like a beast's looking out of deep night. David would have thought he was asleep if his eyes had been closed. He never moved save to lay wood on the fire and he always returned to the same position, his legs crossed before him, his hands on his belly, and his right hand within easy reach of his knife haft.

David felt exhausted and wondered if he could stretch out. Not on his back, nor on his side, for how could he sleep on his side with his hands behind him? Possibly he could if he thrust a leg out at right angles to brace him. He customarily slept on his right side, but with plenty of padding under his shoulder and hip bones. Here there was only the earth, dry and hard from many fires. He moved to look round him, to study his position, to wonder how without hands he could fold himself within the robe; and he was trying to, using his head and shoulders as hands, when the buck leaped up and came around and stood over him. He had drawn his knife.

David looked up at him, unbelieving, and then was so furious that sick rage heaved all through him. "You goddamned red numbskull son of a bitch! What's in your wolverine mind now?" The Indian, holding his knife in his right hand, reached down with his left to feel over David; and David yielded and was silent, like a cow with hands on her udder. The fool was searching him for weapons. The fool felt around his waist and up and down and over him and then went back and sat as before, impassive, immobile, brooding.

Hours later David was lying on his right side, facing the fire, his legs to his knees at right angles to his torso, from the knees down, parallel. He ached almost intolerably in his hip and shoulder bones but he didn't want to move. There were three bucks in the tepee now and he thought they were asleep. What good that would do him he could not imagine, but when they slept he felt a little safer, a little closer to escape. He knew that escape with his hands bound behind him would be madness but he liked to think about it. When, after another hour, he was convinced by the sound of their breathing that they all slept he thought about nothing else. In his mind he made a map of his position, of their positions, of the exit, of the direction he would take once out of the lodge, of the location of this camp on the Saskatchewan. He tried to estimate how many miles an hour he could walk and how far he could walk without food and how he could keep his hands from freezing, and he wondered whether if he found a rock ledge he could rub the leather thongs and sever them. If there was a heavy snowfall would he be able to find his way? He was trying to calculate every risk, anticipate every problem, for he intended to make a break for it before morning. . . .

There could be no doubt that the guards were asleep. He thought it strange that he should be left unbound but for his hands; it looked as if they intended for him to escape, for usually they bound their prisoners hand and foot. Again he was going over and over each step—telling himself that he would do this, he would do that, with everything so carefully planned that he would not have to think at all; telling himself—and then something touched his hand! If he had not been so wide awake and alert he might have cried out, for he hated rats; as it was, he stiffened and all his senses like light flooded the moment. It was not a rat. There was someone behind him. There had been the touch on his hand and then almost at once this person behind him was severing the bonds. He was so amazed that he was breathless. He was amazed because he had been as wide awake as he could possibly have been, yet he had heard no movement; this person had entered and come over to him and he had sensed nothing. With a knife this person was cutting the thongs, gently, soundlessly; this person gently, soundlessly placed the haft of a knife across his fingers; and then there was nothing, no movement, no feeling, and he knew that the person had gone away. It had all taken only a few moments. It had been done with unbelievable deftness. He thought, It is the Cree girl! But no, she was a captive, she could never have come. Was it Sunday?

He lay, possessing his emotions, controlling his breathing; and at last began to work his fingers a little and felt the knife and brought it over in front of him. He was trying desperately to think of everything that must be done: he must bring all the leather thongs forward and take them with him or destroy them in a fire. But the fire had burned too low, he would take them with him, all the pieces. He brought his left hand over and touched the mutilated and aching thumb to his lips: it was a caress to a part of him that was gone: it was a foolish gesture, he supposed, but in this country a man got a new concept of his hands. In London or Glasgow hands were something you shaved with and fed yourself with or twirled a stick with, but here hands were things that kept you alive.

He was thinking fast now and telling himself that he must not blunder. Should he leave the robe or take it? He decided to leave it; he would keep warm by moving. He reached all around behind him to be sure he had every piece of the string, and the pieces he entrusted to his left hand, the dagger to his right. His next task was to disengage himself from the robe. Now and then he paused to listen: the three bucks were snoring but they might arouse themselves any moment; he must move swiftly, but not too swiftly. He must be as soundless as the person who had come in. That, he knew, he could never be; no white man could be as soundless as an Indian, or as a white person raised among them. Freed from the robe, he got to hands and knees and listened; moved slowly and stood; moved noiselessly toward the tepee flap; listened, and heard a buck stirring and felt his flesh rising all over him; stood, almost paralyzed, for several moments, then moved again, holding his breath, listening for the dreadful sound of a dog's bark, almost bursting with emotion when he heard an ember snap, and at the entrance at last listening again . . . and then he was outside, erect and on his feet, limned, stark in a moon-flooded world. He stood a few moments, expecting the sound of dogs, knowing that his feet, no matter how softly he placed them, made crunching sounds in the snow, yet remembering that he had heard no snow sounds from the one who came to him. A phantom horseman, a phantom night shadow. He was no phantom, he was making sounds, and they seemed as loud as blizzards. When he began to move, absurdly straining upward, as though he could take weight off his feet, he thought it queer that no dogs barked. But there was no time to think about dogs, he must be off, he must go; and he went as he had planned it, quickly to the south, out of the lodge camp. And no dog barked! He moved away from the areas where feet had been, to fresh snow, for it would be more silent, and he went swiftly, going east, glancing back, his dagger held in readiness across his belly.

After a hundred yards he began to run, and when he felt safe he held the mutilated thumb up to look at it. Then he looked at his handful of leather thongs and wondered what to do with them. Why not keep them? That was maudlin, he supposed, but after a man had stood at a tree in torture and had looked at death he did not argue about values with those who had never got an arm's length beyond a safe fireside. He would keep the pieces of leather. Someday—yes by God, someday—he would show them to Sunday and he would know by her face if she was the one who came in. If a woman was your phantom rider and your phantom angel in the night it made you feel pretty tender toward her. It made you feel that she was waiting for you and that when this bitch of a war was over—— Lord Jesus, what was that? Incredulous, he put a hand up and found that it was a tear on his cheek. "Why, David McDonald," he murmured, "you damned weakling!"

Where was he, anyhow? That was the thing to think about. He had just left the Saskatchewan and had gone a little south and then east: this meant that he was southwest of the Edmonton fort, maybe fifty miles, maybe sixty or eighty. Maybe a hundred as the river ran, but sixty as the crow flew; if he kept the river growth in sight he would be sure of his way, but that would take longer and he was weak, weak from want of food and sleep, but weak more than that from anxiety and torture, weak because he had been almost drained of hope. He would take his chances with the crow. Still trotting and now holding his hands under his armpits to warm them, he looked up to study the stars and chart his course. He must not hit south of the post, that would be bad: the river from Edmonton flowed northeast, and if he hit very far south of it he would never see it. He would keep north of the crow's line.

He marked his course by the stars and moved on long gliding strides. An hour later, two hours, three hours he was still trotting, with only the white desolate prairie all around him and the first gray of morning upon the sky.

## XXII

It was after daylight and he was walking when up the slope two or three miles away he saw movement. He thought at first it was wolves. What could a man do with a skinning knife against a pack of wolves if they were starved enough to press in? He looked around him but there were no trees—and how stupid to climb a tree and let beasts bivouac you until you froze and tumbled out! There was no shelter of any kind. He stopped, his gaze on the distant objects, and after a few moments he decided that they were not wolves. They kept too close together. It looked more like a dog train. . . .

It was a dog train, it was Jim Dugald on his way to look for him. Coll had chewed the leash in two and the dogs had headed home. David hastened toward the oncoming sled and presently Jim was standing up and hailing him; and then David saw another man a hundred yards or so behind. The dogs, recognizing him, had begun to bark.

They came up, drooling, tongues hanging, harness taut, and Jim threw off his robes and stepped out of the sled. "By the merciful God!" he said. "Where in hell have you been?"

"With a woman," said David, grinning a little.

Jim was looking him up and down. His keen eyes saw the thumb or saw that David was holding his hand in an unusual way. "What's that?" he said.

"What?" asked David, not understanding.

Jim stepped forward and seized David's hand and looked at the thumb. Then he looked into David's eyes. "So the sons of bitches got you?"

"I reckon."

"Did a squaw do that?"

"She had a little boy do it."

Jim was studying David's eyes. He said, "How you feel?"

"A lot like a damned fool."

"How'd you get away?"

David told him what had happened. He told him why his thumb had been cut off.

"Women!" Jim said. "By God, they'll be the death of you."

"I reckoned you'd say that."

Jim dug into his luggage and drew forth a pound hunk of David's favorite pemmican. Then he fetched out a bottle of brandy and pulled the cork, saying, "Here, set your belly on fire. You need it."

David took a deep drink and shuddered. "It never tasted better," he said. He took the pemmican and sank his teeth.

"See Sunday?"

"No," said David.

Jim took David's left hand and studied the thumb. "What you figure to do with all those pieces of leather?"

"Keep them," David said.

Jim glanced again at his eyes and then took the thumb and studied it. He dug into the sled and came up with balsam gum and a piece of cloth. After folding the cloth he poured onto it an ounce or more of the heavy water-colored gum and gently set the thumb stub in the gum and wound the cloth around and around it, making it secure back at the wrist.

"Feels good," David said. He looked over at Payette, who had come up on birch bark skis. "Why you bring him?"

"Thought I might need him," Jim said.

"Then you reckoned the Indians had me."

"Or the girl Sunday."

While digging out more food Jim gave him the news. Colin had seized the pedlar fort of Gibraltar and had taken Duncan Cameron prisoner. He had caught Duncan cold in the act of writing to James Grant to suggest that Indians could make handsome pillage at Red River.

"Still won't do their own dirty work," David said.

Colin had then seized the pedlar express and found, in writing, absolute proof of a plot to wipe out the entire colony the next spring or summer. All the half-breeds had lined up under a murderous wolf named Pangman and had pledged their loyalty and lives to the North West Company.

"Which leaves our honorable company where?"

"In the short grass," Jim said.

"Looks like Colin has taken the bull by the horns. Can he spit in his teeth?"

"He'll have to have angels all around him if he is to live a year."

David was chewing pemmican and looking at Payette. "All the half-breeds have gone over?"

"Every nit, prick, and stillbirth."

"And Lord Selkirk is going to walk into a thing like that?"

"He'll ride," Jim said. "He'll be on a white horse."

"You mean they're going to bribe the half-breeds to wipe out the colony?"

"That's where you come in, but we'll talk about that later." Jim looked into David's eyes and over his face as he might have studied an erring or a stupid son. He said, "I suppose you'd like to go back for this Cree girl. Or was your Sunday girl there?"

"I don't know."

Jim bent over the sled and rearranged the luggage. "Get in," he said.

"I don't want to go back, if that's what you mean."

"Won't you ever understand Indians? We have to go. Only thing is the dogs are so damn tired."

"I'n walk," David said.

"Get in."

"You realize they're on the warpath?"

"We all are," Jim said. "Are you afraid?"

"You'll ask me that once too often," David said.

"All right, goddamn it, get in."

David climbed into the sled, wondering what this man had in mind. It was all right for a man to say he was not afraid, but the red men were on the warpath, their blood was up and boiling, and as likely as not the pedlars were offering them rum for HB scalps. Still, Jim Dugald knew Indians, he knew what he was doing.

"How far, you reckon?" Jim asked, walking behind.

David tried to calculate it but he had only a vague idea of how long he had trotted, how long with his breath like fire in him he had walked. "How far to the post?"

"Twenty-five or thirty miles."

"I guess I walked twenty or twenty-five. Maybe more."

"You think they're about west of the lake?"

"About."

Jim turned to look at the morning sun behind him. "Well, go back over your trail near as you can. We should be there before noon."

And what, David wondered, did he intend to do when he got there? Have a showdown with the Blackfeet? Seeking an answer to the riddle, David felt around him in the sled to learn what Jim had brought. Under the robes on his right he found three muskets, and on his left, knives, powder and ball, rum. There seemed to be a lot of rum. Maybe Jim had brought the rum as ransom.

After an hour David halted the dogs and told Jim to ride. Jim said, "Get the hell on. I'm all right."

"Then let Payette ride. I'll walk with you. We'll talk." David got out of the sled. Payette took his skis off and climbed in and laid the skis alongside.

The dogs trotted gently, easily, and the men had to walk at a killing pace to keep up with them. It ganted a man up in no time.

Breathing hard, David said, "What in hell are we going back there for?"

"A piece of thumb." Glancing over at David's left hand, Jim said, "How is it?"

"Throbs. Feels good."

"Too bad no hide over it. Bone will always stick out."

"Could be worse."

"Everything in life could be, except a man's birth. You were lucky."

Because David's legs were longer he had to shorten his stride to match Jim's. "How?" he said.

Sometimes, Jim said, sort of pumping the words out on heavy breathing, they turned captives over to squaws and squaws had boys cut all the fingers off. Many years ago he had seen a Shuswap with no fingers or thumbs, only stubs. They sometimes cut them off right at the hand instead of at the first joint. By God, it made you wonder about women. He thought of Tum-tum, his mourning bird, and the way she had looked at the blind baby; and he thought of the way squaw mothers stood and watched their sons hack fingers off. It made a man afraid of women. All the talk of mother love, Jim went on, speaking in bursts, was damned nonsense. It was instinct, not love. A mother protected and cherished her young for the same reason a calf bunted at a tit or a dog pissed on a post.

"You sound cynical today," David said.

"Always did," Jim said.

"You're sure a walking fool. Just like Perpetual Motion."

"There was a walker," Jim said, huffing the words out. "What a bastard. Between three and four hundred pounds of marrow and gut and he could walk a moose blind."

"Long legs?"

"Not long as yours."

"That's the river line over there."

"And there," said Jim, turning his head, "is the lake."

After an hour Jim was prevailed on to ride and then smoke from the lodges came in sight. They stopped the sled and Jim dug muskets and pistols out, and he and David strapped pistols to their waists and each took a rifle. Then Jim took David aside, beyond the hearing of Payette but under the lidded watchfulness of his eyes.

"I aim to have some peace smoke with them," Jim said. "I'll ask the principal chief to keep his gun on the young bloods. If he shows any sign of treachery, put your gun on him. Watch Payette. If he makes a crooked move drop him. Use your fist for that." He had been looking at the smoke rising above the river growth. "They know we're here."

"How?"

"I saw a mirror flash. Well, in we go. Just stay cool, that's all you need with a red man." Jim's eyes twinkled at him. "When you lost your temper you lost your thumb."

They headed straight for the village and did not pause until they came to the first lodges. Jim then leashed Coll to an aspen. A score of hostile bucks had come rushing over.

Jim told Payette to ask for Horned Thunder. One of the bucks ran away among the lodges, and in a few moments there came one whom David would never have recognized as the chief, so completely had war paints disguised him. Through Payette, Jim now explained that he had come as a friend, that he had always been a friend to the brave Blackfoot warriors. He wanted to talk to them as a friend and he wanted Horned Thunder to choose a place to sit and to have his gun at the ready, so that he could keep order. Would the chief do that?

Payette and the chief talked and David watched the chief's face. It was so smeared with paint and grease that it was impossible to see any expression in it. Payette turned to Jim and said the chief would do as he wished, and Jim then said he had a present for the great chief, some very fine rum and some tobacco, which would be presented when the powwow was over. The chief sent for his gun, and when it came he took it and sat on a stump about forty feet from where Jim stood, the gun in his hands, the muzzle pointing at the score of young bloods who were looking at Jim. David told himself that he could almost smell the menace in the men. As for the chief, his promise might not mean a thing.

Jim now brought forth a pipe and tobacco and observed those amenities without which any red chief would have been deeply wounded in his pride; and after they had taken their whiffs and made the customary pledge of eternal friendship, Jim spoke to the Indians, uttering a few words, allowing Payette to translate, and speaking again. He said that bitter war had developed between the two companies and he wanted all Indians to know the exact truth of the situation before they took sides. All the land in this vast country, said the prudent Jim, belonged to the Indians really; it had been their home and their hunting grounds for countless generations. The white man wanted only the fur and he would pay for it. Many pelts had been taken, many remained. A long time ago a king, a great white chief, had given the right to the Hudson's Bay Company to buy all the pelts the red men could trap in this whole area, from Thunder Bay to the sea. Other companies had tried to crowd in. The most stubborn of these intruders was the North West Company, which was now trying to turn the red men against the HB men.

When Payette translated the concluding words there were sudden hostile movements. A few of the young bucks drew their daggers, and one, bolder than the others, came forward and made swift flashing circles with the blade. David looked over at Horned Thunder: he did not stir nor raise his gun but sat like a dead man propped up, as he had sat from the beginning. Jim's composure was perfect. He went on talking in his slow, distinct, unemotional way, apparently unaware of the wheeling and flashing blade only three feet from his face. David felt anger and alarm.

Jim went on, quietly, to say that the HB Company and no other had the right to all the furs taken and all the robes—of beaver, marten, lynx, otter, mink, wolf, fox, buffalo, caribou—all the furs and all the robes in all the land. The company would insist on its rights, even if it had to march an army in. There were hundreds, yes, thousands of soldiers who had been in the wars in the area of the big lakes and they could be hired and they would march in and destroy every post, fortress, and lodge of the enemy, and every man, white or red, who stood in their way.

There was a kind of gasping cry from the dagger-wheeling buck and at once several others moved up to flank him, all of them staring with black hostile eyes at Jim and flashing their blades. Horned Thunder gave no sign.

"The pedlars have sure been busy," Jim said to David.

His company, Jim said, had long been friends with the Blackfeet. The Blackfeet had brought many thousands of pelts. All these had been paid for. The company wanted its friends, the brave Blackfoot warriors, to continue to be its friends, to bring all their pelts to the HB posts, to smoke the pipe of peace. He hoped they would not make the mistake of going over to the pedlars—

David started and his hands closed tight on his gun. The foolhardiest of the braves had advanced and with the most brazen contempt was flashing his knife within three or four inches of Jim's face. He was striking down with it, slashing, ripping; cutting across; wheeling it, all with incredible swiftness. David knew that once blood was drawn they would both be goners.

There was no change in Jim's voice when he spoke to Payette. He said, "Tell the chief to take care his braves." Payette spoke to the chief. The chief did not move or speak. Sensing their advantage, another dozen braves advanced, all their knives flashing. In the same unemotional voice Jim said, without turning, "Dave, put your gun on the chief, right on his head. And keep it there." At once David raised his gun and aimed. The response was immediate. The dagger-wielding braves fell back as before a fire and their knives came down and were still against the leather over their thighs. They were looking not at their chief, not at Jim, but at David, who was looking along the sights at the chief's skull.

Jim told Payette to tell the chief to send his warriors away and the gun would no longer point at him.

Payette spoke to the chief. He spoke to his warriors and they moved back, hostile, sullen, sulking.

"Guess I'll change the subject," Jim said to David. He told Payette he wanted the Cree girl brought forth, that he would buy her.

David doubted that she was alive, but a buck hastened away and in a few moments returned with her, clasping the terrified girl by a wrist.

Jim looked the cringing lass up and down. "Tell her to stand up straight."

She made an effort to stand straight but she was trembling and she was too bewildered to know what she was doing.

"A fine lass this," said Jim. "Wouldn't mind delting with her myself."

"Why not?" David said.

Jim told Payette to find out how much the buck wanted for her. He knew that the buck would ask for a hundred times what he was willing to settle for; and so was not surprised when Payette said he wanted much rum.

"How much?"

The Indian who owned the girl seemed to be seeking the advice of his chief. Then he spoke to Payette and Payette said he wanted one hundred made-beaver.

The price was preposterous. "Tell him one quart rum."

Payette talked to the Indian. The buck shook his head no and feigned great anger and outrage.

"Tell him two quart rum."

The buck seemed twice as angry as before. He made moves as if to leave.

"Tell him take girl away then."

David could not restrain a smile at the childlikeness of the Indian's response. Unhappy and confused, like one whose greed had insulted his thirst, like one who had hoped for much more but had been ready to accept much less, he jabbered excitedly to the chief, and the chief, looking at him impassively, spoke to Payette.

Payette said, "He say you rob your bess friend but take two quart."

Jim told Payette to bring a two-quart jug.

When Payette came with the jug Jim gravely presented it to the Indian and, releasing his hold on the girl, the buck clutched it to his belly and ran away. Jim stepped forward and took the girl's arm. He told Payette to tell her to get into the sled, and meekly, almost cringingly, she went over and crawled in. Jim looked at her buttocks as she walked away.

He then told Payette to bring the rum for the chief, and gravely, every movement showing respect, Jim presented the rum and said through Payette that it was a gesture and a token of his love and friendship, of his esteem, of his vast and abiding respect. Jim said he was sure that the Blackfoot warriors, so honorable and brave, would continue to be the friend of his company; that they would bring in thousands of pelts this winter and next spring to trade for rum and tobacco. He said Horned Thunder would always be welcome at the HB posts. While Payette communicated these sentiments Horned Thunder sat like a man of stone, hugging his rum, revealing nothing.

Jim said, "You want to see Sunday?"

David hesitated a moment and said no.

"Why not? You falling in love with this other girl?"

"Have your fun," David said.

"It would do Sunday good to see that you've bought yourself a woman—for a woman never loves a man so much as when she thinks another woman is about to get him." He asked Payette to tell the chief that he would give him another quart of rum if he would summon Princess Sunday for the white men to look at.

David found himself trembling a little. While he was trying to compose his emotions Sunday came alone down the aisle of the lodges, erect, haughty, walking like a princess, her gaze (it seemed to Jim) on David. Jim was watching her and he thought he saw her glance once at the mutilated hand. She came within about thirty feet and looked at David, at Jim, and then at the Cree girl in the sled.

In a low voice Jim said, "Shall I tell her you've bought yourself a wife?"

"Just leave me out of it," David said.

"You're a hell of a fiddle-doup," Jim said. "We've got this girl right across a porcupine back. Now's the time to find out how she feels about you."

"I don't care," David said.

Jim stared at him a moment and then told Payette to bring another quart. While Payette was doing this Jim studied the girl before him. Yes, she was white, all white: no Indian woman ever stood with such scorn, such curling and half-lidded disdain. No Indian woman had ever known how. Had she really been the one who set David free? He tried to think of a sly way to find out.

Payette had presented the rum and returned to his position. Sunday's poise seemed unshakable: in turn affecting a touch of surprise (as when she glanced at Jim), of boredom (as when she looked over at the Cree), or of indifference (as when she looked at David), she stood waiting, as she had stood on the riverbank when she waited for the vermilion. Jim was thinking, There's a hell of a lot of woman in that bitch. Her hurdies were not quite ample enough for his taste

—he didn't like them too slender—but he admitted that in both form and face she had enough to fill a man's dreams and keep him turning all night.

He told Payette to tell her that he thought her very beautiful.

Her eyes opened just a little wider. That was all.

He said to tell her that Chief David—and he indicated David, who stood, uneasy, staring at him—had bought the Cree girl and would take her to the post.

Sunday turned her head a little to one side. Her gaze rested a moment on the Cree and her face darkened. Jim was laughing all over inside. David was angry.

"Tell her Cree girl beautiful . . . David love mucha."

David said sharply, "Why in hell don't you leave me out of it?"

In a low voice Jim said to him, "Shut up, you fool. Just look and listen and you may learn something."

David would have read Sunday's emotions if he had been studying her face. Jim read them. He saw the contempt, the scorn, but he also saw a woman hurt in her vanity. Her lips moved and he heard her speak.

She said, Payette told them, that this was only a slave girl, a stupid thing, and a coward.

Jim said to tell her that the Cree girl was very beautiful and that David loved her with all his liver. Sunday shrugged. Jim said to tell her that this girl would not have let a boy hack a thumb off if David had been among Crees. Sunday drew a full breath and turned. She walked away and no voice stopped her and in a few moments she vanished. Jim turned to David.

"Is it plain enough now?"

"What?" David said.

## XXIII

It was late afternoon when they got away, with David on Jim's insistence riding in the cariole with the girl, the two facing one another, the girl up front with her back to the dogs. Before they turned away Jim had thoughtfully asked Payette to discover her name. After talking to a couple of the bucks and to her Payette said it was Tefronia, or something like that, and meant Tame Deer. Jim said to David, "You have a tame deer all your own, and now let's be off."

David was vexed and humiliated before they turned away and his emotions were no happier when he sat facing the girl and became aware of the emotions in her. She was deeply, abjectly, pitifully grateful that her life had been saved—nobody could have been blind to that emotion in her face. It was in the way she sat, in the way, it seemed to David, she looked off north to the land of her people. Nobody could have missed in her the feeling that she now belonged to this man for life, that he would do with her as he pleased: use her as his lover if he wanted to, or as his slave, his drudge; his to flog, even to kill, or to be kind to; his to sell or to give away; his woman, no, his creature, his thing. He didn't like to see such abject surrender in any human being; it was ugly, it was the ugliest thing in life. But it would all be simple enough: he would send her back to her people as soon as spring broke, as soon as he could. . . .

She had the reddish color and night-black hair and high cheekbones of the Indian but he thought her lovely. She looked warm and womanly.

Tefronia would not meet his eyes. When she looked from right to left or from left to right her gaze passed over his face, but swiftly; there was no meeting of their eyes, not even for an instant. She was looking at the world around her as if interested in it, but he supposed she was feigning interest because she was miserably self-conscious. He wanted to say—and if they had spoken a language in common he would have said, "Look, lassie, it's not going to be so bad. You'll return to your people before long, you will marry a man of your people, and you will be a virgin when you go back. I lost a thumb because of you, lassie, but I shall exact no payment. So relax and stop looking round you in that wild anxious way."

When the trail ascended from a level plane, David climbed out to ease the burden on the dogs. A bitter wind had risen. It was so cold that it went through a man's leather and clear to his marrow. Tonight would be a stinger, Jim said. David thought they should go to the river, where they could find timber shelter, but Jim said they would burrow right on the prairie. They would travel all night but for the dogs. The poor beasties were more than dog-tired.

They halted where nothing was around them but the frozen snow and with an ax and spades they went through the crust, and then the men jumped into the soft white depth under the crust and tramped it down or spaded it back. The girl stood above, fearfully watching them.

Seeing the alarm in her face, David said, "She thinks we're digging a grave for her."

Jim glanced up at the girl. "She wouldn't expect us to take such pains. She thinks we're all going to rape her."

"Would that bother her so much?"

Jim looked up again. David thought maybe he was thinking of Tum-tum. "It might," he said.

"You reckon we had a close call back there?"

"It faired off," Jim said. "The bastards bluff any time they can."

The soft snow under the crust packed down so that soon they had a fairly large chamber under a frozen roof. They spaded snow over and tramped it solid to make a pathway up, a ramp, and then brought the dogs and sled down. David beckoned to the girl and with fear plain on her face she came, clutching the robe which she had been given to put around her. They didn't have enough bedding for all of them, Jim said. He guessed they would just rest awhile and feed the dogs and take off. The dogs were eating the soft snow. David took a double handful and, putting his mouth to it, tongued it in.

"Never camped this way before," he said. "Damned cozy."

"Best way there is," Jim said. He said they would spade the ramp away and the wolves would come up and trot round and round and once in a while look in. They wouldn't know what in hell to make of it.

"Jesus!" David said. "Listen to that wind."

It was going over them at forty miles an hour now, an infernal howling sound that fell into their camp pocket and created strange sobbings and moanings. David shoveled snow back and tamped it to make a back rest, and then indicated to Tefronia that she could sit there and lean back. She acted confused but she sat. David gave her a hunk of pemmican and took a hunk for himself.

"My finest pemmican," he said, chewing. "Think she'll like it?"

It was not likely, Jim said. People were so damned ornery that they seldom liked what they were not used to. That was how bad habits got sanctified.

Payette had banked snow and now sat across from them, leaning back to a snow wall. Jim was feeding the dogs. The Cree girl ate in a nibbling way and David supposed that she did not like his pemmican. He climbed out and went away to ease himself, wondering what the girl would do if her bowels or bladder pressed her hard. He didn't suppose that she would be shy about it. He had seen squaws drinking too much rum who got the backdoor trot and they didn't give a damn where they squatted. When he returned he sat and looked at her curiously. She was almost dainty in her manner of eating: she didn't look like Tefronia, for that name was frosted over with dignity, she was more of a water ouzel. He glanced at Payette. The half-breed, his emotions buried deep, was sitting with eyes closed, chewing pemmican. David thought the eyes were closed. He didn't know Payette. Jim had given the dogs a big supper and they were stretched out, dozing. The wind sounded louder and swifter now but it was empty. It would have been a blinding blizzard if it had had soft snow to pick up. They had dug down to the earth and all around them was dead prairie grass that made David think of the first robin and the first violets; and over there, as dry and flaky as tobacco twist, was a mound of buffalo dung. Yes, it was cozy down here. He felt sleepy, he felt the wholesome relaxing drowsiness of deep fatigue. He let his eyelids sink and almost at once he slept.

In his dream a wind had become visible and he was watching it go through the sky when a voice said, "We'd better go now." In the instant of waking he leaped up, groping for his gun.

"I just said we'd better go now."

"Oh," David said.

"You had about three hours," Jim said, putting the dogs in their harness.

The girl had stood up and David looked at her, wondering if she had slept. Jim had filled the ramp in. The girl walked up it and David thought she would go away to be by herself a few moments but she only stood and looked north to the land of her people.

"How your thumb feel?" Jim asked.

"Fine," David said.

When they were out of the hole and pointing toward home Jim sent Payette on ahead and then entered the sled, and David and the girl walked behind. The wind bore upon them with such aggressive pressures that now and then they almost went down. David moved close to her, and taking one of her arms, put it through his and they walked arm in arm. The touch of her thrilled him like a hot rum drink when sitting in the glowing vivacity of a blazing fire. Lord O Lord, it was good just to feel a woman, to know that a female, lovely and young, was walking with him through the night. It made the maleness come up in him and flush its power all through him.

Thought of embracing her, of drawing her close and entering her deep, made his senses swim and glow and burn, and he had the fancy that again he was in love. He liked it when the wind struck hard, for then he felt her need of him, felt the sudden pressure of her arm or of a shoulder against him or a thigh. He wanted to walk with her all night. An Indian girl was not so different from a white girl after all: he sensed that she liked to feel his arm helping her, liked to walk with him this way. He supposed he was being a sentimental fool but he felt that there was a bond between them, almost a union; and if the damned wind hadn't been so violent and treacherous he would have stopped and folded her in to kiss her. He wondered if she would like that. She would not resist it, of course, since she felt that she was his slave, that it was his right to do with her as he pleased. Poor lass, she might not be a virgin when she went home! His loins were hungering for her mightily but his heart was hungering, too, and his mind and all of him. He had lost his mittens and she wore none: he slipped a hand down and found her hand and enfolded it. She did not resist and, of course, there was no response: it made a man feel like a bloody cad to press himself on a girl if she was unresisting only because she felt she had no rights of her own. Among the beasts it was hard to tell if the female's resistance was unwillingness or merely an aspect of courtship—as with all the grass-eaters, all the rodents, all the cats. Well, he would not go any further. He would hold her hand, that fine strong able Indian hand, her arm; and he would lend her a part of his strength in the murderous wind, in the frozen starlit night upon the great buffalo prairies of the north country. But to the day of his death he would remember this walk with an Indian lassie named Tefronia, the two of them going swiftly with ocean and mountain breath upon them, a man and his girl in the night. . . .

When Jim stopped and told David he ought to ride a while David said no, standing there braced against the wind, the lass close to him; and the tactful Jim, sensing what was blowing, rode on. For hours they walked, as only a mountain man and an Indian girl could walk. Payette at last rode for a while, and at last Jim insisted that David and the girl, or the girl in any case, should enter the sled. David was weary, he knew she was weary, but he would have preferred to go on walking rather than to sit feeling forlorn because there was no longer upon him the touch of her, no longer her presence like heaven upon his senses.

Sitting again, facing her, he observed that she was not tattooed on her chin. He thought it rather strange. Many Cree men were tattooed from head to feet, and Cree women usually had three or four lines from the lip down the chin. He fell to thinking of the Crees and comparing them to the Blackfeet. The Crees were woods Indians, which meant that they were as lazy as hell; the men were eager enough for rum—indeed, next to the Saulteurs they were the worst drunkards in the country—but not eager to work for it, though as horse thieves they would labor day and night. Polygamy was common among them. The Cree men often traded wives for a time and, like the men in some other tribes, they cut off the wife's nose if she was found under another man.

David got out to walk and Jim rode with the girl, and David wondered if Jim would like her for a mistress. Probably not. Long ago Jim had soured on women, and it had been more than Tum-tum. As Jim told the story, there had been nothing in Tum-tum to sour a man: she had been devoted to him, she had given him no trouble at all. Maybe Jim had been soured before he came to this country. Some of the men had; he had been surprised to learn how many of them had left Scotland or another land because of a woman. Anyway, Jim wouldn't want a mistress now, Jim was too full of troubles, Jim said all hell was going to bust loose this year. . . .

With a wind on their backs they made good time, arriving at the post at daybreak. Jim said he was going to throw himself down for a little rest and he went away, and David asked Payette to tell the girl to make herself at home. He said to tell all the men in the post that if they put a hand on her he would break their necks.

"You understand?" he asked, staring at Payette.

"Yes, sir."

"You be damned sure the men understand."

"Thank you."

David asked himself if he was being stupid. Whores in this country were almost as common as mosquitoes: the men, cooped up all winter, needed women but had women only when the Indians came in to trade. Belle-mere, the fat gross woman at the post, lay, David suspected, with most of the men, and little enough Pierre seemed to care. This Cree girl was used to polygamous men who swapped wives and treated all women as whores; she might think nothing of it if the men took her in turn and filled her with disease and babies. Well, he would think about it. He was not going to be a moralist but he just didn't like the idea of seeing a girl debauched by a gang of bastards for whom a woman was only something to get on top of. And he didn't want her either.

He put her to work in the days that followed: she would sit for hours cutting out pemmican bags and sewing them or she would bring wood from the storehouse and pile it by the fireplace. She did other chores, though nobody asked her to. David became conscious of her desire to do things for him; he supposed that was it, for now and then he saw her lurking close to where he worked, her eyes on him, and he thought she was wondering if she could assist him. He never spoke to her through Payette. He paid little attention to her, for he was busy.

Jim had decided not to send David out again, for spring was coming, the post might be raided any day. No express had come for weeks but Jim expected one any day from the southeast. He told David that Colin might be dead, that there might be open war on the Red and the Assiniboine if Selkirk came in with an army. "Better take the Cree girl," Jim said. "Or would you like to take a little journey and bring Sunday back?"

He seldom thought about the Cree girl when she was not in sight. It had been a memorable experience, walking through the night with her; a man did foolish things like that and at the time he saw in them meanings which they did not have and could never have. In such a mood a man might marry a woman and in the gray light of morning wonder why he had been fool enough to do it. He had fancied himself in love with her but he was sure that she had had no illusions about him. Women were not such romantic idiots as men. Some men, anyway—Irish, Scotch, English—they were all fools about women, but not Indians. He had been a mooncalf that night and he still thrilled to remember the touch of her thigh or how her chin came up and her bosom out when the wind smote her and almost knocked her down. Did she remember too?

If David had been observing her closely he would have had no need to ask that. In the Cree girl's attitude toward him there had been a subtle change. He became aware of it only after it was plain to Jim, and plain, he supposed, to every other man at the post.

"You mean she hates me?" David said, staring at Jim.

Hate, Jim said, wasn't the word for it. Possibly contempt was.

"Contempt?" David shrugged.

"I'm no expert on women," Jim said, stuffing his pipe. "One thing, though, I learned in Scotland." He reached for an ember, sucked at the stem and winked, and at last said, "If you don't take a woman when she's decided she'll let you she'll never forgive you."

David stared at him and considered his words. "You mean she wanted to surrender to me? Christ, that's ridiculous!"

"Not wanted, maybe. Expected. Dave, put yourself in her place. Nearly all the white men mount the red women, the younger the better. The women expect it. They might not want it but they expect it. Then if you don't seem to want to, what do they think? Maybe that something is wrong with them."

David shrugged. "Heads or tails, I lose," he said.

Jim turned his bearded face to look at him. "Just what were you doing in that long walk in the moonlight?"

"Damned if I know. Just being a fool, I guess."

"She must have reckoned you had some intimate notions about her. Then she reckoned you didn't, and besides, you told the other men to keep off."

David was feeling angry. "I'm scunnered!" he said.

"You figure you've been pretty selfish about it?"

"No," David said sharply, "I hadn't figured that."

"You didn't want her and you didn't want anyone else to have her."

David got abruptly to his feet. He was furious. He sucked in a deep breath and looked down at Jim and said, "You trying to tell me I'm a damned fool?"

"No, no, I just think you're in love. But don't blow any whitecaps over it. Sit down."

"To hell with you."

"I said sit down. You *are* being a damn fool now. Being bulls, the men just don't know what to think of you."

David sneered. "That I should protect a heifer, you mean."

"If you want to put it that way. Now sit down."

David sank to a bench.

"Truth is, Dave, you didn't protect her so well. She's knocked up."

Again David was on his feet, astounded. "That girl?"

"Look, Dave, I don't want any trouble over that girl. We've got plenty of troubles as it is."

"That's true," David said, coming to his senses. "But what man——"

"I don't know," Jim said impatiently, "and I don't give a damn. I've been here a long time, this is old stuff. You need your head examined if you think you'n bring a heifer into a corral with a bunch of bulls and not get a calf."

"I reckon."

"And what in hell does it matter? If it hadn't been done here it would have been done somewhere else. But I'll find out who the man is. We're going into Cree country soon, so this girl has to have a husband." He looked at David a moment and said, "I had it figured you wanted a woman."

"I do. What man doesn't?"

"This man. I mean——"

"I know. I just couldn't—with her."

"That's why I say you're in love. Well, so much for that. It's silly to talk about such things when we might be dead next year."

"If we forget the little things the big things will forget us."

"Might be." Jim brooded a few moments and said that when the spring brigades came in he would know what they had to do. He would know what his pale solemn lordship was planning. There might be a letter from Colin. "You know," Jim said, smoking, musing, "it's funny nobody has ever pointed out that Hamlet is only the typical Englishman. Why suppose the directors in London could ever make up their minds about anything? Still, Selkirk is a Scot."

"So am I," said David dryly.

"I sometimes wonder about that. This Sunday lass——"

"As you say, we have more important things to talk about."

Jim turned again to look at him. "David, my lad, there's no more important thing in the world than love for a man in love. Remember how she looked? Quite like a princess, I thought. I guess you're in love with her and I guess she's in love with you, but I doubt she'll ever be yours."

David searched in pockets for his tobacco and pipe. He was looking at Jim. At last he knew what Jim meant, and he turned suddenly and left the room.

## XXIV

The worst thing about the north country for David and most of the men was the long slow dragging out of the winter. The first bird did not appear until sometime in March; the ice did not go out of Lake

Winnipeg until late May or June. Spring did come at last, and then the mosquitoes ate a man alive and the mice smelled up his food.

Never before in his nine years here had David been so impatient for spring. Was it because he hoped to see Sunday again? He told himself that was not so, but at his labor, when assorting and baling the pelts or making the records or supervising the manufacture of canoes, sleds, snowshoes, dog harness, he was annoyed at finding his thoughts turning to her. He would force himself to think of other matters—of the deadly Dalles aux Morts on the Columbia, where, it was said, a lot of men had drowned; of MacDonald of Garth, a strange man who, a few years back, had built a fort at the forks of the Red and Assiniboine rivers and had named it Gibraltar, though there was not a stone within miles of it; of Fort William at the mouth of the Kaministiquia on the west shore of Lake Superior, its immense council hall decorated with innumerable trophies, at which the pedlars stared while drinking and feasting and plotting the death of the HB Company; of a sweating and cursing partner of either company making the grand tour of inspection, from York to Norway to the Cumberland to Swan River to the Qu'Appelle to Brandon House, or by another route, fifteen hundred or two thousand miles sitting cramped in a canoe, swatting at a half dozen kinds of bloodsuckers, peering at silent riverbanks for a flash of mirror or tomahawk, and walking his fat legs off over the portages. For most of the partners one grand tour was enough. Not one of them had ever gone the twelve- or fifteen-hundred-mile length of the Saskatchewan, or dreamed of riding the Athabasca from source to mouth. Or he would think about all the landmarks that were becoming more familiar to him than the Scottish moors—Milk and Peace and Smoky rivers, the Sweet Grass Hills and Hand Hills and Cut Knife Hill, the Bear Paw Mountains and the Grizzly Bear Coulee. . . .

And he would wonder if Jim actually had implied that a year from now David McDonald would be dead. Was it because he thought David foolhardy?

Or, watching the men at the canoes, he would think of canoes. Men were queer things the way they named things: the gay canoe, which, they argued, was able to travel on no more than a heavy dew or the steam from a boiling kettle; the tired canoe, loaded to the gunwale and almost submerged; the daring canoe, which took the rapids with an incredible sense of balance; the quiet canoe, moving soundlessly through the night; the fat canoe, a small thing like a bathtub that carried only one man; and the war canoe, carrying a dozen armed men. For the men of the north country they all came to have personalities of their own. This was so because so much of themselves went into the making of these water things: stripping off the bark and keeping it in deep shade until it could be rendered supple with heat; collecting tough stringy roots for threads and splitting them and gathering them in coils and putting them in water to soak; and with the pains of a watchmaker preparing straight-grained cedar for the framework. David had done all these chores. He had set an old canoe on the ground and driven stakes all around it to mark its shape, lashed the gunwale, made thwarts and cross ribs, stretched the bark in strips over the frame, heated the gum and poured it on the seams while it was smoking-hot. It was a man's life and he loved it, but he still thought about Sunday.

Depending on when the ice went out, the spring brigade would come in—by mid-May or late May or early June; and that was a time when men uncorked everything they had bottled up and blew like geysers. Before then there was much to be done. Indians, a few at a time, or a solitary buck, or a score or two score, did come in with pelts to trade for rum, tobacco, and ammunition, but when he examined the furs David was aware that the choicest skins were going to the pedlars. It looked like a nice otter skin, thick and glossy, until he looked sharply and saw that it had been taken not with a trap but with a lance; it looked like a good beaver until he noticed that it had been gut-shot; or like a good silver fox before he perceived that the rascals had sprinkled some kind of stuff into the fur. It was not silver but a cross. And it was that way with all the pelts they brought in. When he said that they were not first quality and fixed the price the chiefs were so offended, so wounded in their pride and esteem, that they would turn away and huddle together, muttering.

"Look!" David would say, turning a pelt over and over to show its imperfections. "Ask why in hell they kill an otter with a spearhead." He thought, The lazy bastards, it's so much easier to shoot or spear than to trap! If he exposed a pelt inside and out and got the chief to look at it, his red face would get redder, if that were possible for an Indian; but a few moments later he would fiercely contend that the fur was perfect, that he was being robbed.

Payette said the chief commanded David to look, to see how glossy the coat, how thick, how combed out——

"Tell him look . . . beaver lost two legs in traps . . . see rutting scars all over. Ask him why they take all the good pelts to the pedlars."

Indians came to trade, including many of the Blackfeet, but there was no sign of Sunday. They pitched their lodges on the river and smoke from their fires against the wintry sky looked like spring and smelled like spring. The squaws did business with those white men who went to them, and February passed, and March, and April came and the first birds. The sky softened a little, the crust of the snow softened, and the sun was so brilliant that those who faced the snow fields had to daub their cheeks with soot to protect their eyes. Then an express came in, in relays from post to post, at great risk and with great daring; and Jim learned of the latest developments down in the southeast. Colin had somehow got hold of a pedlar letter which said that what happened to the colony last summer was child's play compared to what would happen to the next one. Governor Semple was back in Fort Douglas.

"Can't imagine what the fool expects to do there."

"Where is his lordship?"

"Montreal."

"Getting up an army?"

"Oh God, no. He still thinks the pedlars will pack their pemmican bags and leave." Another mission for David McDonald, Jim said. When the brigade came in he would go to Red River.

"Red River!" David was aghast. He had made the journey once, cramped in a freight canoe, on a river that made a thousand or ten thousand changes of mind, as if uncertain whether to flow north or east or south, and so by turn flowed in all directions. "You mean I go with the brigade?"

"Unless you want to go alone."

David had known nothing in the world like the spring brigades. Sometimes he dreamed about them; sometimes when working he had a picture of them, knowing that they were on their way—that some had left York Factory by way of Hayes River and Hill River to Oxford House and the lake, and on through Sea River to Norway House and across Lake Winnipeg to Grand Rapids, into Cedar Lake and up the Saskatchewan to Cumberland House; to Rat Portage, Beaver Lake, Heron Lake, the Lake of the Woods, across Frog Portage to English River, then up to Lake la Crosse and Fort Superior. There the route split, the north line going to Athabasca, the south by Beaver River to Beaver Lake and Lake la Biche, and by La Biche

Portage to the Athabasca. Some came up the North Saskatchewan. For a part of the distance the two companies traveled the same route, for a part of it they did not. David would try to picture the vast area and the brigades, now here, now there, all moving west; and then his thoughts would go off to that stupendous landscape of a million lakes and endless forests and naked outcroppings of granite hills and hummocks beyond Montreal, and to another great river that became five miles wide, then ten, then fifty and sixty; or his thoughts would go west over the Continental Divide to the immense watersheds of the Mackenzie and the Columbia; or north, where distances dwarfed a man's imagination and everything was frozen.

No other day of the year was packed so full of emotion as the day when the brigades came in, bringing their supplies and news of the world beyond and letters from home. Even the dogs behaved like lunatics: they barked themselves hoarse and ran like crazy things until exhausted. But this year the roistering, the good-natured insults, the banter were subdued: it was as if some among them had died since they last met, or as if some among them expected death. How was it here? they wanted to know; and those who had wintered here asked, "How is it out there?"

Out there, they said, both sides were resting on their oars and getting their strength. Both sides were laying in powder and ball under cover of night. In silence and secrecy both were trying to find out who were friends, who enemies, while drawing the lines of battle. Jim and David looked at one another. It sounded ominous.

Not a one of the voyageurs seemed to have a good opinion of Governer Semple. Simple, they agreed with Jim, was a good name for him: it was impossible to tell if his fatal weakness was ignorance or optimism. Ignorance, one said: he had no knowledge of frontier conditions or of defense or of the cunning and tenacity of his opponents. Optimism, another said: he would not face a problem or even admit its existence until it had him by the throat and was kicking his knackers off. Unable to see impending disaster, he refused to set up a defense against it. Indian chiefs had come in to warn him, to let him know that the pedlars were trying to bribe them, to tell him to post sentinels day and night against the half-breeds. He thought it more important to plant cabbages than to get his weapons ready.

"By God, that's it," one of the voyageurs said. "A cabbage government and Semple himself is a cabbagehead. But he'll have on his best uniform and all his dignity when they shoot him."

Was an attack gathering? Jim asked. Oh, none at all, they said, and winked. It was a place of brotherly love, and as soon as Semple could bring priests and ministers in there would be praying everywhere. Prayers and cabbages.

Jim sucked at his pipe and looked at the bearded faces. Was Selkirk going to come over? His lordship, they said, was busy trying to get the Montreal courts to declare all the pedlars poachers, and the Montreal officials to send a couple of policemen to chase them off.

Jim looked at David and grinned.

The Indians always flocked to the posts when the brigades came in, for then their wives did a big business. It was a custom for both white and red to gather around a laden table, with the bucks at one end, their wives and children occupying the lowest social station; and before a huge fire of flaming pitch logs they all ate until in misery, mixing the coarse foods of the country with delicate foods from abroad. But this year there was no feasting at either post, though the chiefs received more than their usual regale of rum and tobacco.

One morning when David was in the trading room Sunday slipped in behind the chiefs; and a little later while examining a pelt David was startled to find her steady gaze fixed upon him. He straightened and looked at her. He had continued his studies in the tongue of the Blackfeet and was now able to talk in simple terms.

In his own language he said, "Why, hello, Princess."

In his language she said, "Haylow."

The other persons in the room were now looking back and forth at the two of them.

Coming forward and looking deep into his eyes, she said, "You have wife?"

She had spoken in her own tongue. In the same tongue he said no. Did she have the Cree girl in mind? He sent an assistant to bring the Cree girl in, and while he was gone David said, "You have husband?"

She shook her head no.

David stood looking at her, thinking, Because she is a princess, but most of all because she is white, she has more privilege than ordinary squaws in the choice of a mate; she does not have to marry Brave Feathers if she doesn't want to, she can marry me and I think she wants to. Brave Feathers, he reflected, seemed to have lost interest in her; maybe Jim had bribed him with rum, for Jim had once said that maybe he could make a deal with Horned Thunder. Or maybe wise old Mink Tails had taken care of it.

When the Cree girl came in David pointed to her belly, though it was not yet swollen, to indicate that she was pregnant, and he explained that she was not his wife, had never been his woman, his squaw. He then called Payette over, whom he now hated, and said that this wolverine, this stoat, this fawning jackal was her husband and the father of her child. He asked Payette if this was so, and in admitting it Payette revealed shame at having had to marry a Cree.

Sunday was looking at the Cree girl as only a woman can look at a woman, her gaze resting a few moments on her face and then going down over her, back up and down, pausing again and again at her belly; her face meanwhile expressing her contempt, her feeling that this was a creature from an inferior people. When she had completed her scrutiny she turned and with a slight shrug indicated that the girl had been dismissed from her consciousness and her life.

To Payette, David said, "Take your wife and go." When they had left the room he said to Sunday, "Very busy now. You come later?" When she understood what he was saying she shook her head no and began to back away. If he went down to the lodges could he find her? She gave no response. He went over to her and asked if she loved him. She hesitated and again backed off, and when her answer came it was no.

Well, he had to get busy now, the chiefs wanted rum, they were like naughty children pressing their pelts on his attention and shyly pulling at his sleeve. They could not understand why a paleface spent so much time trying to woo a squaw when for a keg of rum he might have had her and put her to bed.

David thought he would win her. He had seen something in her eyes that he had never seen there before. He didn't know what it was. While trading he asked himself if it was jealousy perhaps, or impatience at his slow way of wooing, or vexation that he seemed content not to see her for months. He knew little about women but he sensed now that this girl could be won. Still, when evening came and he went among the lodges there was no sign of her, this day or the day after.

The departure of the brigades, like their arrival, was a time to fill a man to the brim and spill him over. The voyageurs dressed in clean buckskin and, smelling of it and of rivers and distances, had gay bands of silk around their hair; and most of the leaders had a bit of gold braid and brass-handled pistols and a fancy dagger at their belts. Again the dogs went mad. When a laden canoe was shoved off it circled and waited, and then the second, the third, all waiting for the head steersman to lower his steel-shod pole as a signal for the take-off.

David was overseeing the loading of canoes when, looking around, he was again startled, for there was the unpredictable girl, her eyes watching him. She came up and looked into his eyes and said in English, "Go?"—because he was dressed for a journey.

"I go," he said, nodding. He pointed away to the southeast, then swung his arm in a great circle to the north and the Athabasca. In her tongue he said, "Maybe come back."

She had followed the sweep of his arm, and her eyes for a moment seemed to speculate on distances. Then she looked again into his eyes, her own questioning, and in English said, "Wen?"

David turned to an assistant and said, "Take over here." He took Sunday's arm and led her away from the river and away from all curious eyes. Then he faced her. He looked first at her hair and saw that it was as saturated with grease as ever; at her cheeks, which were blotched scarlet with vermilion; at her lips, remembering that he had kissed them; and then into the hazel-gray eyes, where a man could see so many things. He opened a fire bag at his belt and, still holding her gaze, took out three or four of the short pieces of leather string that had bound his wrists. He spread them on a palm and looked at them and she looked. Waiting for her to meet his eyes, he returned them to the fire bag, but she did not look up at once. She seemed to be looking sidewise at the earth and thinking. When at last she met his gaze there were strange things in her eyes but no revelation of her secrets.

Speaking in her language, haltingly, groping for words, using only verbs and nouns, he told her he was being sent to Red River, and he indicated the southeast; that he would then go with a body of men into the Athabasca, and he nodded to the north. There would be fighting, killing; there would be many dangers. He might live, he might die. If he lived he would come back. Would she be waiting for him, would she then be his wife? He moved to clasp her arms but swiftly she was away from him, and he was angered. To hell with her! he thought, and moved to go, and at once, just as swiftly, she came forward, looking deep into his eyes, questioning him. "Sunday," he said in English, "wait for me, and when I come back we'll go to

Montreal." He tried to express the same thought in her tongue, when again, feeling great tenderness for her, he moved to take her. But again she was away from him. In that moment he heard the signal and he turned and ran.

He entered the last of the canoes and it shot out and the brigade was ready to go. At a signal from the head steersman all the paddles struck water in the same instant, and they were off, with David standing in a canoe, straining his gaze for a glimpse of Sunday, searching up and down the bank for her, looking—looking as the brigade swept into formation and away. He could not see her anywhere. She was gone and he felt numbed. He felt an ache somewhere in him, of loneliness, of anger and frustration, and for the first time since coming to this country he didn't give a hoot whether he lived or died. Maybe he would be killed, yonder on the Red and the Assiniboine, or north in the Athabasca. And a hell of a lot this girl would care!

He stood and looked up and down the bank as long as the bank was in sight but there was no Sunday.

## XXV

The river was at high water, twenty feet higher than in December, and in the white water it was dangerous, though the HB canoes were sturdier and safer than those of the pedlars—and slower too, the pedlars never allowed them to forget. David stood in what was called a north canoe; twenty-five feet long and from four to five feet wide, it could carry a crew of eight or nine men and their supplies, as well as two or three passengers. It was the largest of the canoes. Made of sheets of birch bark a fourth of an inch thick, sewed with spruce roots split into threads, and made watertight with pine gum in the seams, it had a gaudy appearance, for the sides had been painted with crude mystical figures that were believed to increase its speed. It rode well, even at high water: David stood as firmly as if he had been on earth.

These voyageurs, he reflected, looking round at them, were a life-gulping lot. What men they were and how they loved it! The crew of each boat comprised the middleman and the *boutes,* the latter being the bowsman and steersman, who sometimes helped with the paddles. These voyageurs would rise at two in the morning and take off; pause at eight for breakfast, at two for dinner, at dark for supper and sleep, stroking for sixteen hours with twice the rapidity of an oar, fighting off bloodsucking pests, portaging with burdens on their backs from ninety to a hundred and eighty pounds, smoking their pipes, telling their tales and singing their souls out. They were singing now, every paddler in the whole brigade. It was one of their boat songs. Coming up the big rivers at high water was man-killing work; they swore to God that sometimes they stroked their guts out for an hour or two and never moved an inch, up or down. They merely held their own and cursed as long as they could and then shot for the bank to think it over. Colin Robertson preferred Iroquois boatmen to any other; he said they had more courage and skill in the bad spots. White boatmen said that Colin's skull would be found someday bottom side up on the prairie with a little rain water in it.

David liked to watch the men portage. They moved like a machine, every part in perfect order: the cargo was taken out and four men entered the water, two at either end of the boat; and two more then placed themselves amidships after the canoe was raised and took it out. Men carrying bags of fur or pemmican had a broad leather belt that went across their forehead and back to their shoulders, where, attached, it helped support the burden. These mountain and rivermen would carry a hundred and eighty pounds six, eight, or ten miles, puffing their pipes all the way. The distance of a portage was reckoned at so many pipes.

David carried only his weapons and food and bedding. Through odorous pine woods, with aromatic pipe smoke drifting to his nostrils, he climbed, filling his lungs deep and knowing in such hours why he loved this country. It was a country for men—for men who fell asleep the moment they rolled under a canoe to their robe, who would eat two geese or five ducks at a sitting and smoke enough twist in eighteen hours to kill a horse, who faced hazards almost every day and came to think of them as an indispensable part of life, and who fought or got drunk or raped a squaw with abounding and mounting zest. They made David feel that the men who lived at the posts were losing their maleness.

He liked to watch them pitch camp; no man had to say a word for every man knew his task. Or hear them tell their tales, though they hadn't much time for storytelling if they were to get any sleep at all. This brigade was alive with suspicions. The pedlar brigade was coming behind them: it was a special pedlar insolence to depart after the HB brigade and arrive in advance of it. It was suspected that the pedlars this spring, as during the past three or four springs, would have the best of the pelts and would be full of swagger and brag. It was customary for the brigades of the two companies to journey not too far apart, as protection against Indians, or for the purpose of engaging in drinking or storytelling bouts or in bone-crushing duels.

"They're not on our tails yet," the brigade boss said one evening. "The dirty dogs are up to something."

They had encamped on an island. They were afraid of ambush.

"Ain't never seen their smoke yet," an oarsman said.

"We better look wide," another said. "My squaw, she says to me, 'Dolling, I see mucha theengs besides stars.' I reckon she sees more than we see."

There were snorts of laughter. "Mucha besides stars, good Moses! You mean you always took her outside and done it at night?"

"I mean the few days I had her she spent a lot of time looking up."

Listening to them, it occurred to David that he ought to keep a journal, as many of the officials did. The voyageurs told the damnedest things. One of them, who had spent years in the States, told of a baptism he had witnessed. "Or call it that," he said. A red tribe had captured a white family, the parents, two girls, and three boys. They tomahawked the parents and stuck the scalps up to dry in plain view of the children; and then just for the hell of it, because they were neither beast nor human, they decided to baptize the smallest boy. He was about three or four years old. They filled a huge stone vat with water and kept putting hot stones in it until the water boiled, and then they shoved the boy into it, head over heels. That was their way of showing what they thought of white man's religion and all his cant and preachment about red men down in hell's fires.

One of the men looked thoughtfully at his pipe and said, "'Twas hard on the boy."

After a few moments another said, "This whole country will soon be full of preachers."

"Preachers and cabbages."

"You heard about Adam and Eve?"

"Now who in hell's that?"

"The bull and cow amongst the cabbages." The settlers, the man said, had a shaggy old prairie cow. Selkirk shipped in a glossy bull that was as well bred as an Oxford gentleman and he simply wouldn't look at the cow. He wouldn't even smell to see if she wanted him. Selkirk's governor blessed them and said, "'Multiply, and replenish the earth.'" And by the living God, what did that bull do?

"He the one got out of sight of the stable and got lost?"

"Another one. This one, he went down to get hisself a drink and he fell through the hole they had chopped in the ice. That bull just plumb disappeared and they scratched all the hair off of their heads trying to figger out where he had gone to."

"Didn't they ever?"

"Not till spring. When the ice broke up, why, there he was under the ice."

"Just like an Englishman," a man said. "The bull, I mean."

"And the cow got herself no baby?"

"That cow just laid down and died of a broken heart."

The men smoked and thought about Selkirk and his greenhorns. One of them said, "When his lordship comes he'll have them comb the cows nice and put some ribbon on them."

"It true he's bringing preachers this time?"

"Oh God, yes, all ganted up with righteousness."

"He should bring Father Kelly," one said. "You hell-benders ever hear of him?"

"Irish?" asked a Scot, sucking his pipe.

"More than three hundred pounds of Irish. Bigger'n Perpetual Motion."

"Big as McLoughlin?"

"Oh, Christ. Would make two McLoughlins."

"Big," said another dryly. "Let's not try and figger it out to the pound."

"All right, how did he make medicine?"

Well, David said, it was the pedlars that time—fifty pedlars drunk and raising hell and as blind as a moose with its head under water. Then Father Kelly came along. He began to preach to them. He said they were headed for hell like a herd of buffalo for a precipice. They threw rum all over him and then he got mad and he cussed so hard that every man in Ireland blushed for his own ineptness. He waded in, taking them two at a time, cracking their skulls so hard that you could hear them crack clear to Rainy Lake. Pedlars were lying around as thick as drowned buffalo on a beach. And when Father Kelly couldn't see a single pedlar left standing he was so mighty mad and so full of the holy spirit that he leaned over and stood a couple of them up and cracked their heads again.

One of the men took his pipe stem away and wiped at his mouth. "A preacher, you say?"

"Father Kelly from Clonakilty."

"Ain't this Selkirk a Presbyterian?"

"Approximately."

"He wouldn't figger a Catholic could make good medicine."

"Reckon not."

"How you think the new settlers will make out?"

With a wicked grin the man said, "Quiet-like."

Another said, "Just as soon as old Macdonell can get the half-breeds poured full."

That was the word that came to David all along the line. The new settlers were doomed. If Selkirk didn't understand that he was a fool, and if he did, yet sent them on in, he was a murderer. Could you find any sense in a man like that?

David said one evening, "Wonder why the pedlars are so slow catching up."

"Means something," the steersman said.

"Maybe they won't till they've joined the Athabasca brigade."

"Might be."

"Could we make Cumberland before they overtake us?"

"Oh God, no. They'll be waiting for us about the Churchill."

The steersman was right. They saw smoke in the sky long before they came to the Athabasca junction. They might have portaged and bypassed it but they hoped to find an HB brigade there too, if the pedlars had not taken it prisoner. David thought the situation looked bad.

"What you think?" he asked the brigade foreman.

The boss of a brigade in either company was chosen for experience and boldness. Roger Bruce scanned the distances, his weathered hide looking as thick and tough as parfleche.

"We might have to fight," he said. "But if they mean real trouble I think they'll let us have it at Grand Rapids."

At the foot of Grand Rapids the Saskatchewan emptied its muddy turbulent waters into Lake Winnipeg. It was a beautiful place for an ambush.

"Or Rat Portage?"

Bruce shook his head no. Grand Rapids, he figured. In any case, it would be before Red River.

David said no more. He could think of no reason why the pedlars would attack before Red River, rather than after it, unless Selkirk was marching in an army and they knew it. Bruce and his men camped within sight of pedlar fires, and the next morning the North Westers, sprawled over a big encampment at the junction, were waiting for them. Bruce said they would go right on by if they were not molested, but almost at once some of the pedlars shoved out in their fast canoes and circled the HB brigade, flinging taunts. Were the canoes really loaded with pelts or did they have ballasts of stone across the bottoms? Did they expect to stop at Selkirk's settlement and pick up a few cabbages, and maybe a bag of wheat flour for bannocks and scones? Why in hell didn't they pull over to the bank for a sociable drink?

A bearded giant, standing in a canoe, shouted at them, "Goddamn your hide and taller, you need a regale!"

When it seemed to the pedlars that Bruce was not going to stop, their language became more abusive. They said the hired hacks of the honorable company ought to shuffle off to Scotland and bed down with a lassie before the crows picked their bones. Did they all want to be John Rosses? That question made many a face darken. The violent and illiterate Peter Pond, veteran of the French and Indian wars and out of one escapade only to rush into another, had been the one man, the HB men believed, who knew who murdered John Ross some years ago when the pedlars were exterminating the Gregory-McLeod outfit. To ask them if they wanted to be John Rosses was to make it as plain as words could make it.

An HB oarsman stood up and put his pipe away. He shouted over at Bruce, "Are we going to take these insults?"

Bruce shouted across the canoes at him, "Sit down!"

The oarsman sat but the HB men were getting their blood up. That one about John Ross had stung like a nest of yellow jackets. And to rub vinegar into the sting the bearded giant had his canoe shot close to that of Bruce and he sneered at Bruce as well as a man could sneer whose face was covered with thick coarse hair, and he wanted to know if there was a single damned man in the whole feeble Selkirk outfit who'd like a good fight.

Roger Bruce looked at him. "You talk a hell of a big brag."

"I fight a hell of a good fight," the giant said. "Just give me one smack at you and you'll shit a teurd as big as a moose."

"Put over," Bruce said.

The brigade swung to the north, close to the far bank, where the pedlars were camped. David was wondering if Bruce intended to walk into that camp with only a third or a fourth their number of men. Roger Bruce had nothing like that in mind. He had in mind that only his canoe would beach and he would then tackle this giant himself. He gave orders that all other HB canoes were to remain a hundred feet out, every man alert to the position of his gun.

It was a hell of a thing, David was thinking, for a man as important in the company as Roger Bruce to engage in a brawl. These fights, commonplace enough between the companies when their men camped in the same area, were almost never with fists but with thick tough green cudgels, with which arms were broken and skulls cracked. The pedlar giant, David judged, weighed about two hundred and eighty pounds and there was no fat on him. Roger Bruce was no such giant as that. David had his canoe maneuvered around so that he could speak to Bruce, though he had no right to, for the boss of a brigade was the absolute law and there was no appeal above him.

David called over to him, "Roger, about this fight—"

Roger looked up. His gray eyes swept him, his curt tongue said, "What?"

"Why don't you let some man in the brigade answer the challenge?"

"You mean you?"

"Sure, I'll take it."

"What's wrong with me?"

"Not a thing, but you're brigade foreman, the company needs you."

"You're a chief trader, the company needs you. Are you thinking that bulkhead of bilge can lick me?"

David said no more. He saw that Roger Bruce was deeply angry in a contained unexplosive way. Roger now had his oarsmen shoot him over to the beach and he got out. The pedlars were there, ready for him, the bearded giant at their head.

Bruce looked at the man and said, "What kind of fight do you want?"

The giant said, "What kind you want?"

"Any kind."

The giant turned his bullneck to the right, to the left, slowly, to look at his companions. "Got all his bigs on, ain't he? Kinda brave-like." He looked at Bruce. "Bare knuckles suit you?"

"Fine," Bruce said. "But don't stand there with your brag up all day. Let's go."

The big fellow came in, head low on his thick neck, his mighty arms up, his small bright eyes looking out across the beard that covered both cheeks. Bruce had his guard up but he was not moving like a leviathan; he was stepping nimbly, to right, to left, feinting. He was about six feet tall, David supposed, studying him, and weighed perhaps two hundred pounds. He seemed to be quite fast on his feet. David glanced around him at the position of the guns in his canoe and again looked at the two fighters. Pedlar men were beginning to clamor for action and to fling taunts at their own moose.

"What's the matter, Brig? Can't you see him? He's right there, boy, right under your nose!"

"We shoulda hung a HB banner on him for Brig."

"You reckon Brig doesn't like what he's looking at?"

"Hey, Brig, goddamn it, can't you see him?"

Brig was now advancing and Roger was dancing away from him. The big man held his arms, it seemed to David, not to strike out with blows, but to bring them down, as he might have used clubs. As he came in he raised them as if to club down and then it happened. It happened so quickly that David almost missed it. Roger feinted with his left, in the same moment pirouetting on his left foot and bringing his right foot around and back, toe down; and in the next instant his body rolled behind the blow of his right fist in Brig's solar plexus, knocking a piglike grunt out of him. The big fellow's diaphragm was paralyzed. Without breath, his eyes bulging, his mouth open as if waiting for a nipple, he began to bend forward; and Roger struck again. This time his right fist buried itself in the Adam's apple of the soft throat and the bully's windpipe was paralyzed. Roger turned away, as a man might who had no doubt that a fight was over.

Stricken, paralyzed, unable even to try to breathe, the giant toppled over like a tree. His companions gathered round him, staring at his face, and one of them had sense enough to know that their warrior might die if nothing was done for him. His face was turning purple. His eyes bulged as if he had a tourniquet on his throat. "Water!" a man shouted, and soon they were hurling muddy Saskatchewan water into his face and all over him and they were rolling him over and over, trying to relax him; and when at last the paralyzed muscles gave way his sudden huge gulping of air could have been heard for half a mile. He struggled to his feet and they hustled him off and out of sight.

David was looking with curious interest at Roger, thinking that here was a man it was well to have on your side. He thought he had never seen him before, though he supposed he had, because foremen of brigades had been long in the service and had come up from the ranks. He had seen bullies humbled, he had humbled a few himself, but never before had he seen the job done so neatly and thoroughly. Looking round him, he saw admiration lighting up the faces.

A man caught his eyes and said, "Bloody neat, eh what?"

"Quite."

"What wonders me," another said, "is him and the holy father. Mother McGillivray, would that be a fight!"

## XXVI

There was no further trouble with the pedlars at the river junction but Bruce was worried about ambush at Grand Rapids. David said he would take his own canoe and push ahead and scout it. He went alone. Downstream at floodwater a brigade moved fast but David moved faster, shooting the tiny craft forward with long powerful strokes and keeping his eye on the riverbank. He did not know this country well. He figured that he was still about three hundred miles from half-breed land, but you never could tell where a half-breed would pop up if he smelled a chance at pillage and murder. The first night he found a huge cottonwood tree that, washed away at its roots, had toppled over and lay out across the water but a little above it; and among the dense branches he hid his canoe and anchored to a limb and stretched out in it and slept. Early the second day at Cumberland House, a location occupied by both companies, he concealed his canoe and slipped in to learn if there was any news. He was astonished to hear that the pedlar Macdonell had seized an HB brigade and made off with all its pemmican. Colin had then asked Governor Semple for a declaration of war but Semple was still unable to make up his mind.

"A true Briton," as Jim Dugald would say. "They'll never face a crisis until it has both hands on their knackers. Is he doing nothing at all?"

Not much, the man said. Semple had brought a fresh batch of colonists the seven hundred miles from York to the cabbage patch. They had been so happy that they got drunk and danced all night but at daylight they were praying.

What was Selkirk doing?

Selkirk, his informant said, was trying to persuade ex-soldiers to come over and be farmers. They were Swiss mercenaries and had about as much interest in farming as Selkirk had in the odor of a beaver's sex glands. All hell would pop pretty soon.

"How soon?"

"Any day."

David was soon to learn how true that forecast was, though at the Grand Rapids he found no menace. Nobody was there, or if men were there they were too well hidden to be dislodged. June had come before he reached the lake. He was stroking along close to its west shore when he met a scouting canoe on its way to find the HB fur brigades. This man had bad news. The pedlars, he said, no longer made any bones about it: their henchmen and assassins were openly boasting that there would be red sport on Red River before July came in.

"What do they mean by sport?"

"Murder, of course."

"The settlers?"

Wouldn't the settlers be the easiest to kill? But they were also saying, with no bones about this either, that they would soon seize all the HB posts at the Little Slave, Ile-à-la-Crosse, and Reindeer Lake, and that a little later they would take every post on the Saskatchewan.

David stared at the man and considered his words. Did Semple have enough strength to stand them off?

Nobody, the man said, could figure the governor out. The Indian chiefs had told him what was coming. Peguis had told him over and over and had begged him to do something. All he had done was to give orders to destroy Gibraltar!

"A lot of sense that makes."

"It just gives them more excuse."

"Does Semple think an attack will come?"

"Oh yes, yes, he does. But he told Peguis that he wasn't going to get excited about it until he saw it."

David groaned. "Just the way Elizabeth was when she knew King Philip was building an armada. The British have had a hell of a lot of luck."

Well, he told himself, canoeing on down the lake, the thing for him to do was to scout this country as he went along, and to get to the settlement and find out what Semple had in mind. Were his settlers trained to shoot? Were they organized? Did they have plenty of powder and ball and did they have their weapons in order? Were they prepared on a moment's notice to dash into Fort Douglas, and once there, would they be provisioned for a siege? Was Semple qualified by training and experience to be governor of a settlement that faced enemies on all sides? Why had Selkirk chosen him?

While he was skimming along his thoughts turned to Selkirk. He was Thomas Douglas, fifth Earl of Selkirk, who, after graduating from Edinburgh University, had toured the Continent and returned to marry the wealthy Jean Wedderburn Colvile. With her money he had bought control of the HB Company and with his eyes shut had walked into the fight of his life. His greatest ambition, it was said, was to find homes under the British flag in the New World for the Scottish crofters who were being kicked out of their homes in the Highland expulsions. But the Earl of Selkirk seemed to have no idea at all of the kind of adversary he faced. If he had a good idea, then why in the world would he send out a man like Semple?

Crossing a big lake was not like coming down a swift river. It was hard work. Day after day he stroked and night after night he hid under overhanging foliage. When he came at last to the mouth of the Red River, where it dumped into the lake, he calculated that he was about sixty miles from the settlement. But he had to buck a swift current now and sometimes he had to leave the river and plod along with his weapons and food and bedding and the canoe on his back.

He was walking one afternoon through river growth when he heard sounds that he thought were human. Softly he laid his burden down and listened. He heard voices, male voices, and he thought he could hear the sound of oars. Taking only his gun, he hastened over to the river and then on hands and knees crept forward to the bank. He rose little by little above the foliage until he could look out, and what he saw so amazed him, so filled him with a sense of the dreadful, that he sank back down and sat there, listening and thinking. . . .

## XXVII

Colin Robertson did not like Governor Robert Semple. He said he was gentle and stupid. What he took for stupidity was only a lack of humor; for gentleness, a quiet and fussy devotion to order, pomp, and power. Governor Semple had so strong a sense of the dignity of his own person, of its being inviolable to his social inferiors, that he scoffed at the thought that the half-breeds would dare to lay a finger on him, much less invade his privacy or shoot him down. And so it was with weariness and impatience that he turned once again to face the persistent red friend of the white man, old Chief Peguis.

"And what this time?" asked Semple sharply, his wide-open eyes staring at the humble and self-effacing man before him.

It was the Portage of the Prairie, the old chief said, meaning the voyageur-buffalo-hunting servants of the North West Company. It was the Bois Brulés, he said, the burnt-wood runners, his eyes begging the governor to be reasonable. It was the dreadful and vindictive and murderous half-breeds, and they would be here tomorrow.

"How many?" Semple asked.

The old man thought there would be a hundred or a hundred and fifty. There would be the entire Portage of the Prairie, whatever its number was.

Semple shrugged. "Let them come," he said. "I'll teach those vulgar robbers a lesson."

Peguis stared at him. What in the world did the white man mean? --that he would teach those terrible warriors with the greenhorns, with these dull farmers, these Scotch hillfolk? What about the women and children? he asked. He would be glad to take them away and hide them until the whole thing blew over.

Again Semple shrugged. No, he said, no, no. He dismissed the chief and returned to his office. Let's see, he was making entries in his journal, was he not? What had he been saying . . . ?

Governor Robert Semple knew that Lord Selkirk was racing westward, his temper blazing. He supposed that he was bringing an army to clean out the half-breeds and the pedlars and all the other enemies of the honorable company, whose charter was now a hundred and forty-six years old. He knew that the lord had left Montreal with an armed escort. He might now be as far as Fort William, or even the Lake of the Woods. It was simply inconceivable that the half-breeds would strike again, knowing that an army was coming, with a man at the head of it who had got himself established as justice of the peace for the whole Indian land.

Old Peguis had turned away, shaking his head sadly. He remembered what had happened a year ago. He tried in vain to understand the white man's ways, his contempt of danger, which turned out so often not to be contempt at all but only ignorance; his haughty airs; his complete misunderstanding of the half-breed. Only a few weeks ago Colin Robertson had said to him, "Ignorance will be the death of Semple." Peguis had said yes, he was afraid that it might be. For here was a man who would listen to nobody west of Montreal.

Peguis knew the half-breeds. He had lived among them most of his life. He knew that the leaders, Cuthbert Grant and Bostonnais Pangman, were not ordinary men. They were both the sons of pedlar partners and Grant had been educated in the best schools in Montreal. They were smart and they were bold, as bold as any two men in this whole country, red or white. They had the respect, the confidence, even the devotion of the half-breeds, and when they said they were going to clean a settlement out and throw the last cabbage into the river only an utter damned fool would think they did not mean it.

Peguis knew that they meant it. He knew when they intended to do it. And he knew that it would be a massacre if something was not done—but what could you do with a man like Semple? Should he try again? He asked the sad Marie, Batiste's woman, to whom he had given sanctuary in his lodge, and she shook her head yes.

"Talk to him again," she said.

"I have—once"—he held up a hand and counted his fingers—"four time."

"Talk again. Try and get the women and children into fort."

And so after dark of the night of June 18, Peguis went again to the gate and asked to have the governor summoned. When Semple came, aroused from sleep, scowling, impatient, Chief Peguis begged him to listen a moment and he made another proposal. He offered to bring his own warriors, all of them, to the fort to stand the half-breeds off until Selkirk came. That wouldn't be necessary, the governor said, shaking his head in a vigorous negative. Lord Selkirk was coming at top speed with an army and would arrive any moment. The half-breeds knew it. They wouldn't dare attack.

Peguis looked at him. He felt helpless but he made still another proposal. He begged the governor to get all his colonists inside the fort and keep them there until Selkirk came. For if they slept outside in their cabins they might be burned out, as they were last time, or tomahawked in their own beds.

That was not necessary either, the governor said. Everything would be all right.

And so again, and for the final time, the wise old chief turned away.

The next morning Robert Semple left his bed at the usual hour. The night had been cool. The morning was cool, the air was spiced with the odors of growing vegetables and grains. The colonists were doing well this year. They would have a city here before long, with schools and churches, and broad cultivated fields around it for miles and miles. There might be a kind of kingdom here, or at least a great barony, and he would be the governor and lord of it, with only Selkirk above him. . . .

Nevertheless, he was a little worried this morning. Peguis had been so importunate. How many times had that man come to admonish, to warn, to supplicate, to propose? The governor went outside and climbed to an eminence to look around him, but everything as far as the eye could see was soft and tranquil in the golden light of a June morning. Already some of the men had gone out to the fields, for they were early risers, these thrifty Scots, they worked hard, they would build strong and true. He returned to his cabin and stood there in thought, and he decided after a few minutes to send a boy to the watchtower, with orders to search the areas west and south for sign of the half-breeds. "If you see anyone coming, yell as loud as you can."

It was late afternoon when the lad began to shriek and holler for all he was worth. Semple sent a boy over to see what the trouble was and this boy soon dashed back, gasping, "It's them!"

"Where?" asked Semple, looking south and west. He could see no sign of them. He got his glasses and with a half dozen men he went to the tower. He looked south first, then moved the glasses across the western horizon and to the north; and there, far away, was a thin line of horsemen, approaching from the west, across the swamps of Frog Plain beyond Fort Douglas. Without a word he handed the glasses to one of the men and he looked and in turn the others looked.

One of them said, "It's them."

"I'm trying to count them," another man said, looking through the glasses. "Looks like a hundred or more."

Moving slowly, with dignity, as befitted his position, Governor Semple went down from the tower, saying as he went that he would call for volunteers and go out to meet them. It would be best, he said, to keep them away from the women and children. He would explain to them that if they did not go away Lord Selkirk would exact a dreadful vengeance, and then they would go away.

His men scattered, calling for volunteers, and soon there were twenty-nine of them, with the governor at their head, ready to march out. They were armed but they carried their weapons as men might who had never used them or who felt that they had no use. They went in a group out across the fields to meet the half-breeds, and at once, before Semple understood what was happening, they were outmaneuvered. Seeing them coming, the half-breeds swiftly threw an enveloping semicircle around them, penning them in, their backs to the river, their faces to a half-mile arc of guns. Then an ugly killer named Boucher, eager for the slaughter to begin, rode his horse on a dead run from the half-breed line, his sights on the governor.

Semple saw him coming, his gun at the ready, and he became very angry. His anger became explosive when he perceived that Boucher was painted hideously, like any Indian on the warpath, and when he heard him shouting the most profane and obscene insults in his broken English. Because he was so angry Semple strode out to meet him, his men trailing him. Boucher dashed up and stopped his pony with violent suddenness and the beast reared, the front feet striking; and oblivious of danger, Semple rushed in and seized the bridle reins and shouted up to the man, "How dare you talk to me that way?" He was jerking furiously at the bridle and the half-breed, his gun still ready across his left arm, was jeering down at him and spitting at him and yelling insults.

"You son a biche!" he roared over and over. "You dog ut steenks!"

And Governor Semple, almost too furious to speak, almost strangled by indignities and outrage, held on to the bridle and roared up at him, "You scoundrel! You contemptible scoundrel! How dare you address me that way?"

"You fatass cowert and basserd! You son a biche! You——"

"Scoundrel, scoundrel!"

There they were, the governor refusing to release the rein, Boucher threatening him with his gun and making passes with his scalping knife and hurling upon him every term of abuse and insult known to him in English. Cuthbert Grant had come up and now made a move to stop it. He was shouting at Boucher but Boucher was so furious that his eyes had turned yellow. And Governor Semple was shaking impotently with insult and rage.

Grant might have controlled his men if Semple had not committed an unforgivable outrage and swiftly followed it with another. With all his furious strength he moved closer to the horse and, his wild hands striking and beating upward, tried to seize the man's gun. When he failed in that he swung to his men, his face purple, and roared, "Arrest them, all of them! Take them prisoner!"

He was never to live to explain how he thought his twenty-nine greenhorns would take a hundred armed half-breeds prisoner. There was a shot, and not even Grant was ever to know who fired it. Semple staggered back, a ball through one thigh. In an effort to save the governor's life Grant leaped from his horse, intending to get him up and away; but before he could touch him a second ball went through Semple's chest. He threw himself back, gasping, blood pouring from his nose.

All the other half-breeds had pushed in, eager for a chance to shoot someone, and within a few seconds twenty of Semple's men had fallen around him. Two broke away in a wild run for the river and made it and plunged in. Seven, most of them wounded, were taken prisoner. Twenty and the governor lay dead and not a half-breed had been scratched. A mile away Chief Peguis sat in a tree and watched it and shook his sad old head.

Those over in the settlement had also been watching, and they knew what had happened when they heard the report of guns. They knew what had happened a year ago and their terror now was so wild and uncontained that children stood with hands to their faces, screaming, and women, shrieking hysterically, ran into cabins and out of them or around and around, not knowing what they did. But the half-breeds did not ride over, they did not strike there at once. They went away. In the dark of midnight they returned, to castrate, to tear testicles from bodies and hurl them into the night, with all the bitterness a half-breed and a bastard could feel toward his white father. They ripped bodies open and tore the hearts out, they scalped, they thrust daggers into dead eyes—and left twenty-one ghastly carcasses to the wolves. They had other work to do. Their task now was to gather up the terrified survivors and get them down Red River and far away into the north before Selkirk could come. Their task was to burn the cabins and the crops, to tear down the fort, to leave only ruins and ashes. "Just so you get rid of them," the pedlars had said to Cuthbert Grant. "Get the sons of bitches out of there. . . ."

## XXVIII

David sat back to listen and to think about it, for he sensed at once that these were Selkirk's settlers and that they had been driven out of their homes. The pedlars were taking them to some frozen desolation in the far north, where they would die of famine or loneliness or go mad. What was Colin doing? Where was Selkirk?

David rose again to look. Some of the canoes were passing him no more than fifty feet away and he stared hard at the faces. The terror in them was so stark that he thought he could smell it. It was the half-breeds taking them away, canoeload after canoeload, women, children, men; the half-breeds with their war paint on. Cuthbert Grant was there, he supposed, all the leaders, but he had never seen them, he did not know them. That might be Grant standing in the lead canoe. . . .

They passed in silence, save a human voice now and then and the sound of oars in water; passed and vanished toward the lake, and there was no sign of them. David brought his things over and put the canoe in and bent to the paddle. All the remainder of this day he drove his canoe up the current and all this night until almost dawn, and then he smelled it. He shot the canoe over to the west bank and sat hidden, sniffing the odors on a heavy southwest breeze. He thought it must be the stench from their slain beasts, mingled with the smell of ashes and burnt timbers and prairie grass; but after hiding the canoe close by Fort Douglas and walking out toward the settlement, he came almost at once to the most ghastly scene he was ever to see. His first glance told him that there had been a massacre, his second that wolves had been feasting on human flesh. His nose told him that these persons had been dead three or four days. The bodies, so stripped of their meat as to be unrecognizable, lay within a small radius upon the prairie, only a few hundred yards from the cinders and ashes that had been the colony's buildings. Sickened by the stench, he walked among them, but there was not a face from which the flesh had not been eaten, the eyes picked out, the teeth bared.

Fearing capture, he hastened back to the river and hid. After daylight came he stealthily examined the area, trying to get a picture of what had happened. Fort Douglas had been taken of course, the crops had been burned, the settlement destroyed, and those who had not been slain had been driven to the canoes and taken away. He crossed the river to the east side, and while he was sitting, his gun within reach, eating pemmican and thinking about the slaughter, he heard a sound. Something was coming toward him. He supposed it was an animal, a skunk or a porcupine, but he took his gun up; and a moment later was amazed to see that the thing crawling toward him, not walking but crawling, was a man. David sat very still and watched him. The man had not seen him; he would crawl a little distance and then stop and seem to listen and peer. He was one of the settlers, David supposed: no man from either company would ever go over the earth on hands and knees like that. When the man was about thirty feet away David said quietly, "Where you going?"

The man's response chilled him. Instead of rising to his feet he merely turned and looked at David—looked as he had seen beasts look when unexpectedly confronting him in deep forest, on paths where human feet rarely walked—as the wolverine might have looked at him, or the wildcat. David sat, holding his gun, looking, and the man looked. When David asked the man to come on over he got to his feet, trembling, and glanced round him, like a creature whose only thought was flight. David arose and went over to him and looked him up and down. Yes, this was one of the settlers.

"Where are the others?"

The man looked round him in such a strange uncomprehending way that David suspected that the experiences of the past few days had unsettled his mind. The lower part of his face was shaking, his eyes were wild with memory. David led him over to his things and told him to sit, and the man sank to his rump. David gave him a hunk of pemmican and the man's eyes, looking at it, kindled with a light that was not human and his lower jaw shook so that he had difficulty fixing his teeth in it. David let him eat a little while and then drew him into talk.

In a voice that quavered and died away in the anguished throat the man told his story—the story of the half-breeds, so hideous in their paints, more monstrous than anything he had ever seen; of the massacre; of his dash to the river with all the guns firing behind him. . . . David became aware that the man's impressions of what had happened were so vague and mixed up as to be worthless, but he asked him to go on and tell everything that had happened.

They had called the governor vile names——

"Just a minute. What kind of names?" The man hesitated. David sensed that he was a pious fellow who did not use coarse language and did not like to repeat it. But he confessed at last that they called the governor a son of a bitch and a dog and other epithets of like portent; and that the governor had become simply furious and had said, You scoundrel——

"What?" asked David, astonished. "He called him a scoundrel?"

"He said, 'You scoundrel, do you dare speak to me so?' "

"Oh no!" said David, groaning. If only Jim could hear this!

The man seemed not to understand. He said with dignity, "He insulted our governor. He called him——"

"Yes, yes, he called him a son of a bitch."

"He had no right to."

David looked at him. What did this pious greenhorn from the hills of Scotland think constituted a right in this country!

The governor so completely lost his temper, the man said, that he called the half-breed a damned rascal.

"I can't stand any more," David said. He studied the man's face. He asked, "Didn't any of you fire a shot? Aren't there any half-breed bones out there?" Then he knew that it was a cruel question.

He began to feel pity for this poor half-starved creature. He gave him more pemmican, and to allay his fears so that he might sleep he let him spend the night close by him. The man had told him that he had a wife and three children, and David advised him the next morning to take the trail of the captives and overtake his family. But he knew that such a greenhorn could not long survive in this land. He was tempted to give him his gun but decided that a gun would be of no more use than a walking stick to one of his kind. He offered to take him as far as Cumberland House, where, David said, he could stay until a brigade picked him up. But the man had more character and courage than David had given him credit for. He said no, he would find his family; he had lingered here only because he had hoped to bury those who had fallen. He had seen Chief Peguis out there trying to bury them and, climbing far up a tree, he had seen wolves trotting back and forth.

David then advised him to go to the fort and surrender and say that he wanted to go to his family. The man considered it a few moments and said he would go. Did David know how far away his family would be?

"To hell and gone," David said. "But you can follow the trail by all kinds of signs such as campfires. Better ask them for a small canoe, a gun, some food. . . ."

It was six weeks later when David sat down with Colin Robertson and John Clarke. Having never seen Clarke before, he looked at him curiously, for he had heard, even from such men as Jim, that in the whole company there was no man held in greater fear and respect by white man or red. Clarke was not a giant, measured by white men in this country, but he looked to David like a man who was all sinew and grit. He was an extremely quiet man, a man who never raised his voice, a man of few words. His eyes were blue gray, his hair brown and long, his mouth wide, his beard fine and slightly curly.

Colin was saying to David, "Roger Bruce outmaneuvered the ambush and got through and the brigade has gone on. I took Roger and Jim McVicar and a few others out of it to go to the Athabasca with Clarke and you and the others. They're tough men and you'll need some tough men with all those damned Frenchmen." He looked from David to Clarke, back and forth a few moments, and went on, "Without benefit of barrister, court, or magistrate the pedlars intend to seize every post we have up north, up west; and may have done it by now. Jim Dugald," he said, turning to David, "may be in irons now. They'll capture our men by any ruse, ambush, or deceit they can think of and they may torture them, put them to ordeals, even to the thousand natural shocks that flesh is heir to. So in the Athabasca expect anything."

"We will," Clarke said.

David said to Colin, "Are you going?"

"Clarke will be in command. I have my orders elsewhere."

"John Bowman will miss you."

Colin looked at David. "That's right, he expects me, doesn't he? Well, give him my felicitations. Tell him there'll be other times and places."

"Of course," David said, wondering if Colin was afraid of John Bowman. "And what are our orders under Clarke?"

To drive the damned poachers out of the Athabasca, Colin said, to destroy their posts and forts, to entice all the red men away from them, to fill the pedlars with fright and consternation and terror—

"And just how are we to do that?"

"John will contrive methods."

"I imagine," David said, "the pedlars will be contriving too."

Colin said, a little sharply, "John has one simple order, to assert the property rights of our company and enforce them fearlessly and with the utmost vigor."

"How many of us are going in?"

About a hundred men, Colin said, most of them French Canadians. Some of them would be extraordinary, such as François Decoigne, a top-notch trader with a broad knowledge of the North West Company; or John Clarke here, who had been on the Mackenzie and Peace rivers and knew the whole country. "Or you," Colin said to David, and flashed his quick mechanical smile. There would be a depot post on Jack River; and, as they were all well aware, Selkirk in the previous year had hired Norwegians to build a winter road from York Fort to Lake Winnipeg, and Norway House, on the west side of the outflow from the lake.

David said, "I can't see much sense in a road from York or a depot on the Jack if the Indians won't trade with us."

"You will induce them to trade."

David stared at Colin and shrugged. He was remembering what the man had said on the Saskatchewan last summer: "If we don't have pemmican I don't figure we'll get it." A lot of HB pemmican had been stolen. Jim had asked if the red men would be too scared to trade with the HB men and Colin had said they would be; but now, ordered by Selkirk to recruit men and send them in, he was singing a different song. He was pretending now that all would be fair weather under Clarke, but he knew better. John Clarke was a good man but he had no magic, he couldn't make medicine with the Crees if they all ran away.

"When do we leave?"

"As soon as possible," Colin said. "Maybe by the first of August."

The brigades left on the fourth of August in the muggy depths of the mosquito season and ran into trouble almost at once. At Cumberland House above Lake Winnipeg on the Saskatchewan they were to pick up enough pemmican to carry them to Ile-à-la-Crosse at the entrance to Athabasca land. At Cumberland the crafty pedlars, with half-breeds and Indians scouting for them, ambushed a whole brigade and took it away.

David had made a soft buckskin pouch to cover the stub of his thumb, which seemed always to get in the way of things. He was putting the pouch on and tying it back at his wrist and the eleven men who belonged to him in one of the big canoes were asking how he got his thumb chewed off when suddenly they were surrounded by pedlars with guns at the ready and John Bowman at their head.

"Don't move," John said cheerfully. "You're our prisoners." To his men he said, "Take their weapons."

He had ordered the HB men not to move but they had all stood up. They did not reach for their guns. They were too astounded for that. They merely stared at Bowman, wondering if he was teasing them or if he meant it. Deciding that the man really meant it, David choked up with fury and closed his big hands.

John glanced at the pouch over his thumb and said in his smiling insolent way, "Heard you lost a thumbnail last winter."

"You're pretty big with brag," David said, "when you have twenty men all behind their guns."

"Some men use fists," John said. "Some use brains." He was looking round him. The HB guns had been picked up and John's men were removing knives from belts.

When a hand reached to take his fire bag David said, "Don't touch that."

"Why not?" asked John, looking over. "You got her picture in it?"

Roger Bruce spoke up and said, "How about stepping out from behind your guns?"

"No, Roger, thank you. Now fall into formation, please, and march ahead of us. Don't give us any trouble or we'll put you in irons."

Twelve unarmed HB men marched ahead of them in the direction of their fort. A half hour later John Clarke heard of the capture from one of his scouts. He called his men together, about eighty of them, and told them to line up, facing him; and when they were all looking at him he told them what had happened and asked for volunteers.

Not a recruit from Montreal budged but all the HB men stepped forth.

To the men who stepped forth he said, "I want some pedlars."

Within an hour his men marched in with two prisoners and John Clarke's weathered face almost smiled when he saw who they were. They were the two chief guides and scouts of the entire North West entourage. Clarke looked at them and turned away, saying he would be back soon; and unarmed he went to the pedlar camp and called for John Bowman.

When John came Clarke glanced at him in a kind of offhand way and said casually, "John, it might save some hard feelings if we understand one another. You just took twelve of my men. I just got your two chief scouts. If my men are back right away yours will be too. If they're not I'm going to need a lot of pedlars to keep them two scouts company.

"Now another thing," he went on, giving Bowman no chance to speak, "if this is the way you're going to fight that's fine with us. We just want to know. But, as I figger it, you and your men were just having a little fun."

"Well——" John Bowman began.

John Clarke interrupted him. He knew what that one word meant on the tongue of a Bowman in a situation like this. He also knew that in a situation like this a man of spirit and pride had to save face. So he interrupted to say quickly, "Oh hell, I know how it is. Men get to feeling their pemmican and they do things. Good day, John. I'll see you in the Athabasca."

A few minutes after Clarke returned to his post David and the eleven men walked in, their weapons in their hands. John spoke to an aide and the two scouts were brought out and set free. When they had vanished David said:

"Just how do the pedlars reckon this thing?"

"Don't know," Clarke said. "We'll find out soon enough."

For several weeks there was no hint from the pedlars of their intentions. Their brigades set off first for Ile-à-la-Crosse. Clarke and his brigades followed, with just enough pemmican to see them to that point, a series of small connected lakes, the junction with the Churchill River being at the north end. This was country that David had never been in, nor had more than two or three of all the men with Clarke. Just north of the small lakes was the Methy Portage, the most man-killing of all; and soon after that they would reach the

Athabasca River, which would take them to the lake of the same name; and from there they would follow Peace River, he supposed, deep into the heart of what was thought to be the finest beaver country on earth. But if the Indians wouldn't trade with them what would they eat?

That was a question in many of their minds by the time they arrived at Ile-à-la-Crosse, for their pemmican was gone, they were hungry, they had been almost eaten alive by the mosquitoes, and the green recruits from Montreal were becoming surly and morose. They wished to God they had never seen this land. Taking a few picked men with him, including David and Roger, Clarke at once pushed on ahead to find Indians, with whom he hoped to trade. They shot their canoe across a small lake, up a connecting stream, across another lake; they hid it and went east and west into the timber looking for Indians, pausing to rest or sleep only when darkness forced them to. There was no sign of Indians. Nowhere could they see a wisp of smoke from a lodge fire. None of them said anything, for there was nothing to say: they all knew that the pedlars had frightened the Indians out of this land or had bribed them to leave. It was like this, David supposed, when an army moved across country that had been scorched, burnt out, destroyed. They shot a few grouse and ate them raw but they saw nothing bigger than grouse. Clarke knew that he had to turn back to his waiting men even if he turned back without food; and they canoed all night, arriving at daylight, and got the brigades together and set off for the Methy Portage, which some called Portage la Loche.

The men were now in their fifth day without food and they were ganted up and mutinous and sullen; and they went another day, and another, eating nothing but rose hips, leaves, kinnikinnick bark, moss, water cress. At the portage some of the men were too weak to carry more than themselves, and so the strongest men shouldered the boats and supplies and began the long climb, stumbling over burnt and fallen timber, across streams, over stones; pausing to shoot a grouse or two and share it in tiny morsels, eating all of it, including the guts, and sucking the juice off the feather quills; picking up their burden and staggering on. Clarke was convinced that when they got deeper into the Athabasca they would find game. And they did on the bank of the Athabasca run into six woods buffalo, and killed them all, and some of the men ate so much that they puked and wiped the slobber off their beards and ate again. David, eating only a little at first, looked at the Montrealers and decided that fighting in the French and Indian wars had taught the fools nothing. They ate and puked, they got the backdoor trot, they bellyached, they stared with ugly suspicion at the country around them, they talked as if never before had they seen mosquitoes—these veterans of war. David listened to their complaints and thought, You bastards will be men before you get out of here or you'll be dead.

Most of the buffalo flesh they stripped off and jerked and packed away in leather bags. One day Clarke called his men before him and said that there was a strange new danger which had not been foreseen: they were being followed by some of the pedlars, who were putting pemmican out here and there, in places where Clarke and his men would be bound to see it. What they hoped for was to catch the HB men stealing, so that they would have an excuse to take them as prisoners to Montreal and there have them tried for theft. Any man touching that pemmican would be put in irons.

"Do you understand me?" Clarke asked, looking at his men. "They reckon to starve us till we steal. Then they'll pretend to arrest us and they'll freight us out. If any of you want to go back to Montreal, now is the time to speak up. If you stay with me, then get this in your heads, you're not to touch pedlar pemmican even if you starve to death."

David stared at Clarke and considered his words. They were pretty strong words, it seemed to him. Did he really think that if men saw themselves dying with pemmican for the taking they would turn away from it? Hell, hardly a man in the world would do that. A starving man was a desperate beast for whom threat of irons was no threat at all. Did Roger Bruce think so?

"No," Bruce said. "But if I know John Clarke he won't stop at irons. He'll hang a few up if he has to."

"Men facing death——"

"John doesn't reckon that his men are going to die."

No, John said to his men, "Everything will be all right, don't worry about it." But everything was not all right. The men, even the hardiest of them, were beginning to look gutted out and wan; they had lived through September on half rations of old bull buffalo jerky and wild berries. Every day they searched the woods east, south, and west of Athabasca Lake but there was no sign of life. The red men had been bribed with rum to go away and stay out of sight and the game had all been killed or driven off. This was what John

Bowman had meant by brains. And one day, to add insult to starvation and bitterness, the pedlars sent out from their post a swaggering bully named Hector McNeil to pick a fight with one of Clarke's officers. With him came a score of men. They came over where Clarke's men were sitting around swatting mosquitoes and hearing one of them say that they would all leave their bones here to the timber wolves. David saw the men approaching with John Bowman at their head. Where John was, there you could expect to find trouble.

The pedlars came up, looking arrogant and well fed and busting for a fight. They then stood bunched, looking at Clarke and his ganted-up men, and Bowman looked over at Clarke and said, "Making medicine?"

Clarke said softly, "You look like the man who found the piece of kidney in the pie."

That quip seemed to leave Bowman at wits' end but Hector was ready. He acted like a man who had been drinking. With a gesture intended to encompass all of the HB men he asked, "Got any swordsmen here? There's something that kinda draws me to you."

"Swordsmen?" said John Clarke, looking at him.

"Just giving out about myself a little," Hector said. "Reckoned just to dander up here to see what kinda men you got."

Roger Bruce said, "You pedlars are fighting pretty fancy these days. Did you say swords?"

Bowman said, "Hector, here, he likes a little duel with swords now and then. We reckoned you might have someone." Bowman looked round at the men. "You have Frenchmen here."

James McVicar yawned and got to his feet. Yawning again, he stretched his big long arms to the sky and bent over backwards in a crescent and straightened and said, in the most casual way, "I'm not French, if that makes any difference. But I don't figger you need go yowing all over the place to find yourself a little fight. But, like Roger said, swords is pretty fancy, ain't they?"

John Bowman looked over at Hector.

Hector was looking at McVicar. "Hector McNeil that was, that's me, and I can lick every hog, dog, and divil over here. Is this to be real or just boy-play-around?"

"Wa-al," said McVicar, drawling his words out and yawning, as if half dead with fatigue, "it depends on what kind knives you got. If they're just for cleaning your fingernails——"

One of the pedlars suddenly raised two swords and flashed them in the sun. David knew little about swords: these had a lot of curve in the blade and looked Oriental. He thought possibly they were scimitars.

McVicar stepped forward and took one, tried the haft, balanced the weapon, inspected the point and then the whole blade. He took the other and examined it. At last he said, "Looks like a man could get hurt with one of these things." He looked at Bowman. "Is your man serious?"

"Divil of a note!" cried McNeil. "Tell him it is a fight to the death."

"Fits me like a pair a new drawers," McVicar said. "Which knife is mine?"

John Bowman took the swords and handed them to Clarke. "See if they're the same."

Clarke got to his feet and examined the swords. He said he could see no difference. Bowman extended the two hafts to McVicar and told him to choose one. McVicar took one and backed away from the men, turning the scimitar swiftly, as if testing the action of his wrist.

"Is your man sober?" he asked Bowman.

"Sober as an owl," Bowman said.

"Is this to be a fight till one man's down?"

"Didden you say it!" McNeil said.

Clarke's men now formed most of a circle, with Bowman and his men making up a segment, and the two duelists went into the ring, with McVicar still twirling his blade. David supposed he was limbering up his wrist. Watching him closely, David thought he had never seen a man so calm when facing a hazard that might cost his life. He imagined that Hector McNeil must be a skilled swordsman or Bowman would never have brought him over. Well, maybe Jim McVicar knew what he was doing.

Bowman told them to salute and take their stand. When he came down with his beaver hat the fight would begin. "Are you ready?"

"All ready," McNeil said, "to leave a nice sting in him!"

"Ready to die, you mean?" McVicar said. "Just as well die fighting, for you sons of bitches intend to starve us anyway."

Down came the beaver hat.

The two men stood in the position of swordsmen, balanced, weapons extended. McNeil moved first. He feinted, then made a thrust, and David was astonished to see with what skill, almost with what boredom, McVicar parried him. As swordsmen, he decided, both men were good. Here in the depth of cones and needles and all of a forest's long accumulation it was not easy to maintain that delicate balance so necessary to swordsmen, but these men seemed to. They feinted, advanced, thrust, retreated, and never once faltered or stumbled. For five minutes, ten, fifteen neither scimitar tip touched flesh.

"Wait!" John Bowman called. "Hold it, both of you, a moment!" He turned to Clarke. "How about a little betting on this? Your men wouldn't want any pemmican, would they?"

"They'd only waste it," Clarke said.

"I'll bet you ten bags of pemmican against ten muskets."

Clarke hesitated. David was thinking, Sure, the bastard is after our guns now! Drive all the game away and leave us without weapons. . . .

McVicar spoke up in his slow unemotional way. His guard was up, he was holding his position, his gaze on his foe. He said, "Sounds like a good bet, John."

"Accepted," John Clarke said. "Any more wagers?"

"Any you men want to bet?" Bowman asked.

"I'll take a wager," David said.

Bowman looked at the men in both groups and waited. When nobody spoke he cried, "Ten bags to ten muskets! On with the fight!"

David would never have believed that James McVicar could move with such speed. The word fight was barely off Bowman's tongue when McVicar stepped in and seemed to feint once, though David was not sure of that, and then made a lightning thrust. The blade went clear through McNeil. David did not know that at once. He knew it a moment later when the blade was withdrawn and flashed red an instant and smote, and the blade in McNeil's hand was flung, spinning. McNeil sank slowly. Bowman rushed forward to assist him and, with arms round him from behind, eased him to the earth. As all the men watched him and waited he knelt and tore McNeil's shirt away and examined the wound; and when he got to his feet his face had lost all its smirking arrogance. Bowman looked once at Roger Bruce. He glanced at Clarke.

"All right," he said to his men, "take him to the post."

The men quickly improvised a stretcher of stout green branches and laid the wounded man on it. They bore him away.

John Bowman picked up the swords and looked over at John Clarke. "Ten bags, was it?"

"Ten," Clarke said. Bowman was turning away when Clarke stopped him.

"Now what?" asked Bowman, pausing to look at him.

"I wouldn't put pemmican around if I was you. You might need it."

Bowman was looking at him. "So we might," he said. "But you, with ten bags, you'll be all fixed for the winter."

## XXIX

Ten bags of pemmican, rationed at only one pound per man per day, were gone in ten days. On this ration most of the men spent long hours in the hunt, some of them, like David and Roger, going fifteen or twenty miles and returning before nightfall. The men shot a few grouse, a few beaver and porcupine, an owl or two, a goose or two, a few ducks; they brought to camp the bones and hide of a caribou that had been pulled down by the wolves; but they all knew that they faced starvation if something was not done. And the first snow had fallen.

John Clarke was not a man who sought or accepted advice but he called his officers into council. He said he would have to break it up. He would leave sixteen men on the Athabasca; he would send fifteen men north to Great Slave Lake to build a fort there; he would send thirteen men east to the Pierre au Calumet to build a fort there and trade for pemmican; and with the remainder, six officers and forty-eight men, he would go west up Peace River to build forts along the way.

Like the other officers, David was looking at him. Clarke was a mountain and riverman, and a good one, and he was a brave man, and it was said from end to end of the country that he always came through; but what he now proposed made no sense to David. It certainly made no sense when the fifty-five of them pulled out in eight canoes, with nothing to eat but a few pounds of flour.

"Make sense to you?" David asked Roger.

Roger inclined his head toward a Cree Indian riding in another canoe. Clarke had picked him up somewhere.

"He's counting on him," Roger said.

"Well, it's pretty damned funny. Winter is on us, our guts are empty, and we put our trust in a redskin."

"I'n see us building forts," McVicar said. "Fifty-five men, every goddamn one leaning against a tree to keep from falling over."

Roger said, "Fifty-five dead men under their canoes."

McVicar said, "When a man eats well he thinks of lots of things, but when he don't eat he thinks only of food. That's all life comes down to when you shovel the snow away."

Roger was watching the banks on both sides of the river. "Something else funny," he said. "If our bellies were full we could see red faces all along there. Our bellies empty, we hope to God we can but never will."

"Not even a beaver," David said.

"Not even a sign of cuttings," McVicar said. "The pedlars sure cleaned this part of the country out."

That night the Cree stole out of camp and disappeared.

The next morning the men had nothing to eat, not even a spoonful of flour, but the indomitable John Clarke still pressed on, hell-bent on doing what he had been ordered to do; and portaging around him and his men as they forced their canoes against the current went a group of pedlars, staggering under their kegs of rum, with which they would bribe the red men in the areas ahead, and send them far inland, deep into a wilderness of conifers, far out of sight. It was as plain as day now to Clarke and to his officers that the North Westers expected to starve them into surrender and then give them life and liberty on pedlar terms.

There were eight men in David's canoe, all of them slowly stroking, slowly driving the big boat upstream; their eyes searching—searching—this bank, that bank, for anything that moved, anything that could be eaten. Snow had been falling for days and the banks were snow-laden, the trees bent out over the water, white on their backs and dark and cold under their bellies. Now and then when the men saw open bank they would anchor their canoes and go traipsing off in snow knee-deep, looking for sign of deer, caribou, rabbit, wildcat, coyote, wolf; but there was no sign, the pedlars had driven everything before them. They went up small river tributaries and they saw a little beaver and otter sign, and now and then one of them shot a beast but it didn't amount to much among fifty-five men. A big beaver, even if they cleaned and ate the guts and dug all the marrow out and ate the brains and lungs and kidneys, even if they roasted the bones until they were brittle and could be chewed, dressed out only about thirty pounds.

One morning a gun in the lead canoe was fired, and every man in the other canoes craned his neck round and round and prayed that it was a moose or a buffalo or at least a deer, but it was only a horned owl. The man who shot it picked it up from the water and ripped its feathers off and tore off legs and wings and hunks of breast and gave portions to the men with him, and behind the canoe other men fished the feathers out of the water and sucked on the quills, hoping for a little body juice.

"Rum," McVicar said in his rather droll way. "By God, we have rum. Rum to buy pemmican, but no pemmican, and Clarke won't let us drink the rum. First thing we know he won't let us smoke." McVicar took twist from his fire bag and tamped it into his pipe. "One thing, though, tobacco smells twice as good when your gut is flat."

"Clarke is pretty gant-eyed himself," a man said.

"Why in hell don't we stop and build a fort right here?" asked Jim, puffing, stroking, looking at the virgin timber on either side. "Any idea?" he asked David.

David shook his head.

"Where does this goddamned river go to?" a man asked. "Clarke know?"

"This is the one Mackenzie got lost on."

"No," David said, "it's north of here. This goes west to Fort Vermilion and along about there it turns south for two hundred miles, and then west and north to hell and gone."

"How far to this fort?"

"Don't know," David said. "Maybe two hundred as the river runs."

"God. Ten days paddling and portaging. We won't make it."

John Clarke became convinced that they could never make it. For days, yes, for weeks, his men had been spending the hoard in their bodies, the stored-up fat and meat and strength; and his alert eyes, watching them day after day, saw that even the strongest were now failing. If David McDonald had stood on scales they would have shown that his weight had fallen from two hundred and twenty to a hundred and eighty. Some had lost more. Three or four of the Montrealers were becoming delirious in their sleep. The HB men were all cheerful, unafraid, and resolute, but some of the recruits had blanched inwardly and were talking of mutiny. There was one named Jean.

He awoke one morning to find that the night had buried him under a foot of snow, and when he looked up he could see nothing but the gray underbellies of huge flakes remorselessly falling; and he staggered out of bed and picked up his gun and began to curse and to slobber with rage. He swore to God that he was going to get out of here. He would go alone, he said, this veteran of guerrilla war, his hair falling black and shaggy over his eyes, his starved lips curling in his beard. Was anyone going with him?

The men had all left their beds and stood in the pale gray daylight and some of them were looking at Jean and some of them paid no attention to him. The real mountain and rivermen among them, who had known starvation before, who had known the perils in the depth of winter, who had seen men go out of their minds and curse their God, these men knew that some sort of crisis had come. They had known that it must come. It was these men who did not look at Jean: there was something in a man when he suddenly went weak and afraid that men still strong and unafraid did not want to look at—as they did not want to look at cowardice in a son or faithlessness in a wife; or at a lone grave in a country where other men might soon die.

It was John Clarke's affair, David was telling himself. They would see what John would do now.

The man was shrieking. He said he was going. He was weeping.

God, it was terrible to see a man break and shout that way. A man, David reflected, could smell the end of him. In his pitiable posture as he stood there shaking and sobbing defiance a man could see the end of him. A really strong man never shouted defiance at the north country when he knew that it had licked him: he submitted to it with that grace and humility which were death's right in a thing dying.

John Clarke went over to him. "All right," he said, without raising his voice at all, "if you want to go, go."

"Where?" asked the poor fellow, momentarily brought to his senses.

Under a low ceiling of silent descending storm, in a world with no sound but that of ice floes grinding on ice ledges in the river, Clarke called his officers around him, and with their buffalo robes over them like dark tents they faced one another in a small circle.

"Guess we won't make it up Peace River," Clarke said. "Who in hell would have thought the pedlars could strip a country so clean?"

The men nodded. They would never have thought it either.

"I reckon it's a hundred and fifty yet to Vermilion. I don't know that there's anything to eat there. I guess it's about a hundred back to Athabasca." He now looked at David. "In the lake there at least there's fish, so you take the weakest of the men and head back. You'll be going downstream and if the river stays open you can make good time. In the safe stretches sleep in your canoes and drift while you sleep."

"If the river stays open," David said.

Clarke looked up at the storm. "Long as it snows it will stay open." He looked again at David. "I've counted the ones too weak to go on. Thirteen. Need one or two HB men to help you with them?"

David gave no reply. He thought it a hell of a question.

"I reckon you do," Clarke said. "Any choice?"

"Roger and Jim would be fine," David said. "But I'n try it alone."

"Bruce and McVicar. All right, shove off."

And where were the others going?

Clarke said he would send the strongest with most of the trading goods to Loon River, to rejoin him at Vermilion. He thought they could all make it. They would find Indians before they went much farther, or game; it could not go on forever this way. But he didn't want to be burdened with men gabbling out of their minds or so feeble they would have to be carried. David would take two canoes for the sixteen of them, a little rum, their bedding and weapons. That was all.

John Clarke put out a hand. "Good luck," he said.

David figured that going down-river they could cover the hundred miles to Athabasca in a couple of days, even without food, but he did not foresee a sudden and dreadful change in the weather. It turned cold. The river, most of it, where the current was slow, was already frozen over. In such weather as this it would soon be impassable. They had got the thirteen men into the canoes and had shoved off, even as the weather was changing, and they managed the first day to get twelve or fifteen miles downstream. This would be a bitter night for men with little bedding and no food.

"We'll have to keep a fire all night," David said to Roger.

"Reckon," Roger said.

David was about to say that tonight the river would freeze over in places, but changed his mind. Roger knew it, Jim knew it. Why talk about it? They might have drifted with the current as long as possible, but for the darkness, but for their unwillingness to be in canoes out in a frozen river in nighttime with desperate men. Jean was already hallucinating, and that, David supposed, was bad. The man insisted that he could hear honkers. He would stare up into the sky and say, "There! Honkers!" He meant flying geese. He had some of the other men convinced that geese were flying overhead, and trembling with eagerness, they looked up, guns ready. They had the notion that they would feast on geese this night. David had explained to Jean that there were no geese flying over at this time of year but the man would pay no attention; his eyes shining with lunacy, he stared up at the frozen sky and said over and over that he could hear them. It made a man wonder what kind of soldier he had been.

What kind had any of these men been? Thirteen veterans of the French and Indian wars, with hostility and treachery sticking out all over them.

While the three men were off gathering wood Roger said, "What'll we do with them when they all hear geese?"

"God knows."

"You been watching Butard?"

"Butard?"

"The one with his mouth pulled down on the left side."

"What's he doing?"

"Just the way he looks at us. You think it's safe to let them keep their guns?"

David had wondered about that too. He turned to Jim. "What you think?"

"It's a risk either way."

"We should remember," Roger said, "that these men have all been soldiers. They have killed."

"Maybe," David said.

Jim McVicar said, "They must have brains enough to know they'd be crazy to kill us. What would they do then?"

"Eat us," Roger said.

"We'll just have to watch them," David said.

When they were all around the big fire some of the men tried to sleep, and they had to be watched over like children. Roger thought this night would be about forty below. Even though a man was wrapped in a buffalo robe he was soon chilled through in the part of him turned away from the fire. Half of him froze while the other half roasted. Recalling what Roger had said about Butard, David studied the man in those moments when the man was not looking at him. Butard had an ugly face and looked like a man who was ugly all the way through: the left side of his mouth was pulled down, possibly by a scar hidden in the thick beard; the eyes were black and restless and evasive: the gaze moved over things softly, never pausing in the fixed stare, but moving, always moving. It was now moving in turn over three faces around the fire. When the gaze came to David he met the eyes, but only for an instant; the gaze moved over his face, around and over, never pausing, watching, searching; and then passed on to Roger, to Jim. What was in the mind behind the eyes?

When David got up to throw more wood on, a man whom the others called Gace—it sounded that way as they pronounced it—aroused himself and fixed his morose eyes on David. After David had sat the man said:

"How long before we eat again?"

"Only heaven knows," David said.

"Not till we get to the goddamn fort?"

"We may run into something tomorrow—next day. A deer or something."

Gace looked round him at the night and then overhead. "How long can a man live without food?"

Roger said, "Depends on the man."

Gace now fixed his sullen stare on Roger. "What's the longest you ever heard of?"

Some of the ex-soldiers now showed an interest, their faces still hostile and suspicious but expectant.

When Jim spoke all eyes turned to him. The soldiers had a queer way of looking at Jim, for they remembered how he had run a sword through a man.

"A good man should go forty days," Jim said.

Gace was aghast. "Forty days!" he cried. He looked at his companions to see what they made of that. Then, all the bright suspicion returning to his eyes, he looked at David. "You got food hid away for you three."

"That's a lie."

Gace brooded a few moments. "We could smell your breath."

"The way you hear geese," Jim McVicar said.

Gace looked in turn at the three men. "If the river freezes over we gotta walk?"

"That's right," David said.

"In snow to our asses."

David was about to say that perhaps the snow would freeze in a deep crust but he knew, and he suspected that Gace knew, that it could freeze hard only after a softening.

Gace was pressing in and his companions were listening. "Ninety miles in snow to our asses and no food. You figger men can do that?"

Jim said, "Men can do a hell of a lot of things when they have to."

"What would you do?" Roger asked Gace. "Sit on your ass and freeze to death?"

Again Gace's hard bitter eyes studied the three men. At last, speaking with resentment, with a tone of injury, as though vital truth were being withheld from him, whose life was in peril, he said, "Why *don't* geese fly this time a year?"

"They have better sense," Jim said.

That only whetted the man's suspicions.

David said, "Geese migrate. That is, they go from north to south, south to north, twice a year. They never fly this late."

"Then Jean don't hear geese?"

"I don't," David said, trying to be tactful.

"Mebbe he's got better ears."

"Maybe."

"Then you admit there might be geese up there."

"If there's a million geese up there," said Jim, "they don't do us any good."

"If we just keep shooting up," Gace said, "we might hit one."

David thought, This bastard's crazy too! To change the subject he said, "I think Jean is asleep. Is he all right?"

Gace looked over where Jean was stretched out. To the man sitting next to Jean he said, "Is he all right?" The man only looked briefly down at Jean and said nothing. Gace said, "I guess he's all right." Dark and brooding like a man looking into himself at the prospect of death, Gace set his gaze on the yellow manes of fire and for a few minutes there was silence. At last Gace looked up. He looked at the three HB men, one after the other, his mind obviously speculating about them, their motives, their courage, their endurance. "If some get so weak they can't walk," he said, "what then?"

"We'll have to carry them," Jim said.

Gace gave a low mirthless snort. "We wade in snow to our ass and carry men? I can see that."

"We better try to get some sleep," David said. He turned to Roger and Jim. "I'll take over awhile."

And so during the next three or four hours David kept the fire up and watched the men and now and then turned those who were sleeping if it felt to his naked hand that the part of them away from the fire was too cold. Most of those who tried to sleep kept turning, because one part was too cold, the other too hot. Jean was muttering deliriously. It was a dark night with no moon and almost with no stars; beyond the firelight it looked as black as the inside of the earth, and the snow out there looked colder than any snow had ever looked. The odors were of snow and burning wood; the sounds, of burning wood and sleeping men. David felt responsible for the lives of the fifteen but he could think of nothing to do save to impose discipline. They could keep an eye out for the climbing bittersweet, the bark of which Indians ate after first boiling the stems; for sugar maple, out of which they might suck a little juice; for rose hips. Ninety miles overland in snow three feet deep, in bitter cold without food—and when a man was empty the cold bit into him twice as deep and hard. If the pedlars should tempt them with pemmican could he keep the men from taking it? Should he try? If they were all arrested at least they would be fed. But he doubted that the pedlars would bother: their scouts would report that sixteen men were struggling along through deep snows and John Bowman would write them off as dead. How were Clarke's group and the other groups doing? Dying, he supposed.

Roger then took over and David tried to sleep, but there was too much pain in his belly and too many things in his mind, including Sunday. It was funny how the more famished he became the more his loins hungered for her. He must have dozed off toward morning, all of them must have but Jean, for when they awoke Jean was gone. It was Gace who said, "Where's Jean?" They all looked round them and counted one another. Then the HB men went away from the fire, looking for footprints. "Here they are," David said, and Roger and Jim went over to him and looked down. David said he would follow them, and took off alone with his gun.

They led toward the river. Where had the damned fool thought he was going, and was he still alive or had he frozen stiff? It was so cold that a man ached just lifting one leg after the other and trying to walk. He had all the accumulation of cold gathered in a long night stored in his muscles and bones. This kind of weather took the will to live out of you pretty fast and you just wanted to say to hell with it and give up. Jean had gone to the river in a zigzag way, making a path like a drunkard's; and on coming to the river he had gone out over its ice, though here the snow on ice was so deep that a man like Jean wouldn't have known that he was walking across flowing water. David did not know if the river was completely frozen over here. He soon found that it was not, not quite, and he shuddered with horror, for Jean's tracks led straight on to the open water. It was about seven or eight feet of water in the middle, flowing quite fast, looking horribly black and deep and cold; and David stood and looked at it, knowing that Jean had walked right into it and had gone down. He was dead now, back under the ice somewhere. He had to be dead. Upstream or downstream, either way, the river was frozen all the way across; there was only this short stretch of open water. He had walked into it, the poor miserable bastard, and had drowned or frozen and had been borne away and was under the ice somewhere and, like the bull, would be under ice until it broke up next spring. To be sure of the thing David walked up and down the river in snow on ice, shudders running of horror and of weakness through him. The open water was almost black, and it was gurgling and hissing along the ice edges, and the ice was rumbling and crunching somewhere underneath. There was no need to search: the tracks had gone right up to open water and stopped there.

On his way back he met Roger. Roger looked at him and their eyes met a moment and there was no need to speak. They went back to a dying fire.

Looking round him, David said, "Well, here's where the pedlars get two canoes and some rum." He turned to the men, huddled round the fire. "We take our robes and our guns, that's all. Everyone ready?"

Gace was looking at him. He stood up. "Where's Jean?" he said.

"Under the river ice," David said. "Let's be off."

## XXX

David took the lead, breaking trail in deep snow, pausing every fifty or hundred feet to look back. Roger was next to him, then Jim, with the others straggling along. David was looking into himself at his sensations: when a man was slowly dying from exposure and cold and hunger there were symptoms, he imagined, besides rumblings in his guts and pains in his stomach and stabbing aches all over him. The thing to watch, he told himself, was for signs that his mind was failing. He thought Roger's mind and Jim's mind were as strong and clear as ever and he felt that his own was; but then, so had Jean. In a situation like this only a fool took anything for granted. It was plain that the minds of some of the others were failing and they would fail pretty fast from now on.

Roger said quietly at his back, "A man down."

David stopped and turned. One of them, the last man in the line, had fallen. "Who is it?"

"Like it makes any difference," Jim McVicar said.

David looked at Jim, wondering if he was all right.

Roger said, "I think I've heard them call him Brielle, or something like that. Or is it Brielle?" he asked, looking back down the line.

David called back, "Can't he walk?"

"Guess not," Gace said.

David went back. It was only seventy or eighty feet but a man hated to walk eighty feet twice unnecessarily when he was breaking path to his waist and deciding that his own chances at life were about one in ten. Besides, the bastards stood like tree stumps in the path and he had to move around each man. Gace went back with him. David looked down at the one who had sunk to his haunches, chin resting on his chest. Brielle—if that was his name—was a silent one who rarely spoke, only a youth, a kind of pathetic homesick lonesome-looking kid.

"Can't you walk?"

The youth looked up at him and something went into David, as something might have if he had been a father looking at a son who had fallen. He saw it for a moment in the kid's eyes, the pathetic abject lonely look of one who figured that he was done for.

"Better throw your gun away," David said gently. "Why lug it along? And better come to the head of the line with us."

He saw then that Brielle was no coward. The kid showed it now and he was to show it again. Pushing David's hand away, he struggled to his feet, the effort draining his face whiter still, and stood, sort of wavering, his musket in his right hand. He looked down at it and his Adam's apple went up and down twice before he let the gun fall. David moved aside and Brielle, using almost the last of his grit, went weaving up the path.

"You keep just behind Jim," David said to Brielle.

"I'll break awhile," Roger said.

"Between Jim and me," David said to the youth.

What, David wondered, were they to do with this kid? He was struggling along ahead of David, his shorter legs with difficulty spanning from step to step, as Roger made them, reaching a leg ahead of him and driving it down by lunging forward a little; resting a moment and drawing the leg from behind and up over the snow and then thrusting it ahead. David could tell by watching the kid's back that he was dreadfully weak, that he kept going out of sheer grit and guts; but he couldn't keep going day after day. The whole thing might as well be faced now: some of these men would fall out, one by one, and they would freeze to death and the wolves would come along and eat them. You couldn't be a sentimental fool. You couldn't be a romantic ass and say, We'll all stick together, one die, all die. Men weren't that foolish in the north country. You just faced up to it and asked yourself, How many will get through, if any at all? How many miles a day must we average without food, if any of us are to make it? You had to look deep and hard at yourself and say, If it's ninety miles and I can make fifteen miles a day it will take me six days. Could you live six more days without food and walk that far every day in deep snow? You didn't think you could.

David turned and spoke down the line. "We'll rest now about ten minutes. We don't need all these guns, so any of you want to throw your gun away, throw it away." He went up to Roger and Jim, who sat in snow to their armpits. "If only we got a thaw and then a hard freeze."

"Wonder," Roger said, "if it would be easier on the river ice."

"The river winds too much."

"There'd be ice floes ended up to climb over," Jim said. "And no chance to see anything to eat."

"See off there," Roger said, nodding over to their right away from the river. "Reckon it's a snowshoe path. Reckon the pedlars are looking at us right now."

"The sons of bitches," Jim said.

"Wonder how Clarke and his men are doing."

"Dying," Jim said.

David did not want to raise a matter that, as leader of the group, he had to face. He wished he could put it off. He was silent, hoping that Roger and Jim would go on talking. Then he wondered if in feeling so evasive he was revealing a failing mind and with an effort he forced it out.

"It'll be kinda hard, leaving them one by one."

"Kinda," Roger said.

"You think any of us will make it?"

Roger's temper blazed. "Goddamn you, I should bust you in the teeth for that! Of course we'll make it!"

"Not all of us," David said.

"Not all of us! Jesus Christ, we've lost one already, haven't we?"

"What I'd like to see," said Jim, "is a pedlar. I'd shoot him and eat him."

David looked in turn at the two men, studying them. Roger's explosion, Jim's gleaming eyes scanning the landscape didn't look good to him. He got to his feet and said, "Well, off again."

They all got up but Brielle. David went back to the kid. "Coming?" he asked.

"Can't," the youth said in no more than a whisper. He was looking up at David. His face was pinched and white but there seemed to be no fear in it. He was just too weak to get up. He said he would rest awhile and then come on.

David didn't believe it at all, but what was a man to do in a case like this? Jim had called to him, saying they should be getting along. David was looking at the youth, sitting in snow almost to his ears, his face white and hopeless and very lonely, but not afraid.

"You'll come along a little later?"

The youth nodded.

"Fine," David said. And still he stood there, looking, fixing the pale pathetic face in memory. "We'll be looking for you up the line." Goddamn, what a two-faced thing to say!

As the other men came up to Brielle and passed him they all paused to speak. David could not imagine what they were saying. Ten minutes later they had all passed over a low crest and the young man sitting in deep snow by the trail was lost to sight. David did not think he would ever rise again. He would freeze to death and freezing was not the worst way to die. The worst part of it was his thoughts—of his people back home, of France, so unlike this land, of his youth, of all that; sitting there thinking and growing numb, a young man under twenty yet at the end of his life, and dying all alone with the wolves waiting. There would not be even his bones after a while. For a while it might be said, *Il s'appelait Brielle.* Then even that would be forgotten. . . .

Well, he must put such thoughts away. Jim was cutting straight through now, away from the river, for here it made a great bend to the north. David couldn't see it but he knew about where it was, black and deadly under its roof of ice. He couldn't see any sign of a snowshoe path either but he imagined that Jim had seen one. Jim McVicar didn't make mistakes like that. It meant that some peddlars had moved around them, watching them, wondering how long before they were all dead.

David knew that they were not covering any fifteen miles today, though it was impossible to judge their speed or distance. When he broke trail it was such man-killing work that it seemed to him after half an hour that he had walked several miles but he knew it was only a mile at most, and probably less. When somebody else broke trail he got a sense of how slow they were moving. If it were to turn warm and snow again, putting another foot or two on the three feet they were bucking, they would be goners: a man could buck only so much depth, or a horse or buffalo, even a caribou or a moose. A moose might be found starved and frozen and standing up in five feet. But the sky didn't look or smell like snow, it looked like deeper cold and the world roundabout, as hard and brittle as icicles, felt like it. The eleven men behind were still coming but they were laboring like men using the last of their strength. Leaving the kid behind had made them more desperate, had driven them to keep up.

That's what David was thinking but that is not the way the men were feeling about it. Some of them were thinking that the kid was smarter than they were. He had remained behind for a reason. Jean, Butard said, had gone away for a reason. He was not under the river ice at all. John Clarke had gone off with a bunch of men, leaving all the fools to starve if they wanted to. Jean had finally waked up to that and he had gone after them. Then the kid had waked up to it. He had pretended that he was just going to sit down and rest awhile but as soon as they were out of sight he hopped up and took the trail back and then Clarke's trail.

"Who's going with me?" Butard asked the men looking at him. They had stopped.

"Now what in hell?" Jim said to David, looking back.

"God knows," David said. He took off a mitten and gathered a handful of snow crystals to eat. He wondered how long before they would eat their mittens and shirts.

The eleven men were fifty yards back down the trail. It was plain that they were arguing about some matter.

Roger said, "Mebbe they're figgering to go back and eat the kid."

"Had the same idea," Jim said.

David said he would go back to see what the trouble was. As he approached the group Gace stared at him, more sullen than ever, and Butard's gaze danced all over his face without meeting his eyes.

"What's the matter back here?" David asked.

"Nothing," Gace said. "We're resting."

"Why in hell don't we tell him?" Butard said.

"All right," Gace said, looking up at David. "Where did Clarke go with all the men?"

"He headed for Fort Vermilion."

"Why didn't we?"

"Too far," David said. "You men were too weak."

"That's a goddamn lie," Gace said, and David saw his clasp tighten on his gun. "Jean went. Now Brielle has gone."

So that was it. "Look," David said. "It's two hundred miles or so to Vermilion. It's maybe eighty to Wedderburn."

"You think we believe you?"

"You think I'd starve if I could get food quick?"

"We think you got food." Gace and the men looked at one another. Gace looked up at David and said, "Why did Jean go the other way?"

"Jean fell in the river."

"That's another lie," Gace said.

David looked back at Roger and Jim. He just looked at them and waited, and then Roger and Jim moved toward him. When they came up David told them what the trouble was.

"You goddamn fools," Jim said. "I always did say a Frenchman couldn't tell his ass from his mother's nipple."

Roger said, "Look, there's a snowshoe trail over there. It's a pedlar trail. The pedlars have food, so if you want food, go follow them."

Gace scowled up at Roger. "They got snowshoes," he said.

"Go see which way they went. That's the closest food."

Gace studied the faces of the three men and turned to his companions. "I'll go see," he told them, and struck off through the snow. At once in single file the other men followed him.

David and Roger and Jim sank into the snow to rest, their guns across their legs.

Jim said, "Suppose they can tell which way snowshoes went?"

"Doubt it," David said.

"They'll be eating their clothes next," Roger said. "Then they're through."

"They're through anyway," Jim said. "When in hell do we face it?"

David looked at Jim. Jim had been droll and good-humored until the last day or two. He was getting mean now and he had a mean look. David recalled that he had run a man through with a sword and tossed the sword aside and never looked at the man, as though killing for him were a daily experience. The droll fellows, he reflected, were something else down underneath.

Roger said, "You mean we should leave them and go on?"

"Why fool around with them? If they want to go after Clarke, then to hell with them."

"You two go on ahead," David said. "I have a responsibility."

"Yeh?" said Jim, almost sneering at him. "If you're so damn full of responsibilities why don't you go back after the kid?"

Roger turned to look at Jim. Then, using his gun butt as a crutch, he got to his feet and looked over at the men. David got up, and then Jim.

Jim said, "They wouldn't know a snowshoe track from their ass end. I'm going."

"All right," David said.

Jim went back up the trail and soon was breaking new path. Gace and the men were coming back.

"We can't tell," Gace said.

David nodded to the east, toward Athabasca Lake, and said, "That way."

"How you know? You never looked at the tracks."

"You going with us?" David asked.

He nodded to Roger and Roger went up the trail and David waited; and after Roger had gone thirty yards he turned, his gun across the crook of his left arm, and faced the men and David went up the path. The men stood and looked at them. Roger then went to Jim and spoke to him and he and Jim turned; and David, turning away from the men, went to Jim and Roger.

"I think they would have shot us," Roger said.

"Maybe."

"It's funny," Roger said, staring round him, "that we don't even see a goddamn rabbit track."

Jim said, "Not even the shit of a bird flying over."

"Indians eat moss," David said. "Before long we'll be close to the river."

"Ah, my darling mother!" Roger said. "For a bowl of rose hips!"

"Just some good old pemmican would suit me," Jim said.

They went on and did not look back for some time, and when they looked back none of the men were in sight. From end to end of the vast Athabasca wooded belt were patches of burnt timber, and they were going through one now. David was keeping his eye out not only for the footprint of a living thing, any living thing, but also for a huge tree that had been green but was now dead. Such a tree would burn all night. Maybe they could find some moss or rose hips or old bones, or they might go down into the snow along a feeder stream and find berries still clinging to the vines. Where in hell were the wolves? Raw wolf would taste like buffalo liver now, but all the wolves had been driven away too, or trapped. Curious, again studying his inner sensations, he slipped a mitten off and put thumb and finger into his fire bag and drew forth a piece of the leather string with which his hands had been bound. He bit off a half inch of it and put the remainder back and began to chew. It tasted chiefly of smoke and was tougher than bull sinew. Yet a man, he had heard, could live on hide for days or weeks, or on bones mixed with marrow if you had a way to char and powder them. One danger was that foolish men would eat the leather of their footwear and then freeze their feet and sit like brainless things and die.

At a point not far from the river they found a huge dead tree, and while Jim and Roger were kicking snow away from a spot and scraping with their feet David went to the river to look for moss. He found no moss but saw tied to the limb of a tree a slender leather string and knew that it marked an Indian path of some sort: there would be other pieces if he could get the direction of the trail. He slipped the piece into a mitten and explored around him and found another, and after sensing the general direction it was easy to find still another; and while following the path he came to a down-flung mass of half-burnt timbers and saw under their edge away from the wind a few bones. He set his gun by a tree and crawled under the shelter on bare ground to see how many bones there were, his eyes lighting up at each new discovery as though he were finding bags of pemmican. He shouted over to Roger and Jim and then gathered the bones into a pile. He was examining them to see if the marrow had all been eaten out by insects when the two men came over.

"Bones," Jim said. "Holy Jesus." He also examined them for marrow, but they were old bones and what he saw in their canals was not marrow but the wings and legs and filth of insects dead long ago.

Roger was searching around for grass and bark with which to kindle a fire. When the fire was going they carefully piled bones on pieces of log and with green branches tended them as they charred.

"Wonder what they are," said Jim, looking round him. "Where's the skull?"

"Wolves dragged it off," Roger said.

"It's no man," David said, turning a leg bone. "Look at that."

"A deer," Jim said.

When the bones were charred they moved them from the fire to thick pieces of hot smoking wood and the three men sat together and began to eat. David thought the chief or only flavor was that of chalk, but the bone was hot and that made it taste better. It was something for the stomach. They were still eating when five of the men staggered up, led by Gace. David asked where the others were and Gace said they had gone to find Clarke.

"We're eating bones," David said. "Help yourselves."

The men were not at once convinced that they were eating bones. They suspected that they were eating pemmican that had been concealed all the while, for they had never known men to eat old bones. Gace sank to his knees for a close look at the stuff piled on the hot wood and he stared at it and at the men feeding it slowly into their mouths, and at last with a finger and thumb he broke off a sliver of the brittle smoked-black stuff and put it into his mouth as though it were the head of a serpent. He got to his feet, making signs and gestures of nausea. Seeing his response, the other four men wanted none of it and the five of them stood warming themselves and staring incredulously at the three men eating.

"Suppose there's any strength in it?" asked Jim, crunching bone between his teeth.

"Men can live on it," David said, "a little while." The pieces of leather string he had stuffed into his fire bag. He thought of them as food for the last desperate emergency. Bones would be enough for tonight.

"Don't reckon we should eat much of this," Roger said. "I'm about to puke."

The three had stopped eating and were studying the sensations in their stomachs. If only they had moss to mix with it, David said, looking round him; and he went crawling back under snow-and-dead-timber shelter to find vegetation that a man might eat. He returned, bringing nothing, and the three of them crunched a little more bone and swallowed it and the five of them still stared and wondered.

"Better eat some," Roger said, looking up at them. "Will settle your stomach."

One of the men reached down for a fragment and chewed on it and spit it out.

"Don't do that," Jim said sharply. "There's no food to waste around here."

He divided the bones into three piles and Roger and David took their portions. Then they all got up and carried live embers over to the big tree.

## XXXI

Sometime during the night David thought he heard feet crunching on snow but he was too utterly weary to care. There was nothing in bones to nourish a man. He had eaten the charred blackened stuff until he had almost puked and then felt as if his stomach were full of ground stone. Deciding that it would be better to try to conserve the strength he had than to build more with such food, he made himself as comfortable as he could and lay back, with his big robe wrapped around him from head to feet. The tree was burning at its base, where they had piled dead limbs around it, but long before morning it would be aflame far up its trunk and it might be exploding live embers all over them, but he did not care about that either. He knew now that a man could reach the point where he no longer cared about life, yet would go on living; where he was so drained of purpose and will and meaning that he didn't give a damn if a flaming tree fell across him. He supposed Roger and Jim felt that way too. He was a little afraid that Jim was losing his sanity but felt he was stupid even to think about it, for was he not losing his own?

How could a man tell after he had sunk to certain depths of weariness and hopelessness?

Neither awake nor asleep, he lay in the dim shadowland between, dreaming parts of dreams, coming into fuller wakefulness and bringing a dream with him and taking it back for more dreaming when he dozed again, vaguely conscious of something close to nightmare in which were heat and a sky aflame and the sound of dead limbs bursting and a sense of his body aching and trembling under stabbing pains and of the sound of his breathing. That was the way a man slept when half dead from hunger and weariness. Long before daylight he came awake and thought he should get up but told himself that he ought to relax, to rest, to hoard the little strength he had left until the time again came to thrust legs up and forward, breaking trail. Surely, he thought, they would come soon to a stream with beaver in it. Surely there were deer over the next hill. . . .

When daylight came he had difficulty seeing and he thought it was the poor light. Sitting up, he could see robed forms around him but he had to count them several times before he was sure of the number. One—he told himself that was Roger; two—and that was Jim; and the one there—but where were the others? How many should there be? He tried to remember but got them mixed up with Sunday. He thought there were sixteen and he was looking around for the other thirteen, failing to include himself, when he recalled that a number of them had turned back. There had been Jean. Then some of them had turned back. There had been—— Oh God, what a headache! There had been—— He began to feel angry. His head was splitting and he couldn't remember how many there had been. "Roger," he said. A form stirred, was quiet, then stirred again and struggled to sit up. Roger looked over at him in gray morning dusk and David thought, Jesus, how skinny he is. He said, "Where are they?" Roger looked round him and David said, "How many were there?" Jim now struggled and sat up.

"Can't you bastards ever sleep?"

"It's morning," David said. "I guess some of them have gone."

"Who is that?"

"Don't know. Great God, what a headache."

"Me too," said Roger. "The bone."

"Is that bastard dead?" Jim asked.

David flung his robe back and crawled over. The form looked dead. He felt over it to discover which end was the head and then turned the robe back from the face. This was the oldest one of the ex-soldiers, a man about fifty, with gray in his hair and beard.

"It's the gray one," David said.

"Dead?" asked Roger.

"Can't tell." David put a hand to a cheek and then pulled an eyelid up. "Almost," he said. "He's dying." He reached down and put a hand over the heart and could feel it beating.

"Let's be off," Roger said. He got to his feet and picked up his robe and gun.

David looked round him like one who had turned dizzy on a very high mountain. "We going to leave him like that?"

"Where are the others?" Roger said, looking back down the trail.

Jim went over and thrust at the prone man with his gun butt. "He's dead as hell," he said.

Roger then bent over to look at the man's face. For several moments he studied it, and then reached down and pulled the robe over it. "Rest in peace," he said. He again glanced down the trail and said quietly without any emotion, "The goddamn fools."

They left the man lying there by what was left of the hot smoking tree. He would be dead in a few hours, David told himself, breaking trail; they would all be dead soon and the pedlars would have the Athabasca from end to end, and a hell of a lot he cared. Then he felt shamed by his weakness and told himself that he would not die. He took out a tiny piece of the old string and chewed on it and breathed deep of the cold sunless air and smelled the Indian in his mittens and kept his eye peeled for anything moving. He thought he could see a line ahead that marked a tributary, but not for the life of him could he judge its distance. Oh, he judged it and kept rejudging until it didn't make sense at all. He stopped and drew it to the attention of the other two and said, "How far?" Five miles, Jim said; less than a mile, Roger said. It was only about four hundred yards. If it was not frozen over, Roger said, staring at the thin line in the morning, like a kind of charcoal stroke on a white canvas.

Parts of it were not frozen over for the reason that they flowed too fast. They stood on the ice shelf and stared at the water, upstream, downstream, but there was no sign of beaver or of any kind of life. He couldn't even see a fish, Roger said, looking into the water. The low morning sun now struck patches of it and they were like silver. How in hell, David said, were they to get across? They would have to go down to the river. How far was that? They looked, putting their heads out. They were all behaving, David realized dimly, like men with almost no will left, like men almost ready to lie down and die, as the gray one had done. Death invaded a man and he still walked but he was more dead than living.

They set off downhill for the river. The river was not far but had seemed far. It was frozen over there and the tributary was frozen over for a hundred yards up and they crossed on its ice, going with extreme care, because wind-blown snow and upended floes left treacherous fissures, banked over, into which a man might fall and vanish without a sound. They crossed the stream and stood a few moments, resting. David did not like to look at the other faces. Even beards three inches long did not hide sunken cheeks or lower lids falling away from eyes or the look in eyes. He was afraid of what Jim McVicar might do. Jim looked more and more like a lunatic.

David found it impossible to estimate their distance today. He thought it was because they were walking in deep timber. When one of the others was breaking trail and he was the last of the three he would pause and turn to look back, and in one moment it would seem to him that they had covered eight or ten miles and in another moment that they were within musket range of the burning tree. Until past noon he could see the faint smoke rising from it but could not estimate the distance to the smoke. Of one thing he was dead-sure: they were getting weak fast now, they could not go on like this many more days, perhaps not even one more day. He wondered how the end would come. They would just lie down, he supposed, and wrap their robes around them and never rise again. Thought of the robe made him aware that the weather had turned warmer, and far up in the sky he thought there were signs of gathering storm. If it snowed a couple of feet, as it sometimes did in a day and a night, that would be the end of them. A man with moose legs couldn't buck snow that deep.

Sometime in the afternoon they all grunted with surprise when they found themselves looking at broken snow. Something had been here. It took them a little while to realize that it was men; they walked slowly around where the snow was beaten down and well packed, wondering who had been here and what they had been doing. This was not a campsite. It did not even look like a restsite. Beyond the beaten-down area a trail led away toward the Athabasca, a rather wide path, a snowshoe or ski path. It might be both, David decided; or even a dog-and-sled path, with snowshoes obliterating the sled marks.

"What you think?" asked Roger, looking at David.

David put robe and gun aside and sank to his knees to examine the markings. He thought they were no more than two or three days old but it was very hard to tell in this kind of snow and this kind of weather. He moved over to a stripling tree and looked at twigs that had been bent back by something moving and thrusting against them. Delicately he touched one to see if it would straighten. It straightened a little and he was baffled all the more: how soon a bent twig returned to its position depended on the time of day and the degree of warmth or cold. In midwinter it was not like midsummer, when bent twigs and grasses told you a lot in tracking game.

"Maybe two days," he said, getting up.

"What they doing here?"

Something caught David's eye and he moved to another beaten-down area where trees stood and by a tree he saw bloodstains on the snow. He called the men over and they looked at them. David examined the tree and even rubbed a cheek over its bark, for he had a feeling that a man had been bound to it and flogged.

"What the hell," Roger said, staring round him.

"Better take their path," David said.

Whether following the path was easier than breaking virgin snow they could not decide. Sometimes the path would hold them, sometimes they broke through, and when they broke through it was hell getting their feet back on top because of the crust. But they kept on the path and struggled along for they were sure it led to a pedlar post on the Athabasca. It paralleled the river and went east. After an hour or two they saw that there were more paths than one. There seemed to be snowshoe or dog sled trails all over the country now and most of them seemed to go south. The three men stood together looking round them.

"Indian?" Roger said.

David said, "Crees don't stir much in winter."

"Blackfeet?"

"Too far north, Blackfeet. Maybe Slave land."

Roger was staring south. "How far Edmonton?"

"Oh God. Three hundred, four hundred."

That was nothing, Roger said, for Indians with strong dogs. Or white men either.

"Beaver water here?" Jim asked, sniffing.

They all sniffed and then they plodded on, hoping for beaver water. In this thickly wooded country they couldn't tell if the south trails went deep into the south or were only paths here in the forest. David tried to imagine what they meant. Jim Dugald would have known. David kept sniffing but there was no smell of beaver; in weather turning from cold to warm you could smell beaver for miles. Or beaver and otter and muskrat and all of them put together. Maybe these were pedlar trails. Maybe the pedlars were out in force, going ahead of them to kill or to frighten away every bird, rabbit, and weasel, every living thing. The pedlars, Clarke said, had boasted, on hearing of his coming, that they would starve him and his men into surrender or leave them to the wolves. Brains, Bowman had called it. Thirteen of them, thirteen of only one of the groups, were back along the trail and only God knew what had happened to those who had headed for Calumet or Vermilion or the other places.

They were walking, Roger said, less than a mile an hour now. When they looked back they could see no sign of the tributary or the smoking tree and Jim said they were doing fine, but Jim was becoming foolish. Now and then he cackled. He had made up some sort of ditty which he would sing a time or two in hoarse muttering nasal tones, then cackle, then fall into silence. His behavior was so ominous that Roger and David exchanged glances. "I'd redder burn than be Wedderburn!" That's what the fool was singing. Wedderburn was the family name of Selkirk's wife and the name of an HB post. Then Jim would explode a snort, cackle, and subside. Walking behind him, David looked at him with curious interest. Jim was showing signs of dreadful weakness. They might not have been signs of physical exhaustion in most men but only signs of the weakling, but in a northern giant like Jim they were signs. When, for instance, a foot sank into a hole where Roger's foot had broken through, Jim would make an effort to pull it out and, failing, would rest all his weight on it, set his gun down, lean on it, and seem to doze. He would move only when he became aware that David was going around him. Or if from weakness his knees buckled and he sank, legs bent, he would remain there, kneeling, a ludicrous figure, a pathetic figure who, having spent himself, had no will. David knew the man was getting close to his end, for he was a real mountain man, he was about as tough as they came, he had been in this country fifteen years and had accepted all its challenges as he had accepted

Hector McNeil. David himself was staggering, and in his own way praying, and it seemed to him that he was close to the end too; but when he observed what Jim did he felt stronger somehow. He had had one moment of shameful weakness; since then he had had none and he intended to have none. He would struggle on until he could struggle no more. Well, so would Jim.

Jim McVicar had stopped again. "I'd redder burn than be Wedderburn!" He cackled. It was the wicked hoarse choking cackle of a man half out of his mind but still drawing on unsuspected reserves of strength and in his own way making a face at death. David told Roger that he would break trail now, and he went around Jim and up to Roger.

"Pretty weak," he said in a low voice.

Roger glanced at Jim. "Yeh. It'll storm like hell tonight."

David took the lead. He supposed Roger was right. Indeed, the first flakes were falling, tentative flakes that would dart off on horizontal planes, waver, descend a little, dart again, like things searching the earth below for a place to alight. Now and then he glanced back and his admiration for Jim grew as he sensed the tremendous struggle the man was making. For David, David told himself, was putting forth absolutely all the strength he had just to keep moving—and all the will, the courage, the hope; yet this man behind him who surely had less strength, but maybe more courage, kept coming . . . kept coming; staggering, falling, fighting his way up—but coming; making hideous facial grimaces and singing his silly ditty—and coming! True, he didn't take his turn any more breaking trail but he kept coming. He would be a tough one to keep down. It would have been smart to throw his gun away but no HB man worth his taller ever did that: his gun was a part of him, an extension, a longer reach and a mightier fist. As if the first tentative flakes had looked at the earth and decided that it needed more blanket, the storm deepened and filled the world with twilight. The line of the river had vanished, the sense of forest: it was only three staggering desperate men who could see no farther than a few feet. David knew, Roger knew, that this kind of storm would obliterate all paths in a few hours; then there would be virgin winter world without a sign of living upon it. Then there would be snow, four, five feet deep—soft depths that would make a caribou or an elk plunge for every yard, such loveliness, yet with such power to quiet your life-lusting and bring you to sleep.

Roger spoke from behind. David stopped and Roger came up and said, "Better keep eye open for wood we can burn."

"Reckon. How's Jim?"

"Still comes."

"Long as he sings he'll come."

The trouble was that Jim had switched his song; he was now grunting and muttering over two lines from the "Canadian Boat Song." He couldn't get it all out at once. "'Row, brothers, row,'" he would say, as if that were all of it; but then in another outrush of breath would come, "'The stream runs fast'"; and silence and a grunt and then, "'The rapids are near.'" And after you had almost forgotten to wait for it there would come in a final despairing gasp, "'The daylight's past.'"

David didn't like the change, and he looked hard into the storm for sight of dead trees but it was like trying to look into any dark and mysterious midnight. He could see only about thirty or forty feet; they would just about have to walk into a dead tree if they were to find one. When they were sitting to rest, three figures almost white now, Roger suggested that they leave the path and explore around them. David assented but was afraid that if Jim wandered away he would get lost. Roger went north. David went south, plunging through the snow and falling and rising to plunge again; and after a few minutes Roger whistled and David knew that he had found wood. David returned to Jim. Jim sat in the trail looking like a snowman; he had an inch of snow all over him and only his gun barrel was stark, because snow could not cling to it. Jim was bowed, silent, the gun standing between his legs, held by a mittened hand. When David told him to come on Jim struggled for some moments before he was able to get to his feet. David wanted to take his arm to guide him but knew that his hand would be flung off: you didn't do that with mountain men. He followed David, and David went toward the whistle, following Roger's path; and they came to Roger, who had found a windfall of burnt timber. David said he saw no reason to make a fire now that it had faired off; why didn't they just roll into their robes and sleep? Roger's temper blazed again. He said that for less than a trimmer's steuch he would smash David right in his teeth because he was so damned stupid. Then David was angry, and the two men stood wavering and glaring at one another until Roger's beard parted in a smile and he said he would tell a story. He said that one time when he was a child his family was so poor that there was nothing for Christmas but they all sat before a fire and pretended there was; and in pretending they learned that the important thing about Christmas was not what you could see but what you could feel. Of course they would have a fire.

"Of course," David said, wondering how he could have been so stupid.

He went under fallen timber with Roger and they searched for grass and bark, and after a few minutes they had a blazing fire throwing eerie lights upon a snow-blind world, and David admitted privately that it made him feel more cheerful. He dug out the buckskin strings he had found on trees and gave equal parts to Roger and Jim but he still refused to eat the string with which he had been bound. He was a sentimental fool, he supposed. He would be dead soon. No doubt Sunday had married a buck and was now full of papoose. But he knew better than that: the way she had looked at him that last time, the way she had sucked air into her lungs and turned her head in the peculiar way she had, had told him that she would wait. And by God, he would live.

They laid a piece of the leather on the torn flesh of green conifer and held it for a few moments in the flames to warm it and char it, and then they ate it. David was noting how fast the big flakes perished when they hit smoke or flame; and how the flames seemed less eager in their reaching when they hurled their scarves up into the snow dusk; and what lovely witchery mingled smoke and falling snow made about thirty feet up, as if exposing the hidden illuminations of daylight—for it was still daylight, he supposed. It was hard to tell in storm as deep as this. It would bury them tonight, and what a world they would look on when they arose in the morning!

"That was a nice supper," Roger said, smacking politely.

David looked at him. He had never really known Roger Bruce. Under adversity the real man was coming out, the real man always did.

"'Row, brothers,'" Jim muttered, his eyes half lidded and casting menacing gleams into firelight. He ate like a man who did not know that he was eating but whose instinct to preserve himself ran in deep grooves. He was a man who in his last moments of dying would fling his contempt at death. He was muttering, "'The stream runs fast.'"

This night David dreamed that he was in his boyhood home in Scotland on a Christmas Eve. He had been climbing the Grampian

Hills, that boundary, northwest of the river Dee, between the Highlands and Lowlands; the highest peak in the Isles, Ben Nevis, he had climbed again, as he had so many times as a boy—thinking it a great mountain then, but knowing now that it would be only a hill in the Canadian west; and he was hungry enough to eat leather. His people were so poor that he did not expect a feast this evening, and his astonishment was boundless when, sitting before a fire in deep storm, he saw that there were berry vines all around him, huckleberry and thimbleberry intermingled, and under the vines the lovely shining leaves of the grape. The vines were laden with fruit; the berries hung not singly but in clusters, and he had only to reach out to fill his hands and mouth. Around him was his family, their faces rosy with firelight and snowlight. The thimbleberry seemed to him to have the feeling on his tongue of the nipple of a virgin breast, and he rubbed his tongue over it and around it and then became aware that one of Sunday's hands was clasped in his own. . . .

He felt something striking against his thigh and he stopped eating and looked at his father. The blows continued and he heard voices, and struggling up, he found himself buried under snow and buffalo robe. He heard several voices. Only half awake, he got to his feet, the robe tenting him, and felt hands seizing his arms and heard a familiar voice in his ear. Looking round in the dim light, he saw Roger and Jim and men who were holding them, and then he saw a man pick up his own gun.

"No you don't!" David cried, reaching for it.

A hand shoved him, and he reeled and staggered and fell sprawling. Above him John Bowman was saying:

"Look, you fool, you're so weak you can't stand up."

Struggling to get to his feet, David said, "I can still knock the hell out of you."

"You're my prisoner, David boy. Come along."

"Like hell I am," said David, again on his feet and trembling before him.

"David, you're my prisoner."

"Oh no," said David, and moved to retrieve his gun.

"You determined to be an idiot? You've left thirteen men behind you on the trail—twelve on the trail and one under the ice. Where are McAulay and his men?—Thomas and his men?—Clarke and his men?"

David was thinking, The son of a bitch has been watching us all the time!

"Will you surrender or die?"

"I'll die," David said, and looked around him to see what chance he had to escape. He thought he might make a run for it.

Jim and Roger had also been disarmed and were surrounded by men who were looking at John Bowman and waiting.

"We'll take you to the post," Bowman said, "and fatten you up. It's a great kindness to come away out here and save your lives. I know you appreciate it. Now come along."

"To hell with you," David said. He looked over at Roger.

Roger said, "It seems surrender or death. I'll take death, so let's fight it out right here."

David looked at Bowman. "Give us our guns," he said.

"You miserable stupid bastard," Bowman said, and pushed David and David fell again. "Take them away," Bowman said.

At once his men seized the three and hustled them over to the sleds. Bowman had David and Roger put in his sled and he himself wrapped robes around them to make them snug and then entered the sled and sat facing them, his back to the teams. He brought out a bottle of fine brandy and handed it to David, and he seemed not to notice that David refused to accept it while he dug down for pemmican and roasted goose.

"Don't suppose you're hungry," Bowman said, looking at them. He shoved the pemmican and goose toward them. "You heard about Colin?"

There was no reply. David was thinking, How does the son of a bitch think we'd hear about Colin!

"Took him prisoner," Bowman went on in his easy bland way. "Slapped him into a log jail with a guard over him day and night. That's good brandy and it isn't poisoned. That's the best goose you ever saw. But I'd take it easy and eat only a little or you'll be sick as dogs." He met David's eyes and said, "We've watched you day after day."

"Oh Christ, yes," David said.

"Good thing we did, too. We saved five of the men you left on the trail."

David's mind was a hive of suspicions. "What does the blood mean back there?"

"Blood?"

"By the tree."

"Oh, we've been doing a little persuading of HB men. Some of them are pretty stubborn."

"You mean you beat them?"

"Did you know that Colin is a clever cuss? He invented a cipher code—"

David turned to Roger. "They've been beating our men."

Roger reached for the brandy and drew the cork. "Think I'll have a nip," he said.

"Colin also seems to be quite an authority on Shakespeare. He sent a note over in a keg of whisky—"

David was staring at John Bowman and hating him. He said, "I suppose you beat up John Clarke."

"Clarke? Oh no, not yet. Clarke is to hell and gone out there living on rose hips. We'll let him starve a while longer, then haul him in. We don't intend to let your good men die. You two now, if you'll come to our side we'll give you better jobs and a lot more pay."

David turned to Roger. "Hear that?"

"He's crazy," Roger said. Roger tore off a piece of goose breast.

"You know," said Bowman, watching Roger eat, "that villainous Colin has sent word to Selkirk to ambush all our fur brigades next June and take the furs."

"Where do we do that?" David asked, a little amused.

"At the Grand Rapids. You know, this little quarrel between our companies is getting pretty rough."

"He's telling us," Roger said, looking over at David.

Bowman said, "Why in hell did you come prowling up here in our trapping waters?"

"Your waters!" said David. "All this country belongs to the HB."

"Like hell it does." To Roger he said, "Don't eat that fat. It'll make you sick."

"What you intend to do with us?" David said.

"You? Oh, send you back to your girl someday. I hear she's waiting for you."

David stared at the man, wondering what he meant.

Roger had drawn his knife and was slicing off dark meat. "Dave, we better find out if we'n keep her down."

"Trim off the fat," John Bowman said.

David accepted a piece and sniffed it and began to chew. He was looking at the bottle of brandy, and after a few moments he put it to his bearded mouth and drank. It felt like flame all the way down and was like a pool of fire in his stomach.

Bowman was saying, "These two companies are going to kill one another off, and there must be a better way than that. We can starve you to death every time you come into the Athabasca. Selkirk can spend his fortune getting us into the courts. I've always believed in diplomacy rather than war, but what can we do as long as Selkirk has his hallucinations?"

David was chewing slowly and looking at Bowman and thinking. "No idea," he said.

"What we'll have to do finally," Bowman said, "is to merge the companies. That has been done before. Dave, I'd like to have you think about it, and if you agree with me I'll have a proposal to put to you."

David looked at Roger. "Sly bastard, isn't he?"

Bowman said, "Go on being stupid if you want to, but the next time you come up here we might decide to leave you to the wolves."

## XXXII

When a few days later, feeling strengthened and a little more cheerful, David took his clothes off and looked down over his body he was appalled. He was nothing much but skin and bones. That's all John Clarke would be and the men with him, out there living on rose hips. After he had borrowed Bowman's razor and shaved he saw that his lower eyelids had sunk, that his cheeks had fallen in against his teeth, that his gums had receded. Bowman was giving them the best food he had and telling them to get their meat back on. So as prisoners they had nothing to do week after week but read in the Chipewyan library and wonder what Jim Dugald and Colin and the others were doing. Bowman had told them that they could have their choice: they could be under guard day and night or they could pledge their honor not to try to escape and have the run of the fort. The three of them talked it over and gave the pledge.

"But only for so long," David said. "We don't reckon to stay here the rest of our lives."

Early in February, John Clarke and the men who had survived with him were brought in. They had surrendered rather than die.

David would not have recognized Clarke. Fighting John Clarke, he was called all over this country, but he now looked like a haggard phantom out of the north. From time to time other HB men were brought in, more dead than alive.

"We can do it this way as many times as you're fools enough to come up here," Bowman told David. "Have you thought over my proposal?"

David said he had. He had recovered most of his weight and strength, but he no longer felt that the quarrel between the two companies should be fought out to the death. For Bowman was right: that way could lead only to the death of both.

Bowman had said earlier, "If I turn you free will you try to make them on your side understand that they don't own the whole goddamn world because a debauched king aroused himself from the bed of his mistress long enough to grant a charter? A charter to what? To a country the size of which the blockhead hadn't the faintest notion—nor the slightest title to. Somebody has to back Selkirk up among his delusions and whittle him down to human size. If I turn you free can I count on you?"

And now he said, "What is your answer?"

"I'll go," David said.

David went in May, with a duffel over his back and a musket in his hand. His plan was to go to Jim Dugald first and talk to him. Using the sun as a compass, he struck due south, walking from daylight until dark, never pausing to eat but eating as he walked, and dreaming of Sunday. Now and then he stopped to shoot a rabbit or a grouse, and he stripped the fur or feathers off and ate the thing raw. He was not familiar with this country. Bowman had told him to head for the great bend in the Athabasca and when he came to it he would be only fifty or sixty miles north of Edmonton. He would make the bend if he kept Lesser Slave Lake on his right, Lac la Biche on his left—but he had to walk a long way before these lakes came in sight. It was not easy walking; there were few paths, much of the area was still patched with snow, there were swamps, bogs, small rivers, and cold nights. But he was eager, for he was not only leaving pedlar land, he was approaching the Blackfeet. Months of idleness and good food and sleep had filled him with hungers, and the mightiest hunger in him was for woman. Over and over he said to himself, If only I had her here now!

Toward evening of his third day out Lesser Slave came into view in the southwest. He looked into the southeast but he could see no sign of Lac la Biche. Lac la Biche was much smaller. It did not matter. If he passed Slave a few miles to the east he would be straight north of the bend.

He reached the bend after dark of his fourth day and he was very tired. He figured that he was walking sixty or seventy miles a day. He knew that this was the bend because when he came to the two small lakes the river was there: for many miles it had flowed almost due north and here it turned and flowed almost due south, and for more than twenty miles his path had paralleled it; and at the bend it swung in another loop and flowed north again. These northern rivers wandered all over the map trying to find the sea. This was the bend all right and it looked bad, for the ice was breaking up, the river here was choked with floes and small icebergs. He wondered how he would get across, but he was too dog-tired tonight to think about it and he flung himself down and went to sleep, his right hand on his gun.

At daylight he was up and chewing pemmican while considering his problem. This was a big river, the Athabasca. He was not an expert swimmer but even the best swimmers had no business out among ice floes. He had heard that there were men who could swim a river like this with a musket in one hand but he did not belong to that tribe. He would have to go upstream or downstream to see if it was still frozen all the way across, and if it was he would have to risk it, though a law of the north country said never try to cross on ice when it is breaking. Looking upstream and downstream, he decided to go up, and he had gone two miles or more when across the river on the prairie he saw a horseman. At once he ducked and hid. He looked out to watch the rider, who had stopped and was looking over his way. In the next moment the rider was off on a dead run, but after a hundred yards the horse swung sharply and came back; and memories of things almost forgotten told David that this was Sunday. Perhaps she had known that he was coming.

He went out in plain view. The rider was looking across at him and he was looking at the rider, with a distance of two hundred yards between them. Feeling giddy and full of love and foolishness, he took off his beaver cap and waved it. There was no response until after he had waved a second time; then he thought the person was beckoning to him to come. With his heart beating so fast that he was ashamed of it he went up the river.

He went for another mile, two miles, impatiently plunging through river thicket, and found the river narrower and gray white with ice all the way over. He knelt and put an ear down to listen: he heard crunchings and rumblings as though the current were driving floes downstream under the ice cover. He went out on the ice, his eyes sharp for signs of hidden fissures or treacherous snow pockets; and across from him, sitting on the horse and watching him, was the girl. The river here, he thought, was about three hundred feet wide, and it was convulsed and tortured by the first assaults of high water. If she had not been watching him he might have been more cautious; as it was, he went boldly out until he was almost at mid-channel. He found that the center was open maybe eight feet wide and he looked downstream, where the whole river was a mass of heaving and grinding ice, and then upstream, and as far as he could see upstream the center was open. Ice, millions of tons of it, was being released from the river bottom and was rising against the ice cover and was being driven under it to open waters. David studied the ice of the opposite edge; it looked deep and unshaken. He decided that he could toss his gun over and then go back and take a run at it and leap the chasm. He looked over at Sunday, still watchful, still waiting. Taking the gun in both hands, he stooped and moved it back and forth in the motion of throwing and then gently heaved it across.

The result astonished him. Apparently the ice there was fractured and about ready to move and the blow of the falling gun moved it. A huge chunk of it began to grumble and move, and while David stared at it, confused and helpless, the piece of ice moved with the current and the gun rode with it. He knew now that if he were to leap the center the ice on the far side would give way under him. He stood like the rawest greenhorn, undecided what to do, and watched his gun float away from him.

The girl was not undecided. She was now going downstream and David could tell that her eye was on his gun. He ran back to the shore and then downstream, keeping pace with the horse and the drifting musket; and after a quarter of a mile he stopped in amazement at what he saw. The far bank was open, the ice shelf there had all gone away. Sunday came up to the edge of the bank, spurring the horse, and the horse reared up on its hind legs, trying to hurl itself back from the waters; and then in the moment when David was shouting a protest she smote the beast and dug with heels, and suddenly it plunged in. David felt chilled. It took a lot of courage to put a horse into a river filled with blocks of ice—but there she was, and the horse was swimming furiously toward midstream and he knew now beyond doubt that it was Sunday and that she was going to save his gun. Overcome by admiration and shamed by his own hesitancy, he ran to the ice shelf and dived in.

The sudden impact and the drenching by ice-filled waters took the breath out of him. He reached down to see if his fire bag was secure. Then he moved off, stroking powerfully and telling himself he would have to move fast or he would freeze; keeping an eye on Sunday and the head of the horse and swimming toward them; dodging floes or, failing to dodge, thrusting back from them and going between floating islands, or if one was chiefly mush, floundering across it; getting ice in his nostrils and smelling it, and smelling the winter depths under him; driving on and on, across and downstream, narrowing the distance, exulting within, asking himself what was he if he didn't have the courage of a woman; seeing the morning sunlight upon her hair and face, catching for a moment the brightness of her eyes as she glanced toward him or the bulging consternation and fright in the beast's eyes, sensing its deep fear; feeling the kinship of the three of them, fighting here for their lives in a mighty river where a false move would bear him down and under—and from under a table of ice it was hard to emerge because of its underside softness; seeing her driving the horse toward the gun and seeing her at last reach out for it and recover it and in the same instant glance over to see how he was doing—and telling himself, Good Lord, what presence of mind, what daring she had; saying to himself, What a woman, and then taking a swift view of his inner sensations, his numbness, the chill over his back; looking to the opposite bank to see how far it was; and then seeing Sunday driving the horse toward him and without amazement hearing her say in English, "Grab tail," and replying to her, "No, I'm all right," and then striking out to see if he could swim faster than the horse but knowing that he could not, not in this river, not in heavy clothes with a duffel bag hanging from his neck, not against a horse whose skilled rider guided him from break to break and kept him in open water. . . .

She made the bank first and the horse plunged up and out. He saw her slip down. He saw her lay the gun aside. Then she was over to the bank, bending outstream, looking at him, her eyes grave and anxious and womanly; for David was exhausted and half frozen and he was struggling like drowning buffalo when the dumb things tried to cross on ice and sank by the hundreds or thousands into the river floods. When he got within her reach he gave her a hand and she clasped it, and he felt such melting raptures at her touch that he did not want to climb out at once, but only to lie supine, realizing that this was Sunday's hand on his arm. But he did struggle up and out when she tugged at him, and then they stood face to face, the one drenched all over and flaked with soft ice and half frozen, the other wet to her waist and shivering. He was more than trembling; big shuddering spasms convulsed him, running through him so hard that they stopped his breathing. But the moment she faced him her hands were busy unfastening the strings of his garments and numbly he understood that she intended to strip him naked. One by one she took his clothes off and squeezed water from them and spun round and round with them, spreading them like wings in the breeze and the sun. Then she laid them in tall grass and sat and pulled off her moccasin boots and her trousers; and when he saw her naked to her waist and understood that she had no sense of shame or even sense of being naked he looked down across his body and wondered about himself. She was wringing her own garments and flapping them and when she saw that he was still trembling she indicated that he was to leap around and smite himself and get his blood flowing. "Thees way," she said, showing him. He jumped around, smiting himself, and it now came to him that two or three times she had spoken in English and he wondered about that. He thought perhaps he ought to make a fire. He picked up his fire bag where she had laid it on tall grass and opened it, and the first things he saw were the pieces of buckskin string. He went over to her with the fire bag pouched open and showed her the pieces and took a few out to hold in his palm; and swiftly she looked up at his eyes, looked into them, her own eyes full of what a man had never dreamed of, being a man; and then just as swiftly she took his left hand and pressed her lips to the stub of his thumb. He closed his eyes a moment, feeling dizzy, while both heaven and earth consecrated her as his woman.

The sun had risen and was now warming them. When he saw her putting her garments on he took up his own clothes and got into them and tied the fire bag at his waist. He supposed he had lost his knife for he could see it nowhere, but his gun seemed to be dry. He should have had sense enough to carry his powder pouch in his teeth but it wasn't too far now to the post and he was too happy to care. He told himself that this girl loved him or she wouldn't be doing these things for him. She still used some bear grease and vermilion but he thought her lovelier than ever and he loved both vermilion and bear grease now. He wanted to hold her but he still sensed in her an aloofness, and suspicion, and for a little while he pretended to be busy with his jacket strings. Surely she wanted him or she would never have come to meet him. . . .

He went over to her at last and took her arms at the elbows and faced her. He thought he would be content merely to look into her eyes, for there was so much to see in them—a curious and rather amused measuring of him; a wariness nourished by a woman's insights; and something—he was sure of it—as deep as tenderness.

"I love you," he said.

Something left her eyes and something came. She looked away. Then her gaze returned to his face and regarded him gravely, back and forth from one eye to the other, searching, studying.

"Loov me?" she said, as she might have said, "But how can you know?" She spoke with an accent. He thought it was French, he thought maybe she had got it from French traders as a child. With a faint smile she said, "*Ketuckhomin?*"

"*Ketuckhomin,*" he said, smiling and nodding.

She was still looking from one eye to the other, as though she might see in one what the other refused to disclose. Changing the subject disconcertingly, she said, "You brave."

He tried to hold the smile back but it came through. He shook his head no. "Not very," he said.

She shook her head yes, as a child might have done, without guile.

"You brave woman," he said. "And you do spik English."

"Leetle," she said.

He tried to draw her to him but she resisted. He said, "Sunday, do you love me?"

She still searched his eyes, then his mouth, then his whole bearded face, as a woman searches before she spurns or surrenders. At last, as if her suspicions had melted, she nestled close to him, going inside his arms and turning with a snuggling movement; and somewhere under his chin and close to his throat her lips said, "I loov you."

Drawing her head in against him, David looked away at the sky between the Athabasca and Saskatchewan, telling himself that if he weren't looking into heaven now he never would; telling himself that they would go to Montreal now, by canoe, alone, the two of them, and be married there or have the marriage formalized, for he imagined that they would be married in passion and tenderness long before that. Then he would talk to Selkirk and they would come back. They would go all the way down the long north Saskatchewan, with its thousands of bends and turnings, and through Cedar Lake and Cross Lake and Lake Winnipeg, and the Lake of the Woods and Rainy Lake and the Grand Portage and Lake Superior—God knew how many hundreds of miles—but they would love it, every river and lake clear through the month of June, eating roasted goose and venison, and on their return luscious wild strawberries and raspberries and all the kinds of wild plum, the large red ones, the yellow speckled. Tomorrow he would tell Jim what Bowman had asked him to say, for he did agree that the damned fools on both sides would have to get together or perish. Jim would have him tell Selkirk, the stubborn bastard. Then they would come back and he would be happy in this land with his woman, a mountain and river woman, a woman grown and nourished by the vast out-of-doors, with the sun and the winds and all the days and nights of it, the short summers and frosted autumns and snows of it, in the way she walked, in the way she rode. It would all be there, he had no doubt, in the way she would love.

He moved back a little so that he could see her face. Again for a moment her eyes seemed to cloud with doubt and suspicion, but for a moment only. He looked round him for a mound on which she could stand, hating himself for being so tall; and with her feet on the mound her lips came close to his and he kissed her. He kissed the vermilion on her cheeks, the soot shadows under her eyes—and her eyelids, her forehead, her braided hair smelling of bear grease, and he knew that he loved all these things, bear grease, soot, lodge smoke, vermilion, as he loved the smell of buffalo bush and sage. He held her close, sensing how firm and healthy and wide-awake she was; marveling at her daring and skills; thinking of the Indian in her or what living with Indians had done to the white and wishing it had done more for him. He thought he saw now that you had to take the red man's indolence if you liked what abiding kinship with mountain, river, and sky had done for him; his haughtiness if you admired his courage; perhaps even what white men called his treacheries and cruelties if you were to love your own children.

He had not shaved for several days and he knew he had a porcupine face, but he kissed her again, and felt flooded when she snuggled closer, surrendering, who had so little need to, to the strength in a man's arms. He asked if she would go to Montreal with him and she said she would. Would she go anywhere with him, anywhere on earth? She moved back a little so that she could look around her; she did not answer the question and he did not press it. Clasping her waist, he held her off and looked at her, and when he smiled she responded; and he was thinking that this kind of country did things to a man and to a woman—it gave them the wariness of forest things and the aloofness of high-mountain things and the silences of deep-river and lake things, so that you found it difficult to take off your mask and submit to a thing as defenseless as love.

He asked if she remembered the stampede—the storm—that day far down there when someone was riding—riding to bring him back to camp. "Was it you?"

She looked up and away, her head sidewise in a manner she had when she seemed to be thinking or remembering. She met his eyes again and he saw their mirth. She glanced down at his left thumb and softly touched it, saying, "You brave man." She turned then and picked up his gun and handed it to him. She walked over to the pony, but instead of mounting she took the reins to lead it. She came back to him and he bent to touch his lips to her hair and he enfolded one of her hands, and they walked together into the sun and the south.

## XXXIII

At the Edmonton post David found a brief note from Jim: "You are in command here till I come back." He read it several times. Where was Jim? He had gone down the river, Pierre said, to see Lord Selkirk, who was due at the Seven Oaks settlement in June or July. How long would Jim be gone? Pierre had no idea.

"Didn't he leave any orders? What are we supposed to do here?"

Trade, Pierre said, if the red men came with pelts; lay in stores of pemmican, wood, fish for the dogs; and wait. As Pierre understood it, the center of the struggle had shifted to the east—to the Red River area, or maybe to Montreal and its law courts. The express had brought the news that Selkirk had been served with a warrant, and had spurned it. The governor had then been asked to issue a true bill against him—whatever that was, said Pierre, shrugging—but Selkirk had surrounded himself with a small army and it looked as if there would be hell to pay. The latest news was that his lordship intended to fight the whole thing through the courts, and spend his entire fortune there if he had to.

"The courts," said David, looking at the mirth in Pierre's eyes. "The damned pedlars control the courts. The governor, the judges, the barristers, the policemen, they're all pedlar friends."

"That's what Jim said."

"So what does Jim think he can do?"

"Just find out how things are going."

That evening with a bottle of brandy and Sunday at his side David exchanged views with Pierre on how things were going. David learned that Payette had got drunk and beaten his Cree wife senseless and fled, and Jim had sent her back to her people; that Colin Robertson had been captured and had escaped; that Latude had been seen lurking in this area.

"He has promised to kill you," Pierre said.

"I'm not surprised," David said.

From David, Pierre learned that the Athabasca invasion had been a series of horrors.

"John Bowman says the companies will have to merge."

"Alexander Mackenzie said that fifteen years ago."

"So he did. But they say Selkirk will never compromise."

Almost no Indians came to trade. David had his men cut and stack cordwood, catch fish and dry them, repair and build canoes, and get the post in readiness for winter; and meanwhile, as he was to learn later, Lord Selkirk, the mystic and dreamer, moved with a large armed guard to his Red River colony and for the first time laid eyes on the settlement between a river and a prairie. The surviving settlers had been brought back and had planted grain; and in his four months there Selkirk planned bridges, roads, churches, schools, and shops. But even before he turned east to face the charges against him in the courts, frost had blighted the crops and his settlers faced starvation; Colin Robertson was at the end of his wits; the pedlars were jubilant. Colin still wanted to fight fire with fire but Selkirk said no, he would fight it like a gentleman through the courts and win like a gentleman. It had been founded as an honorable company and it would remain honorable. At that moment he was out on a fantastic bail of six thousand pounds.

Far away in the west David McDonald was finding delight in the ways of his woman, who was neither white nor red, but both: Indian in one mood, almost a Scottish lass in another; always unpredictable, never the same. He thought of himself and wondered if it was not a curse to be all Scot by blood and training, or English, or Jew or Dutch —or anything, yes, even Indian. He felt that he must be pretty dull to one like Sunday, who, being white, had the white heritage, yet who, having lived all her life with the red people, had so much that belonged only to them. How Indian she was in her ways he was to discover one day in early fall.

Because he was bored waiting for Jim, or angered by a man's threat on his life, he went almost daily outside the post with Sunday to walk in the early autumn chill and talk and dream, or to ride with her over the hills. He always went fully armed. He felt self-conscious when riding with her because she was such a superb horsewoman and had a much finer horse than his own. He did not indulge her in equestrian rivalries even when she challenged him, but was content to be inferior to her, content indeed to learn from her. Now and then she would touch her horse and be off like the wind, her face turned to mock him a little, her long soft hair (he had washed all the grease out of it) flowing from her head like a scarf; and he would follow at a gallop but he never tried to race her. When he drew up she would look at him with questions in her eyes, her head tilted to one side, one eyebrow raised a little; but he was never offended by her excellences, only proud of them. In his opinion white people who tried to match red people in horsemanship or in contempt for death were ridiculous fools. She was not a red woman but she was red in those ways.

She was a red woman in so many ways. There was her secretiveness. He was teaching her to talk more and more English—he intended also to teach her to read—and he was trying to learn something about her background, her people, but Sunday would not talk about those things. "My peep-l here," she would say, and gesture at the north country. If he pressed the matter she became secretive and sullen and hostile, just like an Indian. Like an Indian, candor was not her way, nor spontaneity, nor complete surrender. He became aware that there was a part of her which he would never know or touch.

One day they were out riding with an eye peeled for Latude, for David had learned from his scouts that the half-breed was on his trail. He was carrying his gun, as usual, across the crook of his left arm, and they were galloping along side by side, three or four miles from the post, when suddenly she screamed and hurled herself like a thunderbolt from her horse. She threw herself toward him and with such force that she cleared her horse and fell across his pommel, almost knocking the gun from his grasp, and in the next moment he thought the earth had fallen out from under him. Later he was to recall that he had heard a shot, but he was not conscious of it at the moment because of her scream and the impact with which she had struck him and the sudden falling away of everything under him.

He had the sensation of falling into an abyss, though actually nothing fell away except his horse. His horse dropped, and he and Sunday went down with it; and at once her hands were on him with more strength than he would have imagined she had and she was dragging him out of the saddle and down behind the horse. She was crying in his ear and forcing him down and he still had no clear sense of what had happened. He knew now that his beast had fallen and that he was out of the saddle and stretched out on the ground. He knew that Sunday was cowering low and pressing him down and looking warily around her. Then he heard blood gurgling in the horse and felt its hide twitching against him and knew that it had been shot.

He did not yet realize that the bullet had been intended for him. Truth of this came to him in the next few moments as he became aware of Sunday's behavior. With the swiftness and stealth of an Indian she had flung herself back and turned, and was holding two heavy strands of mane up a little, in the form of a narrow V, and was peering between them. She did not peer long. With what David thought was a gasp she went flat on her belly and began to move around the rump of the horse, a hand reaching back to grasp him and jerk him after her; and he crawled after her, still a little dazed, knowing now that someone had shot at him but not knowing why Sunday was going around the dead horse.

He was to know that a few moments later. He heard the hoofbeats of a galloping horse. He saw Sunday crouching and peering across the saddle; and, listening, he understood that the horseman had left his position and was circling. He drew his gun forward. She moved close to his ear and in fierce whispers made him understand that the rider might soon present himself and that David was to be ready to fire. He brought his gun up and examined it. He reached round to see if his knife was in his belt. He listened, and then rose a little to peer across the horse to see where the horseman was. The horseman was not moving in yet. He was two or three hundred yards out in the prairie, going at full speed in a great arc. He was east of them, David and Sunday were behind the dead horse on the west side. The rider went to the northeast and turned and rode back.

David's wits were clear now. He knew that the rider out there was trying to determine whether David McDonald was dead or alive. It was now that David recalled having heard two shots, or possibly three. He imagined that the man out there was Latude who had been bribed with promise of a keg of rum to kill him. He was kneeling, hugging the earth, his gun ready; and when it seemed unlikely that the rider would move in he detached his fire bag and gave it to Sunday and told her to have powder and ball ready. He had decided to shoot the horse rather than miss the man on a running shot.

But he would wait a little. The horseman had gone to the southeast and had paused there and was looking over.

David whispered to Sunday, "What'll he do now?"

"He look. Then he ride."

After two or three minutes the rider galloped off to the north. The prairie was more than knee-deep in grass and low bushes and it was obvious that the man was unable to see their dead horse clearly or to tell what had happened. Did he imagine that he had killed a horse and two persons with two or three shots? Sunday's horse had galloped away toward the post.

The rider went north and turned and came in closer, his pony in a dead run. David was staring hard and trying to judge the distance; he thought it was still over two hundred yards and he again decided to wait, knowing that eventually the man would come nearer if he saw no sign of life. The man came, after again dashing to the south and turning. He came at full speed. Tense, crouched, hidden behind the pommel, David waited; and when he thought the rider about a hundred yards away and ready to swing out, he swiftly brought his gun across the horn, sighted, and fired. The horse dropped. David swung to Sunday to reload and he was ready to fire again by the time the rider, flung down, had freed himself from the saddle. The man was on his feet and for a moment stark and clear. David fired again and the man went down. But David did not stir. For a man to fall as if hit was the oldest ambush in the world and a favorite with Indians. David was sure that he had hit him but he could not be sure that he had killed him and he was wondering how to find out when again Sunday amazed him. She leaped up and went off into the west screaming like a thing wounded.

Still crouched low, David now looked both ways, over to the man, hidden from him in the tall grass, and over at Sunday, racing away in wild zigzag leaps and filling the sky with her cries. He knew that this was another Indian trick: she thought that if the man was alive and able to fire her running away would bring him into view. David peered across the horn and waited. When after a few minutes there was no sign of life where the horse and man had fallen he got warily to his feet, his gun ready and his finger on the trigger; and after looking and listening another minute or two he stepped across the dead horse and walked east. He heard Sunday crying to him and, like a greenhorn, he turned, leaving himself defenseless and broadside to the enemy. But the enemy was dead. Sunday came running up and together they went over. The horse was dead too.

"You good shot," she said, touching his arm.

In that moment she appalled him, for she had the red man's indifference to death. He was looking down at the dead face of Latude and feeling sorry for him. He was thinking, The poor miserable bastard, a half-breed who probably didn't know his white father, whose red mother probably had syphilis! In all the world what was there but vengeance for him? But when David turned to Sunday and looked at her eyes he sensed that she was thinking of the man's scalp, of the scalping knife at David's waist.

David stripped the saddle and bridle from Latude's horse. He then handed the musket to Sunday and said, "Come," and they went to his own horse; and with two saddles on his back and with Sunday carrying the gun they headed for the post. He was feeling wretchedly unhappy, not so much because he had had to kill Latude as because in such moments of supreme crisis he did not feel together with his woman, as he felt in the embrace. In crisis he was white and she was red, and what a world there was between them! She had admired his markmanship. She had thought he ought to take the scalp, yet she was a woman, she would be a mother. Worst of all, when he got into a mood like this she withdrew from him, she became distant and suspicious and almost hostile. She became again a daughter of prairie and lodge smoke and raw liver; a squaw hacking at a blinded buffalo to bring it down. Still, maybe at heart she was another Tum-tum.

He could not doubt her devotion to him. She had seen Latude ready to fire and had thrown herself across David to shield him; and when, after returning to the post with her, he got another horse and a spade and rode back out to bury the dead man, he discovered that she had trailed him. He did not know that she had trailed him until after the grave was filled and he was ready to return. Then, looking round him, he saw her sitting on her pony fifty yards away, a musket across her left arm. It was plain that she had been standing guard over him. He mounted and rode over to her and for a moment they looked into the eyes of one another. Then without speaking they rode back to the fort.

He got to know her better after the long deep winter set in. She had seen him reading and she wanted to learn to read; and so before the fireplace he laid buffalo robes to form a soft mattress and robes to form a back rest and he would sit and stretch his legs out and Sunday with her back to him would put her head under his chin, her loose hair flowing over her, and with both arms around her he would hold a book up before her and point to words and pronounce them.

He tried to define abstract words in terms of things known to her. One evening he pointed to the word small and said it meant little; and he reached out to hold a palm eighteen inches above the floor. "Little David," he said.

At once she left his arms and turned to look at him. "Leet-l David?" she said. Cocking her head to one side, as was her way when perplexed and thinking, she was silent, her gaze moving back and forth from one of his eyes to the other. Then a hand slipped down to her belly and her open palm against it seemed to be listening. "No leet-l David," she said.

David chuckled. "That's all right," he said. "We'll keep trying." He had to say the words over and over to make her understand what they meant.

Then her face opened in the widest smile he had ever seen on it. She sighed and slipped back into his arms and turned her face up so that her lips could kiss his chin. "Now?" she said.

She had such firm lovely breasts that David liked to hold one gently in his two hands, cupping it like a ripe fruit; or to move the tip of his tongue across a nipple, softly back and forth until, gasping, she covered it. He had known that red men were not like white men in making love. Sunday had known it too, and she was curious about it. She said that red men never put their tongue to a woman's nipple that way or fondled her breasts. She wanted to know what white men called it, and he used the words breast and teat and she liked the latter because she found it easier to pronounce.

"Paleface like teet?"

"Uh-huh," said David, nodding and grinning.

"But teet for ba-bee."

"Uh-huh," he said.

Then he told her that far away back home he had known a man who took one nipple when his child took the other, and together they nursed; but Papa was so greedy that he got more than his share and baby was starved and Mama had to wean Papa. She had moved away to look at him, her gaze going from one of his eyes to the other, back and forth, as it always did when she suspected him of jesting. He saw that she was quite disturbed. He did not fully understand why until she said:

"Leet-l David you rob?"

He felt something like shock. Goddamn, he didn't want her to get the notion that out in the white world all the husbands were sucking their wives! "No, oh no!" he cried, shaking his head. He tried to explain to her that only rarely did a paleface do that, but she was not fully convinced and he wondered what she had seen in the lodges when squaws lay under white men.

She was an apt pupil, she learned fast. Sometimes he would mix a hot rum drink and they would sip it together while they studied; and sometimes he had a servant bring their supper to them before the fire. She hungered for raw liver. She hungered for a child. When languorous and warm and a little sleepy she would snuggle against him and look up and say, "Leet-l David now?" It was the happiest winter David had spent in the north country but it was also a winter of anxiety and foreboding.

What, he asked himself every day, was happening far away to the north, far away to the east? He knew that there could be no answer until late spring, but before the first birds came he climbed often to the tower to look downstream at the line of a frozen river, hoping that by some magic an express would come in. Had there been another invasion of the Athabasca or were the two companies trying to fight it out in the courts?

There was no answer until early summer. Then an express came, a lone man as tough as bull hide named Angus Clouston, bringing tidings to all the HB posts west of Cumberland House. Only an expert riverman as hardy and fearless as Angus would have been given such an assignment, for in the war between the companies it was essential that the expressmen got through. David regaled him with liquor and food and cocked both ears for the news.

The news was bad, all of it. There were now forty or fifty charges —no man pretended to know how many—against Selkirk and the HB Company, covering everything from assault to riot, larceny to kidnaping. All of eastern Canada was talking about it and books were being written about it. Selkirk and Colin and others had brought charges against the pedlars, two or three hundred charges, for looting, burglary, arson, murder, and God alone knew what else. The courts were choked with allegations back and forth, barristers were swarming like wolves after the caribou; but those close to Selkirk, like Colin, saw that his health was breaking, suspected that his mind was breaking, and believed that in a few weeks or months the man would be dead.

The recital had filled David with anger. "And what in hell do we do now? Just sit on our goddamned asses?"

Angus shrugged and poured brandy through two hedges of beard into his mouth. If it couldn't be settled in the courts, he said, it would be settled in the field.

"Athabasca, you mean?"

Colin, he said, would lead another invasion this coming winter.

"The fool. John Bowman is right."

"Lord Selkirk thinks he is right."

"Well, if Colin gets up there and starves his guts out as we did maybe he'll get some sense in his head. Where is Jim Dugald?"

He was at Red River, Angus said. The crops of the colonists had all frozen and Jim had led hunting parties to find meat.

"He send any message?"

"Just keep the post up and wait."

"On the courts?"

He was to stay here, Angus said, until further orders came. He was to keep lookouts day and night, for the pedlars were boasting that they would take every HB fort within a year. Colin said that was more brag. David was to buy pelts and pemmican if he had rum and things to trade with.

"Damned little," David said. It was plain that honorable old HB was going broke.

And so he stayed and he posted lookouts, he did a little trading, he led a few hunting parties, he became impatient and short-tempered—but never with Sunday. She was with child, leet-l David was coming, but when David tried to keep her in the fort or asked her to lie down in the afternoon and rest she would have none of it. What nonsense was this? A squaw worked right up to the day of birth and on the day; and if her people were marching that day she would fall out of line and vanish into a thicket and have her baby, and an hour later would be marching with them again. She was not a squaw, he said, but his statement meant nothing to her. She went with him hunting, fishing, after wood, everywhere. In late fall another express came to say that Lord Selkirk's health had broken completely and he was sailing for home. Colin had led an invasion into the Athabasca. Everyone on both sides knew that a crisis was swiftly approaching but nobody had a ghost's notion of what it would be.

Next year would tell, they said. That was all.

So David spent another winter, cursing his luck and waiting. On Christmas Day their son was born. David had asked Mink Tails to bring Sunday's mother in—the only mother she had known; and the old squaw had helped her deliver the babe and had then gone back to her people, her belly warm with rum.

"Leet-l David," Sunday said, holding the child up and looking at his father, her eyes mirthful.

"Little David," he said. "Now we'll have a little Sunday."

Her face sobered. "Leet-l Sunday?" she asked, looking back and forth at his eyes. Then she smiled. "Now?"

"No, goddamn it, not now. There, give him both teets and don't accuse me of robbing him."

## XXXIV

Five months later an express brought the news that David had waited for. It was Angus again. Colin had led an armed invasion into the Athabasca and the pedlars had captured him and kept him for months in a small log prison. They were going to bring him down with the spring brigades and boot him out of the country and skin him alive if he ever came back. But Colin, though imprisoned, had managed to send word to Governor Williams of the Red River colony: with all the soldiers he had he was to meet and ambush the brigades at the Grand Rapids and take all their furs and send the pedlar partners east for trial.

Staring at Angus, David said, "Colin always did believe in miracles. Have I permission to go?"

"They sent no orders for you to stay."

David put Pierre in charge of the post, chose the toughest of the one-man canoes, a bag of pemmican, plenty of powder and ball, and was ready to shove off when Sunday came and stood before him. She was dressed for a journey and over her back was little David in a papoose bag.

"Oh no," David said. "You stay here."

"I go where you go."

"No, no—"

"Yes—yes!"

"There'll be fighting. There'll—"

"I keen fight."

"There'll be snow, cold, storm. Our baby."

She shrugged. Her eyes again shone with hostile contempt. Did he think that papooses were hung up by the fire all winter? She said that if he left her behind she would follow him even if she had to walk.

"All right," he said, and seized another bag of pemmican, another robe, a slightly larger canoe. Sunday asked for a musket for herself and for a hunting knife. He got them for her and, like a professional hunter, she examined them and her fire bag, with little David standing up her back and blinking gravely at his father.

Then they were off, down a great river at floodtide. It was the twenty-eighth of May, 1819. David supposed that the fur brigades had left the far northern posts. He knew that he would have to row from daylight till dark if he were to get to the Rapids in time for the fight, but he soon learned that far from being a burden Sunday was another right arm. She said little but she always knew what to do—if it was when, rowing, he showed a sign of food hunger, or in getting a quick breakfast or supper, or in scanning the banks for a chance to kill fresh meat, or in portaging or keeping the child clean or taking the paddle. Little David, like Indian babies, never once whimpered but turned on them a toothless baby grin if they looked at him or gazed round him out of immense curiosity when they did not. He slept without a cry all night, a tiny thing in his own moccasins, beaver cap, and leather garments.

One evening she startled David by saying, "Bath." She stripped the baby and herself and he took off his clothes and they all sat in the river and bathed, the baby with just his head out. After the bath she gave the child a swimming lesson. David thought, When he's three he'll be able to swim better than I can, and when he's eight he'll make me look ridiculous on a horse.

He thought he was covering a hundred miles a day but no man could guess distance on a great river that meandered endlessly, like a thing with its head cut off and its body still moving. At one point it went away south, as if eager for the junction with its south fork, but then flowed away back north, forcing the south fork to cover another hundred miles to find its confluence. After this junction David proceeded more warily, for he was approaching the Churchill, down which the pedlars would come; and at the junction with the Churchill he examined the banks but found no signs. He did not know if they were behind him or ahead of him until he smelled the delicious woods smell of campfires. He examined the ashes and thought the fires were only two or three days old, for when he stirred them they gave off a faint wraith of smoke that was not all wood ash and there was a slight fire warmth in a segment of unburnt log. He would have to overtake them, and this night he stroked all night and Sunday sat up all night, refusing to sleep when he did not sleep.

The next day he came in sight of Cumberland House. It was here that he and a group had been ambushed and taken prisoner on their way to the Athabasca with John Clarke. He hid the canoe and, leaving his wife and child with it, he went warily through the woods to reconnoiter; and at the HB post he learned that a little way up the river Colin had escaped and had fled to the post here and had challenged the pedlars to attack. That was only two days ago. The pedlars had refused the challenge and had gone on down with their furs, with Colin and a dozen men in pursuit, knowing that Governor Williams would have an ambush waiting. Two days ago and it was only about a hundred and fifty miles to the Rapids! David ran to his canoe and in a few minutes was again stroking swiftly over the muddy waters, Sunday facing him, her gun ready. He had no doubt that there would be a fight at the Rapids and he wanted to be in it.

He went at full speed for hours and passed a spot on the bank where campfires were lazily smoking. He stroked until after dark in the first of two big lakes, close together. They got only a little sleep, and long before daylight he was stroking again. When they approached the swift channel of rapids connecting the two lakes, he thought he heard voices, and now and then he paused to listen. Letting the canoe drift, he chewed pemmican and looked at Sunday, wondering if her marvelous insights revealed anything to her. He said white water was not far ahead. And when at last he could look ahead and see white water he decided to take the canoe into the woods and hide it and leave Sunday and the child with it, and then hasten downstream to see what was happening. He shot over to a bank and tossed food and robes out and dragged the canoe back into hiding. He said, "Wait here," and took the portage trail and ran, his gun at the ready.

A few minutes later his wits were standing on end. He had raced down the bank about half a mile with the sound of roaring white water in his ears and he had gone out to the edge to have a look. On glancing upstream the first thing he saw was a canoe with a person in it. Who, he wondered, would be fool enough to venture down over that cascading hell of water! He stared. The person was taking the hazards with superb skill. He turned to look downstream and saw a great barge of logs in mid-river with a lot of men on it and they seemed to be hauling in on ropes. On the far side he could make out what looked like a part of the fur brigades and a group of large canoes closing in. He thought, Those are Colin and his men and I should be over there; and again he looked upstream to see what the canoeist was doing. The canoeist was bearing toward him, the canoe dipping and rising—vanishing momentarily in the swirling saucers, poising an instant on the crests; and with astonishment that left him numbed and witless he perceived that the person in the canoe was Sunday. He stared, transfixed. He glanced downstream, he shook himself and moved. He leaped down the bank and was about to plunge in when he saw her motioning to him to go back; and while he stood in water to his waist, staring, unbelieving, she shot toward him, balanced on a crest, disappeared downward into spray and mist, and then was almost within reach, spinning in a whirlpool. While she fought to control the canoe he saw dully that his son was in the papoose bag on her back, that her gun was across her lap. She was using a paddle better than any white man he had ever known. She backed water on it until she had the canoe poised and then shot it forward, and it was right at his side and his hands were on it and he was scowling at her drenched face and crying, "You damned fool, you!" but his words were lost in the roar. He looked downstream but from his low position could see only tumbling water. He backed up and out, pulling the canoe after him, and when she leaped out he dragged the canoe back into the bank and anchored it. He reached out to take her hand but she threw his hand off and he then rushed a little way downstream for a better view and she was right at his heels; and when at last he stopped and turned for a moment to look at her he saw his son's face and the wet silk of his hair and his eyes, like his mother's, gravely staring at his father.

They were opposite the barge now and they stood on the bank looking over. It looked to him as if most of the fur boats had been caught and anchored but men were out in canoes fighting to capture or overturn one another. The river was calmer there but at some distance below the barge it broke again and plunged in a great fall. The men in the canoes were struggling, they were striking at one another with oars but they seemed to have lost their weapons; and in one canoe he thought he saw the face of Colin Robertson. He was sure of it a moment later when the face turned toward him. Colin, standing up, seemed to be trying to lash his canoe to one of the larger canoes and climb into it; he seemed to be fighting single-handed against six or seven men, and the two canoes all the while were drifting toward the fall. Men on the barge appeared to be shouting warnings but nobody could hear anything in the roaring of the water; and then the men in the big canoe tipped Colin's canoe over and he was spilled out, he went head first in and down; and a few moments later surfaced and was swimming. He was trying to swim to the shore now. David stared at him, fascinated, and muttered, "He'll never make it!" The men in the big canoe were trying to make the shore now; standing, they were paddling desperately but they would never make it. They were being flung to the brink and Colin's empty canoe was going with them and Colin was borne after his canoe; for the river was deep there and it was moving down over a great escarpment to make its plunge. The men on the barge were silent, staring. David had taken one of Sunday's hands. Everyone looked now, waiting; the men in the big canoe had ceased struggling and seemed to be sitting, their hands clutching the sides; and Colin and his canoe were bobbing like corks; and then all of them seemed to dip in a long smooth arc downward and up and they stood limned an instant against blue-green forest, three objects on a mighty crest of muddy waters; for an instant only and then they were gone.

"Jesus!" David said, but his voice was lost in the roaring of waters.

He touched Sunday to indicate that she was to come, and they ran down-river. The earth was tumbled and torn here but they clambered over stones and fallen timber and down, with little David jouncing while his round eyes surveyed the foaming waters and the forest; and when on a level with the bottom of the fall they went so close that spume and spray drenched them but nowhere in the boiling white cauldrons, nowhere in the down-sucking whirlpools or in edge waters bursting against stones and hurling their might upward and falling back—nowhere was there sign of man or boat. David looked up at the wide curved wall of descending water, of water plunging like planed gray stone, of water bursting open at the edge in gigantic lacework shot full of sunlight and silver; he looked at the gray slippery stones, in one moment half out like resting river beasts, in the next almost submerged and drenched over, that lay between him and the wall; and he looked downstream again. Either the men and boats had gone through the boiling pools and been carried away or they were back behind that wall of water. The latter thought seemed to him fantastic but he knew that at the bottom of a fall like this, where the waters burst open and churned and swirled round and round, things in their depths did not get out in a hurry, not in the brief while it had taken him to rush down the bank. Still, if men and boats were in those whirlpools they would surface now and then and he had seen no sign of them, nor sign of anything darker than white foam with shadows on its sunless side.

What was it like back behind the wall? Could men live there? He had seen a fall far up against the headwaters of Peace River that had a vast chamber behind it, a huge wet cool mausoleum back under stone, with the ledge above overhanging, over which the river fell. He looked at the slippery stones at his feet and, handing his gun to Sunday, he went forward to the edge of the fall; and standing there with water smiting him and raining over him, he thrust his head through the curtain and peered. Then he went back close to the stone, where the curtain, he thought, would be thinner, and with heavy spray drenching him and water pouring from his hair down into his eyes, he bent forward, his head under the downpour, to look in and behind the fall; and what he saw brought a cry from his lips.

The big canoe had somehow got itself anchored and the men were there clinging to it like drowned things, their bodies stretched out in the whirling pool around them, their arms stretched out and their hands grasping. How in the world could he get them out of there? He shouted but it was stupid to shout, for his voice was lost even in his own ears. He went back and looked round him for a long slender pole and with the pole he returned and thrust it forward to the man nearest him; and one hand loosed its clutch on the canoe and seized the pole and drenched eyes turned, trying to see him; and David drew the pole toward him and pulled the man out, pulled him across the whirling waters and up to the stones. Half drowned and still dazed, William McGillivray, the brains of the North West Company, got to his feet and shook water from his hair and eyes. David led him over to the bank and at that moment a number of HB men appeared, with soldiers, with Governor Williams at their head.

Nobody could hear another's words. David pointed, and then with the pole returned and thrust it in, and this time the man he dragged out was Colin Robertson, blowing water from his lungs but trying to grin. They brought the other men out and then they all took the portage trail downstream, with David and Sunday in the rear. Once, years ago, David had seen William McGillivray; the man was fatter now, with large round buttocks that rolled with each step, with fat cheeks grown up against small close-together shrewd Scot eyes. They went to the HB camp and there the roaring of the waters was distant and they could hear one another; and McGillivray, standing in his drenched leather, faced Colin in his drenched leather, his eyes laughing with cunning, his eyelids drooping.

"Twice you've escaped. This time we're going to kick you out of the country and if you ever come back we'll skin you alive."

"A lot of rodomontade," Colin said, grinning back at him.

Men shoved in, thinking perhaps there would be a duel, but McGillivray was not the dueling kind. He said:

"I don't know what Roddo Mont had but you won't have enough skin on you for a pair of moccasins for a child."

"Brag. The big pedlar wind. Goddamn it, man, you're our prisoner."

"Your prisoner?" said McGillivray, staring round him. He seemed only now to become conscious of the soldiers.

Colin was saying, "Two years ago you starved Clarke until he couldn't walk. Then you tied him up to a tree and beat him. Then——" He broke off. Several of the pedlar partners were approaching, with huge violent Ben Frobisher in the lead.

When Ben came up, soldiers surrounded him, bayonets fixed, and Ben with both hands slapped the bayonets right and left and roared curses upon the HB Company. HB men were admonishing him but he still struck the bayonets away until behind him he felt the blades through his leather and into his hide. He stood as if listening.

McGillivray was saying, "If you are arresting us I suppose you have warrants. This is a country of laws——"

Governor Williams, as hotheaded as Frobisher, exploded. "Warrants?" He advanced, shaking a fist at McGillivray. "Sir, do you dare to speak to me of warrants? What warrant had you when you threw Colin Robertson into a jail all last winter? What warrant had you for hanging John Clarke up to a tree and flogging his hide off? You have the gall of a royal ass to talk to me about warrants! Your governor of Canada is a damned stinking rascal and warrants are all damned nonsense in this country! Out of this land you go, McGillivray, and every infernal pedlar with you!"

Colin had walked over to David, bending his head to indicate that they would walk away. When they were a hundred yards distant they stopped and Colin looked at Sunday and then at the child.

"Well, David, I see you got your woman—and a baby. A boy?"

"A boy."

"Let me hold it a minute," Colin said. Sunday took the bag down and lifted the child out. Colin held it up at arm's length. It looked like a doll, its feet encased in tiny beaded moccasins, its body in tiny buckskin trousers and shirt, beaded and fringed, and above its round face a tiny beaver cap. Colin looked at it, snuggled it for a moment close to him, and returned it to Sunday.

Turning to David, he said, "Williams doesn't know it, Selkirk doesn't know it, but it's about all over. Why don't you take your wife for a trip to Montreal?"

"Had thought of it."

"You have a few months to do as you please." He gestured over at the camp where soldiers were standing guard over their prisoners. "Selkirk has spent his fortune, his health, his mind. He's dying. We pay no attention to him any more." Lowering his voice, he said, "I've learned that McLoughlin and some others intend to slip away to London to see the directors." His eyes twinkled at David. "I reckon to be on the same boat. As for the pedlars over there, we'll take them east for the hell of it but we could never get them into court.

We'll have to turn them loose." He looked curiously at Sunday. "Where your man goes you go. That right?"

"Leet-l David too," she said.

"Of course, little David too. Learning English and everything. Well, David, do as you please awhile and Jim'll be back before long." He turned away, raising a hand in farewell.

David and Sunday went back up the river and climbed to an eminence back away from the sound; and they stood there together, his arm around her, David speaking. Pointing to the south, he said Lake Winnipeg was there, Red River, and beyond them, the United States; and to hell and gone over there was Montreal—he was slowly turning as he talked; and then away off there were James Bay, Hudson Bay, Thunder Bay, and the north country farther than any man had ever looked or dreamed; and the Athabasca yonder and then the magnificent bulk of the Rocky Mountains and the great rivers, the prairies and the buffalo herds, the smell of buffalo bush and sage and lodge smoke, of buckskin tanning, of ice floes and snowfall, the smell of big country. Which way should they go?

"That way," she said, looking west.

An hour later they were in their canoe and they were going back up a long river, a mighty river, a river that had its source in a glacier lake in the top of the Rockies, that carried its waters clear across the vast Canadian prairies to dump them into a great lake. How many voyageurs, how many brigades had gone up and down this river? How many men had bent to the oar as he was bending now? Colin said the companies would merge and when they did, then all of the men could sing Tom Moore's boat song:

> *"Soon as the woods on the shore look dim,*
> *We'll sing at St. Anne's our parting hymn!"*

He broke off in the song, rested his paddle, and drew Sunday back to kiss her. He glanced back south and could see campfire smoke above the spray and the mists and the river.

> *"Row, brothers, row, the stream runs fast,*
> *The rapids are near and the daylight's past. . . ."*

19850

Ft. Chipewyan
Ft. Vermilion
L. ATHABASCA
PEACE R.
C
A
N
A
Methy
Portage
LESSER SLAVE L.
ATHABASCA R.
Augustus
NORTH SASKATCHEWAN R.
Edmonton
Scene of Capture and Torture
Acton House
and
Rocky Mt. House
Area of Buffalo Hunt
ROCKY MTS.
ALBERTA
SOUTH SASKATCHEWAN R.
U.S.
Scale of Miles
0
100
200